WOMEN and
CHILDREN
FIRST

THEY SURVIVED THE
TITANIC, BUT THEIR LIVES
WERE CHANGED FOREVER...

GILL PAUL

——✦——

AVON

The facts surrounding the sinking of the *Titanic* are portrayed
accurately in this novel, but otherwise it is a work of fiction.
The names, characters and incidents portrayed in it are the work
of the author's imagination. Any resemblance to actual persons,
living or dead, events or localities is entirely coincidental.

AVON

A division of HarperCollins*Publishers*
77–85 Fulham Palace Road,
London W6 8JB

www.harpercollins.co.uk

A Paperback Original 2012
1

Copyright © Gill Paul 2012

Gill Paul asserts the moral right to be identified
as the author of this work

Images on page 465, 466, 469, 470 and 473 courtesy
of the Library of Congress

A catalogue record for this book is available from the British Library

ISBN: 978-1-84756-325-5

Set in Minion

Printed and bound in Great Britain by Clays Ltd, St. Ives plc.

MIX
Paper from
responsible sources
FSC **FSC™ C007454**
www.fsc.org

FSC™ is a non-profit international organisation established to promote
the responsible management of the world's forests. Products carrying the
FSC label are independently certified to assure consumers that they come
from forests that are managed to meet the social, economic and
ecological needs of present and future generations,
and other controlled sources.

Find out more about HarperCollins and the environment at
www.harpercollins.co.uk/green

For Ana, Rhuaridh, Barnaby, Harvey and Florence

Prologue

Reg's hands were shaking so hard he couldn't hold the newspaper still enough to read. He sat on a bunk and smoothed the pages open on the shabby grey blanket, ironing the creases with his hand. Lists of names in tiny type covered the surface, organised into uneven columns of surnames, forenames, the class in which each person had travelled, and finally their country of origin.

Straight away he saw an error: Luigi Gatti was listed as Spanish rather than Italian. How could he trust this list if they could make such a simple mistake? Was anything in it reliable? Abbing, Abbott, Abelson . . . Ernest Abbott. That must be Ernie who worked in the mess, but they had him down as a third-class passenger. Poor old Ernie.

His finger scrolled down the page. There was Colonel Astor, with the same number of words by his name as anyone else. All that money couldn't buy him a place on the other, shorter list, the list of survivors. There was Bill, who had slept in the next bunk, and Ethel from the pantry, the one they called Fat Ethel. If only they'd been kinder . . .

A couple of columns across, at the 'J's, his stomach turned over and his heart began pounding hard. It was a most peculiar feeling to see yourself listed as dead. He looked away and refocused his eyes just outside the window where he could see unfurling buds on the topmost branches of a linden tree. Someone was moving around in a greystone office building opposite. He couldn't make out if it was a man or a woman, but they were holding some papers, which they put down then disappeared from view. For a few minutes he breathed quietly, keeping his head empty, until he felt able to look at the newspaper again.

The first name that appeared before his eyes was 'Grayling, Margaret, 1st class, American', and his eyes filled with tears for the generous old woman who had been his favourite passenger. Not even that old: she was probably only in her forties, about the same age as his mum. Then into his head came the peculiar scene he had witnessed between her husband and a striking young girl on the boat deck. Everything in his mind was now divided into 'before' and 'after', and that had been before: exactly forty-eight hours before the unthinkable happened.

PART ONE

Chapter One

It was one in the morning and first-class victualling steward Reg Parton should have been asleep in his bunk, but a restlessness took him to the ship's galley where he knew Mr Joughin would be pulling steaming trays of bread out of the ovens. Joughin was a good sort and always ready to slip you a fresh roll or two, especially at this time of night when he'd had a few whiskies. Chief baker was the right job for him, because he liked feeding people.

The ship was almost twelve hours out of Queenstown, on the southern tip of Ireland, and gliding her way across the Atlantic. There was less swell than with any other ship Reg had been on. She was as steady as if you were in your own parlour at home, with only the muffled roar of the engines indicating that you were on the move. The *Titanic* was a beautiful beast, with everything brand new and sparkling. It was nice being on a maiden voyage – there was the sense of every surface being untouched and pristine, and this ship was the most magnificent he'd ever seen. Woodwork gleamed, chandeliers shot pinpricks of light around the vast salons, and every surface that could possibly be decorated was clad in gilt, mosaic or milky mother-of-pearl.

Reg had been on board for two days and he'd spent all his off-duty time exploring. There were ten separate decks, each almost 300 yards long, joined up by elevators and staircases in hidden corners. Every deck had a different layout of interminable corridors with faceless doors and he'd got lost more times than he could count. It would take months to get to know this ship properly. He doubted anyone knew it from bow to stern, except maybe the designers. Mr Andrews, the chief designer, was on board and was often seen wandering the decks making notes in a little notebook.

Reg burnt the roof of his mouth on the hot roll and swore.

'That's what you get for being a gannet,' Mr Joughin remarked in his broad Birkenhead accent.

Reg ran to the sink to pour a glass of water, and while he was drinking, Second Officer Lightoller put his head round the door.

'Tea and biscuits for the bridge, Mr Joughin.' He didn't so much as glance at Reg.

'Right you are, sir.'

Lightoller disappeared and Mr Joughin began to set a tea tray. 'Where's that bloody Fred when you need him? He went for a fag half an hour ago and hasn't come back. Who's going to take this tray?'

'I'll do it!' Reg nearly jumped with excitement. 'Please let me.' He was dying to see the bridge with all its gleaming, state-of-the-art equipment. Maybe Captain Smith would even be there.

'It's not your place,' Joughin grumbled. 'It should be Fred.'

'But Fred's not here. They won't even notice who brings their tea. Let me do it.'

'Go on with you, then.'

Reg took the elevator up to the boat deck and walked to the short flight of steps that led up to the bridge. The moon was waning, the night was so black there was no dividing line between sea and sky, and the few stars were distant dots in some other galaxy. Onboard lights had been turned to a dim glow as the 1,300 passengers slept below. The steps were slippery with salt spray and Reg took them slowly so as not to slosh tea from the pot.

When he entered the bridge, he was disappointed to see that it wasn't the captain on duty but another officer, one he didn't recognise, who was standing alone by the wheel gazing out at the ocean ahead.

'Put it down there,' he said, without looking round, just pointing vaguely.

Reg had hoped he might be able to get into conversation and ask questions about the function of all the fancy modern buttons and levers and dials, but there was no encouragement to friendliness in the square set of the officer's shoulders.

'Thank you, sir,' Reg said before turning to leave. If it had been Captain Smith, he could have asked his questions. He'd sailed under the captain two years earlier, had been his personal dining steward on the voyage, and he'd found the grizzly-bearded old man to be a genial, fatherly sort. Whenever he was dining on his own, he'd been happy to answer questions about the propellers and bulkheads and top speed of the ship. He loved his ships, and encouraged Reg's boyish curiosity.

Reg stopped just outside the bridge to examine the sextant, with which the captain checked the ship's position at noon every day, then he gazed down the length of the vessel, past the huge funnels and towards the stern. It was a floating hotel, like the Ritz at sea. Of course, he'd never been to the Ritz Hotel, never even been to London, but he'd read all about it in the papers when it had opened six years earlier. The upper classes went there to sip tea in the opulent Palm Court, among

13

real palm trees. Even King George was sometimes glimpsed there. One day Reg would like to visit, he thought, but in the meantime, they had their very own Palm Court and Verandah Restaurant on the *Titanic* and it too had real palm trees in exotic wooden tubs. No detail had been spared; there was nothing but the best for their well-heeled clientele.

A movement caught his eye and he turned to see a girl standing behind one of the lifeboats, right next to the railing. Her back was to him but he could see that she was very slim, with copper hair secured by a diamond clasp, and wearing a shimmery white dress. She was holding something bulky and brown and, if he wasn't mistaken, furry. Could it be an animal, perhaps a pet dog? It seemed rather large for that.

She turned and Reg shrank back, not wanting to be caught staring, but she didn't once glance up towards the bridge. She was gazing beyond the lifeboat towards the entrance to the Grand Staircase and shifting her weight from foot to foot as if she were agitated about something. Suddenly she turned back towards the ocean, lifted her brown bundle and tossed it high into the air, right over the railing. Reg jumped in horror and opened his mouth to yell, the thought that it might be a dog foremost in his mind, but as it flapped in the air he saw that it was a coat. A fur coat. It seemed to float in slow motion, caught on an ocean breeze, before disappearing from view.

Why would anyone do that? It was a gesture of such extravagant abandon that he was struck dumb.

The girl glanced over her shoulder, presumably to check whether anyone had witnessed her bizarre behaviour. In the lamplight, her face was small and exquisite, like a flawless china doll. She had diamond earrings to match her hair clasp, and

14

her robe plunged open at the front in quite the most revealing manner Reg had ever seen on an upper-class lady.

Yet, there was no doubt that she was upper class. Everything about her seemed genteel and expensive, and the gown was cinched in around a waist so tiny Reg felt sure he could have linked his hands round it.

'She's perfect,' he thought to himself. 'Truly perfect.' But what was she up to? She took a step towards the Grand Staircase, then turned back again as if not sure what to do for the best. She leaned against the railing and bent over to look at the ocean 75 feet below. Reg took an instinctive step towards her. Was she planning to jump? Or just trying to see where her coat had landed? Should he rush over and be ready to grab her if she started to climb the railing? She would die instantly on impact with the water. That tiny neck would snap as surely as if she had leapt off a ten-storey building and hit the pavement below.

He stood, torn by indecision. What if she leapt and he didn't get there in time to stop her because he'd been too busy gawping? He'd feel terrible, knowing he could have prevented it. Should he make some kind of sound so she knew he was there? He could approach and ask if he might fetch anything for her. He rehearsed the words in his head. 'Good evening, ma'am. May I be of assistance?'

She turned again and just at that moment, Reg noticed a figure coming up the Grand Staircase and emerging onto the deck. He walked past a lamp and Reg saw that it was Mr Grayling, an American gentleman whose table he waited on in the first-class dining saloon. He could easily have spotted Reg hovering on the steps to the bridge, but he didn't look that way. Instead, he strode directly towards the lifeboat where the girl was waiting. As she saw him approach, she gave a little cry, ran towards him, and threw herself into his arms. Her tiny white figure was enveloped in his large, dark-suited one.

Mr Grayling held her close for a while then he leaned back to cup her chin in his hands. He said something to her, but Reg could only catch the word 'sorry', before he bent to kiss her full on the mouth. She raised her pale, thin arms around his neck, while he placed a protective hand in the small of her back. It was a posture so intimate Reg knew that they had to be lovers, and not just new lovers. There was a familiarity about their passion. Perhaps they had been apart for some time and this was their reunion.

An awful fact nagged at Reg's brain as he stood watching. Mr Grayling was married to a woman Reg knew and liked, who was with him on this trip. He'd waited on Mrs Grayling on a Mediterranean cruise the previous year, when she'd been travelling with a woman friend, and they'd had several friendly conversations. Reg had been touched that she remembered him this time and professed herself delighted to see him once more. She was nicer than any other passenger in first class, where familiarity with the staff was somewhat frowned upon. How could Mr Grayling betray her? What kind of a man would bring his mistress onto the same ship as his wife?

The lovers slipped in behind the lifeboat, still caught up in their embrace, and Reg decided he had best get a move on before he was spotted. They wouldn't be at all pleased if they thought they were being spied upon. He knew to his cost that if a first-class passenger made a complaint against a steward it would always be believed, no matter how unjust the circumstances. On his last voyage, an elderly gentleman had lost a silver cigar case and accused Reg of stealing it. His belongings were searched and of course it wasn't found. It finally turned up under a table in the smoking room, but Reg knew the incident was recorded in his particulars at the White Star Line office. He'd seen it with his own eyes when he signed on for this voyage. There was an indelible shadow on his record because of it. He'd protested indignantly to the secretary at the employment office but was told it was just a record of an event, and nothing would make them remove it.

Reg stamped his foot on the step and walked down with a heavy footfall, so no one could accuse him of sneaking around. At the bottom of the steps he turned left towards the port side of the ship so as not to pass Mr Grayling and the girl, who were on the starboard. When he reached the Grand Staircase, he didn't look back but hurried down. He caught the elevator to D deck, said good night to the night shift operator, then descended a further flight of stairs to Scotland Road, a corridor stretching half the length of the ship, where he had a berth in a dormitory with twenty-seven other saloon stewards. It was one-thirty, and he had precisely four hours to sleep before it was time to get up and prepare for breakfast service.

Chapter Two

Lady Juliette Mason-Parker knelt on the bathroom floor, acid scorching her throat and the taste of vomit in her mouth. The floor was tiled with a black and white diagonal diamond-within-diamond motif. Some diamonds had black centres while others were white. She counted the number from the toilet across to the bath: exactly fourteen. Who decided that? Was it calculated precisely to work that way? She supposed it must be. Everything on the *Titanic* seemed meticulously designed, nothing left to chance.

The bathroom fittings were real marble. It seemed remarkable to her that the ship could stay afloat with the weight of all its fixtures and fittings: the library full of books, the swimming pool, the extravagant cut-glass chandeliers in every public room, the carved oak panelling on the walls and the enormous pieces of mahogany furniture. It was much more luxurious than their draughty family pile in Gloucestershire. A student of decorative styles could learn all they needed on board, Juliette mused, as they wandered from the Jacobean dining saloon to the Louis XIV restaurant to the Georgian-style lounge. Their suite had a French feel, with tapestries in rococo frames on the walls and heavy patterned drapes closing off the sleeping areas during daytime.

In the next room, her mother slept soundly, occasionally snuffling and murmuring in her sleep. The last thing Juliette wanted was for her to awake and start fussing. If ever there was a woman who enjoyed fussing, it was Lady Mason-Parker. She had been irritating Juliette beyond measure on this voyage. If it wasn't her endless advice on which hat to wear for breakfast, and which gown was suitable for walking on the promenade in the afternoon, then it was her lectures on how to ensnare a husband, with methods that Juliette considered had gone out with Jane Austen. Men nowadays liked women with a bit of conversation in them rather than smiling fools, but Lady Mason-Parker felt that Juliette's forthright opinions scared them off. So far mother and daughter hadn't argued outright but tetchy barbs had been fired back and forth.

Suddenly Juliette spotted the lid of her pot of cherry tooth powder in the gap between the washbasin and the toilet. Throwing up in the middle of the night had its uses after all. She squeezed her hand in to retrieve it, then considered whether the nausea had subsided enough for her to wash out her mouth and return to bed. She rose tentatively, holding onto the basin's edge, and regarded herself in the mirror.

Her blonde hair was pinned into waves, which were supposed to hold it in the style of the moment once the pins were removed in the morning. Whoever designed it had paid no regard to the fact that ladies had to attempt to sleep while being stabbed in a dozen different spots on their heads. Her eyes had bruised circles underneath and her skin without makeup had a faint greenish tinge. She would never get a husband looking like this, certainly not the rich American one her mother had in mind. And there was the added complication that it had to be done within a couple of months, from first meeting to proposal to marriage ceremony. The problem was that Juliette was pregnant. It was only eight weeks since the one and only time she'd had intercourse, but the signs were unmistakable. When she first caught her daughter throwing up and prised the truth out of her, Lady Mason-Parker had swung into action like a military commander.

'We need to find you a husband straight away. English men dither so, but a rich American would be ideal. They would be over the moon to get themselves a real English Lady for a wife, and they tend to be more impulsive than Englishmen when they fall in love.'

Juliette was horrified. 'Mother, you can't be serious! I'm not interested in tricking some poor Yankee dupe into holy matrimony. It's hideously immoral.'

'What you did to get yourself into this condition was immoral. Getting married is the way to fix it, and your husband will be delighted to have a child so soon. It will prove you're good breeding stock.'

'I'm not a farm animal! And I refuse to cooperate with your schemes.'

Juliette's protests were in vain. Her mother booked them a passage on the *Titanic*'s maiden voyage, calculating that the ship would be overflowing with eligible American millionaires. Since they sailed, she had occupied herself making enquiries of crusty dowagers in the lounge and arranging introductions to crass Americans who sold automobile components or garden fencing. Juliette had no choice but to converse with the men in question, but at some stage she would find a way to put them off. Mentioning her support for women's suffrage seemed a foolproof method.

'Have you chained yourself to the railings at Parliament yet?' one gent had asked tentatively at dinner that evening.

'No, but I rather think I might some time,' Juliette had replied. 'It looks fun.'

'She's joking, of course.' Her mother leapt in to try and salvage the relationship, but the merest hint was usually enough for them to take fright. No man wanted a suffragette for a wife.

Quite apart from the dishonesty of tricking someone into marriage, Juliette didn't want to be legally entwined for eternity to an American millionaire. She had a strong suspicion she wouldn't like living in America, even though she had never been there before. She liked Gloucestershire and her horses and her friends; she enjoyed the fundraising she did for charity, which she knew she was good at. If only this whole unfortunate pregnancy could be over as quickly as possible then life could go back to normal.

She favoured Plan B, which was that, in the event her mother failed to entice some rich gent to propose to her during the crossing, they would rent a small house in upstate New York, sit out the remainder of the pregnancy then have the baby adopted through a Christian adoption society. Juliette could return to England and the life she'd known before with no one any the wiser. Even her own father and brother had no idea about her pregnancy; they thought she and her mother were simply visiting some distant American cousins. And as for the baby's father, he would never find out.

Charles Wood was their local member of parliament, and quite high up in the Liberal party. Juliette had been introduced to him because of her charity work, and one weekend he had invited her to a house party on his estate. It was there, after an invigorating evening of discussion with distinguished guests who even included the prime minister's daughter, Violet Asquith, that Juliette had allowed Charles to come to her bedroom while the others slept. She had been flattered by his interest in her. Her head was turned. She had heard whispers of other girls who had done 'it', but not of any who got caught out. It was her own stupidity to develop a crush on a married man and get carried away without the least thought for the consequences.

There had been no point in telling Charles. What could he have done? In the unlikely event he offered to divorce his wife and marry her, he would have destroyed his parliamentary career. In 1912, no one would countenance a divorced MP. Besides, her mother would never have allowed the marriage. She had much grander plans for her eldest daughter. Juliette must either marry money or she must marry landed gentry, as her younger brother would inherit the Mason-Parker estate. She had been born to a titled family and must uphold the standards set by her own upbringing, which meant no commoner was good enough (unless he happened to be sufficiently loaded to make such criteria insignificant).

Juliette dabbed a little cherry tooth powder onto her brush and scrubbed her teeth, then rinsed and spat. She wouldn't let herself think about the creature growing inside her belly because she knew it would be the undoing of her. Their Labrador Tess had given birth to five puppies just last Christmas – little blind pink wriggly things – and they had given away four of them as soon as they could. Her baby would be the same. It would go to decent people and have a happy life, and one day in the future when Juliette was married to a man she loved, she would have children of her own.

She crept back into bed and pulled the satin coverlet up to her chin. Why was it always women who had to do the hardest things? How much easier it must be to be a man. Juliette wished with all her heart that she could fast-forward time to seven months from now when they would be on the return voyage to Southampton, footloose and unencumbered.

Chapter Three

Annie McGeown sat on the edge of a bunk and watched her four children breathing. They were so peaceful now, like little angels. Shame it hadn't been that way earlier. They'd only been on the ship for twelve hours since boarding at Queenstown, but the eldest boys were running riot, feeling cooped up in the limited space. Back home she could kick them out into the fields between meals, but here there was just the third-class outdoor deck and the long corridors where they bashed into other passengers and got told off for making a racket. Her oldest, Finbarr, had already kicked his ball over the railings into the Atlantic and they had nothing left to occupy them except a set of quoits provided by a friendly deck steward.

Oh, but they were lucky, though. Look at this place! They had a cabin of their own with six bunk beds, two of which were empty since the baby shared with her. There were real spring mattresses and clean pillows and blankets. There was a tiny porthole and even a washbasin crammed in between the beds. And the food! It was the best she'd eaten in her life, no question. She'd felt so grand, sitting with her brood in the restaurant, each in their own places and a highchair for the baby, and waiters serving them with three courses at dinner. A lovely soup and bread, roast meat and potatoes and then a plum pudding for afters. She was stuffed to the gills. And the menu for the next day had been pinned on a notice board, promising ham and eggs for breakfast. Any more than a week of eating like that and she'd be the size of a house when she got to America and met up with Seamus again.

It was a year and a half since she'd seen her husband, and even that was only for a month when he'd managed to wangle a cheap passage and come back to Cork for a visit. He'd never met his youngest, didn't know any of the children well, because he'd been out in New York for five years, working on the railways and saving enough money to afford a good home there. And now at last he was ready for them to be reunited. He'd written that he had leased a three-room apartment in a place called Kingsbridge, a suburb of New York City where there were lots of other Irish. There was a Roman Catholic church and good Catholic schools, and the people were friendly and welcoming. The local priest was helping him to find some furniture so it would be all homely when they arrived. In that last letter, he'd sent the money for their tickets: thirty-five pounds and five shillings, a vast sum. But in America, Seamus earned two pounds a week, which was unthinkable back home in Ireland. Annie didn't even know anyone who got two pounds a month!

It was a new life for all of them. Their children would better themselves and get good jobs one day. The only bitter-sweet edge was the sadness Annie felt for the relatives she'd left behind: her elderly mam, her brothers and sisters and cousins. Would she ever see them again? Or would they just write letters once a month with mundane news about marriages and jobs and mutual friends and never be able to put into words how they really felt? Her mother couldn't write, but one of her sisters had said she'd take dictation.

Look on the bright side, Annie, she urged herself. *Here you are on the most luxurious ship in the world having a rare old time of it, and in five days you'll be with yer man again.* She felt excited at the thought. Married thirteen years and she still felt as much passion for him as the day they were wed. She hugged herself, thinking of the moment they'd walk down the gangplank with all their bags and there he'd be, grinning from ear to ear with his arms stretched wide.

The people in third class were friendly as well. Earlier that evening, after dinner, there had been a quick knock on the door of her cabin. She'd opened it to find three women about her age grouped outside.

'I'm Eileen Dooley,' one said. 'This is Kathleen and Mary. We noticed you earlier with your brood. Aw, will you look at them all peaceful now, God bless them.' The other women poked their heads round the cabin door for a peek. 'Anyway, we're going for a cup of tea and a chat while our menfolk are in the smoking room and we thought you might want to come along for a bit of adult company.'

Annie had been planning to spend the evening embroidering a blouse for her daughter while she had a bit of peace with them all asleep, but she was tempted. 'That's neighbourly of you, but I'm worried about leaving the little ones in a strange place. What if they wake up?'

'Your eldest looks old enough to cope. What age is he?'

'Ten.'

'Sure and they'll be fine. Turn the key in the door so they can't run off and get up to shenanigans.'

Still Annie hesitated. 'Am I dressed all right? Some folks looked so smart at dinner time. Maybe I should wear a hat?' The woman called Kathleen had a hat on but the others didn't.

'You're fine, love. Keep your hat for Sunday best.'

'If you're positive,' she said, picking up her bag and searching through it till she found the cabin key. 'They're all out for the count here, so I'll just come for a quick brew.'

They'd led her to the third-class general room, where there were polished tables and chairs, teak wall panels and white ceramic fittings. Kathleen turned out to be an old hand at transatlantic travel, and she kept exclaiming how much better the *Titanic* was than any other ship she'd been on.

'Some of these ships just pack you in like cargo,' she said. 'And you have to take your own food along, so by the end of a week's voyage everything is stale and the bread's mouldy. This place is a palace compared to them.'

'Aren't you the brave wan travelling on your own with the children like that?' Eileen told Annie. 'We're a big group. Fourteen of us, all from Mayo, so we're company for each other. You'll have to sit with us for your meals or those childrun will drive you to the demon drink by the time we reach America.'

'I'd love to,' Annie said. She'd been feeling a bit shy on the ship, not sure about the correct etiquette. Was there a dress code? Could she ask the stewards to heat a bottle for the baby? He liked his milk warm. Which bits of the ship were they allowed to wander in and which were off limits? Now there were some people she could ask, who had crossed on these ships before and could tell her what to do. They seemed a lovely bunch.

When she got back to her cabin, the children were still sound asleep, without a clue that she'd been gone a while. She climbed into bed, shifting the baby over beside the wall so he couldn't fall out. Strange to think that on the other side of that wall were thousands and thousands of miles of ocean, all the way from the Arctic to the Antarctic, and up above them only stars. She said her prayers in her head, before dropping off to sleep.

Chapter Four

Reg lay awake mulling over what he'd seen on the boat deck. Of course, he knew that rich men had affairs. He'd sometimes see them sneaking shoeless out of the wrong cabins when he passed in the early morning on his way to the dining saloon. From the girls' point of view, he could understand if they were short of money and a wealthy older man bought them jewels and fashionable gowns; that probably happened the world over. He knew from gossiping with the other lads in the mess that Mr Guggenheim had his mistress on board with him, a young French singer called Madame Aubart. They'd taken separate suites, but everyone understood that hers wasn't occupied because she stayed with him. His wife was back home in New York. Perhaps she knew about the mistress and turned a blind eye? These things happened.

Was that the case with Mr Grayling and the girl? He had a large fortune made in South American mining. Did he buy her expensive gifts in return for her favours? Somehow it didn't fit with the scene Reg had witnessed. The girl had an air about her as if she had grown up with wealth. Why would she need Mr Grayling's money if her family had plenty of its own? She could obviously afford to dispense with a fur coat that had cost goodness knows how much . . . Reg couldn't imagine what it might be worth but he knew it would be more than he earned in a year.

If it weren't about money, why would a stunning girl like her be having an affair with a man who must be more than twice her age? Reg guessed she wasn't any older than himself, and he was twenty-one. It certainly couldn't have been physical attraction because Mr Grayling wasn't a looker. He was a round-faced gent with sleek greying hair and a waxed moustache, who gave the impression of a sea-lion when first you met him. His figure was sea-lionish as well. It disturbed Reg to visualise his ample belly pressed against the girl's slender frame. If truth be told, it made him feel a bit sick.

It wasn't just the physical side that disturbed him, but also his loyalty to Mrs Grayling. She had been friendly to Reg from the first day of her Mediterranean cruise the previous year, complimenting him on his proficiency at silver service, praising the food, the views and the décor of the dining saloon. One afternoon she had eaten lunch alone because her friend felt poorly, and afterwards, while Reg was clearing the plates, they got into conversation.

'Where's home for you, Reg?' she asked.

'Southampton, ma'am.'

'Do you live with your family? Or your wife?'

'I live with my mum and three younger brothers. I've got a girlfriend, Florence, but we're not married.' He wasn't usually one for opening up to anyone about his personal affairs but Mrs Grayling was so amiable he found himself confiding in her.

'Do tell me how you met Florence,' she urged. 'I love hearing about the beginnings of relationships.'

Reg paused in his work and leant on the back of a chair. 'It was just over a year ago,' he told her. 'I was down at the docks one afternoon because there was a German ship moored – the *Prinz Friedrich Wilhelm* – and I'd never seen her before.

Florence happened to be there with her friend Lizzie and we got talking about the ships.'

In his head he relived the scene. He had overheard the girls wondering where the *Prinz Wilhelm* came from so he called over to tell them. 'She sails out of Bremen, and comes here first, then to Cherbourg and on to New York.'

'Is it a passenger or a cargo ship?' Florence asked, moving closer, and Reg explained that the transatlantic routes made most of their money ferrying emigrants to the States, but that they also took mailbags and a few tons of cargo. He told them he worked for White Star Line on their transatlantic steamers and was just back from a voyage on the *Olympic*.

'Is that a fast one?' Florence asked. The friend, Lizzie, was prettier but she seemed much shyer. All the questions were coming from Florence, so he found himself focusing his answers on her. They were easy questions, ones he could respond to knowledgeably.

'Did you ask her for a date?' Mrs Grayling asked, interrupting his reverie.

'I invited them both for a cup of tea in the Seaview Café, then as soon as the words were out of my mouth I remembered I wouldn't have enough money to pay if they both wanted cake.' He grinned. 'Fortunately, they just asked for tea.'

'What did you like about her?'

Reg considered. 'She was easy to talk to,' he said. 'She works in a stately home and we compared notes about how some upper-class folk can be a bit unreasonable. Not you, of course,' he added quickly. 'I told her about a lady I served on the *Olympic* who made a big fuss because we didn't have strawberries in December, as if we should have altered the course of the sun to change their growing season just for her.' Mrs Grayling laughed. 'And then Florence told me she got so shy sometimes when serving drinks at the big parties where she worked that her hands would shake, and the posh folks would glower at her as if she had the plague. And I looked at her and felt I understood her somehow. Do you know what I mean? I thought we might be the same.'

He remembered that was the moment when he noticed Florence had a few tiny freckles on the bridge of her nose, and thought he might like to have a chance to count them. She saw him looking and smiled back and it was a nice feeling. She was well turned out, in a blue coat with loads of tiny buttons up the front, and she wore a little hat that had a fabric flower pinned on the hatband. She held her teacup nicely, like a lady, even though her accent was similar to his own. He liked everything about her.

'So what happened next?' Mrs Grayling was lapping up the story, completely absorbed. All the other stewards had left the saloon and they were on their own in the vast room.

'I asked if we could meet again on her next day off, and said I'd bring my friend John. You know – the Geordie lad I work with?'

'I know exactly who you mean – the steward with the red hair. I've seen you chatting to him.'

'Yes, that's him. Lizzie didn't really hit it off with John, though. I don't think he was enough of a looker for her.'

They'd paired off into couples and walked up to the public gardens, and Reg felt nervous at first. He wasn't experienced at making conversation with girls and couldn't think what to talk about apart from ships, but Florence made it easy. She chattered away, full of stories about her huge, chaotic family with umpteen siblings and cousins, and about all the staff politics at the stately home where she worked, then she asked a few questions about him. When Reg told her his dad had left home when he was eight, she squeezed his arm in sympathy, and he thought that was nice. Not too much of a reaction and not too little; just right.

Before she stepped onto the tram that evening, Reg took her hand and raised it to his lips, and she giggled, obviously pleased. She kept waving at him for as long as the tram was still in sight.

'So you've been stepping out for more than a year now?' Mrs Grayling asked. 'Isn't it difficult to see each other with you being away at sea so much?'

'My trips are about two or three weeks each, then I've got at least a week off in between, sometimes more, and we'll meet up on her days off. It works out all right.'

If she could get the afternoon off, Florence would be waiting at the quayside when his ship docked. It made him feel all warm inside when he saw her tiny figure standing there waving up at him. No one had ever cared about him like that before: not his dad, not his mum, and his brothers were all young and self-obsessed. Florence was smart and insightful and he liked talking to her, liked walking arm in arm with her, liked giving her a cuddle. He'd had dinner with her family, she'd met his mum, and now a year on there was a sense that everyone was just waiting for an announcement. Wedding bells, a baby within a year, a little terraced house near the docks and her bringing up the kids while he was away at sea earning the cash.

'Do you love her? My goodness, listen to me,' Mrs Grayling laughed. 'I'm being so nosy. Please tell me to mind my own business if you don't want to answer.'

'No, it's fine.' For some reason, Reg didn't mind the directness of her questioning, although he never talked to anyone else in this way. 'I do love her, but I just don't know if I'm ready for marriage and I think that's what she wants. Her friend Lizzie got engaged recently and I could tell by the way Florence looked at me when she told me about it that she would like me to propose. Other people keep dropping hints or asking outright when I'm going to make an honest woman of her. It's what you do round our way.'

'Why don't you feel ready?'

Reg considered. 'I suppose I worry about the money. I want to have enough put aside to get us a decent place to live, and before I have kids I want to be confident that I'll be able to put food on the table for them. Working on ships, you only get a contract for each voyage and you can never be sure you'll ever be hired again. That worries me.'

There was more. Reg dreamed of bettering himself and being able to afford some of the luxuries his wealthy passengers enjoyed. Just one or two, nothing excessive.

'I want to get my own car one day,' he'd told Florence. 'Have you ever seen a picture of a Lozier? They're pure elegance on wheels. A bargain at only seven and a half thousand pounds!'

'You admire the rich more than I do,' Florence mused. 'You're more impressed by them.'

He suspected it was true. Not the ones who'd simply inherited their wealth but he admired the self-made millionaires from America, the ones who had started their own car dealerships and hotels and property empires. He wished he could make enough money to have a better life, but there was nothing he could do besides wait on table. And so they carried on as they were.

'Marriage is a tricky thing,' Mrs Grayling told him. 'It's hard work and sometimes it feels as though you are the only one trying.' Suddenly she looked very downcast. Her grey-blue eyes had depths of sadness in them. 'But it sounds as though you had better be careful not to let that girl slip away. Aren't you worried she'll meet someone else while you're at sea?'

Reg thought about it for a moment then shook his head. 'She wouldn't ever mess me around. She's an honest, straightforward girl, and that's what I like.'

'You should hang onto her then. Take my advice.'

A year after that exchange, Reg was overjoyed when he looked at the *Titanic*'s first-class passenger list and spotted Mrs Grayling's name. He asked the chief steward, Mr Latimer, if he could wait on her table and as soon as she walked in to dinner on the first evening and saw him holding her chair for her, she exclaimed, 'Reg! How wonderful you're here. Tell me, how is the lovely Florence?'

He was touched to the core that such a grand lady would remember anything about his life. 'She's fine, thank you, ma'am,' he said.

'And are you married yet?'

'Not yet,' he grinned.

'But still together?' Reg nodded. 'That's good. I'm delighted to see you again.'

Then two nights after that reunion, Reg saw Mrs Grayling's husband with the young woman on the boat deck and he felt simply awful about it. The knowledge weighed heavily on him. It was as if being witness to her husband's infidelity had somehow made him culpable himself. Should he tell Mrs Grayling? Or do something about it himself? But what?

Chapter Five

Next morning at breakfast, Reg couldn't meet Mrs Grayling's eye, scared that something in his countenance might give away what he had seen on the boat deck. The situation was compounded when he overheard Mr Grayling being irascible with his wife. He seemed a bad-tempered sort, forever complaining about something: his food wasn't hot enough, or the next table were making too much noise. That was forgivable, Reg supposed, but speaking discourteously to such a sweet-natured person was not.

'Will you try out the gymnasium today, George?' she asked. 'You could have a Turkish bath afterwards. It's supposed to have glorious mosaics.'

'Have you taken leave of your senses? When have you ever known me go to a gymnasium or a Turkish bath?' Mr Grayling's tone was impatient, and as Reg arranged the cutlery for their chosen dishes, he couldn't help noticing the hurt look on Mrs Grayling's face. He remembered her commenting that marriage was hard work and watching her with Mr Grayling, Reg could imagine why she might feel that way.

'I plan to stroll along the promenade this morning, then perhaps I shall write some postcards in the reading room,' she told her husband. 'How about you, dear?'

'I haven't made up my mind yet but when I do, I'll be sure to inform you.'

His tone was heavy with sarcasm and Reg flinched. Mr Grayling seemed to be in a particularly foul mood, which was rum considering that, from what Reg had seen, he was having his cake and eating it. What right did he have to be bad-tempered, when he had both a charming wife and a willowy, goddess-like mistress?

He wasn't the only grumpy one that morning. At one of Reg's tables there was a young Canadian couple, Mr and Mrs Howson, and the wife was a silly, giggling girl who kept making eyes at Reg right under her husband's nose. It was a game to her. Maybe she was trying to show hubbie that she was attractive to other men, but it put Reg in a very awkward situation. He tried to be strictly formal and avoid any eye contact, but Mrs Howson insisted on clutching his arm and asking inane questions.

'What's the difference between a herring and a haddock, Reg? I only like fish that don't have any bones.' She clutched his arm and peered up at him with doe eyes.

He felt like telling her that jellyfish were the only fish without bones and they didn't have any on the menu. He also wanted to ask her to let go of his arm, but he did neither. 'The herring have tiny bones throughout so you might be better with the haddock, ma'am.'

'You always look after me so well,' she purred, and her husband snorted. It was embarrassing, and Reg moved away from their table as quickly as he could.

As he worked, he kept an eye on the saloon door watching for the girl from the boat deck to arrive. He was curious to find out whether she was travelling with a husband or, if she was unmarried, who was chaperoning her. They certainly weren't doing a very good job. Women like her would never travel alone. It simply wasn't done.

First class was full of beautiful women. Some had looks that owed a substantial debt to artifice, but others were natural stunners. Even at breakfast, they wore fancy gowns in expensive velvets and silks with lace trimmings, and they all had hats with feathers and bows pinned to their heads. Every lady in first class wore a hat for breakfast and lunch and some kind of headdress for dinner. It was a regular fashion parade. Florence would have enjoyed looking at the clothes, he thought. She liked nice clothes. He'd gone with her a few times to browse through the rails in Tyrrell & Green's department store, although she could seldom afford to buy more than a new pair of gloves or a length of lace to trim a petticoat.

Breakfast service ended at 10.30 and there had been no sign of the girl from the boat deck. Maybe she was having a lie-in, or perhaps she had chosen to dine at one of the ship's cafés or the à la carte restaurant. He cleared the last plates from his tables and set them for luncheon, then caught his friend John's eye and motioned with two fingers to his lips that he would meet him down in the mess for a fag. John nodded, but he had a table who were being slow to finish their meal, so Reg went on ahead.

He stopped in at the dorm to pick up his fags and wrinkled his nose at the vegetable smell of farts and feet and armpits; the twenty-seven men who slept there wouldn't have a bath till they reached New York so it was sure to get worse each day. There were only two baths for the eight-hundred-plus crew members, and a separate one for the officers. Reg opened a couple of portholes and jammed them ajar with iron shoots from the store cupboard. That should help. Then he took the fags and matches and made his way to the stewards' mess, where he sat down and waited for John to arrive so they could light up at the same time.

Reg wasn't a big smoker. Some stewards were always nipping off for a fag and getting antsy when they were forced to go too long without one, but for Reg it was just a punctuation mark in the day, a chance to put his feet up and socialise. He collected the cigarette cards for his little brothers, and they'd never forgive him if he gave up, but generally he could take it or leave it.

'You'll never guess what I saw last night!' Reg told John after they'd both exhaled the first drag. 'One of my passengers, Mr Grayling, fooling around on the boat deck with a girl less than half his age while his wife is in their suite just a couple of decks below.'

John was unsurprised. 'Goes on all the time with these people. They have different rules to you and me. It's not just the men either. The women do it as well.'

'Get away with you.' Reg frowned.

'Colonel Astor's first wife had an affair and the whole of New York knew about it. They say his daughter isn't really his. Now he's got divorced and married again and they're all pointing the finger and saying he shouldn't have remarried, but if you ask me his wife was the one that started it.'

Reg had heard something of the kind before but hadn't paid much attention. 'They sit in your section, don't they? What do you think of the new wife?'

John wrinkled his nose and gave it some thought. 'Bit of a mousy thing. She'll let him be the boss, though. She won't be running off with fancy men, not like the last one.'

'She's only young. Eighteen, I heard, and he's nearly fifty. I don't know why a girl would want to do that.'

John rolled his eyes comically. 'Hundred million dollars in the bank? I'd marry him for that!'

'I don't think you're his type somehow.' John would never win any beauty contests, but he was the nicest chap you could ever hope to meet.

They'd become friends on Reg's first voyage after some of the other lads played a practical joke on him. He'd been working flat out from five in the morning and got to the dorm at eleven that night so faint with exhaustion that he was hoping to fall straight into his bunk. But as he walked in the door, he heard stifled laughter and sensed something was up. Sure enough, there was a huge metal object jammed into the space between his bunk and the one above: a dessert trolley from the dining room. It was about five feet long, two feet wide and felt as though it weighed a ton.

'You bastards!' Reg swore and the room erupted into laughter. He grabbed the trolley's handle and tried to yank it out but it was jammed in tightly and hard to manoeuvre. 'Bloody hell, I don't believe it.'

'Here you go, man. I'll give you a hand.' John skipped round the other side of the bunk to push from behind, while Reg pulled, and soon they had the dessert trolley back on the floor again.

'Thanks, mate,' Reg nodded, and from then on they were pals. They covered for each other on the ship and watched each other's backs when their shipmates were fooling around. It was like having a brother on board.

Reg had hoped John would have some advice for him regarding Mr Grayling's infidelity, and in particular if there was anything he should do about it. 'You should have seen this girl who was with him on the boat deck,' he reiterated. 'She was the bee's knees. I'll point her out at luncheon. It didn't make sense somehow.'

It was only afterwards he realised he'd forgotten to tell John about the fur coat, in some ways the strangest part of the scene he had witnessed. He made a mental note to mention it later.

Chapter Six

After breakfast Margaret Grayling found a deckchair on the promenade and sat staring out at the ocean with a huge lump in her throat, her eyes watering in the salt breeze. George, her husband, had been more than usually difficult during this voyage. He'd always been a cold man but his rudeness to her had previously been confined to their moments alone. He would never have spoken discourteously to her in front of the servants at their Madison Avenue home, yet he was prepared to do so in front of a steward on the *Titanic*, when all around them sat the cream of New York high society, no doubt listening in.

In private, George had renewed his demands that she should divorce him, but the idea was anathema to her. It was against every religious principle she held dear. They had been married in the sight of God and the minister had clearly said, 'What God hath joined together, let no man cast asunder.' How could she go against God's commandment?

George didn't share her religious beliefs and seemed to think she was merely worried about what society might say. In 1912, divorce caused a scandal and there was no question that both parties were stigmatised by it, even when one was blameless. But Margaret had never given much weight to the opinions of society. She didn't engage in the complex sets of social rules that dictated the parties and dinners to which you were invited, the box in which you appeared at the opera, or which ladies left visiting cards at your door. She had more or less stopped appearing in society seven years earlier, after great tragedy had rent her life apart.

Theirs had never been a passionate marriage but it had produced a daughter, a gentle, artistic girl called Alice, who was the sun around which they both revolved and the cement that kept their marriage civil and sometimes even happy throughout the seventeen years of her life. When Alice died of scarlet fever in February 1905, everything had collapsed inwards. In the cruellest of all the cruel things George had ever hurled at her, he screamed that it was her fault, that she had been responsible for killing their daughter, and from that fatal wound their marriage had never recovered.

Rationally, Margaret knew it was simply not true. She and Alice had visited friends of hers and two days after the visit, it transpired that one of the friends had succumbed to scarlet fever, despite showing no signs of it when they were there. And then Alice developed a sore throat and pink cheeks and a sandpapery rash on her chest and neck. Her friend recovered within a week but Alice's condition had continued to deteriorate. She struggled for breath and was rarely fully conscious during her last days. George paid for the advice of every specialist in New York and beyond, throwing money at the problem, but to no avail. In the small hours of the night, Alice's breathing became fainter and fainter, then stopped altogether.

A solitary tear trickled down Margaret's cheek. Grief like that never left you. It abated sometimes, just for a while, then returned to thump you in the gut and knock you backwards when you least expected it. It was something she would always live with. But George turned all his grief into anger directed towards his wife. All the intimacy of their marriage, such as there had been, mutated into cold silence or bitter recrimination. She missed the days when they used to be a team, lying in bed together discussing Alice's small triumphs. She missed the occasional gesture of physical affection. Even a simple peck on the cheek would mean so much now but there was no chance of that. Never again.

She'd hoped this trip to Europe could achieve some kind of rapprochement. She'd begged him to bring her along, hoping that the unfamiliar surroundings might re-ignite some companionship at least, but to no avail. He had left her on her own for several weeks in a hotel in Bologna, claiming that he had business to conduct, then insisted on cutting short the vacation and rushing to catch *Titanic*'s maiden voyage. Nothing had been gained by the trip. They were returning to the aching loneliness of the mansion where they lived separate lives under the same roof.

Should she go against God's will and give George his divorce so that each had a chance of happiness in the future? The more she observed other marriages, the more she believed that women seemed most content who lived on their own.

There was a Canadian couple in the dining saloon, the Howsons, who were a terrible advertisement for the institution. Married less than a year, they were already disappointed in each other. Neither had fulfilled the other's expectations. Margaret knew them slightly and could see where the fault lines lay. She hated that he gambled or, more particularly, that he gambled and lost. He hated the money she spent on clothes and fripperies. He'd been a bachelor throughout his twenties and had never realised quite how much a new gown cost, nor how many were required to see a fashionable woman through the season. On the *Titanic*, first-class women would never dare turn up to dinner in a gown they had worn before. Each evening required a lavish new creation.

There was something more, Margaret mused. They had moved to New York after their marriage and he had hoped to gain immediate acceptance in high society through his wife, who came from a better family. He had no concept that to reach the inner circle of the kind of high-society grandees travelling on the ship would take careful calculation and manoeuvring over at least a year, and even then they might never get there since he worked in property. Being Canadian stood against them as well. They might be endured for the course of the voyage but no new invitations would be delivered to their butler on their return.

Margaret could view all this from a distance and see the futility of their ambitions and desires in the context of a life. So many other things were more important, but the young could never understand that. To them social position was everything, since a wag had said back in the 1880s that there were only four hundred fashionable people in New York (the exact number that would fit in Mrs William Astor's ballroom). The term 'The Four Hundred' had been coined and instantly everyone began scrabbling for their place in the hallowed ranks. The irony was that the harder you tried, the less eligible you appeared, and she knew the Howsons would never get there. Would that prove a rupture that would tear their marriage apart?

Mrs Howson's flirtatiousness with Reg was awkward for the boy. He dealt with it professionally, but it couldn't be easy when you are trained to be polite to all passengers. You can't take sides between husband and wife.

She wondered if marriage would be easier when you came from Reg's class. Surely things would be simpler without all the rules about status that bedevilled her own class? His girl, Florence, sounded like a sweetheart, but Reg had intimated that he was hesitating about taking the step of getting engaged. Maybe it was hardly surprising given all the bickering couples he saw on the ships where he worked. He didn't want to make a mistake. He was a good person, and wouldn't have led her on for – what was it? – two years now if he didn't genuinely love her.

Margaret had taken a liking to Reg. He had the looks of a moving picture star but seemed unaware of it. There was no trace of the vanity that afflicted many handsome men she had met, who checked their appearance in every reflective surface and strutted arrogantly into rooms, watching for a reaction. Reg seemed modest and introspective, and an all-round good sort.

During the Mediterranean voyage, she had witnessed an incident that he didn't know she had seen. His friend John had been looking very queasy during breakfast service one morning, as if he had a stomach upset, and he had suddenly rushed off, leaving a pile of soiled plates on a table near the entrance, where arriving guests would see them. The chief steward noticed them and became instantly enraged. His eyes swept the room looking for someone to blame, and in an instant Reg was by his side. Margaret was close enough to overhear their exchange.

'I'm sorry, sir, I only put them down for a moment. It won't happen again,' Reg said, and relayed them quickly to the pantry, letting John off the hook.

That's one of the reasons he was Margaret's favourite steward, but she also liked a sense that he had hidden depths. He was a sensitive person, who thought about the world and all that he saw of it. When they talked, he really looked at her and seemed to see beneath the surface.

There was something else, as well. Reg was an independent type. Deep down, despite his bosom friendship with John, she sensed a loneliness in him, and that's what attracted her. They were alike in that, for she was herself perhaps the loneliest woman in the world.

Chapter Seven

At luncheon, first-class passengers could choose from a set menu with soup, fish, chicken, eggs or beef; they could have items from the grill, such as mutton chops or sirloin steak; or they could select from a buffet with salad, cold cuts and sea-food dishes, such as salmon mayonnaise, Norwegian anchovies or potted shrimp. Reg hovered near the buffet to help serve passengers when they'd made their decision, or to retrieve the food they dropped while serving themselves.

Most of the ladies had changed since breakfast. First thing in the morning they wore skirts and blouses but for lunch they wore suits with long jackets – some of them caught at the back like a bustle, others slim and fitting on the hips – and all topped with the obligatory hat. Personally, Reg thought it was silly wearing a hat to eat a meal because they kept having to flick back those long floaty feathers and ribbons to stop them dipping in the food.

The Howsons sat down at their table and Reg spread the napkin on Mrs Howson's lap in a swift fluttering motion, with-out touching her or encroaching on her line of sight, just as he'd been taught. Straight away she began bothering him with her dozens of inane questions.

'Have you ever been skiing, Reg? You'd love it. You should visit Calgary some time and we'll take you out on the slopes.'

'Thank you, ma'am, but my work keeps me too busy.'

'You've got such a good figure, you must play some sports. What do you play, Reg?'

'I like a bit of football when I'm back home.'

'What in God's name is football?'

'It's a game with two teams where you kick a ball into a goal, ma'am.'

The husband sat scowling throughout their exchange; then as soon as Reg left the table, he heard the hiss of their argument.

'It's vulgar to talk to the staff like that. You shouldn't be overfamiliar. Didn't your mother teach you anything?'

'You're such a snob.'

'You're so common.'

The tension grew as they ate, and Reg tried to keep himself well clear of them. When he came to collect their plates, Mrs Howson's face was pink with fury.

'My husband thinks I shouldn't fraternise with you, Reg. What do you think?'

'Oh shut up,' her husband snapped. 'Leave the poor boy alone.'

Reg was balancing their plates and a serving dish on one arm as he scooped a stray piece of cauliflower from the table-cloth. Mrs Howson turned and yanked the pocket of his jacket just at a moment when he was twisted at an awkward angle, leaning sideways towards the table.

'I'll talk to him if I feel like it,' he heard her saying as he struggled to regain his balance, but it was no use. He managed to twirl at the last moment so that the dishes fell to the floor behind rather than into her lap, but the dining salon fell silent at the resounding crash of breaking crockery. It echoed round the Jacobean carved ceiling then died away to an expectant silence.

Instantly Reg spun into action, crouching down and picking up the jagged pieces in his hands. John appeared by his side with a dustpan and brush and between them they had the floor spotless again in less than a minute. But the chief steward, old Latimer, was watching and as Reg scurried past, he said in a cold voice, 'Wait behind after service.'

Reg was glad to see that the Howsons had left when he emerged from the galley. Mr Grayling had gone as well, but Mrs Grayling sat alone at their table, so he approached to ask if he could fetch anything for her.

'I saw what happened with those plates,' she told him. 'It wasn't your fault. Will you get into trouble?'

'Please don't worry on my behalf, ma'am.'

'I could explain to the chief steward what I saw, if that would help.'

'Thank you,' Reg said. 'But I simply lost my balance. I'm sorry if the noise disturbed you.'

She looked at him with her kind eyes. 'They'll make you pay for the breakages out of your salary, won't they? I know how these liners operate. And I'm sure this porcelain is expensive. Please will you at least let me give you the money?'

'We're not supposed to accept money from passengers, but thank you very much for the offer.' For a moment, he felt like crying under her maternal gaze. She was much nicer than his own mum, who'd never had any time for him. She couldn't wait to send him out to work so he could contribute to the household coffers, which seemed to be his only value to her.

'Nonsense. Plenty of the other staff members accept tips, and you will accept one from me. I insist. I will slip it to you quietly, when no one else is looking, some time before we reach New York, but for now I don't want to hear any more about it.'

She stood up to bring an end to the conversation. 'I'll see you at dinner.'

'Thank you, ma'am.' Reg pulled back her chair for her, wrestling with a powerful wave of embarrassment mixed with gratitude.

He would accept the money, he decided, after Old Latimer told him that the three porcelain plates he had broken cost two and six each. Reg's wages were only two shillings and four-pence per day, so that breakage would cost him more than three days' wages – in other words half of what he would make on that crossing.

'Worse than that,' he told John later, 'it's going on my report. I explained what happened but he wasn't having it. It's one law for them and another for us and I'm fed up to the back teeth with it.'

'It's just the way it is. No point fighting the system.' John never got into trouble, never got caught on the rare occasions when he did transgress the rules.

'It's all right for you with your squeaky clean record. I'm trying to better myself and all I get are setbacks.'

'It'll be fine so long as you keep your nose clean from now on. They won't do anything about one misdemeanour. Anyway, I wish I had your problems with all the lasses fancying me.' John grinned at him. 'You've always got lasses chasing after you. Remember those ones at the fairground last week? It must be your dark, brooding looks.'

'What a load of rot!' Reg punched his arm. It was true that two girls had latched onto them at the fair and wouldn't leave them alone even after he mentioned he was stepping out with someone. They hadn't been interested in John, just him. That kind of attention was discomfiting. He hated it.

'Did you see your lass at lunch?' John continued. 'The one from the boat deck?'

'She never turned up. She must take her meals elsewhere.' Reg had forgotten about her till John brought it up but suddenly he recalled the vision of the silvery-white dress silhouetted against the dark ocean, and the fur coat flapping as it fell through the air.

'Way you described her, I think you've got the hots for her,' John teased. 'You like the lasses with a bit of class.'

'I wouldn't touch her with a bargepole,' Reg exclaimed. 'I don't like girls who mess around with other women's husbands.'

'I'm sure she'll be heartbroken to hear it.' John imitated a lady sobbing into her sleeve.

Reg laughed, but he meant it. He felt contempt for women who did that. He bet they never thought of all the people their affairs affected, and the repercussions it could have. They were selfish creatures, only in it for what they could get.

Back home in Southampton, when Reg was a young boy, he used to lie crushed up in bed with his three younger brothers, hearing sounds from the next room of his dad groaning and the bedsprings creaking and then a woman uttering little sighs. Reg knew that his mum was at work – she worked nights at a laundry – and his dad was in there with someone else. He was too young to know exactly what sex was, but old enough to know that shouldn't be happening. 'Keep yer mouth shut or I'll clip yer ear for ye,' his dad snapped in response to Reg's reproachful stare over breakfast.

He wanted to tell his mum what he'd seen, because he was young enough that he still felt he ought to tell her everything, but he didn't because she always looked so sad. When she was at home she often sat at the kitchen table and wept

51

and Reg didn't want to be the one to make her any sadder. Then his dad left home when he was eight and he heard his mum saying it was all because of 'that floozy'. She took longer shifts at the laundry and drank gin and got sadder, and it was up to Reg to look after his younger brothers, scraping together haphazard meals and forcing them to wash every now and again.

Reg went to sea when he was fourteen. It's what you did when you came from the Northam district of Southampton. All his mates were doing the same. Some became firemen or trimmers, electricians or greasers, but Reg always wanted to be out front meeting the wealthy passengers, so he trained as a saloon steward and worked his way up from third class to first. He had to learn silver service, and be able to explain all the dishes on the menu, and most of all he had to become adept at gliding in beside the diners without them feeling as though he were in their space. He must never touch or lean over them. His exhalations of air should not brush their cheeks. He should be in and out before they even noticed he was there. It was an art, and he reckoned he was pretty good at it.

He started out working on Mediterranean cruise ships, and when they were given shore leave in Gibraltar or Genoa, Nice or Naples, the other lads would go to a local knocking shop, but Reg never joined them. He and John discovered a mutual love of swimming, so whenever there was time they'd go for a good splash-around in the clear blue-green waters. If it was too cold, or it wasn't a good spot for swimming, Reg would go for a long walk, getting his bearings in the town and watching the people who lived there. He liked imagining what their lives were like: what they ate for dinner, what they did in their spare time, whether they loved their families.

'He's an odd fellow,' the lads said about him, but he didn't care. He didn't even care when they hinted he might be homosexual. Let them say what they liked, he'd decided to wait until he fell in love before having sexual relations. He wanted it to be nice, not sordid. He wanted to find someone he loved and stay with that person for the rest of his life. When he worked in steerage on transatlantic ships, there were women who'd offer themselves to him in the corridors: earthy-smelling, dark women with huge soft bosoms and missing teeth. One had lifted her skirt and pressed his hand against her mound.

'Get me a souvenir from first class, love? An ashtray, or a cup and saucer? I'll make it worth your while.'

He grabbed his hand back. 'Sorry, ma'am. We're not allowed.'

The other lads did it, though. He'd come upon them in storerooms, trousers round their knees, panting as they thrust into some fleshy creature who was pinned against the wall. It disgusted Reg. He didn't like to mix with those sorts.

When he met Florence, he knew straight away she was different. She didn't flirt with other men. When he kissed her it felt nice, not sordid. He couldn't imagine swapping her for anyone else, especially not these first-class ladies with their airs and graces, who flirted with him as though he was their personal plaything. It was no way to treat another human being. There was a term for it nowadays. They called them flappers: young, mischievous, impetuous types who flirted with anyone who took their fancy. The girl on the boat deck was a flapper. So was Mrs Howson. Reg didn't like either of them. They were dangerous. If you knew what was good for you, you'd keep out of their way.

Chapter Eight

The stewards were free from the end of lunch service, at around three o'clock, until just before dinner began at six. They ate a meal in the mess on E Deck, usually whatever was left over from the third-class dinner, then had a couple of hours free. Reg liked to walk around the ship, exploring. He folded a white tea towel over his arm so that it would look as though he was engaged on an errand, but in reality he was spying. He liked to watch the passengers and see how they chose to spend their days, trying to imagine what it must feel like to be them.

That Saturday, he started up on A Deck where, on the first-class promenade, he overheard a group of passengers discussing whether they might see a pod of dolphins. 'On our last crossing they followed the ship for ages and they were simply divine creatures, so intelligent.'

Reg didn't interrupt to tell them that the North Atlantic was far too cold for dolphins in April. They were intelligent enough to be sunning themselves down in the Caribbean at that time of year.

He walked the length of A Deck and into the first-class smoking room, where there was already a card game in progress. Men's heads were bowed in concentration and a blueish fug of cigar smoke hovered above them. In the Verandah and

Palm Court next door, some children were playing with hoops on sticks, whooping as they wove among the tables, while their nursemaids sat talking in low voices. He walked down the stairs to B Deck. A few young folk were relaxing in the Café Parisien and, as he walked past, one of them called out, 'I say, could you fetch us some pink gins?'

'Of course, sir,' Reg nodded, and he passed on the order to one of the French stewards employed there. Every room on the *Titanic* was an exquisite copy of something or other and this was supposed to be a Parisian pavement café, so the staff were all French (or at least spoke in mock French accents). He glanced along the length of the room, wondering if the girl from the boat deck might be spending her time there, with the younger set, but there was no sign.

He worked his way along the B Deck corridor and level by level wandered down into the depths of the ship. The reception room on D Deck was empty; most first-class passengers were either upstairs or in their cabins having an afternoon nap. Down on E Deck, he helped a gentleman who was looking for the barber's shop but had wandered into the crew quarters off Scotland Road instead.

'Good lord,' the gent exclaimed. 'How did I get into a staff area?'

'It's easily done, sir,' Reg told him.

When he reached the third-class cabins on F Deck, there was a strong smell of garlic and cheap hair oil and the chatter was in Eastern European languages he couldn't fathom. He'd picked up a smattering of Italian and French and Spanish from his trips round the Med, and thought he had a good ear, but these languages had lots of 'schm' and 'brr' sounds and no roots that he could identify.

The aft end of third class accommodated the Irish and it always sounded as though there was a party going on as they called from cabin to cabin, and groups of them congregated in the corridors. They were excited to be going to America, excited to be on this ship. One bunch of women hovered directly in his path and he couldn't help overhearing their conversation.

'Eileen, did you see yon toothy fellow dancing in the meeting room last night? He nearly tripped o'er his own feet trying to catch your eye.'

'Away with ye,' Eileen drawled. 'He was just clumsy.' She stepped back to let Reg past and there was a silence then a whispering behind his back. He sensed they were nudging each other and gesturing towards him.

'Well, isn't that lovely now,' an older woman's voice said, and they all laughed out loud.

Reg blushed, glad they couldn't see his face, and turned off at the next doorway that led to a staircase. He descended to G Deck, where the post office was situated right next to the squash court. Suddenly there was a commotion. A door leading to the boiler room opened and an engineer emerged holding two scrawny, tousled children by their arms. Spotting Reg, he called over, 'Can you find out where these two come from? I just caught them sneaking around the engines without a by your leave.' He shook the boys' arms, but they were giggling and didn't look in the least abashed. 'If I catch you in here again, I'll have you scrubbing the decks,' he warned.

Reg wasn't looking at the boys, though. Over the engineer's shoulder he caught a glimpse of the huge machine with all its pistons and cylinders and shafts, pounding back and forwards in order to provide the power that made the ship move. It emitted impressive hissing and clanking noises, and Reg could well understand why the two boys had sneaked in for a look. He'd have liked to do the same himself, but the engineer slammed the door, leaving him in charge of the children.

'Which class are you in, lads?'

They looked at each other. 'Third,' the older one said. 'With me mam and baby brother and sister.' The accent was Irish.

'What're your names?'

'I'm Finbarr and he's Patrick.'

'Where was your mum when you last saw her?'

'She was in our cabin, changing the baby.'

'I bet you don't know your cabin number,' Reg challenged. 'Young lads like you would never remember.'

'We do too. It's E107.' The older one was doing all the talking. He was a gangly lad wearing short trousers that he was too old for. Surely his mum could have got him some long ones for the voyage to cover those awkward kneecaps?

'Let's go up there, then. She'll be worried about you.'

On the way, he told them what he knew boys would want to know: that the ship had two four-cylinder triple-expansion steam engines that drove the propellers, and a low-pressure turbine that recycled steam from the engines. He told them that it had a maximum speed of twenty-three knots but that they were currently only doing about twenty-one. He told them there were twenty-four double-ended boilers and six single-ended ones and that firemen worked day and night to feed coal into a hundred and fifty-nine furnaces. He told them the length and the breadth and the tonnage of the ship, and he was still talking when they arrived up on E Deck outside number 107.

Hearing voices, Annie McGeown opened the door and immediately grabbed her sons and pulled them into the room.

'What have they been doing? Oh, I hope they haven't been up to mischief and causing trouble?'

'Not at all,' Reg told her. 'We were just having a chat about the ship.' He saw the boys' expressions of surprise when they realised he wasn't going to tell on them for going in the engine room. 'They're clever lads,' he continued. 'I bet they do well at school.'

'I'm so grateful to you, Mr. . .'

'Parton. Reg Parton.'

'I'm Annie McGeown. I wonder, could I ask you a question? Is there somewhere I can warm the baby's milk? I filled his bottle from a jug at lunch so I could give him a feed later, but he doesn't like it cold. I haven't seen any other babies down here and I don't want to cause a fuss.'

'Do you want it now?' Reg asked. 'I can pop down the corridor to our mess and get someone to do it straight away. Other times, you ask any steward in the dining saloon.'

'Oh, if you're sure it's no trouble?'

'Tell you what,' Reg suggested. 'Why don't your two eldest come with me and they can bring it back again?'

This was readily agreed and Reg led them along the corridor and through the crisscross metal gate into Scotland Road. He showed them where the crew dorms were, and the storerooms and the mess, then he took them to meet Mr Joughin, who warmed the bottle and gave them a teacake each. The boys kept nudging each other in their excitement. Finally, Reg showed them back to the gateway into third-class aft, and pointed them in the direction of their cabin.

'Will we see you again?' Finbarr asked wistfully.

'I should think so,' Reg smiled. 'I'll keep an eye out for you.'

'Grand!' Finbarr breathed, and Reg realised with amusement

that they looked up to him. They must be the only people on the ship who did.

Once they'd gone, he wandered back to his berth for a lie-down. He had a Sherlock Holmes novel with him but he wasn't in the mood for it. He spotted an old newspaper among John's things and pulled it out. It was dated the 8th of April, the day before they'd sailed. Reg climbed up onto his bunk and opened it.

The headlines were all about two steamers that had collided on the River Nile, and they estimated around two hundred were dead. Reg shuddered. He hoped they had drowned rather than being devoured by Nile crocodiles. Seamen hate reading about deaths in the water so he quickly turned the page. The PM, Mr Asquith, was about to introduce his third Irish Home Rule Bill. Good luck to him, Reg thought. No matter what he offered, he'd never manage to keep all the parties happy. Some suffragettes had been chaining themselves to the railings at Parliament again. And then he came to the society pages and settled back to read properly.

There was a photo of some lords and ladies in full evening dress huddled under umbrellas outside the Savoy. The accompanying story congratulated them for coming out to a ball on such a filthy night and risking getting rain or mud on their expensive gowns and black tie dinner suits. The picture was grainy but they looked radiant and not the slightest bit damp. What you couldn't see were the footmen off to the sides who were holding the umbrellas. They'd probably look like drowned cats, but he supposed that wouldn't be the kind of picture the paper would want to print. Not on the society pages.

He glanced at the names. They were all called Charles, Edwin, Herbert, or names like that. None of them was called Reg or John. The ladies had flowery names: Violet, Charlotte, Venetia.

John came into the dorm. 'There you are. I thought you'd jumped overboard after your little accident at lunch.'

Reg sighed. 'You can bet the stupid flapper who caused it won't be losing any sleep. Tell me, John, d'you ever wish your mum had called you Herbert? D'you think your life might have been different?'

'If I had a different mam, my life would have been different. A name's a name.'

'What's wrong with your mum, then?'

'I dunno. I never see her. Haven't been home in a while. We're not a close family, not like yours.' John came from Newcastle and he always claimed there wasn't enough time between sailings to nip back and see his folks, but Reg guessed he didn't make much effort.

'The only thing close about our family is the way we all live on top of each other. I wish I could afford to get digs, like you.'

'You'll have your own place soon enough when you and Florence tie the knot.' John put his finger in his mouth and popped his cheek.

Reg threw a pillow at him. 'Don't you get on my case as well! I've got enough people telling me what I should do. There's a whole big world out there and you and me should be off exploring it instead of rushing down the aisle.'

'That's why we came to sea, isn't it? To see the world, meet the rich – and clean up after them. Did I tell you I had to mop up after a yappy little dog had a widdle in the dining saloon yesterday? The owner knows she's not supposed to bring him, but she sneaks him under her shawl then he sits on her lap eating bits of fillet steak and whatnot.'

Reg smiled. He'd noticed the lady in question, with a tiny nose poking out of her oversized handbag. 'I bet she's American.'

'Course. An English lady wouldn't do that. You can tell a mile off which nationality they are before they open their mouths, can't you?'

'Definitely. It's the way they hold themselves. Americans slouch.' John nodded agreement. 'And they talk about themselves all the time without listening to other people.'

'I can't stand watching them eat,' John added. 'They shovel the food in. And their table manners would make your hair stand on end. They just reach across the table for things instead of asking and they use all the wrong cutlery.'

A steward lying on a nearby bunk, a chap called Bill, butted into their conversation. 'I had one American gent complaining because his knife wouldn't cut the steak, and he was actually using his fish knife. I didn't say anything, though. Just went and got him another steak knife and then he was happy.'

'I've got one who brings his own cutlery with him because he doesn't trust ones that anyone else has used. He's an odd one. Won't share the sugar bowl with anyone else on his table, but wants one of his own. I just set completely separate things for his place. He's not even one of the millionaires. He's down on E Deck.' This came from a steward named Harry.

It seemed everyone had a story about the passengers on their tables, although some thought the English were worst because they were so perfectionist and snooty. 'Lady Duff Gordon won't take food from a serving plate if I've served anyone else from it. There's six of them at the table but I think she reckons she's the grandest.'

'You work in Gatti's, don't you?' Reg asked, because the last speaker had an Italian accent. Gatti's was the à la carte restaurant on board, run by Luigi Gatti, who also ran the restaurants at the Ritz in London. Passengers paid extra to dine there.

The chap nodded. 'Why do you ask?'

'I don't suppose you have a girl who comes in there, really slender, with copper-coloured hair? She's drop-dead beautiful, about twenty-ish I'd say. I saw her on deck last night in a silvery-white dress, very low neckline,' Reg motioned with his hands, 'but she hasn't been into our restaurant so I thought maybe she eats in yours.' He wondered why he was asking. It made him sound obsessed. What would they all think?

The Gatti's waiter shook his head. 'They are mostly older couples in ours. I can't think of a girl like you describe.'

'Reg is in love,' John teased, and this was met by a chorus of whistles and 'wey-hey' noises.

'Course I'm not.' Reg was regretting opening his mouth. 'I only saw her once. I just wondered why she never comes to the dining saloon. I 'spect that's why she's so skinny.'

'She might eat in the Parisien or the Verandah,' one chap suggested. 'Lots of the young ones eat in the Parisien.'

'A few of them get food sent to their rooms. Only if they're feeling under the weather, though.'

'Perhaps she's not in first class?' Bill suggested. 'There are some lookers downstairs as well.'

Reg considered it for a brief second, but there was no question in his mind. 'She's definitely in first. Keep your eyes peeled for me, will you?'

'For you? Not if I see her first,' Bill rejoined, and they all chuckled at the idea. In reality, none of them would ever try getting it on with an upper-class lady. It wasn't the way things worked. You were born to a certain station and that's where you stayed. For a saloon steward to have an affair with a first-class passenger would be like a donkey squiring a thorough-bred horse.

Reg wished John hadn't said he was in love. It was quite the opposite really. He was curious about the girl from the boat deck but he instinctively disliked her for what she was doing. He was still wondering if there was anything he could do to protect Mrs Grayling from finding out about the affair. He considered asking John's advice, but when he thought about it, he was pretty sure he could guess what the answer would be: 'Ye daft eejit! Keep your nose well out of it.'

Chapter Nine

By dinner time on Saturday evening, Juliette was restless in her gilded prison. No matter how large the ship, there was no escape from the exasperating presence of her mother, and from the burden of class expectations, which were magnified a thousand times on board. Here were the *crème de la crème* of American society and a good few British aristocrats, all mingling together and watching each other closely for any lapse in standards. Not for a second could you swear, or burp, or put your feet up on a table, never mind attend breakfast without a hat. Brought up with a brother who was close in age, Juliette enjoyed tennis, cricket and tree-climbing rather than needle-point and bridge. She liked male conversations about politics and exploration and technology but when she tried to engage their companions in the reception room outside the dining saloon in speculation about what might have happened to Captain Scott, her mother was desperate to change the subject.

'Really, Juliette, I'm sure the ladies don't wish to talk about such things.'

Juliette ignored her and continued. 'Mr Amundsen has returned triumphant so at least we know it's possible. But the papers are saying that Scott's party did not have enough supplies with them for this length of time. I do hope they are all right.'

A middle-aged American woman called Mrs Grayling, whom they had met just that evening, smiled at her. 'I'm fascinated by the stories I've read about both men. They seem infinitely resourceful. I have a hunch that Captain Scott will be fine. He might even have turned up while we've been at sea.'

Her husband didn't agree. 'They'd have told us. Someone would have telegrammed news like that to the ship and the captain would have announced it. Remember we heard the news that Amundsen had returned safely while on our voyage across to Europe.'

'That's true, dear,' Mrs Grayling said, smiling in his direction. 'At any rate, I wish Captain Scott and his team all the best.'

There was some discussion about who was dining at which table that evening and they decided to ask the chief steward to move them so they could sit together as a party. Juliette was pleased because there was no obvious suitor in the group that her mother could thrust upon her but humiliated when, over dinner, she guessed that her mother was asking Mrs Grayling if she knew of any possible marital candidates. Their heads were close together, voices lowered to little more than a whisper, but Juliette could tell by the way they occasionally glanced in her direction that she was the subject of their discussion. It was insulting. She was only twenty and perfectly capable of finding a husband for herself once the present unfortunate matter had been dealt with, yet her mother seemed to think it was her role now.

Juliette was seated between Mr Grayling, who didn't seem to want to make conversation, and a Canadian couple who weren't speaking to each other. She got talking to the husband, a man called Albert Howson who came from the Calgary area, and who proved to be a most agreeable companion. They talked about the rumour that King Edward VII had been married bigamously to Queen Mary, after a secret marriage in Malta while he was serving in the Navy, which meant George V wouldn't be the lawful King of England. Neither believed it. Juliette was interested when he described Calgary as cowboy territory, but said that there were fortunes to be made for those prepared to speculate. But when she brought up the subject of women's suffrage, she found Mr Howson unsympathetic.

'Men are the ones who understand finance and business. How would a woman even begin to vote knowledgeably on fiscal policy? They would vote for the most handsome or charismatic candidate rather than attempting to review the issues.'

'Don't be such an idiot, Bert,' his young wife cut in sharply. 'Women would bring an emotional sensitivity to politics that would improve them for the better. We have more insight into human behaviour. We care about others.'

Her husband turned to her with a curl of his lip. 'All you care about is fashion: who has the newest gown or the biggest diamond ring.'

Juliette turned quickly to Mr Grayling so as not to be drawn into their squabble. 'Are you enjoying the crossing?' she asked. 'Is the *Titanic* everything you expected it to be?'

'I don't have any complaints,' he replied. 'Except that the soup is never hot enough. And the meat is frequently overdone.'

Their waiter was collecting plates at that point and Mr Grayling raised his voice to make sure he was overheard. Juliette felt sorry for the poor boy, who certainly bore no responsibility for the standard of the cuisine. When he lifted her plate, she turned to him.

'The fish was quite delicious. Please pass my compliments to the chef.'

The waiter gave a slight smile and nodded. 'Thank you, miss.'

She tried again to engage Mr Grayling, but he didn't seem to want to join in the general conviviality. Was he shy perhaps? Or just not good at small talk? On the other side of the table, the conversation turned to the speed of the ship, and Juliette listened with interest.

'I do wonder if they are going for a record crossing,' remarked one gent. 'They say we covered 519 miles yesterday, which is rather more than the day before.'

'Would that mean we'd get into New York early?' his wife asked.

'In theory, yes. It could be Tuesday evening rather than Wednesday morning.'

'That would be rather a bore as our chauffeur won't be there till the morning.'

The Canadian woman, Mrs Howson, joined in. 'You could send him a Marconi-gram. Have you sent one yet? They're ever such fun. I sent my sister one yesterday, simply saying 'You'll never guess where I am!' She thought we were coming back on the *Lusitania* so she'll be astonished when she gets it.'

Mrs Grayling asked how Marconi-grams reached the people concerned, and one gent took it upon himself to explain about radio waves and how they were sent from ship to ship then on to base stations on shore.

'How clever!' she remarked. 'What will they think of next?'

'I imagine they will think of a way of using the telephone across an ocean. That will rather change the world, won't it? Imagine being able to place a telephone call from New York to London!'

'I can't see it happening in our lifetime. How would they run the telephone wire along the ocean floor?'

'Do you have a telephone yet?' Mrs Howson interrupted. 'It's very convenient but I never say anything private on the line because the operator always listens in. You can actually hear her breathing. It's most off-putting.'

Mrs Grayling said that her telephone always gave her a start when it rang. 'It's so loud and shrill. I'm not sure I like it. You use it more than I do, darling.' She turned to Mr Grayling, trying to include him in the conversation. 'What do you think?'

'Technology has never been your strong suit, has it, my dear?' He looked round the other guests at the table. 'She doesn't like to touch the light switches in case she electrocutes herself.'

Juliette was astonished by his patronising tone. It seemed a nasty way to talk to your spouse.

'But there was that case in the *New York Times*,' Mrs Grayling protested. 'It can happen.'

'I read that story,' another gent burst in gallantly. 'It *was* rather alarming.'

Juliette was interested to hear that so many Americans had telephones and electric lights in their homes. Back in Gloucestershire they had neither. She'd been trying to persuade her father to install a telephone but so far he hadn't agreed.

Over dessert, the Canadian couple's argument erupted into a fierce skirmish and Mrs Howson rose and stamped away from the table without saying goodbye to anyone. The husband quaffed the remainder of his wine in one swallow and remarked to the gentlemen, 'At least that frees me up for the evening. Shall we retire to the smoking room?'

As the ladies rose to leave the dining saloon, Juliette caught eyes with a man at the next table. He was sandy-haired, with an intelligent face. She got the impression he must have been listening in to the Howsons' quarrel and felt vaguely disconcerted that he might imagine they were friends of hers. He gave a slight smile and she smiled back and it was over in an instant. She followed her mother to the reading room and once they were seated, Lady Mason-Parker regarded her with a twinkle.

'Mrs Grayling has invited us to dine with them the week after we arrive in New York. Isn't that kind?'

'Very kind,' Juliette replied suspiciously. 'Will it just be the four of us?'

Lady Mason-Parker played with a button on the sleeve of her gown. 'She said she might try to find some young people to join us. That would make it more fun for you, I expect.'

'Please tell her not to worry on my behalf. I'm sure it will be a charming evening anyway.'

It was an ambush, pure and simple. Juliette wondered which poor dupe was to be seated next to her. Would he be told that she was a titled English Lady looking for a husband? Probably. She dreaded the evening already.

Her mother went on to talk about the gown worn by Lady Duff Gordon at dinner that evening, speculating on whether it came from the Maison Lucille fashion house she owned, and remarking that ladies' silhouettes were certainly getting narrower this season, no matter what the old-fashioned houses like Paquin might say.

Juliette listened for a while then, claiming a slight nausea, got up to return to their cabin. She stopped on the outdoor promenade to look out at the inky ocean and the star-speckled sky. She felt like a four-year-old confined to the nursery for bad behaviour at the tea table. She felt as though she were being punished for the brief affair with Charles Wood, something that really didn't feel as though it were her fault. *He* had been the one who seduced *her*. As she had often done in the past, she wished she had been born a boy. Men had so much more freedom, and the increased responsibilities that went hand in hand with it would have suited Juliette just fine. The life she was being forced to lead was suffocating her. She put a hand to her throat, for a moment feeling almost literally as though she couldn't breathe.

Chapter Ten

Most tables in the first-class dining saloon seated eight people. If a party was travelling together they were naturally seated together and you could put in a request to be placed near your friends, but otherwise the chief steward designed the seating arrangements. Reg had watched with secret amusement the shuffling around that had taken place after the first dinners on Wednesday and Thursday evenings. Some people asked to be moved if there were Jewish passengers at their table. Others asked the chief steward to seat them further away from the Astors, who were still being ostracised by New York society after the scandal of his remarriage. And yet more were simply bored to tears by the dining companions allocated to them.

It was all done with outward shows of politeness: 'Oh goodness, they seem to have moved us to another table. I can't think why!' But there was a playground ruthlessness about it. 'You're not good enough to sit with us,' they were saying. 'I'd rather be with the Wideners or the Cardezas, thank you very much.' Reg found it fascinating that in a society that already had so many stratifications, yet more were designed by the top stratum to further segregate themselves.

The Graylings' table companions had been different for each of the four nights of the voyage so far. Reg doubted that she would have requested any change and he could only assume that other people wanted to get away from them because they felt uncomfortable around the obvious tensions in the marriage. He eavesdropped on a lot of the conversations as he made his way round, holding out silver platters from which diners could help themselves to appetisers, entrées and vegetables, and he thought Mrs Grayling was uncommonly polite and well-bred. She asked about other people rather than going on about herself, and she made everyone she spoke to feel good about themselves.

On Saturday evening, Mrs Grayling spent much time whispering to another woman, a titled English lady, while her daughter talked to the Howsons about Canada. Reg was more interested when the discussion turned to the speed of the ship. He'd felt himself that they were pushing along at a rate of knots. They seemed to be testing her, and she was running beautifully, all those pistons and cylinders and propellers doing exactly what they were designed to do.

As he moved round the table collecting plates, he heard them discussing the probability that one day telephone calls could be made from America to England. Reg had never made a telephone call. He'd only ever seen a telephone in the White Star Line offices and when it rang, it was so loud and insistent he'd almost jumped out of his skin.

He took the plates back to the pantry, as the wine waiter circled the table topping up glasses. Why didn't the Graylings get divorced, he wondered? It happened more often these days and although there might be a brouhaha for a year or so, at least you could move on. Perhaps they were religious. Or maybe money was the tie. He supposed Mr Grayling would have to give her a large settlement from his multi-million-dollar fortune if they divorced. Having said that, he'd heard that the first Mrs Astor only got a small stipend from the vast family fortune because of some legal agreement she had signed before they married.

As he walked back out into the saloon to see to his other tables, Reg scanned the room for the boat deck girl, as he now thought of her, but yet again she wasn't there. It was a spacious room with upwards of fifty tables, but he was convinced he would have spotted her. He'd always had a good memory for a face, especially one as remarkable as hers.

The Howsons were arguing again, and it transpired that Mr Howson had lost some money gambling that afternoon. As Reg approached to take their dessert order, their voices rose and she pushed her chair back and stood up. Reg kept well back so she couldn't grab hold of his jacket this time.

'I didn't realise when I walked down the aisle that I was marrying a loser,' she spat.

'Well, I didn't realise I was marrying a spoiled child,' he drawled.

She threw her napkin on the floor and flounced over to Reg. 'Will you bring some dessert down to my room?' she asked in a cloying voice, deliberately loud enough for her husband to overhear. 'You choose. Whatever you think I'll enjoy.' It was such blatant flirtation that Reg didn't know where to look.

'I'm sorry, ma'am, but I'm not allowed to leave my post.'

'I insist!' she demanded and stamped her foot. 'I absolutely insist.'

'In that case, I'll see to it,' Reg promised with a nod, and she smiled coyly. As soon as she had left the dining salon, Reg spoke quietly to Mr Howson. 'I'll have your room steward take something to your wife,' he said, anxious there should be no misunderstanding between them.

'Make it arsenic,' the man muttered under his breath.

What was it about his tables that attracted the unhappily married, Reg wondered. Was it him? There were dozens of happy couples on the ship. He'd seen the Strauses, a couple in their sixties, holding hands as they sat on the promenade watching the sunset over the ocean. There was a young Spanish couple who were always laughing together, like a pair of little songbirds. Loads of couples seemed very much in love, but it was the ones who weren't that gave you pause for thought. If he married Florence, would they end up bickering like that one day? He couldn't bear to live that way.

Towards nine o'clock, the dining room was thinning out and Reg noticed that Mrs Grayling was once again sitting on her own at the table. He assumed Mr Grayling had gone to the smoking room for a brandy.

'Would you like me to bring you something else, ma'am?'

She smiled. 'No, I'm fine. I've been watching you and it makes me quite exhausted to see how hard you work. You don't stop for a second, do you? And you're so graceful as you weave your way around us all. It's almost like a dance.'

Reg wondered if she had drunk too much wine at dinner, and coloured slightly, unsure what to say.

'Goodness, listen to me going on. I was hoping to catch you.' She glanced over to where the chief steward stood at the entrance. He wasn't looking their way. 'Hold out your hand.'

Reg did as she asked, holding it out flat. Her gloved hand came down on top of his and she placed something there then bent his fingers over so that it wouldn't show.

'This is from me, not my husband. It's to say that I'm grateful for the way you've been looking after us. I don't want to hear any more about it, though. I'm going down to my room now and we won't mention it again.'

Reg pulled back her chair. 'Thank you very much, ma'am,' he said quietly. 'It means a lot to me.'

'You're very welcome, Reg. I'll see you at breakfast.'

Reg could feel that there was some kind of banknote in his palm but he didn't dare check which denomination, so he put it directly into his trouser pocket and finished clearing his tables, then set them for breakfast. It was only later when he went to the lav that he fished it out and nearly fell backwards with shock. It was a five-pound note. He whistled out loud. He'd never even held one of these in his hands before, never mind one that was his to keep. It was green, with a picture of King George on it. Straight away, he decided not to tell anyone, not even John, because it would make the others jealous. They might even report him and he'd be forced to hand it back. He would keep it in his trouser pocket and never be separated from it. There was too much chance of pilfering if he left it unsupervised with his few possessions in the dorm for even five minutes.

Good old Mrs Grayling. What on earth would he say when he saw her the next morning? How could he ever thank her? Did she have any idea that it represented more than a month's wages to him? Reg felt his cheeks grow hot with excitement. With money like this, maybe he could get a stall and sell meat pies to the seamen who came ashore at Southampton. The Seaview Café wouldn't be happy about the competition, but all was fair in love and business. Where would he make his pies, though? His mum would never let him use her kitchen and he'd have no income to pay rent on a place of his own. Was there anything else he could do?

He wished he could ask advice from some of the million-aires on board. What gave Mr Straus the idea of setting up

Macy's department store in New York? Why did Mr Cardeza decide to get into manufacturing blue jeans? How had Mr Grayling raised the money to invest in South American copper mines?

But then none of them had been born in a two-bed terrace in Albert Street, Northam, with no father to look after them and no money. Someone had surely helped them take the first step up the ladder. The likes of the Astors and Guggenheims and Vanderbilts were a different kettle of fish because they had inherited their wealth, but how could you leap from poverty to business success? He needed to have a good idea, and save money until he had enough to start up. Think about what people need and don't yet have, he urged himself, but no matter how hard he concentrated, that crucial bright idea wouldn't come. He didn't have the technical know-how to invent a way of transmitting telephone calls from New York to London. All he knew was the restaurant trade.

He lay on top of his bunk fully dressed, listening to the sounds of all the other stewards in the dorm chatting quietly to each other, their voices disappearing one by one as they drifted off to sleep. Reg knew he wouldn't sleep for ages because he had too much on his mind. He felt restless and unsettled. He was twenty-one years old and still waiting for his life to begin, but he didn't know how to get started, didn't even know what it was he really wanted. John wasn't ambitious like him, and he was probably a much happier person as a result. All John wanted was to find a good woman to marry, and maybe to make it up the ranks to be a sommelier or chief steward one day – although privately Reg couldn't see that happening because he was too broad in his accent, too coarse in his looks. They liked their head waiting staff to be easier on the eye. Reg could have done it, but he was insubordinate at heart. He followed the White Star Line rules but sometimes felt as though his head might explode. He'd rather be his own boss one day.

Maybe too much contact with the rich had spoiled him, giving him airs above his station. Face facts: the only thing he was good at was waiting on table; the only money he had was a five-pound note. He should accept his lot, go home and put down a deposit on a nice engagement ring for Florence. Mrs Grayling would probably be delighted if he told her that was the way he planned on spending her money.

But he knew he wasn't going to do that. That's not what it had come to him for. It was his chance to do something that would change his life once and for all. He got fed up lying there with his thoughts swirling round and decided to get up. He jumped lightly to the floor, pulled on his shoes and wandered out into Scotland Road. He hadn't consciously chosen a destination but his feet led him, almost without thinking, up the five flights of staff stairs to the boat deck

It was peaceful up there. The ocean was like a millpond. No wonder there was no swell on the ship because there was none on the ocean either. The stars seemed a little brighter than the night before, which meant there was less cloud in the upper atmosphere. The ship's engines made a mere humming vibration up on deck, like a cat purring in its sleep. They were noisier down below where he slept.

An officer descended from the bridge and walked across to the officers' quarters. Reg looked over the railing towards the surface of the water and saw someone's head protruding through a porthole, smoking a cigarette. Otherwise all was still and silent as the grave. It occurred to him to wonder whether

Mr Grayling might have another assignation with the boat deck girl. It had been around that time the previous evening when he saw them. Neither of them appeared, though. Why would they? It was after one a.m. on the White Star Line 'Honour and Glory' clock when Reg slipped down the Grand Staircase and back to his dorm.

Chapter Eleven

After breakfast on Sunday morning, Annie McGeown went with her children and her new friends from Mayo to the church service led by Captain Smith up in the first-class dining saloon. She wore her best green frock, her only hat and a beige wool jacket, and she combed the boys' hair over to the side the way she had seen on the boys up in first class.

It was only one deck up from their cabin, on D Deck, but there was no mistaking it was another world. Her feet sank into the plush carpet. She could see her reflection in the dark wood panels. Everything gleamed with polish and it smelled more expensive than their third-class dining room, in a way that you couldn't quite put your finger on. But Annie wasn't one for yearning after what she didn't have. She was excited to be there among the first-class ladies in their jewels and towering hats with peacock feathers. She was curious to see Captain Smith, and when he came in she was impressed by his smart uniform and air of authority. He had kind eyes, she decided, and a gentle voice. She clutched the baby – fortunately asleep – and squeezed her daughter's hand tightly.

The captain read at length from a prayer book Annie didn't recognise, and the boys soon began to fidget. She had to swipe Patrick on the back of the head when his whispers grew too loud. Annie wasn't listening to the service herself, though, too busy gawping at the grand clothes, the fine fabric of the gents' suits, the fancy plasterwork on the ceiling, the elegant curve of the legs of the chairs. The tables were covered in spotless white damask cloths and the sunlight streaming in through the big picture windows sparkled on the chandeliers up above. Annie felt overwhelmingly privileged to be there.

When the captain finished speaking, a quintet began to play and the congregation of some three or four hundred all sang along to the hymns. There were nervous glances when it was announced they were to sing the one entitled 'For those in peril on the sea' but Annie felt it had a nice tune to it. As she sang, she thought about fishermen way out on the ocean in their tiny craft trying to earn an honest living. That's who it was about.

And then it was over and people were filing out towards their cabins to freshen up before luncheon.

Finbarr tugged at her sleeve. 'Ma, is he really the captain of the whole ship?' he asked. When she said he was indeed, Finbarr continued, 'Can I go and talk to him?'

'He's busy right now, my love, but what would you go and say?'

Finbarr blushed. 'I want to ask him if I can work on this ship one day. I think it's the best place I've ever been.'

Annie smiled. 'I expect he would tell you to finish your schooling first and be a good boy and you would be in with a chance.'

She dawdled as they walked out through the first-class reception room towards the stairs down to E Deck. She wanted to feel that carpet under her feet for just as long as she could. There were huge bouquets of spring flowers on side tables and their scent floated through the air. How come they looked so fresh when the ship had already been at sea for four days? Was it the lilies-of-the-valley that had such a sweet smell?

Her new friends Eileen and Kathleen and Mary were chatting nineteen to the dozen about the grand ladies they had seen.

'Did you notice the diamond bracelet on yon lady in the lilac? It looked so heavy it must strain her arm.'

'I should have such problems!'

'It was the size of the hats that got me. Who would have thought you could balance so much on your head without getting a headache?'

Annie was only half-listening. She looked at the rich reds and greens of the embroidered upholstery and wished she had shades like these for her own work. Embroidery threads could be expensive and she'd only brought four basic colours with her. She imagined herself sinking into an armchair by one of the big picture windows with their vast views of the ocean and summoning a steward to bring her a glass of stout as an aperitif before dinner.

The baby wakened and smiled sleepily up at her, and she kissed his perfect plush cheek and breathed in his milky smell.

Chapter Twelve

As passengers began arriving for breakfast on Sunday morning, Reg rehearsed in his head some ways in which he could thank Mrs Grayling for her generosity. She had hinted that she didn't want her husband to know about the gift, so it was tricky to decide how to phrase it without giving the game away. He decided that he would simply say 'Thank you very much for your kindness yesterday, ma'am', and if Mr Grayling demanded an explanation, he would say that she'd been very supportive after the accident in which he dropped the plates. That should cover it.

When Mr Grayling arrived and walked over to the table, he was alone. Reg hurried to pull out his chair.

'Would you like to wait for Mrs Grayling before ordering, sir?' Reg asked.

'My wife's unwell. She won't be taking breakfast today.'

Reg immediately felt concerned. 'I'm sorry to hear that. Shall I ask the ship's doctor to call on her?'

Mr Grayling dismissed this with a shake of his head. 'It's just a touch of seasickness, or perhaps she ate something that disagreed with her. She'll sleep it off in no time. Now I think I'll have the lamb collops this morning.'

'Very good, sir.' As he walked away to place the order, Reg thought cynically that Mrs Grayling's illness would be very convenient for Mr Grayling and his young mistress. Most fortuitous for them, but less so for him. It didn't feel the same in the dining saloon without her kindly face.

Reg was tired and after breakfast service finished, he nipped back to the dorm for a nap. John and some of the others had gone to the church service but Reg had never been religious. It was all hocus-pocus to him, a great big fairy story designed by the ancients to try and make us behave ourselves. He couldn't bring himself to believe in a giant bearded figure in the sky who decided when you lived, when you died, who was born rich and who destitute. There was no logic to it.

Reg reckoned he'd be wakened in time to have a bite to eat before lunch service, because the lads'd be making such a racket when they got back from the sermon he'd never sleep through it. He was wrong, though, because John thumped his shoulder when there were just five minutes left to rush upstairs to work.

'I thought you needed your beauty sleep,' he explained.

'But I'm bloody starving,' Reg complained. 'I need my grub even more than I need my kip.'

'Sorry, man; thought you'd eaten earlier.'

When he reached the dining saloon, with all the smells of soup and gravy and roast meat wafting through from the galley, Reg's stomach began to gurgle and he had to press it hard with his fist.

'Your jacket's creased,' Old Latimer chided, and Reg pulled it down firmly by the hem, smoothing it flat with his hands.

The occupants of his tables arrived all at once, and he had a flurry of trying to greet them and take their orders without anyone waiting for too long. Mr Grayling was once again unaccompanied and in answer to Reg's enquiry, he said he was sure that his wife would be better in time for dinner that evening.

Everyone placed complicated orders, for starters, soups, mains, side dishes and puddings, as if church had made them ravenous. Having already thanked God for their food, they felt free to eat it without guilt. He carried plate after heaped plate of piping hot meals to tables, and hunger gnawed at his belly, as if the acidic digestive juices were trying to digest his own insides. He comforted himself by imagining all the helpings of food he would devour down in the mess at three that afternoon. He would heap the food as high on his plate as it would go without collapsing over the sides.

One o'clock came and went, then one-thirty, and then two. By two-fifteen, Reg only had a couple of tables left, and one of them was on desserts. He cleared the main course plates from the other, deftly stacking them with the fullest on top, and as he did so he noticed an untouched piece of filet mignon in gravy. The lady concerned had toyed with her mashed potato but the steak was still a perfect oval, just as he'd brought it out from the galley. Reg had never tasted filet mignon but he'd heard the meat was so tender it would melt in your mouth without chewing. His belly gurgled like a rusty old water tank.

He pushed the swing door into the pantry and headed towards the washing-up area, his eyes darting round the room. It was crowded but everyone was busy with their own tasks: finishing the individual decorations on desserts, scrubbing the cooking pots, covering leftovers and taking them into the store. Reg balanced his plates on the edge of the table, had one more swift look round the room then lifted the filet mignon and took a bite. It was sumptuous; everything he'd heard and more. The texture was like velvet, the flavour rich and meaty. He swallowed, and then he couldn't resist one more bite. It was the fatal flaw, he thought later; the greed that means a burglar returns for one last piece of silver and is caught red-handed. His mouth was full and the filet mignon was still in his hand as Latimer strode into the pantry and came straight over.

'What are you doing, Parton?'

If he tried to swallow the chunk of meat whole he would choke, but he couldn't be seen to be chewing it, so Reg tried to slip it under his tongue and speak normally. 'Nothing, thir,' the words came out, then he started coughing and had to spit the meat into his hand. It hadn't melted in his mouth after all.

'Any guests passing by could have glanced in the door and seen you guzzling their leftovers like a wretched dog. This will go on your report, Parton. I thought you would have been more careful after yesterday but it seems you don't care about your position here.'

Reg hung his head and whispered, 'I do care, sir. I'm sorry.'

'Get back out to your tables.' Latimer marched off, enjoying his status in officialdom.

Reg was sunk into gloom. He was booked to wait first class on the *Titanic*'s return voyage to Southampton, but after that he would almost certainly be relegated to second or third class. They expected impeccable standards in first, with no room for imperfection or slovenliness.

'Bad luck, man,' John said once they were standing in the dinner queue in the mess. 'We all do it from time to time, but it's rotten that you should be caught straight after that eejit woman got you into trouble yesterday. You'll just have to work twice as hard and impress them so much they realise they can't manage without you.'

'Do you ever get the feeling that you just want to turn back the clock by thirty seconds? That's what came into my head. Thirty seconds, and I'd have had the plates scraped and stacked by the sink and I'd be on my way back out to my tables.' He sighed. 'I dunno, John, I think I've just about had enough of this life. I can't see me going on like this, year in, year out. But if I'm going to leave, it would be better to do it with a clean record. I should have resigned before this trip. I should never have come on the *Titanic*.'

John was shocked. 'You've got a great career here. Everyone wants our jobs. Why not talk to the glory hole steward and explain what happened when you dropped the plates? He could maybe talk to Latimer and sort things out for you.'

The 'glory hole' steward was the one who looked after the stewards in each dorm – the term being ironic, of course.

'I thought I might have a word with the Tiger.' The Tiger was the name given to the captain's personal dining steward, the role Reg had filled on a previous voyage with Captain Smith.

'Good idea. I'm sure you'll straighten it out one way or another before we get to New York.'

Reg tucked into his beef stew, and almost immediately had to remove a piece of gristle from his mouth. Despite long slow cooking, this beef needed vigorous gnawing before you could swallow it, unlike that divine morsel of filet mignon. He'd talk to the Tiger, that's what he would do. If he mentioned it to Captain Smith, Reg was sure things would be all right. The captain liked him. They'd been, if not friends, at least friendly companions on that last trip.

'Hey, Reg,' a steward called from another table. It was the Italian one who worked in Gatti's à la carte restaurant. 'I didn't find your dream girl yet but I'm still looking for her.'

'Who's your dream girl, Reg? Do we know her? Is it Fat Ethel from the pantry?' There was general laughter at the table behind theirs, which Reg ignored.

It did make him wonder where the girl was eating her meals, though. Why would you come on a ship that was famed for its luxurious amenities and then not avail yourself of them? She was a mystery passenger all right. Could she even be a stowaway? All these big ships had some. No one could ever tell exactly how many were on board, and it would be easier to stow away in first class than in any other because no one would expect it. Friends of passengers were allowed to come aboard at Southampton to have a look around, and the ship's whistles warned them when the gangplank was about to be drawn up. What if some just stayed behind and found an empty cabin to sleep in? Would anyone even notice?

He considered this option as he ate, but it seemed unlikely that a girl whose appearance oozed wealth and position would risk the disgrace of being caught not paying her fare. Much more likely that she was eating in one of the other restaurants while he was busy at work. The ship was a labyrinthine floating city. It would certainly be possible to miss someone.

After he'd finished his heaped bowl of stew, Reg turned down John's offer of a game of rummy and went to walk it off. First he headed up to the à la carte restaurant on B Deck, just on the off chance the girl might socialise in there. It could be her kind of place, he guessed: an elite social club as well as a restaurant, where the décor was even swankier than on the rest of the ship. There were festoons and swags and polished walnut, under an elaborate chandelier that was secured in position so that if the ship swayed, it wouldn't move around and cause alarm. Their chief steward, a man Reg didn't know, hovered by the door to prevent undesirables getting so much as a toe over the threshold.

'Message for Miss . . .' Reg mumbled an invented name as he peered past. 'Can I just check to see if she's here?'

He glanced round the room, but his colleague had been right. It was an older crowd in there, the dowager duchess types who donned their jewels and furs for breakfast and didn't take them off all day. There was no sign of the boat deck girl.

He walked through the adjoining Café Parisien, which was lively today. Some young folks were playing a game that appeared to involve balancing cocktail cherries on their noses, and drinks had been spilled on the tables as each clamoured to have a go. Reg raised his eyebrows in greeting at the steward who was standing by, waiting to get access to mop up.

Next he walked along the port side cabins on B Deck and his feet slowed outside the door to the Graylings' stateroom. He knew from the passenger list that they were in B78. He listened hard but there was no sound from within. Should he knock and ask if he could fetch anything for Mrs Grayling? But that was the bedroom steward's job and he wasn't sure who their bedroom steward was. Crew on a ship like this could get bad-tempered if you tried to do their job for them. Every role was clearly defined and even a simple thing such as Reg taking that tray up to the bridge the other evening could have upset Fred, the steward whose job it was, if he had ever found out. You could never have the assistant vegetable cook touching a dessert, or a steward pouring wine, and there would be hell to pay if a scullion put something away in the pantry. Stupid when you thought about it, when you were all there to serve the passengers. Eight hundred and eighty-five crew serving thirteen hundred guests: Reg calculated that was almost seven-tenths of a steward per passenger. Did the Ritz Hotel in London have such a high ratio?

He stood outside B78 for a few minutes but there was no sound from within so he walked on. When he reached the end of B Deck, he walked back along the other side, then descended a staircase to C. Ahead of him, he saw an English girl from one of his tables in the dining saloon rushing towards him with her hand over her mouth. Suddenly she gave a cry and bent double. Reg hurried over and saw that she was retching. A pool of lumpy yellow vomit was on the carpet at her feet and some had splashed the front of her gown. She looked up at him and they caught eyes before a fresh convulsion seized her gut.

'Here. Please use this towel, ma'am,' he said, handing her the one folded over his arm.

She grabbed it and held it to her mouth, her eyes signalling thanks.

'May I walk you to your cabin?' he asked.

She nodded. 'It's C43. But what about…?' She motioned towards the mess on the carpet.

'I'll have someone see to that, ma'am.'

She took his arm and leaned against him, holding the towel to her mouth as they walked down the passageway and round the corner to her cabin.

'Shall I ask a doctor to call on you?' Reg asked. 'He could give you something to settle your stomach.'

'No, really,' she insisted. 'It's just that the food is richer than I'm used to. I probably made a pig of myself at luncheon. I'll be fine now. I can't thank you enough.' She peered at him properly. 'I know you from the dining saloon, don't I? What's your name?'

'It's Reg Parton, ma'am. Reginald, my mum calls me.'

'I would shake your hand, Reg, but I've probably got sick on it. My name's Juliette Mason-Parker. I expect I'll see you later at dinner. Goodbye for now.'

After seeing her safely inside her cabin, Reg hurried back along the corridor but when he reached the spot, someone had already cleaned up the pool of sick, leaving a barely discernible damp patch on the carpet and a slightly sweet odour in the air.

Chapter Thirteen

John was worried about Reg. He seemed distracted on this voyage, and if he got himself demoted he might leave the service of White Star Line altogether – a prospect that filled John with gloom. He couldn't face carrying on without his mate beside him. They'd sailed together for seven years, since they both started out as kitchen skivvies under a tyrannical chef on the *Oceanic*. They'd survived that experience by working as a team: when one had been given a mountain of potatoes to peel or thirty saucepans to scrub, the other would quietly relinquish their time off to help. They'd never put it into words but they were a unit on board rather than individuals, and that made it all more bearable.

John would miss their jaunts when they had time off in a foreign port. In the Med, they'd find a quiet spot to jump off some rocks and swim far out, ducking each other or flinging handfuls of seaweed. Reg had been the one who saved John when he panicked after swimming into a shoal of jellyfish, coming to drag him out even though he got stung himself. Whenever they had time off in New York, they'd choose a landmark and head for it. A few times, they'd not realised how far it was and had to sprint back to the ship, arriving just as the deck hands were pulling up the gangplank. They hadn't missed a sailing – not yet – but a couple of times it had been touch and go.

John didn't understand what was up with Reg on this trip, but he wasn't himself. He seemed overly disturbed about one of his passengers having an affair, and in John's opinion it all stemmed from his family background. He knew that Reg's dad used to play around, driving his mother to the gin bottle. That's why he was a bit puritanical about the opposite sex. He didn't ever join in the banter among the lads in the mess about which were the best-looking passengers, or speculate on the ones in third class that might be up for a spot of how's your father. It was unusual that Reg had commented on the looks of that girl on the boat deck. That's why John had been pulling his leg about it; he hadn't meant any harm.

The truth was that John loved Reg like a brother. He considered him family, perhaps more so than his own family, whom he rarely ever saw. They weren't bad people: his mam had been loving, but unimaginative. When John announced he wanted to go to sea they hadn't understood it. Why didn't he stay in Newcastle and work in a factory, where there were regular wages, day in, day out? John felt he needed more colour than that. He liked a change of scenery and he loved the weather at sea: the dramatic, multicoloured cloudscapes, the way the ocean was sometimes grey-green, sometimes petrol blue, sometimes balmy turquoise. He was more of an outdoors person than Reg. Being at sea suited him.

That Sunday afternoon, John decided to try and help Reg's situation. He wandered up to the boat deck and hovered near the officers' quarters until he saw James Paintin, the captain's personal steward, known as 'the Tiger', who had worked with him for almost four years now. Reg had filled the role briefly in November 1911 when James took time off to get married, but there was no doubt it was James's position. He was the captain's closest confidant in many ways, and a decent man as well.

John stopped him on the boat deck and briefly outlined the situation. 'I know Mr Latimer is just doing his job, but he doesn't see the problems Reg can have with the female passengers due to him being such a handsome fellow. He never encourages them but some of them are a law unto themselves. He deals with it quietly and never complains but I'm worried that if he has a bad report after this voyage, he'll leave White Star altogether. Is there anything you can do to help?'

'What about you, John?' Mr Paintin teased, his voice thick with a cold. 'No problems with the girls for you?' He blew his nose into a big white handkerchief.

'Nothing I can't handle,' John grinned.

'Well, leave it with me. It sounds as though he deserves a reprieve on this one. I won't have the chance to talk to anyone tonight because the captain's at a party, but maybe I'll see what I can do tomorrow. Don't mention anything to Reg until then.' His nose was red and shiny, his eyes watering.

'You all right, sir? Want me to get you a hot toddy?'

'I might pop down and have one with Joughin later, but not till after the party.' He looked out towards the horizon. 'So what do you think of the ship, John?'

'She's the best ever, sir.'

'She's a grand beast, isn't she? Sometimes I get a queer feeling about her, but the passengers seem to be happy and that's the main thing.'

He sneezed as he walked off towards the captain's cabin. John stayed outside for a bit to watch the ocean until it was time to get ready for dinner service. There wasn't a cloud in the sky but there was no warmth in the low white sunshine.

Chapter Fourteen

'I hope there isn't some kind of illness being passed around,' Reg remarked to John on their way to dinner service. 'Two of my ladies are unwell now.'

'It'll be the way you've been putting your dirty great thumb in their soup,' John quipped. 'I don't like to think where it's been!'

'Rather my thumb than your feet,' Reg replied. John's feet always gave off a rank odour when he removed his socks at night and he was frequently joshed about it by stewards in the surrounding berths. Someone even left a pack of Odor-o-no on his bed.

John ignored him. 'The Wideners are throwing a party for Captain Smith at seven. I'm going to be rushed off my feet. Will you watch my back for me?'

Reg agreed. That meant he would keep an eye on John's tables as well as his own, and signal to John if he noticed anyone waiting to place an order or for plates to be cleared. If things started backing up, he would step in and help directly, although they would try to avoid it coming to that because passengers in first class preferred their own personal steward.

Perhaps it was the party for the captain, or perhaps it was because there were only two nights left before they reached New York, but all the ladies seemed to have made a special effort with their appearance. The younger ones wore quite daring décolleté gowns in vibrant shades; the older matriarchs appeared to have been unable to decide which jewels to wear as they peered into their jewel boxes and had just piled on the lot. Diamonds and precious stones glittered in tiaras, necklaces, earrings, bracelets and armlets. Light sparkled in them and split into multitudes of coloured dots that bounced off walls and ceilings. The men looked handsome – or at least as handsome as nature permitted – in black tie and with brillantined hair and waxed moustaches. As each party walked in, there was a surreptitious turning of heads in their direction, just long enough for an opinion to be formed on the outfits and for the *mot juste* to be found.

The chef had pulled out all the stops, serving ten courses and several options for most: oysters, salmon mousseline, the infamous filet mignon, roast duckling, roast squab, foie gras, éclairs. There were going to be a few groaning waistbands, a few people groping for indigestion remedies in the middle of the night.

To Reg's surprise, Lady Juliette Mason-Parker was back, looking fetching in an ivory gown trimmed with lace at the sleeves and neckline. Her complexion seemed rosy, although he supposed that could be rouge.

'I trust you are feeling better, my lady,' Reg said quietly as he fluttered her napkin onto her lap.

'Yes, thank you so much,' she whispered, and gave him a quick smile with her eyes. It was obvious she didn't want her mother or anyone else at the table to hear of her misadventure.

Once again Mr Grayling came into the dining saloon on his own and when Reg asked about Mrs Grayling's condition, he didn't have much to say.

'She's fine. Just didn't want to risk it tonight.'

Reg speculated that he could have dined with his mystery boat deck girl in the absence of his wife, but for some reason he preferred to sit on his own at the corner of another table. At first the occupants tried to engage him in conversation then gave up at his monosyllabic responses. Yet again, Reg's eyes swept the busy saloon looking for the girl; yet again, he didn't find her.

The Howsons had wangled an invitation to the Wideners' party so Reg didn't have to serve them, and he found all his other passengers in celebratory mood. Bottles of champagne, Madeira, Château Lafite and aged cognac were broken open and quaffed. The noise level in the room rose as the levels in the glasses dropped. Faces reddened and smiles broadened. The Wallace Hartley trio played ragtime classics out in the reception room and a couple of young men did a Turkey Trot on their way into the saloon that had diners laughing and applauding.

Behind the scenes, some young scullions in the galley were playing up. As Reg picked up plates from the hot press, a movement caught his eye and he looked down to see one of them crouched beneath the press, piping mounds of mashed potato onto the toecaps of another steward's shiny black shoes.

'Watch out, mate,' Reg pointed, and the chap swore as he had to put his plates down to wipe his shoes clean.

'Bastards! I'll get you later,' he snapped at the guilty party, then turned to Reg. 'Be careful with that pole by the soup tureens. They've put goose fat on it. I nearly came a cropper earlier.'

Stewards often grabbed that pole for balance as they swivelled round the corner to pick up a tray of soup dishes. It was a mean trick. Next time Reg passed John, he whispered to watch out for the pole and keep an eye on his feet at the hot press, because he didn't have any time for accidents.

Reg kept his head down and worked hard, hoping to impress the chief steward with his diligence. It was after ten by the time the last diners drifted away to the smoking room or the reading room, or to one of the cafés to continue the party. Reg finished his own tables then helped John to sweep up any last crumbs and lay fresh linen for the morning.

'I'm gasping for a smoke. You coming?' John asked.

'Let's go outside,' Reg suggested. 'I fancy a breath of fresh air.'

John grinned. 'Are you still looking for your mystery lass by any chance?'

'Course not. Anyway, we'd better go down to the crew deck if we're having a smoke. One more misdemeanour on my record and Latimer will make me walk the plank.'

They stopped by the dorm to pick up their cigarettes then made their way outside, and the second they stepped through the doorway in their thin uniform jackets, they clutched their arms and shivered.

'Bloody hell. It's chilly out here. The temperature's plummeted since this afternoon.'

'We must be getting close to Iceberg Alley,' John said, peering out into the pitch black. 'Wonder if we'll see any?'

'Only if you fancy sitting out here all night. I can just about manage five minutes for a smoke then I'm going in before my bits freeze off.'

They lit up and took simultaneous drags. The smoke they exhaled mingled with the mist of their breath.

'How long have we got in New York?' Reg asked. 'Do you think we'll manage any sightseeing this time?'

'I think it's a quick turnaround but we might get an afternoon.'

'What do you fancy? Times Square? Broadway? You know me, I just like to have a wander.'

'All right, I'll come and have a wander with you. I fancy seeing Central Park.'

When they finished smoking, they flicked their cigarettes over the side and the glowing butts were instantly swallowed by the blackness. They made their way down to the mess and had a cup of tea with some of the other stewards, but most were too tired for conversation. It had been a long five days.

Reg and John were in bed by eleven, and Reg dropped off to sleep rapidly. His limbs felt like lead, his head sinking deep into the pillow, and even the sounds of the other stewards' bedsprings creaking and their shoes landing on the floor with a clunk weren't enough to keep him awake.

But at eleven-forty, he woke straight away and sat bolt upright when his berth was jolted, as if a giant hand had shoved it. He felt the ship juddering and heard a drawn-out scraping sound. He'd been on steamers for seven years and he knew right away that it was odd. It would take a lot of force for such a huge structure to be rocked in that way.

'What the bloody hell was that?' someone asked.

Reg was already out of bed and pulling on his trousers.

Chapter Fifteen

The engines had stopped almost immediately, and the silence that followed was eerie. They'd got used to the constant roar down there on E Deck and modulated their voices to be heard above it, so the next person who spoke sounded unnaturally loud.

'The dampers are shut down.'

Reg didn't know the speaker.

'We definitely hit something. Maybe it was a whale,' Bill speculated.

'Poor thing. It's going to have one hell of a sore head,' someone else chipped in, and the mood of slight alarm lifted.

'That's going to take the shine off the paintwork. Maybe we'll have to go back to Belfast for a repaint.'

Reg knew it wasn't a whale, though. A whale wouldn't account for that unearthly scraping sound, which had lasted several seconds, and even the largest whale couldn't have jolted a ship of this size quite so hard. As he tied his shoelaces, he was turning over two theories in his head. Either it was a problem with a propeller – he'd been on a ship before where one of the propellers came loose and it caused a cacophony and made the ship judder like crazy – or they'd hit something solid and hard. Maybe another ship. Maybe an iceberg. Whichever it was, he had an overwhelming urge to get out on deck and see it.

'Where are you going, man?' John asked sleepily.

'I'll find out what's happened and come back and let you know.' He grabbed his jacket and before John could reply, he'd hurried out of the dorm and along the corridor to the staff deck at the front of the ship.

As soon as he opened the door and stepped outside, he found his answer. Small chunks of ice littered the deck, most of them no bigger than his clenched fist.

A seaman was idly kicking some around.

'That was a close shave,' he commented when he noticed Reg standing there. 'Big as the Rock of Gibraltar, she was. Came out of nowhere.' He had a Scottish accent.

'We hit her, though,' Reg said, peering backwards over the rail to try to see the berg, but the night was too black. He couldn't make out a thing, apart from a sprinkling of stars up above.

'Just a side swipe. Did you not feel us pull hard a-starboard? It's as well someone up on the bridge had their eye on the ball.'

The ship had come to a standstill without her mighty engines powering her. Reg picked up a chunk of the ice and smelled it, and was surprised to detect a faint scent of rotting vegetation. Surely icebergs were just frozen water? It seemed odd.

'It'll be two or three hours before we're on our way again,' the seaman was saying. 'Captain Smith isn't one for cutting corners, so it'll be a full inspection, prow to stern.'

His last words were drowned by a deafening hiss as the turbines, now at rest, let off built-up steam. Surely anyone who had slept through the collision would be woken by this?

Reg considered taking a piece of iceberg back to show the lads in the dorm. Maybe he could get revenge on one of those galley scullions who'd been messing around earlier by slipping it into their bed, so they woke up freezing cold and lying in a damp patch. More than that, Reg wanted to tell everyone in the dorm what he'd heard about the collision and see what they made of it. Maybe some of them had been on ships that struck icebergs before. There were lots of them about when you took the northern transatlantic route in the spring, because all the Arctic glaciers were melting and icebergs broke off and floated south.

He nodded goodbye to the seaman, picked up a chunk of ice and went inside, walking in the direction of the dorm. But as he passed the staff staircase, some instinct made him change his mind and head up to the boat deck instead. There were bound to be officers on deck and by eavesdropping on their conversations, he'd get more information. He wanted to know what was going to happen next. Had the ship been damaged? How long would they be stuck there before they continued on their way? He tossed his chunk of ice overboard as soon as he got out onto the boat deck and wiped his hand dry on his trouser leg.

There were lots of people standing around but the first person Reg recognised was Second Officer Lightoller. He was a stern, very formal man, always impeccably turned out, but now he was dressed only in pyjamas. He wasn't even wearing a dressing gown and must have been freezing in the night air, but still he walked with military posture, an incongruous sight striding across the deck towards the officers' quarters in his bedroom slippers.

Small groups of crew and passengers stood around talking in low voices. The hiss of the escaping steam drowned them out and all Reg got was a vague impression of murmuring, and a sense of curiosity. Everyone was waiting and wondering, or peering into the dark trying to see what they had struck. He stopped close to one group and listened in.

101

'I've never seen an iceberg before. What do they look like?' a woman asked, but no one answered her.

'I heard Colonel Astor said to the bar steward, "I asked for ice in my drink but this is ridiculous."'

'Someone told me it was Ismay who said that.'

'Well, someone did.'

One man pointed out to sea and several more turned to follow the direction of his finger. A couple of crew members joined the group and Reg wandered over to see what had attracted their attention.

'She looks as though she's stopped for the night,' he heard someone say and, glancing towards the horizon, he thought he could just make out tiny pinpricks of light. He squeezed his eyes shut then refocused on the spot and was pretty sure they were right: there was another ship out there. It was good to know they weren't completely alone in the vast darkness – just in case. He didn't clarify to himself what the 'case' might be.

Just then, he saw Captain Smith coming down the steps from the bridge and he hurried in his direction to try and be close enough to hear what was said. Before he got there, an order was given and several men scurried towards the lifeboats and began unfastening the cumbersome tarpaulin covers. Reg felt a twinge, like a fist clenching round his heart: why were they preparing the boats? It must be bad news. Then he told himself it was most likely a precaution. There was probably some maritime rule about it, and Captain Smith would, of course, follow it to the letter.

Near the entrance to the Grand Staircase, the captain was hailed by Colonel Astor and this time Reg was close enough to make out his words.

'We're putting women and children into the lifeboats. I suggest you and your wife go below and don your life preservers and some warm clothing.'

'Thank you for your frankness,' the colonel said.

Reg wanted to grab the captain's arm and ask all the questions that were swirling round in his head, but he strode off in the other direction, all brusque and busy.

We must be holed, Reg decided, *and they want to get passengers off for their own safety while we carry out the repairs.* Lots of doubts assailed him, though. Why put thirteen hundred passengers, including some of the world's wealthiest families, into wooden rowing boats in the middle of the night if it wasn't strictly necessary? In all his years at sea, he'd never experienced anything like it. Even when they dropped a propeller that time, they had limped to port with everyone still on board. But then, they had been in the Mediterranean and not far off shore, while the *Titanic* was still two days' sail away from New York.

How was it going to work? They hadn't had a lifeboat drill on the *Titanic*. No one would know where to go. Most other ships made the passengers take part in a mock evacuation during the first day on board, so they could find their way to their allocated lifeboats if need be, but no one had bothered on this voyage. He supposed it hadn't been thought necessary, but now it meant they risked chaos. People might start swarming up to the boat deck and crowding onto boats.

And why women and children first? Surely they would remain calmer with their menfolk by their sides? Of course, there weren't enough boats for every passenger to have a place all at once, but he imagined the ship he'd seen on the horizon would be radioed to come and pick them up so the lifeboats could return for more. If it came to that. Which it probably wouldn't.

He felt charged up, anxious to be doing something to help, so he walked across to the officer who was overseeing the preparation of the lifeboats on starboard side.

'What can I do, sir? Can I help with the boats?'

The officer glanced at his steward's jacket. 'Go and rouse passengers. Tell them to make their way up here wearing warm clothes and life preservers. No panic, though. Tell them it's nothing to worry about.'

'Aye aye, sir.'

Reg walked to the Grand Staircase, and he must have assumed a new air of authority and purpose because now passengers stopped him and asked what they should do. He passed on the message, adding some elaboration of his own.

'It's maritime rules after an incident such as this, sir. A few hours and we'll be on our way.'

On A Deck, he looked into the smoking room and saw some men sitting round a card game, drinks by their elbows. There was concentrated silence apart from the flare of a match as someone lit a cigar, and a clinking sound as the barman tidied his stock.

Reg stood in the doorway for a moment wondering if he should say anything, but he didn't recognise any of the men and shyness made him reluctant to make an announcement to strangers. They probably wouldn't take him seriously in his victualling steward's uniform. What did he know? No one so much as looked round, so after a while he closed the door and carried on down the stairs towards the first-class cabins on B Deck.

Chapter Sixteen

Annie McGeown was lying in her bunk unable to get to sleep when the ship struck the iceberg. She'd been imagining the new home they would have in New York. It was hard to form a picture of it in her head, because all Seamus had told her was that it had three rooms – three! – and a yard out the back where the childrun could play. It was an *apartment*, a word that had been new to her until a few weeks ago. They would be on the ground floor and there were neighbours living upstairs, and more again above that. Annie wasn't sure if they'd have to share a kitchen but she hoped not. She'd like her own kitchen, where other wives couldn't pinch her flour and salt or leave burnt pans steeping in the sink. The lavvie would be out in the yard and everyone in the building would take turns. She hoped they were clean people; there was nothing worse than clearing up the mess others left behind.

She thought about how she would decorate the apartment and turn it into a real home. She'd find fabric to make pretty window curtains, she'd embroider some pictures for the walls, and she'd pick wild flowers and put them in jars, just like those huge bouquets of flowers she'd seen up in the first-class lounge. She was a good housekeeper. She'd learned all the old tricks from her mother, like using vinegar and newspaper for the windows and wiping down walls with a solution of washing soda to discourage mould. She'd maybe plant some vegetables in the yard, if she could just find a few seedlings to start off with. Oh, but she had so many plans for their new life . . .

Annie felt the ship turn sharply just before the collision. The movement almost made her roll on top of the baby. Then there was a jolt, and a noise that seemed to her like the sound of the big cogwheels grinding the corn at Dunemark Watermill. That was her first thought: why do they have a watermill at sea? She got up and crept to the porthole but outside all was black.

The engine noise stopped abruptly and now the only sounds were her children snuffling and sighing in their sleep. *Something's broken in the engine*, she thought. *They'll have to fix it. I hope it won't make us late arriving in New York. I don't want Seamus to be hanging around.* He was taking the day off work to meet them, and she wanted them to have as much time together as they possibly could.

In the corridor outside, she heard voices. People were emerging from their cabins to discuss the reason for the unscheduled stop. Annie stood with her ear to the door to listen, not wanting to go out in her nightclothes, but then she heard voices she recognised as belonging to her friends from Mayo. She pulled her coat over the top of her nightdress and quietly eased the door open.

'You all right, love?' Kathleen asked. 'Did it wake you?'

'What happened?' Annie looked from one to the other and they shrugged, but a man further along the corridor had more answers.

'We hit an iceberg. There's a small hole in the front of the prow but they've closed the watertight doors so the water won't flood in.'

'Mother of God,' Annie exclaimed, clutching her hand to her mouth. 'Are you sure? Who told you that?' She peered at the speaker, who was wearing an overcoat and cap, his face indistinguishable in the dim lighting.

'I've come from downstairs. There's an inch of water on G Deck and the staff are hauling the postbags up the steps so they don't get wet. But they told me the damage is contained now. They'll mop the floors and we can all go back to sleep.'

'Holy Jesus,' Kathleen gasped, crossing herself. 'You think we're going to go back to sleep while the ship's taking on water?'

The man sounded impatient. 'It's not taking on water any more. That's the beauty of the design. They've closed off that area and we're right as rain. That's why she's unsinkable.'

'I don't know, I still don't like it,' Kathleen murmured. 'I'm going to find a steward.'

Annie felt her guts twisting. She tried to focus on the positive things the man had said, but in her head all she could think was that they were in the middle of a vast, freezing ocean, there was a hole in the ship and she was alone with four children to look after. What would Seamus do if he was there? He'd probably go and find a crew member to ask about it. Well, that's what Kathleen was doing. She couldn't go because she had to mind the children. There was nothing she could do except wait.

'Are you all right, love?' Eileen asked, taking her arm. 'You look all shook up.'

'I wish Seamus, my husband, was here. He'd know what to do.'

'You're with us, now. Our men will look out for you. I'll be sure to tell them to.'

'You won't go anywhere without me? I'd never find my way around this place. It's the most I can do getting to the dining

107

room for meals then finding my way back to the cabin again.' Annie tried to speak lightly, but her voice caught in her throat.

Eileen put an arm round her shoulders and gave her a quick squeeze. 'I promise we won't go anywhere without you. Let's wait and see what Kathleen says when she gets back. She's bossy enough she'll be sure to get some answers out of the crew.'

It wasn't long before Kathleen reappeared. 'Storm in a teacup,' she called with a grin. 'The steward says we should all go back to bed. If anything more happens, they'll come and let us know. We probably won't be moving on till morning, he says. Oh, and that hissing noise you can hear is just the engines letting off steam. They have to do that when the ship stops.'

Annie listened and now she could hear the hissing. She'd half thought it was inside her head.

'You go and have a lie-down,' Eileen patted her shoulder. 'Most likely the next time we see you will be at breakfast, but if anything happens before then we'll knock on your door.'

Annie thanked the two of them and watched as they walked off down the corridor, then she turned the handle and let herself back into the cabin. The children were in the depths of sleep, their breathing barely detectable. She remembered that when Finbarr and Patrick were younger she sometimes panicked and woke them in the night just to be sure they were still alive. You never did that with the third and fourth.

She smoothed a curly lock back from the forehead of little Roisin, her precious daughter, and noticed the thumb resting on the pillow where it had slipped out of her mouth. She'd promised she would stop sucking her thumb when they got to America, but Annie didn't believe it for a moment. She didn't even know she was doing it half the time, and three was very young after all.

Finbarr started dreaming. She could tell from a change in his breathing, some little sighing noises, a slight restlessness. Maybe he was dreaming of working on a big ship like this. Annie didn't plan to encourage it. She didn't ever want him to leave her side. If he got married, she supposed he and his wife could rent the apartment upstairs but she didn't want him going any further than that.

Finbarr was special because he was her first-born, but he was also the one with the most spirit. He reminded her of herself at that age, always asking questions, wanting to understand how everything worked and why the sky was blue and the grass was green. He was braver than her, though. She had always been obedient and didn't like to make a fuss, but Finbarr would never put up with perceived injustice. He often got himself into bother at school by questioning the teachers' decisions. He thought for himself, and they didn't like that.

Finbarr was the main reason they were moving. From the day he started school, he had been bright beyond his years and Annie could tell there wasn't enough the teachers back home could teach him. Who knows, but with some clever American teachers he might become an office worker? She wanted that for him, that he earned his living with his brains rather than his muscles, like his dad. She wanted him to go out to work in a suit and tie and carrying a case of important papers. It wasn't that Seamus wasn't clever. He could have gone far if anyone had ever persuaded him to stay on at school and take his exams, but that hadn't been an option because his dad had needed help on the farm. They would do better by Finbarr in America – the land of opportunity, everyone called it.

Oh God, she just had to get them there first. She'd been anxious before when all was plain sailing, and now it seemed the ship had taken on water. Even if it was just a small hole, it meant they were a fraction less safe than they had been yesterday.

She pulled her rosary beads from a little embroidered bag in her handbag, and knelt down on the floor.

'Our Father, which art in heaven,' she began, fingering the first bead. If she did the whole rosary before going back to bed, then surely no harm would come to them?

'Hallowed be thy name. Thy Kingdom come, thy will be done . . .'

Chapter Seventeen

As Reg walked along B Deck, passengers were beginning to emerge from their cabins, fiddling with the ties on their cork life preservers.

'Do we need to put these on now?' someone asked him.

'No, just take them up on deck with you,' he improvised. He wasn't sure if that was the correct advice but reasoned that the officers on deck would soon set them straight.

Since he seemed to be in possession of information, a few people crowded round him with more queries.

'Is it true that the ship's taking on water?'

'No, sir, not that I've heard.' He wondered where they got that from. Funny how rumours spread.

'Do we all have to get in the lifeboats? Are they safe?'

'Safe as houses,' Reg told them. 'The captain will decide whether they're to be lowered or not.'

'Should we take our valuables with us? I've got some money lodged with the purser.'

'No, just take yourselves. Even if the lifeboats are lowered, you'll be back on board again before long.'

Once they had assured themselves that he knew little more than they did, the group dispersed and Reg continued along the corridor to the Graylings' suite. Most other doors were ajar, evidence that the room steward for the floor had already

111

knocked and passed on the message. Reg listened, but couldn't hear any sound from within the Graylings' suite. Were they there? He knocked and waited, but no one came. He knocked again, more loudly this time. Still there was no reply. Finally, he tried the handle and found the door locked. That was odd. No one locked their doors on board. Still, he assumed it meant they had gone up to the boat deck already.

Reg saw the steward coming along, checking rooms and turning off the lights if the occupants had departed.

'Hey, what are you doing?' he called, in a less than friendly tone.

'I was looking for the Graylings. Have you seen them?'

'If they're not answering the door, they must have gone already. What do you want them for anyway?'

'Nothing.' He blushed.

'Well, go and mind your own beeswax.'

Reg made his way down to C Deck, but the stewards appeared to have roused everyone there as well. There was nothing for him to do. Suddenly, too late to duck out of the way, he saw the Howsons coming towards him. She was bundled up in a pale mink coat and matching hat, and Reg couldn't help but think her outfit seemed too glamorous for climbing into a ship's lifeboat in the middle of the night. But then, come to think of it, most of the other first-class women were dressing up in their furs and fancy clothes. It was yet another opportunity for a fashion show.

'Reg, isn't this all a bore?' Mrs Howson asked. 'I was sleeping like a baby when we were awoken. Do we really have to go up on deck?'

'I'm afraid so, ma'am. Captain's orders.'

'How long will it take?'

'I couldn't say.'

'Well, I think it's outrageous, and I plan to complain to the captain personally.'

'Don't be an idiot, Vera,' her husband admonished. 'Let's go.' He grabbed her arm, prompting a sharp and most unladylike response, which Reg took as his cue to press on along the corridor.

Half a dozen passengers were clustered outside the purser's office, clutching their receipts, and Reg could see the two lads inside were being run ragged trying to track down each individual deposit box filled with money and jewels.

'We'll be back in a couple of hours. There's really no need, ma'am,' one of them was insisting.

'I'm not going anywhere without my Fabergé egg,' an elderly woman told him.

Reg stopped for a moment, considering whether to volunteer his assistance. He wanted to keep busy but there was nothing for him to do. The pursers would never let a victualling steward into their hallowed office, so he decided to go down to the crew dorm and find John.

As he passed the first-class restaurant, he noted the time: twelve-thirty-five. It was only fifty-five minutes since the collision, but it felt like hours. Time seemed to have slowed down – or could the clock have stopped?

Descending the staff stairs to E Deck, Reg noted that the steps felt odd. He hadn't felt any difference on the richly carpeted passenger stairs, but the hard staff ones seemed to be at a strange angle, so that when he put his foot down there was a curious sense of tilting forwards. The ship was listing, he realised. Noticeably listing. His heart began to beat just a little bit harder. That seemed to imply they *were* taking on water. Maybe that passenger had been right.

There was no one in the dorm. No John, no Bill. Someone had come and given them instructions, and Reg felt a little panicky that he hadn't been where he was supposed to be and now he'd been separated from his fellow workers. It seemed imperative that he found them as soon as possible. Before leaving the dorm, he went to his bunk and retrieved his passport and a St Christopher Florence had once given him, which he kept under his pillow. He checked his trouser pocket and made sure the five-pound note was still there. Then he reached under the bunk and pulled out a life preserver. There was only one left, which meant John must already have taken his. Clutching it to his chest, he hurried out of the door and back to the tilting staff stairs, which he bounded up two at a time, all five floors to the boat deck.

When Reg emerged panting for breath on deck, lifeboats were being loaded. A nearby boat was hanging on its davits, suspended over the side and Fifth Officer Lowe was standing with one foot in the boat and one on the railing as he helped an elderly woman to step in. She was terrified and in the end Lowe had to hoist her across and deposit her in the boat, where she sat down heavily on a bench, looking dazed and scared. Others hung back, glued to their partners, unwilling to commit themselves to a wooden rowing boat hanging seventy-five feet above the surface of the ocean. *And who could blame them?* Reg thought.

'Who's next? Any more women or children here?' Lowe called out. 'We're about to lower away.'

As Reg watched, the crew tried to persuade a large American woman to get in but she was adamant she wasn't leaving the ship. Suddenly a slender figure appeared clutching a velvet cloak around her. Her back was to Reg but as she stepped up to the rail, she turned and he saw from her profile that it was the beautiful girl from the boat deck, the one who had thrown her fur coat overboard. She had an elegance about her as she skipped, light as air, into the boat. It was as if this was a fun new game at a cocktail party, rather than a mid-Atlantic emergency.

Reg hurried to the rail to get a better look and saw that he hadn't been wrong; she was exquisite, with the kind of face you would want to keep looking at from different angles, so you could memorise its perfection. She took a seat near the rear of the lifeboat and looked back as if waiting for someone else to follow. The crew had begun to untie the ropes, when another figure stepped forward.

'Room for one more?' asked a man's voice. It was Mr Grayling. Without waiting for an answer he stepped smartly up to the rail and climbed straight over into the boat, where he sat down beside the girl and smiled at her.

'But it's women and children first!' Reg wanted to call out. He looked at Officer Lowe, waiting for him to issue a reprimand, but instead he gave his men the order to start lowering.

Reg leaned over the rail as the boat began to descend jerkily towards the glinting ocean surface so far below. The girl was holding onto Mr Grayling's sleeve and saying something to him that Reg couldn't hear. But where was Mrs Grayling? Could that be her in the black shawl? No, it wasn't. He scanned the occupants of the lifeboat, noting that there were a few other men on board – but no sign of Mrs Grayling. How could her husband abandon her? Surely married couples should try to stay together and protect each other at a time like this? Reg felt furious that Mr Grayling would prioritise his mistress on that of all nights.

The boat was only half full; there would have been plenty of room for more. He wondered if they were planning to load more passengers from a lower deck. Would Mrs Grayling board there? Where on earth was she?

As the lifeboat disappeared into the gloom, Reg took a mental note of the number on the side: Lifeboat 5. It seemed important to remember that.

He peered out towards the horizon, to left and to right. Where was the other ship they were going to offload passengers onto? Surely it should have drawn closer? It must be round on the port side now, he guessed. He hoped they wouldn't take too long transferring passengers and sending the lifeboats back, because the *Titanic* was beginning to feel distinctly queer underfoot.

Chapter Eighteen

When she woke, for a few seconds Juliette couldn't remember where she was. Her mother was shaking her shoulder.

'We have to get up, dear. The captain wants us all up on deck.'

Juliette opened her eyes a fraction and mumbled 'Why?'

'Something about an accident. It's nothing serious but we have to get into the lifeboats.'

Juliette closed her eyes again. All she wanted to do was sleep. 'Can't you go without me?'

'It seems everyone has to go. I hope it won't take too long. Honestly, have you ever heard the like? Waking first-class passengers in the middle of the night and making them go out in the cold air? I'll be asking for a refund of some of the fare if we're not back in bed within an hour.'

Her mother was bustling around, and Juliette heard the wardrobe doors open.

'I thought you could wear the tweed coat with cherry velvet trim over your blue wool dress. They're probably the warmest clothes you have with you. I didn't bring much winter clothing because it never occurred to me we'd be out in the night air.'

'What's the time?' Juliette asked.

'Twelve-thirty. Hurry now. The steward is coming back for us in five minutes and you've got your hairpins in.'

There was no option but to get up and drag herself over to her dresser to start pulling out the carefully positioned pins and let the locks of hair fall to her shoulders. She wound her hair into a quick chignon, secured it with a tortoiseshell comb and got dressed. When the steward arrived she was bent double fastening the fiddly buttons on her boots.

'Please put on your life preservers, ladies.' He retrieved them from the top of the wardrobe and demonstrated how to slip them over their heads and tie the ribbons around the side.

Rubbing her eyes, Juliette followed as he led them up the Grand Staircase to the boat deck. As they emerged she heard the orchestra playing a ragtime classic: 'Come on and hear, come on and hear, Al-ex-an-der's Rag-time Band'. She saw groups of first-class passengers hovering: Benjamin Guggenheim talking to his valet, and the Howsons standing with several other couples she recognised but hadn't been introduced to.

'This way, please.' Their room steward indicated and beckoned them towards a lifeboat that was being filled. 'Fifth Officer Lowe will take care of you.' He turned to Lowe. 'These women are travelling alone.'

'Please allow me to assist you into a boat, ma'am.' Lowe extended an arm to Lady Mason-Parker.

'Is it strictly necessary, officer? My daughter hasn't been feeling at all well. She's still queasy and this won't do her any good.'

'I'm afraid it's captain's orders, ma'am. We'll get you and your daughter safely back to bed as soon as we can.'

'Oh well, really,' Lady Mason-Parker grumbled, but something about his polite accent and smart officer's uniform made her obey.

There were four other women in the boat as they stepped in, and Lady Mason-Parker nodded in greeting before taking a seat right at the back. Juliette followed her, still groggy from her sudden awakening from deep sleep and overwhelmed with a sense of unreality. All the passengers seemed confused by the contrast between the gaiety of the music and the seriousness with which the officers were issuing orders, the glamorous outfits many were wearing and the bulky and distinctly unglamorous life preservers tied on top. Juliette looked over the side of the boat and gasped at the sheer drop downwards. It was perhaps the first time she understood that the situation might be dangerous. They wouldn't off-loading passengers like this unless there was a good reason – but what could it be?

She and her mother watched in silence as their boat filled up with women, none of whom they knew. The cold was beginning to bite and Juliette pulled down the sleeves of her coat to cover her fingers. Why had she not thought to bring her muff? Her mother was uncharacteristically silent. Normally she would have been commenting on the other women's clothes or their hairstyles but she didn't say a word, even when one woman got in wearing her coat over a nightgown. Juliette glanced round and caught an unguarded expression on her mother's face. She was afraid.

'Lower away,' someone shouted, and their boat lurched down about five feet and tipped to the side, causing several women to scream in terror. Juliette gripped her mother's arm, her throat too tight to make a sound. She felt a cramping in the pit of her stomach, as if the baby objected to this nocturnal activity.

Suddenly there was a scuffle above them. A man of Mediterranean appearance stood poised as if about to jump into their boat, but Lowe grabbed his arm and pulled him to the deck, amid much shouting. Two other crew members came forward to restrain him and Lowe himself came to the edge of the rail and jumped down into their boat, causing it to swing dangerously on its ropes. A fresh outbreak of shrieks pierced the air.

'They must know what they're doing,' Juliette tried to assure herself. 'They wouldn't risk our lives.' She counted five men on the boat and around forty women. Were there sufficient men to row and steer? Did they know what they were doing? Where had they been told to go?

Suddenly there was a white flash in the sky far above and, shortly afterwards, another, then another. Was it a fireworks display, part of the onboard entertainment to accompany the lively music they could still hear playing?

'These are rockets,' her mother said quietly. 'They're trying to attract the attention of other ships.'

Juliette felt goose bumps all over. 'What does that mean?'

'I wish I had brought our jewellery. I could kick myself for leaving it behind.'

'Do you think we are being transferred to another ship? If so, I'm sure they'll have our luggage sent on.'

'If it's possible, I'm sure they will,' her mother replied in a tone that suggested she thought otherwise.

Juliette struggled to process her meaning. Some words came into her head: *Things like this don't happen to people like us.* Her existence over the last nineteen years had been cushioned by money and social status, and untouched by tragedy. Her grandfathers had both passed away when she was young, too young to remember them, but no one else she knew had ever died. They had been safe, because they were Mason-Parkers. They were the privileged few.

The lifeboat lurched downwards again and she gripped the side hard, keeping totally still so as not to contribute to the alarming rocking motion. Down they went steadily now, past lit portholes with no one behind them, past sheer metal sides studded with rivets, until there was a bump as they hit the ocean.

'We're taking on water,' a woman cried.

'Get the plug. Find the plug!' Men shouted at each other and pushed women out of the way until the plug had been located and lodged firmly in place. Juliette bent over to touch the bottom of the boat and found half an inch of water sloshing around. She lifted the hem of her coat and tucked it under her thighs so it wouldn't get wet.

'Man the oars,' Lowe shouted, and their craft began to glide away from the side of the *Titanic* that towered above them like a smooth vertiginous rock face. Another lifeboat was just in front and it seemed as though theirs was following it.

Juliette wished they could stay close to the ship. It seemed safer than heading out into dark nothingness. There was no lamp on board and the only light was that cast by the *Titanic*'s lights. What if they got lost at sea? What if a big wave tipped them over?

But the water was as smooth as glass, the only ripples those caused by their oars.

Chapter Nineteen

'Annie? It's Eileen.' The words were accompanied by urgent knocking. 'We're to go up on deck.'

Annie flung the door open. 'What's happening?'

'You'll have to wake the little ones. A steward just told us all to get dressed in warm clothing and put on our life preservers and make our way up to the boat deck.'

'Why? What's going on?'

'I think we're being loaded into the lifeboats. No need to worry, love. Just keep moving and we'll be fine. Do you want me to give you a hand with the childrun?'

'No, I can manage them. But you'll wait for me, won't you?'

'Of course. We'll be right back for you when we've got our things together.'

'Are we to bring our cases?' Annie asked, alarmed. It would take her ages to repack all the children's clothes.

'The steward said not to. We're just taking our money and papers. See you in five minutes, love.'

Annie didn't allow herself to think. She shook Finbarr and Patrick awake and gave them their clothes to put on. Startled by the sharp edge to her voice and too sleepy for questions, they obeyed. Annie laid out clothes for Roisin then started to dress her little girl while she slept. She'd always been a sound sleeper from the day she was born. The house could

122

have fallen down round her ears and Roisin would sleep through it.

Annie dressed herself quickly, without thought, just pulling on the first items that came to hand. Her heart was thumping hard, causing a rushing sound in her ears. *Keep moving, keep moving.* She had all her papers and money in her handbag anyway so now she just had to get a change of clothes for the baby, little Ciaran. He was sleeping in a cosy sleeping suit her sister had passed down, so she'd only need to bring a change of clothes for him, and some nappies and a bottle, and they could be stuffed into her handbag, leaving her arms free.

'You ready, Annie?'

There was Eileen at the cabin door, and one of the men behind her, whom she remembered as Kathleen's brother. 'Would you like me to carry one of the children?' he asked.

'Oh, would you?' Annie asked. 'That'd be a big help.' She picked up the sleeping Roisin and handed her over. The alternative would have been to waken her and make her walk, but this would be easier all round.

'You'll need your life preservers. They're under the bunks.' Eileen squeezed into the cabin and crouched down to haul them out herself, then helped the boys to pull theirs over their heads.

'Where are we going?' Finbarr asked in a puzzled tone.

'In the lifeboats. It'll be an adventure,' Eileen told him.

'Why are we going in the lifeboats?' he asked.

'Finbarr, will you give it a rest. Not now.' Annie knew that his stream of questions would continue ceaselessly once you let him get started.

The life preservers were miles too big for her youngest two. They were twice the size of the baby and almost as tall as Roisin, so she pulled on her own and left theirs behind. Maybe someone up on deck would have smaller ones they could use. 'That's us all set,' she said, picking up the baby in one arm and her handbag in the other.

'They're waiting for us by the stairs,' Kathleen's brother told her.

Just along the corridor was the staircase they normally used to go down to the dining saloon, and there were the rest of the Mayo party all wearing their life preservers over outdoor clothing.

'A steward said they're not ready for us up there yet,' someone said. 'The gate up to D Deck is closed. He said he'd come back for us when it's time.'

'I don't know about you but I'm not hanging about down here,' someone else replied. 'If they're loading lifeboats, I'm going straight up there.'

'But you can't get through this way.'

Annie's stomach was in knots. She reached for Patrick's hand and gripped it tightly as the men went into a huddle to discuss the situation. She would stick with these people and do whatever they thought best and then she would be fine. There were loads of them and they seemed like good people. Thank goodness she wasn't all on her own trying to work out what to do for the best.

'Ma, why are we going in the lifeboats?' Finbarr whispered.

She sighed. 'There was an accident. We hit something and the ship took on a bit of water. It's not serious. We'll be fine.'

'What did we hit?'

'I think it was an iceberg.'

'How big was it?'

'I don't know, Finbarr.'

'Didn't you see it?'

'No, I was in bed, like you.'

'Who told you it was an iceberg?'

'Stop it,' she hissed. 'You're driving me mad. I need to hear what the grown-ups are saying.'

Groups of passengers were heading in different directions but no one seemed to know for sure what they were supposed to do and there wasn't a crew member in sight.

Kathleen's brother came over with Roisin sound asleep on his shoulder, oblivious to the commotion. 'We're planning to go down through the crew area to the third-class outdoor deck. There's a ladder from there up to the boat deck. Us men will give you a hand with the kids, so don't worry about that.'

'Are you sure it's all right?' Annie asked. 'Shouldn't we wait for the stewards to come and get us?' She didn't like to break the rules.

'They're going to be busy with all these folk.' He gestured around and, just at that moment, a large crowd swarmed up the stairs from below, dozens of them, all chattering in a mixture of languages.

'There's a foot of water down there,' someone called in English, and Annie's mind was made up. If water was flooding in, she wanted to be higher up in the boat. She wanted to be close to the lifeboats and able to see the night sky above her.

'I'll come with you then. Thank you.'

They pushed forwards down the now-crowded corridor and through a gate into the staff quarters. Annie struggled to stay right behind Kathleen's brother. He was tall and fair, and easy to spot with her little girl's mass of dark curly hair on his shoulder, but he was walking fast. She tugged on Patrick's hand and called to Finbarr to hold onto his brother's other hand so they formed a chain. Some folks were dragging suitcases, but the Mayo party was rushing now, overtaking the ones with luggage.

'See in there, Ma?' Finbarr called over the voices. 'That's where Reg took us, it's where he sleeps. There's the stairs up to the galley where we got a teacake from the chef. This is called Scotland Road. At least, that's what Reg called it.'

'Keep up, Finbarr. Stop dawdling and yammering.' Annie was exasperated by the effort of rushing with a baby in her arms, her bulky handbag dangling from her elbow, her son's hot little fingers in hers, and keeping sight of Roisin and the man who was holding her, a man whose name she didn't even know. If only Eileen had stayed behind to help with the boys, but she was somewhere up ahead, probably with her husband, who Annie knew was called Eoghan. Annie pushed through the crowd. 'Excuse me,' she murmured. 'Excuse me, I have to reach my friends.'

Scotland Road seemed to go on for ever but at last they reached a staircase that led upward with no gate blocking it. A mass of people was already on the stairs, all shoving together, and Annie was scared that if one toppled, they would all fall down and crush those below.

'Keep a tight grip on each other's hands, boys,' she told them and, glancing down, she saw their scared little faces. They were half the size of some of the biggest men there. It must be terrifying to be caught up in such a mob. 'We just need to get up these stairs to the deck. Stick right beside me.'

As soon as she stepped onto the stairs someone pushed in behind her and she had to nudge backwards with the sharp point of her elbow to make space to haul Patrick up onto the step. She held his hand so tightly she knew she was hurting him but there was no choice. Under her breath, she began to pray. 'Holy Mary, mother of God, help us please.'

They moved slowly but steadily upwards. She saw the doorway to the open air up ahead and counted the steps till they would reach it. Kathleen's brother was through it now and he turned back and waved at her and pointed to indicate he was going to the left.

'Wait for me, don't go,' she wanted to shout, but he had already vanished.

When she reached the top, she peered over in the direction he had indicated and saw Eileen climbing a big metal tower. Her heart sank. It wasn't a ladder at all, but a crane for loading cargo, and at the top she would have to shimmy along the beam and over a railing onto the boat deck. The others were crowded below, watching. Annie hurried across.

'I'll never manage that with the children in tow,' she cried.

'Eoghan here will take the babby for you and I'll manage this little 'un.' Kathleen's brother nodded his chin down to Roisin. 'The boys can climb by themselves if they've got a man right behind in case they slip.'

Annie looked up. It seemed a long way. 'What do you think, boys?' She turned round, and her heart skipped a beat. Patrick was there, still holding her hand, but there was no sign of Finbarr.

'Where's your brother?' she screamed, shaking his hand fiercely. 'Where is he?'

'I don't know,' he murmured. 'I tried to tell you but you didn't hear me.'

'When did you let go of his hand?' Annie could hear the hysteria in her voice.

'On the stairs. I couldn't hold on.'

She ran back to the top of the stairs and screamed 'Fin-barr! Fin-barr!' The baby wakened and began to cry.

Kathleen's brother appeared by her side. 'Fin-barr,' he yelled.

Annie scanned the crowd, her eyes roving across all the faces, looking for a gap between the people where a little boy might

127

be trapped. He wouldn't have the strength to haul himself up if he got knocked to the floor with all these people tramping over him. '*Finbarr!* Where are you? Can anybody down there see a boy with black hair?'

Most people ignored her but a few turned to look, then shook their heads. 'Sorry, no.'

Kathleen's brother tapped her on the arm. 'I'll go back and find him. You take the other three up and I'll meet you at the top.'

'I'm not going without Finbarr. I'm not leaving him.' She was wild with anxiety.

'Of course you're not, love. He'll turn up like a bad penny any second. Come on, now.' He pulled her away from the top of the stairs and back to where the others stood round the foot of the crane.

'I've lost my eldest,' she told them, choking back tears.

'I'm going to look for him,' Kathleen's brother explained. 'Someone take this wee girl.' He handed her over to Eoghan.

'But you don't know what he looks like,' Annie protested.

'Course I do. Black hair, skinny legs, cheeky smile. I'll find him. I'll see yous all up at the boats.' He turned and strode off towards the stairs, pushing his way through the crowds coming in the opposite direction.

'Come on, love. They'll be right behind us,' Kathleen urged Annie. 'You stick with us an' we'll get your childrun up there. I'll go up wi' this fella.' She nodded at Patrick.

Annie struggled with herself. Every instinct in her body wanted to go back down those stairs and hunt and hunt until she found Finbarr, but how would she manage to get through the crowd that was still pressing upwards when she had her other children in tow? She'd end up losing them all. Instead, she shushed the crying baby.

'Maybe I'll just wait here for him,' she told Kathleen.

'No, you go up to the boats, love,' Kathleen urged. 'They might come up by another route. Maybe the gate on the stairs is open now. We'll all meet on the boat deck. I promise.'

'Come on, Annie,' someone else urged. 'I'll take the babby for you.'

The man called Eoghan had started climbing upwards with Roisin on his shoulder and suddenly she opened her eyes, wide awake, and began to shriek: 'Ma! Mammy!'

'I'm coming,' Annie called to reassure her. 'Be a good girl for the nice man.'

Another man took Ciaran from her arms and started climbing. She let Kathleen help Patrick onto the crane and waited until he was a few steps up before getting on behind him. It was hard to climb with her bulky skirts wrapped round her legs, slowing her. Patrick was much faster, like a monkey scampering up to the top, where someone held out a hand to help him along the boom to the deck. As she got closer, Annie saw that it was Eileen. She'd waited for them up there.

When Annie reached the top of the crane, she sat astride the boom and inched her way along then Eileen helped her to swing her legs over onto the boat deck. As soon as she was on her feet, she turned to peer back down below. Had Kathleen's brother found Finbarr? Were they on their way yet? Half a dozen people were still climbing the crane but none of them was her boy. Oh Jesus, where was he?

She had such a tight feeling in her chest, she knew she wouldn't be able to breathe properly until Finbarr was back by her side. She clutched Patrick and Roisin and baby Ciaran and stood at the top of the ladder, peering down to the

129

third-class deck below and the doorway beyond. She scrutinised each new head that emerged and prayed they would appear any moment.

What could have happened? Why was it all taking so long?

Chapter Twenty

Reg walked over to the port side of the boat deck and scanned the horizon, but there was no sign of the other ship he had spotted earlier. The implications of this struck him immediately. If there wasn't another ship to empty the lifeboats into, then most people would have to remain on the *Titanic* until help arrived. But how much longer would that be? They were obviously taking on water. You could feel a distinct list to port now, and the lifeboats on this side hung away from the ship's edge, so there was a gap passengers had to leap across.

Second Officer Lightoller, now properly attired in his uniform, was in charge of loading the boats on the port side and Reg soon realised he was being much stricter than Officer Lowe in his application of the 'women and children' rule. Only a handful of seamen got into his boats – just sufficient to row them – and the rest of the occupants were women. As Reg watched, Lightoller extended his arm forcefully to stop a young man embarking.

'We are all gentlemen here, sir,' he said.

The man's reply was drowned out by the noise of rockets being fired above. Reg had never seen this done in all his years at sea and it was a sobering indication of the gravity of the situation. Everyone stopped what they were doing to look up at the giant white starbursts. Then Reg decided the rockets were good news. Surely that ship he'd seen would turn round now? The captain must think it was close enough.

'Excuse me.' Someone tapped Reg's arm. 'My wife is pregnant and I don't want to send her off in a lifeboat on her own. Do you think we will be safe if we stay behind on the ship?'

The couple were pale and terrified. She had an obvious pregnancy bump, which she rested her hands upon, and they gazed at Reg as if he were the fount of all knowledge, the one person who could save them.

'Go over to the other side,' Reg advised, pointing. 'Speak to the officer in charge there. He might make an exception and let you get in a lifeboat together.'

They hurried off, and Reg walked to the railing to peer out at the boats that had been launched on the port side. He hoped Mrs Grayling was in one of them, but they were so far below it was impossible to discern individual faces. However, he could see that several boats were only half-full. Why hadn't they filled them up at least?

'Reg!' He turned at the sound of his own name and was overjoyed to see John running towards him. 'Where the hell have you been, man?'

They threw their arms round each other and hugged for a moment, overwhelmed with relief to be together. They'd never hugged before and felt self-conscious as they broke away.

'I've been wandering around. It's hard to know what to do for the best.'

'She's going to sink, you know,' John said gravely, and Reg felt a plummeting sensation at the shock of his words.

'How do you know?'

'An engineer from the boiler room told us. Soaked to the skin, he was. He says straight after the collision the water was

132

gushing in and they had to run for their lives. They closed all the watertight bulkheads but the hole is too big and the water's flooding over the top.'

'Christ! How long have we got?'

'A couple of hours, he told me, but that was maybe an hour ago. There's help on the way. The boys in the radio room are beavering away, but it's not certain anyone'll get here on time.'

'I thought I saw a ship on the horizon earlier but it's gone now.'

'It's such a black night, it's hard to see anything. But listen, Reg, you and me are going to stick together, aren't we? We're never gonna get into a lifeboat so we need a plan.'

Reg tried to still the panic in his chest, in his head, so he could think clearly. 'These lifeboats are pulling away half-full. If we could only get to one of them when the ship goes down, they'd have to take us on board. We've got an advantage here, John. We're both strong swimmers. That's what we have to do if it comes to it.'

'It's going to be bloody freezing in there.' John jerked his head towards the ocean. 'We won't last long.'

'We'll wait till the last moment when she's really low in the water. If we tried to jump from up here, we'd break our necks anyway. Wait till we're about twenty feet off the water then jump with your arms up high. Remember they told us that in training?'

'We'll do it together, won't we? The jump, I mean?'

'I'll be right beside you and as soon as we hit the water, we look for each other then choose a lifeboat and swim for it. We'll make it. You know we will.' Reg squeezed John's shoulders.

'Aye, remember that time we got caught in a current off Malta and were getting swept out to sea? I thought I was a goner, but you said "just keep swimming" and we did and we made it. That's what we'll do. We'll just keep swimming.'

They looked at each other and Reg saw that the defiant words were at odds with the terror in John's eyes. His own were probably the same, but being with John gave him courage. They would make it if they stuck together.

'Hey you! Stewards!' Reg turned to see Lightoller beckoning them over. They hurried across. 'One of you go down to the galley. Joughin's baking some bread. Bring up any batches that are ready and distribute them among the lifeboats. And the other, find the captain and give him this message.' He handed a folded piece of paper to John. 'Be quick about it.'

The last thing Reg wanted was to go below again. Instinctively he wanted to stay in the open air and Joughin would be on D Deck, four floors down from the boat deck, but John was clutching the message so it looked as though it had to be him.

'I'll meet you by the captain's bridge soon as I'm done,' he told John. 'Good luck.'

'You too.' John gave a quick smile then each went off on their respective errands.

Reg ran all the way down the Grand Staircase to D Deck. The first-class corridors were eerily empty now, and he could hear odd creaking and groaning noises as the ship leaned in an unnatural direction and her timbers and metal plates complained. He sprinted through the first-class dining room, where the chandeliers were hanging askew and the tables were set for a breakfast that would never be served. The pantry was empty but in the galley Joughin was sitting by the bread oven, looking bleary-eyed.

'Hello, young Reg. Did your belly bring you down here? It always seems to let you know when I've got fresh bread on the go.'

His words were slurred and Reg caught the smell of whisky on his breath.

'I've to take some bread up to the boats.'

Joughin waved an arm at a batch of loaves that was cooling on racks. 'Take all you can manage. It would be a shame for it to go to waste. Make sure you get some yourself. There's butter on the side.'

'Are you coming up to the boats soon?' Reg asked, curious about his sense of calm.

'By and by,' Joughin grinned. 'By and by.'

Reg grabbed some white towels to protect his hands and lifted a rack of a dozen hot loaves. It was unwieldy but he'd manage. 'I'll see you up there then,' he said. 'Good luck, sir.'

He hurried back along the route he'd come, just as fast as he could while balancing the rack of bread. The clock on the Grand Staircase read just before one-thirty a.m. 'I should be tired,' he thought, but in fact he had never felt more wide awake. Every muscle, every nerve was alert, and his brain was working overtime.

He carried the tray to Lightoller, who nodded and motioned for a seaman to take it. Reg didn't see what happened to it after that. He'd meant to break off a piece for himself and John but his stomach was in knots and he wasn't remotely hungry.

There was only one lifeboat left on the port side now and Reg heard an argument among an Irish crowd nearby.

'Annie, will you see sense? Finbarr could be off on another boat already. Take this one and save yourself and the childrun.'

'I can't leave him. He's my first-born, my angel.' Her voice was high, sharp, desperate. She whirled round and saw Reg watching. 'Oh!' she exclaimed. 'You're the one who brought the boys back that day. Do you remember?'

'Yes, of course I do, ma'am.'

'My Finbarr is lost. This lady's brother has gone to look for him but they're not back yet and everyone says I should get on a boat. But how can I leave my precious boy? It would be

135

wrong, plain wrong. You tell me. What must I do? I don't know what to do.' A baby cried continuously in her arms, and two scared children clung to her skirt.

Reg swallowed hard. 'Your friends are right, ma'am. You should get on the boat to save these three little ones. Finbarr was a smart boy. I expect he'll find his own way to a boat. Where did you see him last?'

'In the corridor they call Scotland Road. Finbarr was showing me the dorm where you sleep, then we got crushed on the way up the stairs at the end and when I got to the top he wasn't with us any more.'

Reg took a deep breath. All he wanted was to go and find John and look out for himself, but he couldn't walk away from this woman's distress. 'I tell you what . . . If you get on this boat now, I'll go down and find Finbarr. I'll look after him for you and we'll catch up with you later. How about that?'

'It's not right for me to leave the ship without him. My bones tell me it's not right.'

'Ma'am, it's your duty.' Reg took her arm and steered her towards Lightoller. 'You have to protect your little ones. I'll find your boy for you. I promise I will.'

She looked up at him with such trust and faith that he felt dreadful. He couldn't promise any such thing with all the chaos and confusion. He just knew he had to make her save her other children, and so he lied.

'A woman and three little ones, sir,' he called to Lightoller, who immediately picked up the girl and passed her to a seaman on the lifeboat. 'Come along, ma'am. We're about to lower away.'

Annie turned to Reg. 'I beg you with all my soul: please find my boy and bring him to me safe.'

'I will,' he said. 'Trust me, I will.'

He watched as Patrick, then the baby and finally Annie were helped on board, then he turned to begin his search.

Chapter Twenty-One

A surge of third-class passengers arrived on the boat deck, excited to be in the open air after a tortuous journey through the innards of the ship. They were gabbling in a mixture of European languages – Swedish, Greek, Portuguese, Czech – and gazing around, trying to work out where the lifeboats were located. Davits swung empty along both port and star-board sides. As this dawned on them, they looked puzzled and accosted any uniform-wearing crew they could see, straining to make themselves understood.

'Where we go now?' someone asked Reg, and he pointed to the roof of the captain's bridge where some seamen were struggling to detach one of the ship's four collapsible boats. 'Try there,' he suggested.

He ran over to the bridge himself and climbed a few steps, just high enough to give him a view over the heads of the crowd. Could a young Irish boy be somewhere within that mass of humanity? They kept moving, making it impossible to search efficiently.

'Finbarr!' he yelled, but his voice was lost in the din of anxious voices, distant crashing noises, and the strains of the orchestra who were still, unbelievably, playing their hearts out just by the entrance to the Grand Staircase. The whole deck was slanted towards the bow, and Reg could clearly see she was sinking nose first. Oh God, where were those rescue ships? There was no time to lose.

He swallowed his panic and scanned the boat deck methodically, section by section, looking for Finbarr and looking for John as well, but there was no sign of either. What would a ten-year-old boy do if he lost his mother in a crowd on Scotland Road? What would he himself have done at that age? Reg jumped down the steps and pushed his way through to the railing that overlooked the third-class open area. There were groups of passengers huddled down there but none of them was Finbarr. With sinking heart, Reg realised there was nothing for it but to go back down to E Deck himself and have one last look along Scotland Road.

The staff staircase was listing so badly that he had to cling to the banister with one hand and balance on the edges of the steps. Once inside the ship, he could hear more clearly the crashes as furniture toppled over, huge soup tureens clattered across dining rooms and other, more catastrophic damage was done to the pistons and turbines within the engine casing. The ship was shuddering like a huge wounded beast in its final throes, trying desperately to resist its fate.

His mother will never know if I turn back now, Reg thought. *I could just say I didn't manage to find him.* The idea was incredibly tempting, but then he remembered the boy's eager face, his fascination with the engineering of the ship, and knew he couldn't abandon him. Finbarr was just like him at that age. He deserved a chance.

As E Deck came into sight, Reg saw it was submerged under a few inches of water. Little waves were lapping up the stairs, and he swore. 'Finbarr!' he yelled and listened hard, but there was no answer. 'Finbarr!'

He decided he would wade halfway along as far as the stewards' dorm, then turn back, and he bent to unlace his shoes and slip them off. He reached behind him and placed them several steps higher up.

The water was cold but not as cold as he'd expected. The edge of iciness must have been mitigated by the heat of the ship's furnaces. There was a current pulling him down Scotland Road, though, and he hooked his fingers around door jambs so as not to be swept off his feet. 'Finbarr!' he shouted. 'Fin-barr!' He listened hard but couldn't hear anything above the gushing of the water.

Reg inched down past the crew WCs, alternately shouting and listening. Miscellaneous items floated by: a book, a pair of trousers, a striped towel. He passed the cooks' dorm and the bedroom stewards' dorm and at last he reached his own. It was barely recognisable, the bunks squashed against the end wall and one of them upended. The water was getting deeper by the second and now swirled up to his knees.

'Finbarr!' he shouted one last time, and was about to give up when he heard a faint cry of 'Help!' coming from further down Scotland Road.

'Is that you, Finbarr?' he called.

'Yes,' came the reply.

Reg swore under his breath. He couldn't turn back now. He waded further along the corridor, still calling, and the boy's voice got closer then he came into sight. Just by the elevators, there were stairs down to the laundry area on F Deck. A metal gate was pulled shut across them and Finbarr was trapped behind that gate, submerged up to his waist in water. His face was bright scarlet with crying. The poor kid was scared out of his wits.

'How on earth did you get in there?' Reg exclaimed, trying to make his voice sound calm. 'Your mum's been going crazy looking for you.'

'I lost me ma in the crush and someone said there was water coming in down below and I wanted to see it. But I got lost and I couldn't find the way back up again.' Finbarr was sobbing and stuttering, overcome with emotion.

Reg waded over and grabbed hold of the gate and wrenched, but it wouldn't move. The floor catch on his side needed to be released so he groped under the water to find it. 'We'll soon get you up on deck,' he soothed.

Surely he'd be able to find him a place on one of the collapsibles? They might be in short supply, but Finbarr was just a kid. That should get him to the front of the queue. The catch sprang loose and he pulled at the gate, using all his strength to drag it across against the weight of the water until there was just enough of a gap to haul Finbarr through.

'Where's Ma? Is she mad at me?'

'She's not mad, just worried. She had to get on a lifeboat with your little brothers so I said I would look out for you. We'll find her later.' No point in alarming the boy yet when he was still shaking with the horror of his ordeal. 'We've to get along this corridor and up the stairs to the boat deck. Quick as you can.' Reg pushed him forwards.

'Is the ship sinking?' Finbarr asked.

There was no point in lying. 'Yes, it is. But don't worry, because help is on the way. It might even be there by the time we reach the deck.' Reg felt cheered by his own words, but seconds later the ship gave a huge judder, causing a wave to sweep along Scotland Road, nearly knocking them off their feet. They hurried faster, clinging to door frames, until they got to the staff staircase.

141

'Damn!' Reg swore out loud. The water had reached the step he'd left his shoes on and they'd been swept away. They'd cost eight shillings and sixpence. He couldn't afford to lose them.

'Start heading up,' he told Finbarr. 'I'll be right behind you.'

He followed the direction of the water and spotted one of his shoes in a mound of detritus just round the corner from the cold store. The other one was further along outside the engineers' mess. Both were completely sodden, but they were better than no shoes at all.

Back at the stairs, he had to use the handrail to drag himself up because it was impossible to get purchase on the lopsided steps. Finbarr was waiting for him, shivering, his teeth chattering, and Reg hoped the exertion of the climb would warm him. Goodness knows how long he'd been in the water. Beneath their feet, the ship kept shifting, and behind them the ocean crept upwards step by step.

When they emerged onto the boat deck, they had to grab hold of the nearest railing because the deck was at a slant and anything unsecured was hurtling down towards the bow. Reg slipped his wet shoes on, tied the laces, and inched forwards till he could see the bridge. Some men were still on the roof struggling with a collapsible but they hadn't managed to shift it. There were folk huddled on the stairs to the bridge and around the base of it, but no sign of John – at least not that he could make out.

Suddenly, Captain Smith appeared from the radio room on the port side and strode towards the bridge, for all the world as if everything was normal, the deck wasn't tilted at a strange angle and they'd soon be serving breakfast in the dining saloons. He pushed through the crowds on the stairs and disappeared up into the bridge without stopping to talk to any of those who turned to him in expectation.

Reg wished he could get over to the bridge to join him. The captain must know how close the rescue ships were, and he would tell them what to do in the meantime. But there was nothing to hold onto in the area between where they were and the bridge and Reg worried that Finbarr might lose his balance. Could they make it if they ran for it? He reckoned he probably could but he wasn't sure about the boy, who was wide-eyed and silent with shock.

While Reg hesitated, there was a deafening crash deep within the bowels of the ship. Something gave way and they were thrown back against the doorway to the stairs. Seconds later, a huge wave washed over the boat deck, sweeping several people over the side into the ocean. Their terrified screams hung in the air.

Finbarr grabbed Reg's arm. 'What's going to happen to us?' he sobbed.

Reg felt like sobbing himself, but having someone else to look after made him calm. 'OK, Finbarr, this is how it is. I don't think we're going to make it to a boat on deck. We'll have to jump into the water and then one will pick us up. You're wearing your life preserver so that's good. It means you'll stay afloat. I need you to listen to me very carefully and do exactly what I say.'

Finbarr nodded, his face so trusting that Reg felt a lump in his throat.

'First, we're going to make our way over to that railing. That's where we'll jump from. It's not far. We'll just run and grab hold of it. Are you ready? Go!'

Finbarr dashed first and Reg followed directly behind him. When he reached the edge, he saw they were still around thirty feet above the water, which seemed too high to risk it. Some people were already floating on the surface but none looked as though they had survived the drop. The nearest lifeboats were about fifty or sixty feet away. He reckoned they could make that, so long as the boy stayed calm and didn't thrash around in panic.

'We mustn't jump too soon or it will be too far to fall. I'm going to tie our life preservers together so we don't get separated. When I say jump, you jump.' As he spoke, he unfastened the ties at the side of his own life preserver and looped them through Finbarr's, tightening all the knots carefully. 'As you jump, put your arms right up in the air so you hit the water feet first in a straight line, like a pencil.' Reg demonstrated. They'd been shown this in staff training. If you didn't do that, the impact could force the life preserver upwards and break your neck. 'Do you understand?'

Finbarr nodded, too overcome for speech.

'Once we're in the water, we'll find the nearest lifeboat, and later, when the rescue ships come, we'll get you back together with your mum.' *Oh God,* Reg prayed silently. *Please make it true.*

His stomach was churning as he watched the movement of the ship carefully, making his calculations. If only John were there, they could have discussed it together and worked out the best time to jump. He didn't want to wait too long because they had to swim clear of the ship to avoid the suction when she finally went under. He'd make his move just as soon as they got a bit closer to the surface.

There was a bonus to having the boy with him. If places in lifeboats were at a premium, surely he would get priority with a child to look after? He'd be hailed as a hero for rescuing Finbarr. That was a heart-warming thought. Shame he wasn't a first-class passenger or there might even have been a reward.

Something odd was happening below decks. With a deafening crack, the bow of the ship disappeared completely and the stern upended. Simultaneously the ground disappeared from beneath their feet so they were left hanging by the arms from the railings. The deck was almost vertical and the water was close by. Reg heard screams as people all around them fell away into the bubbling whirlpool below.

'Pull up and swing your feet over the edge,' Reg yelled at Finbarr, and with his free hand he pushed the boy's legs to demonstrate what he meant. He did the same himself, and now they were poised, maybe twenty feet above the ocean. Out of the corner of his eye, he saw a collapsible being washed overboard.

'See that boat?' he shouted to Finbarr. 'When I count to three, we're going to jump in that direction. Are you ready?'

He looked at the boy, and Finbarr nodded. Reg grinned, to give him courage, and Finbarr smiled back.

'One, two, three . . . jump!'

Together they made their leap out into the blackness.

Chapter Twenty-Two

The water came faster than Reg had expected and he shot down through it like an arrow. There was no time to notice the cold. He was conscious only of the pressure pounding in his ears. When he stopped plummeting, Reg immediately started to swim upwards. He had to reach the surface so he could breathe, but which way was up? He could only trust his instincts and push in the direction he seemed to have come from because it was pitch black and there was no reassuring light above. Just when his lungs were fit to burst, his head broke the surface and he sucked in huge gulps of air. His heart was beating so hard he could hear it.

That's when he began to feel the excruciating cold biting into the back of his neck, his hands, his legs. His flesh felt raw with it. 'I have to keep moving,' he told himself, and then his next thought was to look round for the boy. The knots between their life preservers hadn't survived the impact with the water but he couldn't be far off.

'Finbarr?' Reg called, his voice sounding weak even to his own ears. 'Finbarr?' he called, slightly louder.

Yells and screams and cries for help filled the air but they all seemed a long way off. Behind him, the stern of the ship was perpendicular in the water and Reg guessed that she could slide under the surface any moment. He had to get clear or he could be sucked down with it, but where was the boy?

'Fin-barr!' he yelled, as loud as he could this time. He turned in each direction yelling the boy's name and scanning the water but there was no sign. What could have happened to him? Reg began shuddering with the cold and knew that if he didn't start swimming soon, he would die.

'Where are you? If you can hear me, swim away from the ship. Follow my voice.' He had one last look round then struck out blindly, his normal strong strokes hindered by the cumbersome life preserver. *Just keep swimming. Just keep swimming.* John would probably be in the water now, the same thought in his head.

'Finbarr! This way!' he yelled from time to time, his voice breathless from the effort of propelling himself forward. He raised his head and looked around but there were no lifeboats in sight. *Just keep swimming. Just keep swimming.* The cold bit into him, and he knew it was a killing cold. It sucked your energy, sapped your strength, made you want to close your eyes and give up.

Suddenly the ocean moved. Reg was pulled under again and he struggled to find the surface. He opened his eyes but all around was black. Panic set in and he kicked out with all his might. After all this effort, was he going to drown anyway? His lungs were agony. Would his life flash in front of his eyes the way they said it did? *Don't panic, don't panic.* He released a dribble of air from his mouth to see which way the bubbles went, then swam in that direction. Just when he thought he was lost for sure, he found the surface and gulped at the night air. His lungs were overstretched and burning. All those years at sea and no one had ever told him how much it *hurt* to drown.

He trod water for a minute, trying to breathe his fill, and then he looked around to get his bearings. He turned one way then the other and a new horror filled him. Where was the ship? She had gone. Disappeared. In the water there were bits of fractured wood, life preservers – some with people in them and some without – a deckchair, a barrel of some kind. But no *Titanic*. How could something so enormous have simply vanished?

He tried to lift himself higher out of the water to spot a lifeboat but found he had little strength left. It was ebbing from him as the cold gnawed into his muscles and bones. He turned ninety degrees and scanned the horizon, then another ninety, then again, and finally he spotted a collapsible. It was upside down in the water and half a dozen men were sitting on it.

'If I can get there, I'll be safe,' Reg thought. Like that time in Malta, he knew he had to keep swimming. Easy to say, but his arms felt as though they belonged to someone else and were no longer under his control, and he had lost any sensation in his legs. He was working as hard as he could and didn't seem to be moving at all.

I have to do this, he spoke sternly to himself. *I have to live. I'm only young and I haven't done anything yet.* He wanted to start his own business, buy a car – a Lozier, preferably – and get married. He couldn't die before he'd achieved all those things. His arms and legs had stiffened up, making it harder than ever to move forwards, but he pictured himself behind the wheel of his car, driving down a road on a sunny day with Florence by his side, laughing. *Just keep swimming, just keep swimming. Not far now, you can do it.*

By the time he reached the collapsible there were a dozen men on it, some standing, some sitting and one, just near Reg, who was lying with his leg trailing over the edge. Reg grabbed hold of that leg for something to haul himself up by and the man said 'Hey!' but that was all. Reg tried to get a grip on the wooden slats but there was nothing to hold so he used the body of the lying man and with the last of his strength he crawled onto the upturned boat.

Instantly he was out of the water, he felt colder. His teeth were chattering and he couldn't stop shaking.

'Stand up. You're taking too much room,' someone nagged him.

His legs were so wobbly he wasn't sure he could make it and he had to grab hold of another man to steady himself. Once upright, he looked at the scene around him and blinked. As far as the eye could see, the ocean was littered with bodies and broken pieces of the ship. He couldn't see any other lifeboats. A swimmer approached and was told there was no more room on board and Reg felt a pang of guilt about that. And then suddenly he remembered Finbarr, and began to yell his name.

'Shut up, you,' someone growled.

Reg called even louder. Surely the boy must be nearby. Guilt pierced his heart like a knife wound. He had promised to protect Finbarr. His mother had put her trust in him. And instead he had saved himself.

Someone else was climbing onto their raft, and Reg was delighted to recognise Second Officer Lightoller. He felt euphoric. They would be all right now, because Lightoller would take charge. He'd tell them what to do. First, it was imperative that he told Lightoller about the boy.

'Excuse me, sir,' he called. 'Excuse me, Officer Lightoller.'

'Who are you?'

'Reg Parton, sir. There's an Irish boy, a passenger, in the water nearby. I promised his mother I'd look after him. His name's Finbarr. We have to find him.'

'Everyone who can, on their feet,' Lightoller ordered, and Reg thought with relief that he was getting them all to search for Finbarr. 'Easy does it. Lean towards me, men.'

149

The boat wobbled and almost overturned, but every time it tipped in one direction, Lightoller gave an order and they managed to lean and steady it.

He's looking for Finbarr now. He's bound to find him, Reg told himself, and it was a while before he realised that Lightoller was simply directing their movements so that the collapsible didn't capsize.

More swimmers came towards them but were told they couldn't climb aboard or the boat would sink. One man tried his luck and was beaten off with an oar. He fell back into the ocean with a groan of utter despair. All around them were groans. The cries for help gradually subsided as swimmers realised there was no one to come to their rescue and they needed all their breath simply to keep moving.

'Finbarr!' Reg called his name one last time, but without any hope. It had taken all the strength of his twenty-one years and all his skill as a swimmer to make it this far. A skinny little lad of ten wouldn't have stood a chance.

Chapter Twenty-Three

Annie sat huddled on a bench in Lifeboat 13, so traumatised she couldn't move. Baby Ciaran had been crying and there was sick down his front, Roisin was sucking her thumb and whimpering, and Patrick was white as a ghost, but Annie couldn't help them. She was enveloped in a sense of dread so heavy that it made her oblivious to everything around her.

She had done a wicked, evil thing leaving her first-born behind on the ship. Seamus would never forgive her if any harm came to him. It was obvious now that she'd made the wrong decision. She should have sent the other three on a lifeboat with Kathleen and stayed behind to find Finbarr herself. Why hadn't she thought of that? It hadn't been fair to put such pressure on Kathleen's brother and then on that young steward. Neither of them knew the boy. Neither of them loved him. They might search for a while but then they'd give up because after all he was nothing to them. But she, Annie, would never have given up until she'd found him. Surely her mother's love would have been fierce enough to save him? Yet instead she had let herself be talked into leaving him behind.

How would he feel when he heard that she had saved the others and left him? How would he manage if he was lost, or injured? Would someone take pity on him? He was only a boy and looked younger than his years.

In her head, she repeated the rosary, over and over, and it formed a backdrop to the pounding anxiety, the fears and suppositions. She kept turning to look back at the ship, although they were too far away now to make out the faces of those on the decks. Rows of portholes in its sides were still brightly lit but it was obvious the vessel was fatally damaged because of the slant at which it sat in the water, its bow almost submerged.

Was Finbarr one of those little black figures on deck? Why weren't they launching any more lifeboats? Could he maybe have disembarked on the other side? Pray God that he had.

'Don't look!' someone said to her in a kind voice, and she turned to see that the huge vessel had upended itself in the water, like a broken child's toy. Some of the little black figures, mere dots, were slipping and falling overboard, and their cries for help reached her ears and pierced her soul. What kind of a mother was she that she left her son to go through this on his own? She didn't deserve to have children, didn't deserve a loving husband.

Now she couldn't take her eyes off the vertical ship, so unnatural it seemed a crime against the law of gravity. The lights flickered off, then on again, but it seemed as if it might stay poised there forever, providing refuge for those left on board. 'Please God, please,' Annie repeated over and over. If it could just stay like that, there was hope.

But then it began to slip, smoothly and quietly, into the oily blackness. In just a few seconds it was gone completely and they were plunged into almost complete darkness. There was no moon that night, no lamps on the lifeboats, just the dim glow of the stars to see by.

There was a delay before the wave of sound reached her: a prolonged howl of anguish unlike anything she had ever heard.

All those people on deck had plummeted into the North Atlantic, all those tiny specks swallowed up by the water that must be close to freezing point. She couldn't see them any more, but could hear the sound and it made the blood freeze in her veins. Was her son one of them?

'We must go back,' she insisted to the men who were rowing their boat. 'My son might be in there.'

'We've no room, ma'am,' a seaman replied. 'We're full to bursting.'

It was true that they were crushed against each other and every space filled, but Finbarr was only little.

'He's small for his age. He's only ten. We must go back.' She pressed them, trying to get them to understand.

'He'll be on another boat already,' a woman nearby told her kindly. 'There were places for all the women and children. Those in the water are grown men and pray God they will find something to float on until help arrives.'

'You'll find him when the rescue ship arrives,' someone else told her.

'Oh, please can we go back just in case?' Annie wailed. 'What if he's in there?'

'The boat would be overwhelmed if we went back. Every man and his brother would try to climb aboard and we'd all drown. If he's a young child he'll be safe on another boat. You mark my words.'

After a while there was no more point in arguing because they weren't going to change course, so Annie strained her ears to listen, trying to pick out individual voices. There were cries of 'Help me!' and 'My God!' and lots of names – Ethel, Anna, Marie, Clara – presumably men calling for their wives. A couple of times she thought she heard shouts of 'Ma', but none

153

with Finbarr's distinctive Cork accent. There were curses and groans and sighs, and gradually, as time went on, the voices got fewer and farther between.

Still Annie strained to hear every last sound that echoed across the fathomless ocean, even though she knew by now that none could be her son. If he had got onto a boat, he would be alive, but if he had toppled into the ocean he had no chance. He couldn't make his way to a lifeboat, wouldn't know how, because none of her children had ever learned to swim.

By her side, Patrick was shaking with silent sobs. The others were too young to understand but he knew the worst. She should put her arm round him. They should all hug and share their body warmth and try to give comfort, but Annie found she couldn't move. She was paralysed in her fear. She wasn't sure if she would ever be able to move again.

Chapter Twenty-Four

As she watched the *Titanic* sliding beneath the water, Juliette's first emotion was terror. She became convinced they were all going to die out there in the black, fathomless night. The piteous screams of the men pitched from the ship into the ocean were like some awful hell chorus and she imagined she and her companions on the lifeboat would soon be joining them in the freezing water; either that or they'd be left to drift in the darkness until they froze to death.

'We must go back and save as many as we can,' a woman declared.

'Not yet,' Officer Lowe told her. 'We'd be overwhelmed by swimmers.'

An argument broke out, with some passengers urging Lowe to turn back while others claimed it was too dangerous, and Juliette listened, unsure what to think. Her mother was being uncharacteristically silent.

Lowe seemed to have a plan in mind, though. He called to the men rowing some other craft in the vicinity and five boats converged and were tethered together.

'Ladies, I'd like to transfer you into these other boats so that I can go back and pick up survivors,' Lowe announced. There was a collective gasp of fear, so he continued: 'There's no need to be alarmed. We'll hold the boats very steady so there can be no risk of falling. As you see, the ocean is very calm.'

Juliette's heart was beating hard. Some months previously, she had been trained in lifesaving by the Red Cross. It was one of the charities for which she organised local baking and craft sales to raise funds. Normally she just handed over a bag of cash to the Red Cross representative and received his fulsome thanks, but on this occasion she had been asked if she would like to attend a one-day lifesaving course, and she agreed. Should she mention this to Officer Lowe? For the life of her, she didn't think she could remember a single thing they had taught her. These men in the water would have hypothermia, and the only treatment she could imagine being effective would be to make them warm somehow – but without blankets and flasks of tea, how would that be possible?

Women were standing up carefully and stepping across to the other boats, causing theirs to rock alarmingly in the water. Juliette's mother was breathing with short little pants as she stood to take her turn. Two seamen held her elbows and she shrieked as they lifted her into an adjoining boat.

Juliette stood up, still wrestling with her decision. Should she say anything? Officer Lowe reached a hand towards her and the words spilled out.

'I have Red Cross training. I'm not sure . . . maybe I could be of assistance?'

'Good,' he nodded, appraising her. 'Stay here then.'

She sat down, feeling sick. Now she would be expected to know what to do, to save lives, and she couldn't think of anything useful. She was a fake, a sham, and this was no time for pretence. Juliette's mother looked across from her seat in the new boat and seemed surprised but didn't say anything.

Once most of the women had been distributed among the four other boats, Lowe ordered his men to row back towards the area where they could still hear voices crying out for help. Juliette ran through her scant knowledge: check if they are breathing, feel for a pulse. Would she have to do mouth-to-mouth resuscitation? Goodness knows what would be required.

When they reached the first figure in the water, Lowe leaned over to check for vital signs but quickly decided there was no hope. Juliette was too far away to see the face. All she could make out was the life preserver and a slick of wet hair. They stopped again, and again, but none was alive. The groans and cries were getting fewer and weaker as men succumbed to the brutal water temperature.

'I am hearing their last utterances,' Juliette realised. Sometimes they were snatches of prayer or distinguishable names, but more often just sighs of utter despair.

Lowe found a man who was still breathing, semiconscious, and all the crew gathered to help haul him onto the boat, causing it to rock wildly. They laid him on the bottom, with his head by Juliette's feet and she sprang into action.

She placed her fingers on his neck and felt a pulse, a faint one. He was murmuring under his breath so that meant he was breathing. She took off his life preserver, loosened his collar and tie to help him breathe more easily and started rubbing his arms and chest vigorously in an attempt to warm him. He was young, in his twenties, clean-shaven, with dark hair. He could be handsome; it was hard to tell in the dark but she suspected he might be.

'Mother,' he mumbled at one point.

'I'm here,' she whispered. 'You're safe.'

Three more men were hauled on board and some other women took care of them, following Juliette's lead.

Juliette sat on the floor of the boat and pulled the man's head onto her lap, so she could more easily continue to warm and soothe him. It was good to have something to focus on rather than her own safety. She just hoped she was doing the right things.

Lowe circled the area several times and checked dozens of bodies floating in the water but no more were pulled on board. It was mostly quiet now, apart from the splashing of their oars. Occasionally a lone voice cried out and Lowe tried to row towards it, but it had always faded by the time he reached the scene.

They're all dead, Juliette realised. *And I listened to them dying.* She had no idea of the number of casualties but guessed it must be in the hundreds. The extent of the disaster was unimaginable. Every time she glanced over the side of their boat, there were floating life preservers as far as the eye could see, most of them holding a body suspended inside.

She bent down and hugged the man on her lap, trying to transmit her own body warmth to him. 'There's nothing I can do for the ones out there,' she decided. 'But I am going to save this man if it's the last thing I do.'

'Hold on,' she whispered to him. 'Help will be here soon.' She brushed the dark hair back from his forehead and kissed his brow with all the gentleness of a lover, and he murmured something unintelligible in reply.

Chapter Twenty-Five

Reg was shivering convulsively and if it hadn't been for the men who surrounded him, he would have fallen and slipped over the edge of the collapsible. He had no feeling at all in his feet and that bothered him. There was a very real danger he could lose them to frostbite. He stamped one then the other but they were so numb it was as if they belonged to someone else.

Lightoller had turned in their direction. 'That man lying down. Is he alive? Could someone check?'

He meant the man whose leg Reg had used to haul himself up onto the collapsible. Someone crouched to listen for signs of breathing.

'He's gone.'

'Roll him overboard then,' Lightoller ordered. 'We need the space.'

It felt cruel to do so, but it was an order given by an officer. To his surprise, Reg found himself making the sign of the cross. Despite his lack of religious faith, it felt as though some gesture were needed and that's all he could think of. The man rolled off and was soon lost from sight.

All was quiet now, apart from Lightoller's occasional orders for them to lean to the left or to the right. Oars were virtually useless on an upturned boat, so they drifted aimlessly through the blackness. Reg didn't think he knew anyone on the collapsible apart from Lightoller, but then he heard a Birkenhead accent he recognised.

'Mr Joughin, is that you?'

'Yeah, an' who's that?'

'Reg Parton, sir.'

'Young Reg. I'm glad of it.'

They lapsed into silence again, and now Reg simply focused on the act of staying upright. His legs were like jelly and he knew he was leaning on his neighbours too heavily because they nudged him and snapped that he should get off the boat and swim for it if he couldn't stand up by himself. He blew into his fingers to warm them, and all he could think was that something had to happen soon because he couldn't go on like this much longer. And yet he must.

The night seemed interminable. At one stage, Reg began hallucinating. He thought that Lightoller was his father and felt euphoric that he had come back to look after him in his hour of need. He was a good man after all, no matter what they said about him. 'Father, I wish you could meet Florence,' he said, and all of a sudden Florence was there and Reg was delighted. He couldn't see her but he could hear her introducing herself to his father. 'Reg is a good boy, Mr Parton,' she said.

'Will you put a bloody lid on it?' a harsh voice scolded. 'You're going doolally.'

'Is he talking to me?' Reg wondered. And then he realised he had been speaking out loud, and that Florence wasn't on the boat and Lightoller wasn't his father.

He looked out across the ocean, and there weren't so many bodies floating around now; they must have drifted away on a current. On the horizon he could see faint grey dawn arriving, its rays curving around the edge of the planet. It was probably about four in the morning, he reckoned, although he had no way of checking. They could have been standing on that collapsible for hours, or days even. He couldn't remember.

Gradually he became aware that the other men were talking among themselves: just quietly at first, and then the tone changed, became more animated. What were they saying?

'I reckon she's twenty minutes away.'

'Less than that.'

Reg looked out towards the horizon and first he saw an iceberg, glistening in pale pink rays of sunlight. Next he saw a lifeboat full of people. That must be what they were talking about. And then the sun slipped a little further over the horizon and he made out an indistinct glowing shape and his heart gave a little skip. Could it be? He kept his eyes glued to that spot and the shape got bigger and closer and soon there was no doubt at all. It was a ship. They were saved. He was going to live.

Chapter Twenty-Six

'Was that a shooting star?'

Juliette looked up. A carpet of stars was blinking against the black sky but she couldn't see any trails. And then she saw what they were talking about: a white starburst that exploded outwards before petering down towards the water.

'It's a rocket!' Lowe declared. 'It must be the *Carpathia.*'

'Is that a ship come to rescue us?' one woman asked, and Lowe told her that it was.

Juliette leant down to whisper the news to the man on her lap. 'Not long now,' she told him. 'Hang on in there.' She ran her fingers through his hair and ruffled it affectionately.

Lowe was giving orders and the men were rowing with renewed vigour. She could feel them pulling through the water. It was getting lighter and as she looked out over the edge of the boat, she saw other lifeboats dotted in the water around them, all full of huddled figures. She counted six boats, each of them crammed with survivors. Maybe more people had lived than she thought. Perhaps only a few had perished and the rest had been picked up and saved, like the man in her lap.

She wondered if she should check his pockets to see if he had any identification, but it felt impertinent. Instead she cradled him and whispered reassurance. 'I can see the ship now,' she told him. 'It's huge. We'll soon be on there, in dry clothes, with blankets and a warm drink. They'll have doctors too.'

As she watched, the first lifeboat arrived alongside the *Carpathia*, and Juliette could see there was some kind of opening halfway up the side of the ship, and tiny figures were lifting people onto ladders to reach it. The sky was brightening by the minute.

'Ladies, we're going to have to squeeze up and take some more on board,' Lowe told them.

They were pulling up alongside a lifeboat in a perilous state, half-submerged so that its occupants were standing in several inches of water. There were about thirty of them, crowded together like sardines, all soaked to the skin and teeth chattering. Juliette pulled her patient closer and bent his knees up to make room. One by one the men from the half-submerged vessel clambered on board, and she felt their craft lowering in the water with the extra weight.

When everyone was loaded, they started rowing towards the ship. Juliette felt impatient now, but it took at least another half-hour before they pulled alongside the *Carpathia* and some of her crew began helping them on board. She saw there was a rope ladder stretching upwards.

'Will you manage to climb, ma'am, or would you like us to lower a chair?' someone asked her.

'I can climb myself, but what about this man? Look after him first, please. He needs help.' She lifted his head from her lap and extricated her skirt from beneath him.

A *Carpathia* crew member came on board and crouched to assess the condition of her patient. After a minute, he looked up gravely. 'I'm sorry, ma'am, but he's gone.'

It was like a punch in the heart. 'He can't be. He's not,

he's alive!' she insisted. She grabbed his wrist and felt for the faint pulse she had detected not long before. She bent her head to listen for any hint of breath. She shook him by the shoulders. 'He was alive just now, I swear.' Tears came to her eyes and began to flow. 'Oh God, he has to be alive.'

'Let me help you on board.' The seaman took her hand and raised her to her feet. She stepped across onto the rope ladder and began to climb, and that's when she started to sob in earnest. She felt intense grief, as though he had been a close relative, or a lover. Maybe he could even have been her future husband. But in truth, she hadn't even found out his name.

Chapter Twenty-Seven

Throughout the night, Annie sat still and silent, her chest tight with fear. Roisin and Patrick snuggled into her sides and slept fitfully, the baby lay cradled and snuffling in her arms, but she remained wide awake, her ears alert for a Cork accent on one of the boats they occasionally drifted near.

As dawn broke and the *Carpathia* was sighted, she felt a mixture of hope and fear. Now she would know for sure if Finbarr had reached a lifeboat. Maybe they would soon be reunited. She wanted to believe it, had to believe it. Theirs had been the last boat she had seen leave the ship, but surely either Reg or Kathleen's brother would have saved her boy. She'd put her trust in them. They mustn't let her down.

Their boat pulled up alongside the *Carpathia* and the crew lowered a sling for baby Ciaran. She nestled him into it and he was hauled up to an opening in the ship's side, then it came back down for Roisin, who started crying. *For God's sake, why did she keep crying?*

'Can you climb by yourself?' she asked Patrick, conscious these were the first words she had spoken to him since the *Titanic* sank. He nodded.

She climbed the ladder directly behind him and immediately she reached the ship, she demanded of the crew there: 'Have you seen a young Irish boy, black hair, so high?' She held her hand at a height just a few inches taller than Patrick.

'Yours is one of the first boats but there are lots more coming,' she was told. She turned to scan the ocean behind them and her spirits lifted as she saw at least a dozen other boats struggling towards them. In the distance the craggy peaks of icebergs glinted in pink dawn light.

'If you go upstairs they've got blankets and hot food and drinks,' a crew member told her. 'We need to keep this area clear.'

She led the children up the stairs he indicated, but instead of going inside for food, she took them onto the deck and found a spot where they could see out over the railings.

'Can you count all the boats for me, Patrick love?' she asked, and he began counting out loud.

'Nineteen, ma. There are nineteen boats out there, and ours makes twenty.'

More than she'd thought. Annie's heart gave a leap. 'Which one do you think Finbarr is on?'

'That one,' Roisin pointed to the closest one.

'I think that one,' Patrick said, pointing to the boat that was furthest away, a mere speck on the horizon.

An elderly American couple approached them. 'You poor things, you've been through such an ordeal,' the woman said. 'Would you like to rest in our cabin? We're in first class. There's room for you all to have a proper sleep.'

'I have to look for my eldest son,' Annie told her abruptly, then added 'thank you' as an afterthought.

'I'm sure he'll be here soon, but you should at least come into the warm. The children are shivering.' The woman was soft-spoken, with a gentle manner.

'It's kind of you,' Annie said, 'but I have to keep watch in case I miss him.' She had failed to keep a proper eye on him when

166

they were on the ship, so it was the least she could do now. She couldn't risk missing him when he came on board, in case he got lost. These ships were huge.

The couple conferred with each other in low voices then wandered off, but five minutes later they were back, the woman carrying blankets and the man bearing a tray with three steaming cups of tea, a jug of warm milk and a bowl of sugar. Annie's eyes filled with tears at their kindness.

'God bless you,' she said. 'Thank you so much.'

The woman wrapped a blanket around Roisin and stirred sugar into a cup of tea for her. Annie found the baby's bottle in her handbag and filled it with the milk, and Patrick sipped some tea as well, but Annie wouldn't touch it. It wouldn't feel right to take any sustenance until she knew where Finbarr was.

As each boat approached, her eyes moved from head to head, quickly at first, and then more methodically. *Not you, not you, not you.* Each time she realised he wasn't on board, she switched her attention to the next boat that was drawing near.

'He must come, he must. Holy Mary, mother of God, I beg you with all my heart.'

And then a particularly crowded boat appeared and she saw Reg being helped to his feet ready to disembark. Her heart skipped a beat as her eyes roved the faces in the throng but there was no Finbarr. Had Reg not found him? He made his way to the rope ladder and she could see he was having a lot of trouble climbing. His hands wouldn't grip the rope and it looked as though his feet were too painful to take his weight. He slipped and twisted round the ladder and one of the crewmen had to help him up. Annie grabbed the children and rushed down the stairs to meet him, questions fit to burst from her lips.

Reg almost collapsed in the arms of the seaman who hauled him off the ladder. He was in a shocking state, white-faced, blue-lipped, with his clothes frozen to his skin. He looked up and saw Annie watching and straight away shook his head.

'I'm so sorry. I found him then I lost him again.'

'What happened?' she breathed.

'I tied him to me as the ship went down and we jumped but the knots came undone and I couldn't find him in the water.' He took a step towards her and staggered.

'You need to see the doctor, lad,' someone cautioned.

Annie felt like lashing out at him. *Why had he survived and not her son? How could he find him then let him go again?* Instead, her knees collapsed beneath her and she sank to the floor, the babe still in her arms.

'Ma!' Patrick yelled in terror. Roisin screamed, a shrill, horrible sound.

I can't break down, she realised. *It's not an option. I have to pull myself together for the sake of these three.*

Someone appeared with smelling salts, but she waved them away. She hadn't lost consciousness; her legs had simply stopped supporting her weight. A woman took the baby from her while she leaned on a gentleman's arm to get to her feet. Reg had disappeared, led off somewhere by the crew.

Now I know the worst, she thought. *I just have to find out if there is any way that I can carry on living.* At that moment, it didn't feel as though there ever would be.

Chapter Twenty-Eight

In the doctor's consulting room, Reg was stripped of his wet clothes and wrapped in blankets. A nurse manoeuvred him into a chair and lifted his feet into a basin of warm water. Still he had no sensation in them. They were big white blocks of flesh attached to the ends of his legs. The same nurse held a cup of tea for him to sip because his fingers couldn't grip anything.

'We'll find some dry clothes for you,' she said. 'Once you've warmed up a bit.'

People were bustling around and he wanted to nod off to sleep, but his brain was too active. The main thought in his head was that he had to find John. He wanted to tell him about trying to save Finbarr. He wanted John to tell him that it was OK, that he'd done his best, because he was stricken with guilt. The sight of Annie's face, the way she collapsed when he told her that her son was lost, would stay with him for the rest of his life. He replayed the events in his mind and knew he should have done more. He should never have swum off without the boy. He'd been selfish. He'd thought only of saving himself.

His feet were starting to hurt now, as if they were being jabbed by hundreds of needles.

'That's good,' the doctor said. 'The circulation is returning. A couple more minutes then I'll dry them and put on sterile dressings.'

I don't deserve this, Reg thought. *They wouldn't be so kind to me if they knew.*

The nurse brought a set of clothes for him: a grey suit, a white shirt and some socks and underwear. They looked about the right size. He wondered whose they were but didn't ask. She showed him to a cubicle where he was able to pull them on. The jacket was a little wide in the shoulders, but otherwise it was fine.

'Where are my other clothes?' he asked, and the nurse showed him a pile by the door.

'We'll launder and dry them and you can pick them up tomorrow,' she said.

Reg slipped his fingers into his trouser pocket and felt something soggy. Very carefully, he turned the pocket inside out so he could extract Mrs Grayling's five-pound note without tearing it. The paper was soaked through but still intact. If he dried it carefully, it would survive. He placed it in the inside pocket of his new jacket, making sure it was flat. In the other pocket he found his passport in three disintegrating pieces, and placed them in the jacket, hoping they would dry eventually. Deep down, he found the St Christopher Florence had given him, and transferred it to his new trousers.

The doctor applied bandages to his feet, carefully separating the toes so they didn't stick together as the flesh healed. He wasn't able to put his shoes on, but the bandages were thick and would cushion his feet while he walked around the ship.

'There's space downstairs in the crew dorm. Go and have a sleep,' the doctor advised, but Reg had no intention of sleeping before he found John. He limped painfully out of the surgery holding his shoes in one hand, determined not to rest until they were reunited.

The ship was unfamiliar and much plainer than the *Titanic*. Reg hobbled along the corridor and up some stairs and found he was in a lounge. Survivors from the *Titanic* were huddled in every chair, and some were on the floor propped against the wall, wrapped in blankets and talking in hushed tones. He walked through, scanning all the faces, but they were passengers rather than crew. In one corner he recognised the Howsons and slunk past, careful not to catch their attention. He couldn't face talking to them. Just beyond the lounge, he found a *Carpathia* steward filling a tea urn.

'Where have the *Titanic* crew gone?' he asked.

'There's some down below in crew quarters. Do you want me to take you down?' The lad spoke so kindly that Reg felt tears spring to his eyes. He felt he could handle anything except other people's kindness, especially that of a lad his own age.

'I can find it.'

The steward showed him the entrance to their staff staircase and patted him on the back. Reg hobbled down the stairs, reliving the memory of his final trips on the staff stairs during the last couple of hours of the *Titanic*'s life. These stairs were level and filled with the healthy purring sound of the ship's engines.

He found the crew dorms and walked round, peering down at the heads on pillows. He recognised a few *Titanic* crew members he knew by sight but none he knew to talk to, and no John.

He must be looking for me, Reg decided. *Chances are, we'll keep missing each other.* Where would John look? Either here, in the crew dorm, or out on deck perhaps? Reg turned and hobbled slowly, painfully, back up the stairs again. When he reached the lounge, he continued out onto the observation deck.

There were some *Titanic* passengers there, either sitting on deckchairs or standing by the railings looking out across the water. Reg followed their gaze and was astonished at the number of icebergs he could see stretching out to the horizon. They were easy to spot now, sharp and glinting in the morning sunlight. The water was choppy and little remained to tell of the catastrophic events of the night before: a piece of wood; something red in colour that he couldn't make out, a stray life preserver with no one inside.

He continued further along the deck and there, by the railing, was Mr Grayling. They caught eyes, and Mr Grayling nodded to Reg.

'I hope Mrs Grayling is all right, sir,' Reg ventured, approaching.

'I haven't been able to find her yet,' he replied gravely. 'I put her on a lifeboat last night but there was no room for me to board, so we became separated. I expect she's here somewhere.'

It was on the tip of Reg's tongue to mention that he had seen Mr Grayling boarding Lifeboat 5, but he didn't. It wasn't his place. 'If she got on a lifeboat, I'm sure she'll be fine, sir. I'm very glad to hear it.'

'If you bump into her, do tell her I'm looking for her.'

Reg agreed that he would but still he felt cross with Mr Grayling. It wasn't right at a time like this to be fooling around with someone less than half your age. And why was he standing out on deck rather than searching high and low for his wife? It wasn't right at all.

Reg walked on and everywhere he went he peered at the occupants of chairs and corners, searching for John. He bumped into Mr Joughin and they shook hands. Joughin slapped him on the back and said 'Well done, lad, well done!' but when Reg asked, he said he hadn't seen John.

I have to search more thoroughly, Reg told himself. He decided to zigzag down the ship, walking the length of each deck before descending to the one below. His feet were hurting badly, but that's what he had to do. He looked in the restaurants, the gents' bathrooms, the lounges, the crew dorms, and on every outdoor deck. He asked each member of the *Titanic* crew he came across, but no one had seen John. Once he had finished searching every deck, right down to the cargo area of the ship, he started zigzagging his way back up again. Maybe John was doing the same but in the opposite direction and they kept missing each other?

There was a hard nugget of panic deep behind his breastbone that nagged more with each step. *What if John hadn't made it?* Surely he must have. He was strong and brave and sensible, more sensible than Reg. If only they had been together at the end, John would have helped him to save Finbarr and they would all have been rescued together. Reg needed John. He ached for him. Frankly, he didn't care who else had died so long as John had made it. Each time he reached a new part of the ship, he allowed himself to hope that John would be just around the corner. Each time his hopes were dashed, and panic began to take hold.

I can't go on without him, he thought. There was no reason why he should have survived and John hadn't. It was random, arbitrary and unspeakably cruel. If it turned out that John was dead, Reg thought he would rather swap places with him. He would rather be dead himself than carry on living in such a hostile, unpredictable world.

Chapter Twenty-Nine

Annie stood on deck watching until the last lifeboat had been unloaded. She knew there was no longer any hope of finding Finbarr but she didn't know what else to do. Sleep would be an impossibility. So would eating and drinking. She should tend her three remaining children but she was paralysed by the shocking acuteness of her loss. Her son was there one minute, gone the next, and he was never coming back. How would that ever make sense?

The *Carpathia*'s engines started and the ship sailed in a big circle around the area where the *Titanic* had disappeared. Annie's eyes never once left the water. If she could find his body and take it back to Seamus, that would be something. They could have a proper funeral with all the holy rites and she could begin the process of mourning.

She heard some sailors down below were keeping a lookout for bodies, but there was nothing to be found. Where had they all gone? There was barely any wreckage in the water. There must be a current pulling everything away. Could some survivors have clambered onto the nearby icebergs? She squinted at them, but there was no sign of bodies, either dead or alive.

The kindly American couple came back. 'They are holding a religious service in the saloon,' the woman told her, taking her hand and patting it gently. 'I thought you might want to be there.'

Annie nodded her thanks. That was something she could do. She followed them indoors to a spacious room where a crowd had already congregated. There was standing room only as the *Carpathia*'s chaplain stood in front of them with a prayer book in his hands.

'This is a service of respect for those who were lost, and gratitude for those who were saved,' he began, but his words were soon drowned out by sobbing. Baby Ciaran wakened and began to cry, Roisin and Patrick were crying, and as Annie looked around, she saw that even grown men had tears streaming down their cheeks. She envied them. She couldn't seem to cry herself.

She strained to hear the chaplain's words above the weeping but could find no comfort in them. *Why had it been God's will that Finbarr died? What good did it do anyone?* As they bent their heads to pray, she pictured Finbarr's grin, his unruly hair, his blue eyes and his skinny ten-year-old frame and she tried to visualise him being welcomed into God's kingdom, but she couldn't see it, couldn't feel it in her heart. He was too young. He had his whole life ahead of him.

Afterwards, the American woman, who seemed to have taken a special interest in Annie's family, led them to a dining room where the tables were set for breakfast. She helped Patrick and Roisin to order food, got a steward to fill a bottle with warm milk for Ciaran and put a plate with some toast and jam in front of Annie.

'You're being so kind and I haven't even asked your name,' Annie said, ignoring the toast.

'Mildred. Mildred Clarke. My husband is Jack.'

Annie introduced herself and her three children.

'And Finbarr is the one you've lost?'

Annie nodded, grateful that she had used the word 'lost' rather than 'dead' or 'drowned', grateful that she had used the present tense.

'What kind of a boy is Finbarr?'

'Oh . . . he's curious, headstrong. A bright boy, with an answer for everything. He could talk the hind legs off a donkey, that one.' It felt good to speak about him. She was glad Mildred had asked. It made her feel as though he was somehow still around.

While they sat talking, Reg limped into the room. His complexion was no longer quite so sickeningly pale, but he had dark circles under his eyes and one side of his face kept twitching with tiredness. He hesitated and looked as though he was about to turn on his heel when he saw Annie, but she held out her hand to him. *It wasn't his fault Finbarr had died, not really. It was unfair to blame him. He was only a boy himself.*

'Have you eaten? Would you like some food?' she asked.

'I can't eat,' he said, his voice a husky whisper.

'No, me neither.' She hesitated. 'Do you feel able to tell me what happened? There's no rush. Just when you can manage.'

Reg nodded, his eyes cast down. 'Now is fine.'

They moved to an unoccupied table, leaving the children sitting with Mildred, and Reg began to talk, in a voice that was shaking with emotion. He described finding Finbarr trapped behind the gate between F and E Deck and about how they made their way upstairs only to be separated as they leapt into the ocean.

'Was he scared?' Annie asked. She wanted every last detail.

'He was scared when I found him but just before the jump, he seemed fine. He trusted me. He was sure I was going to save him.' Reg's hands were trembling and he couldn't meet her eye.

'Did he ask where I was?'

'Yes. He was worried that you would be cross with him, but I said you weren't. I said you just wanted him back safe and sound.'

'What were his last words?' she asked, trying to visualise the scene. She needed to picture it.

Reg couldn't remember exactly. 'We talked about running to the railing and when we were going to jump, and he said he understood and then, just before we jumped, he smiled at me. He seemed fine.'

Annie placed her hand on his. 'He thought you were quite the hero after that day you took them to the galley. I'm so glad he had you for comfort, and that he wasn't alone at the end.' She tried to smile.

Reg was distraught. 'I wish I could have found him in the water. I don't know what happened. He just didn't seem to surface from the jump. I looked for as long as I could but he didn't appear.'

'Didn't he tell you?' Annie asked. 'Finbarr couldn't swim.'

At that, Reg broke down and wept into his hands, and the sound was awful.

It's because we're not used to hearing men cry, Annie thought. *The act of crying seems more suited to higher-pitched female voices.* She rubbed his shaking shoulders, feeling protective towards him.

'I didn't know,' he sobbed. 'He didn't say.'

'But what could you have done if you did know? It wouldn't have changed anything. He's in God's hands now.' If she said it often enough, maybe the time would come when she was able to believe it. 'We're all in God's hands.'

Chapter Thirty

Juliette found that she couldn't stop crying. It was humiliating how readily the tears flowed. A *Carpathia* passenger came over to her in the lounge and asked 'Have you lost your husband, dear?' and Juliette had to explain that she wasn't married and that she hadn't lost anyone. *Control yourself*, she urged. *Pull yourself together.* But the tiniest thing would set her off again, especially the sight of others' grief.

The Howsons came to sit with her and her mother, and Juliette noticed that the hostility towards each other that she had witnessed at the final dinner on the *Titanic* was long forgotten. They held hands now, grateful not to be widowed, and full of news about those who had survived and those who hadn't.

'Colonel Astor is lost and Madeleine is quite inconsolable. Utterly beside herself. She's pregnant, you know. And did you meet Eloise Smith, the senator's daughter? She's in the same situation: pregnant and her husband drowned. It's tragic for the little ones who'll never know their fathers.'

Juliette thought with distaste that Vera Howson appeared almost to be enjoying her role as emissary of the bad news.

'They say that fewer than one in three survived,' Bert Howson chipped in. 'There simply weren't enough lifeboats. It's a disgrace. I hope White Star Line will be forced out of business.'

Juliette's mother joined in. 'What are they going to do about compensating us all? I've lost some priceless family jewellery. If only the steward had said to bring it with us onto the lifeboats, it could have been saved. I'm very cross about that.'

'There will have to be compensation,' Bert agreed.

Juliette felt sick listening to them as they reduced the whole disaster to a financial transaction. She stood up abruptly, announcing that she was going out on deck for some fresh air, and walked off swiftly before her mother could decide to come with her.

Out on deck, she stood gazing across the water. They were speeding back towards New York now, and would be arriving on Thursday, only a day later than scheduled. For them, life could carry on as before, yet she felt that she would never be the same again. She felt as though she had been a naïve child before. She'd never understood the nature of the world, never understood that someone could be alive at one moment and dead the next, with no warning. Of course, she had known it intellectually; she read the newspapers. But she had never before felt the sheer fragility of existence. She had never before had a young man die in her arms.

'Are you all right?' a man's voice asked, and she looked up to see a fellow passenger. She recognised him as the man with the sandy hair who had smiled at her as they left the first-class dining saloon after that last dinner.

'I haven't lost a loved one, if that's what you mean. But no, I'm not all right.' Tears filled her eyes yet again. 'I can't seem to stop crying, and then I feel guilty because I have no right to cry when the ship is full of people who have lost those to whom they were closest in the world. How about you? Did your wife survive? Your family?'

'I'm not married and I was travelling alone. Now, now, you mustn't feel guilty for crying. You are in shock – we all are. It will take some time before anything feels normal again.' He had a warm voice, and an American accent, but not a broad one. He sounded cultured.

Tears rolled down Juliette's cheeks and she opened her handbag to search for her handkerchief.

'Normally I would be able to offer you my own handkerchief but I'm afraid these are not my clothes. I was given them by a nice woman who underestimated my size somewhat.' He opened the jacket to show Juliette how the waistcoat buttons were straining across his chest, and she smiled through her tears.

'What happened to your own clothes?'

'Wet from my swim. They'll be dry in the morning, I'm assured.'

Juliette gasped. 'You were in the water and survived? Please tell me what happened – if you don't mind, that is.'

He explained that he had waited until the *Titanic* was very low in the water, fixed his eyes on one particular lifeboat that was only half-full, then dived in and swum to it. 'They had no choice but to haul me on board.'

'And you are fine? You feel no ill effects?'

'I'm fine now. I wouldn't want to repeat it though.'

Juliette told him about the man she had looked after, who had a pulse and was mumbling when he was hauled onto their lifeboat, and her shock when a sailor from the *Carpathia* pronounced him dead. 'I feel such a fraud,' she admitted. 'I told Officer Lowe that I knew about first aid, and then the only patient I was charged with caring for died.'

'It sounds as though he'd been in the water too long. Nothing you could have done would have made any difference.

But it must have been very traumatic for you. No wonder you are still in shock.'

Juliette's eyes welled up again and she dabbed at them.

'My name is Robert Graham,' he introduced himself. 'And you, I know, are Lady Juliette Mason-Parker. I noticed you in the dining saloon and someone at our dinner table told me your name. Are you travelling with your mother? Do you have no male escort?'

Juliette shook her head. 'My father is back home in England.'

'In that case, I would be honoured if you would allow me to be of assistance to you and your mother on the ship. If there is any service I can perform, please let me know.'

He had an open, friendly face, Juliette decided, and the offer seemed completely genuine. 'Thank you so much. We might well take you up on that. In fact, perhaps you could advise me how we can send a Marconi-gram to my father to tell him we are alive? I expect the news of the sinking will reach England and I don't want him to worry.'

'I'll see to it straight away. I've already sent one to my mother and sisters. The Marconi operators aren't charging a fee, for compassionate reasons. Would you care to come with me and choose the wording yourself?'

He offered his arm, and Juliette took it. As they walked to the Marconi office, she could feel the reassuring warmth of his arm through the fabric of his jacket.

Chapter Thirty-One

Reg was badly shaken by his conversation with Annie. He felt sick and dizzy with exhaustion but knew that if he lay down, his head would fill with nightmares of drowning and loss. He couldn't bear to be still. If he kept moving, maybe he'd find John around the next corner and they'd hug and things would be all right. He needed to talk to someone about what had happened, needed it badly, and John was the only person he could think of who would do.

A *Carpathia* crewman was walking round with a list of names. *That's it!* Reg thought. *He will know if John is here because his name will be on the list. I need to get him to check his list.*

The man was talking to another group of passengers, but Reg waited patiently to attract his attention. They took a long time and Reg wasn't close enough to hear what was said but he imagined they were asking after their friends on board, checking who was there and who wasn't. At last they finished and the man turned towards Reg.

'Passenger or crew?' he asked.

'Crew.'

'Name?'

'John Hitchens.'

He scanned the list then wrote the name down. 'What job?'

'First-class victualling steward.'

He wrote that down as well. 'You look like you need some kip,' he told Reg. 'Go down to our dorms. Pick any bed that doesn't already have someone in it.'

I don't want to sleep. I want to find John. The man had turned to walk away, though, and Reg realised his last words hadn't been spoken out loud. Did that mean that John was on the list? Or not? Why hadn't he said either way? Reg's brain felt as though it was full of fog. He started to follow the man with the list, but realised he had disappeared from sight round a corner. Which way had he gone?

Reg turned into a carpeted corridor with cabins leading off. Was this the first-class area? It was hard to tell on this ship where each section led into the next. While he was hesitating, a cabin door opened and Mr Grayling emerged and stared at him.

'What are you doing here?' he demanded.

'I was looking for someone, a friend of mine.'

'I see,' he frowned. 'Well, I hope you find your friend. I still haven't found my wife and I'm starting to become rather alarmed. You haven't come across her, I suppose?'

'Oh no!' Reg cried in despair, and struggled to hold back his tears. 'She must be here. Where could she be?'

Mr Grayling looked surprised. 'I wasn't aware you were so fond of her.'

Reg nodded. 'I am.' He looked at the floor. 'She's been very good to me.'

'I suppose she gave you a ridiculously generous tip. She's like that.' He tutted. 'I can't imagine what's happened to her, unless she got off the lifeboat I put her on to go back to our cabin for something. I couldn't keep an eye on her because I was ushered to a boat on the other side of the ship. Did you see her at all after the collision?'

Reg shook his head. 'I came and knocked on your cabin door but there was no one there.'

'You didn't go in?'

'It was locked.'

Mr Grayling looked startled for a moment, but recovered himself quickly. 'Yes, of course. It would have been. I see. I suppose . . . I'm afraid I'm beginning to think the worst.' His voice was grave but emotionless.

Fresh tears came to Reg's eyes. 'There's a man going round with a list,' he suggested. 'Maybe she is on it?'

'The roll call? I've already checked that.'

Reg smeared the tears from his eyes with his sleeve. Poor Mrs Grayling. It was horrible to think she might have perished. Why would she have got off her lifeboat? What had been so important?

'You're in a bad way, my boy. Have you seen a doctor? Look, your feet are bleeding.'

Reg glanced down to see that blood was soaking through the bandages.

'You should go and rest somewhere. Shall I call for someone to help you?'

'I'm fine,' Reg mumbled. 'You're right. I'll go and rest now. Thank you, sir.' Then he added, 'I do hope you find Mrs Grayling.'

He turned and hobbled back the way he had come, going over the conversation in his head. How could Mr Grayling be so calm about the loss of his wife? Did he even care about her? Or was he happy that she was out of the way so he could spend more time with his young mistress? You'd think he would put on a show of grieving at the very least. She deserved much better.

And then something else Mr Grayling had said came to mind. He had talked about a roll call. That's what the list was, and Reg's name wouldn't be on it because he had given John's name instead of his own. *Idiot!* He'd have to find the man with the list and get him to change it. Not until he'd had some rest though. He was so very tired that if he didn't lie down soon, he would collapse. Somehow he made it to the crew dormitory, selected a bed in the farthest corner from the door and was unconscious as soon as his head hit the pillow.

Chapter Thirty-Two

The first- and second-class areas on the *Carpathia* were much smaller and dowdier than their equivalents on the *Titanic,* while the third-class areas were larger, with basic furniture and fittings. The ship had been sailing towards the Mediterranean with almost all her cabins occupied, so it was a crush for the seven hundred and eleven *Titanic* survivors to be fed and found places to wash and rest. Every bed, every chair was occupied and many slept on the floor, while the *Carpathia* staff worked flat out to serve extra sittings at mealtimes.

Walking into any room, you could tell at a glance which were *Titanic* passengers and which *Carpathia*, for the *Titanic* ones looked dazed, full of disbelief about what had happened to them, while the *Carpathia* passengers observed them with a mixture of sympathy and curiosity, as if they were rare specimens in a zoo. Virtually everyone behaved with consideration towards the others on board – everyone, Juliette thought, except her mother.

'It's unacceptable that we have to queue to get into the dining saloon for meals,' she proclaimed loudly. 'Do they know who we are?'

'Do be quiet, Mother,' Juliette hissed.

'We paid more for our tickets than the *Carpathia* passengers, so we should be given priority.'

'It's a different shipping company. We haven't paid these people anything at all.'

Robert was the only person she could bear to be around. He was calm and practical, finding solutions to any problems that arose. He found a small second-class cabin for Juliette and her mother to share and collected some basic toiletries from the barber's shop on board. He arranged for Lady Mason-Parker's blouse to be laundered, and procured some aspirin when she complained of a headache. Whenever she could, Juliette liked to escape with him for a walk round the decks, where they talked endlessly about what had happened, and why, and tried to come to terms with their experience.

Juliette wanted to find out the name of the man who had died in her arms, so together they approached Officer Lowe to ask if he had been identified. He told her that it had been a twenty-five-year-old first-class passenger called Frederick Baines, a sales representative for a pharmaceutical company, who had been travelling alone.

'Like me,' Robert said, 'but two years younger.'

'Yet you survived,' Juliette pointed out. 'I still feel that I should have done more to help him.'

'I was a college athlete and still play hockey. Perhaps Frederick Baines was not so fit, or perhaps he simply didn't reach a boat so quickly.'

Officer Lowe nodded agreement. 'He had been too long in the water. The pulse was only ever very faint. I expect his organs were failing well before we hauled him on board. The doctor told me that twenty minutes is the most he would expect a fit man to live in such water temperatures. You did all you could for him, Lady Mason-Parker.'

'Thank you for saying so.'

'If I might make one more suggestion . . . Perhaps you could write a letter to his mother, telling her about his final hours. I'm sure it would bring her great comfort to know he was so well cared for. If you feel able to write such a letter, I will make sure that it is delivered.'

Juliette agreed that she would, and was glad to have a task that absorbed her for some of the time at least. Robert read her drafts of the letter and made suggestions and at last declared it perfect so she copied it out neatly and he took it to Officer Lowe.

It seemed that most of Juliette's acquaintances from the ship had survived, but Robert was with her when she heard the news that Mrs Grayling was not among them.

'How could that be?' she exclaimed, distraught. 'I thought all the first-class women were escorted to lifeboats by their room stewards?' She couldn't fathom what might have happened.

'Something went wrong, I suppose. I believe she was one of only four first-class ladies to perish. Two waited behind with their husbands and one, I hear, was too fearful to get into a boat, but neither scenario was the case with Mrs Grayling. I expect her last moments will remain a mystery.'

'Yet her husband survived. Why did he not attend to her safety?'

'You were fond of her, I see,' Robert commented.

'In truth, I didn't know her well, but she had invited us to dine with her on arrival in New York. I think she and my mother were scheming to find me an American husband.' As soon as the words were out of her mouth Juliette blushed, wishing she hadn't mentioned it, but Robert smiled.

'I can't believe that you are not entirely capable of finding a husband for yourself. They must be queuing up at your door.'

Juliette blushed even deeper. 'I shouldn't have told you about that,' she stammered. 'Forget I spoke.' Since the catastrophe she hadn't given a thought to the small matter of her pregnancy. It was no longer the overriding concern in her life. She hadn't even felt nauseous on the *Carpathia* because there were much more pressing worries to attend to.

'Not at all. I'm curious to hear that the Graylings planned to entertain. They are notoriously reclusive. I don't think I've heard of them giving a dinner party in many years, despite the fact that they have a large Madison Avenue home with perfect amenities for entertaining.'

'How sad that the dinner will not come to pass now. I would have liked to get to know her better once we were in New York.'

Tears came to Juliette's eyes again, and to distract her, Robert continued, 'Speaking of our arrival in New York, do you have a hotel reservation or will you stay with relatives?'

'I believe we are staying at the Plaza. I hope they will hold the room although we will arrive more than a day later than expected.'

'I'm sure they will. I would be honoured if you would allow me to escort you there on arrival. There is bound to be a scrum at the port, with worried relatives and reporters all trying to get close, but my driver will be waiting. May I offer my protection?'

'Oh, please. Yes.' The prospect of wrestling their way through a crowd and trying to find a taxi in an unfamiliar city was daunting. She didn't want to be separated from Robert on arrival. She felt safe with him around.

Chapter Thirty-Three

When Reg opened his eyes, he was momentarily confused to find himself on a lower bunk instead of the top one above a sleeping John. He was close enough to a porthole to see that it was broad daylight outside, but which day? And then it all came back to him in a great rush: the horror of struggling for his life in the water; the stricken look on Annie's face when he told her he hadn't managed to save her son; the absence of John. Missing, almost certainly dead. It was unbearable. His heart was thumping so hard he felt as though he might die any second, but he couldn't open his mouth to call for help. He was slicked with sweat, breathing hard, totally consumed by panic.

What am I going to do? he thought. *What on earth am I going to do now? How will I carry on?*

'Are you OK?' someone asked. 'Are you in pain? It's just that you were moaning.'

Reg raised his head and saw it was a steward from second class, whose name he didn't know. 'I'm OK,' he managed to say. 'What day is it?'

'Tuesday. They say we moor in New York on Thursday night, then we're being loaded straight onto another ship, the *Cedric*, for the journey home. Have you ever sailed on the *Cedric*? Any idea what she's like?'

Reg was filled with horror at the idea. He wanted to run down the gangplank on arrival in New York, plant his feet on solid ground and stay there. Another transatlantic voyage straight away would be more than he could bear. What if the *Cedric* hit an iceberg and the whole thing happened again? He realised he hadn't answered the question, so he said 'No.'

'Talkative one, aren't you?'

Reg turned his face to the wall. He knew he couldn't face another ocean crossing. After tomorrow evening, he never wanted to set foot on a ship again. In fact, he wanted to get as far from water as he possibly could. He felt numb, but his brain was racing, trying to think of a way he could manage on his own if he left White Star Line. He had his wages for this voyage – minus the cost of the breakages – and he had Mrs Grayling's five pounds, but would that be enough to rent a room somewhere and tide him over until he found a job? America was supposed to be the land of opportunity. If he made a fresh start there, he wouldn't ever have to go back on a ship. That was his overriding concern.

There was a loud clatter in the corridor outside and Reg dived under the bedclothes, trembling with fear.

'It was only a tray,' the steward in the next bunk told him. 'Someone dropped a tray. You're in a bad way, ain't ya? Come on, let's go and find some grub. I'm starving.'

'No, thanks.' He couldn't face eating. His stomach was twisted up in knots so it didn't feel as if there would be any space for food.

'Suit yourself,' the steward said. 'I'm off.'

How could anyone eat with the cries of all those dying men still ringing in their ears? It seemed disrespectful. Reg wanted to stay in bed with the covers pulled over his head. That way he wouldn't risk bumping into Annie again. Her kindness was almost more than he could take. He didn't want to see Mr Grayling either, or the Howsons, or anyone really – apart from John, and it didn't seem that was going to happen. *Don't think about John. It hurts too much.*

He forced himself to consider what kind of job he might be able to get in New York. Perhaps he could be a waiter in a top-notch restaurant. He'd read about some very smart places, all of them in the area around Fifth Avenue and Central Park, but he would need a reference to get a position there. If only his record at White Star Line didn't have those blemishes on it: breaking crockery, eating a passenger's leftovers, and then that accusation of theft from the previous year. It didn't occur to Reg to wonder whether Latimer had already recorded his recent misdemeanours, and if so whether the record – and Latimer himself – had survived.

He wasn't thinking logically. Instead, he felt an overwhelming sense of doom. He would starve on the streets of New York, unable to work to pay for food and shelter because of that bad report. No one would want him. He didn't know anyone in the city he could turn to. Back in Southampton, he could have asked neighbours to help him get a job with the town council, or begged them to let him serve tea and scones at the Seaview Café, but here he was on his own. Yet he couldn't go back to Southampton because it would mean crossing the ocean and he knew he simply wasn't capable.

What would John advise? John was smart. John always had an answer for everything. If he were there on the *Carpathia*, what would he do? Surely he wouldn't be able to get straight on another ship as if nothing had happened, as if he hadn't narrowly survived while dozens of people died in the water around him, as if he couldn't still hear the sound of their groans ringing in his head?

If John was still alive, they could have stayed in New York together. John had a squeaky clean record with White Star so he could have got work in an élite restaurant while Reg could have found something less lofty, and maybe one day they would have started their own business together. Their wives could have been friends, their children could have gone to the same schools, they could have lived in the same street, perhaps started a football team.

Stop it! Stop! You're torturing yourself. These things could never be and it was Reg's fault. If only he had found John at the end and they'd stuck together. If only he had rescued Finbarr and emerged from this a hero of sorts, maybe White Star would have overlooked his misdemeanours. But he had failed and as a result a boy had died.

For most of the day, Reg lay in the unfamiliar bunk turning over the problems in his head but without finding a solution. It was as though his brain was encased in fog. It felt as though the answer was somewhere nearby but he couldn't quite reach it.

As darkness began to fall, hunger forced him to get up and ask directions to the staff mess. They were serving a stew with mashed potatoes and he let them pile his plate high. He began to eat and was surprised how much better he felt after only a couple of forkfuls. He looked around the room at the other diners and spotted the man who had been taking the roll call the day before.

I should talk to him later, give him my real name, Reg thought. But then another idea sprang into his head, and it was so obvious he was amazed he hadn't thought of it before. He was already on the survivors list as John . . . so why not continue to be John? On arrival in New York, he could use John's name when he looked for work, and when the restaurant manager called White Star for a reference, he would be told that John's record was spotless. It was a perfect plan.

The idea made him feel close to John again, as if they were still linked after death.

Of course, he would need to write to his mum and Florence to explain. They would try to persuade him to come back, but he'd have to make them understand that he simply couldn't cross the ocean again. Maybe in a year or so he'd feel differently, but for now he had no choice.

He would have to write to John's family as well. He should tell them he was using John's name. It would be a tricky letter to write but surely they wouldn't mind when he explained his reasons? It was just for the sake of getting on his feet. He felt sure John wouldn't have minded.

'Course you can use my name, man,' he imagined him saying in his Geordie accent. 'Happy to be of service!'

Chapter Thirty-Four

Mildred persuaded Annie to share her first-class suite, which had two separate bedrooms, while her husband slept in an armchair in the first-class lounge. Annie argued against the plan but she didn't have the energy to resist when Mildred tucked Roisin under the counterpane of her soft four-poster bed and invited Patrick to have a soak in their *en suite* bathroom. The children had taken to Mildred, and they clung to her, seeking a sense of security they were unable to get from their distraught mother.

When Annie awoke the next morning, more than twenty-four hours had passed since Finbarr disappeared. The sun shone outside, there were sounds from the corridor of passengers heading to the saloon for breakfast, and the baby was squawking for a feed. Life would go on – cruelly, relentlessly – whether she wanted it to or not.

'Patrick's been asking me what happened to Finbarr,' Mildred told her quietly. 'I said he is with God now, but I think he would like to know more. He feels it is his fault, because he let go of Finbarr's hand. Are you able to talk to him about it?'

'Of course. I must do that.' She buried her face in her hands, trying to think of what she should say. It seemed she had to deal with one difficult thing after another and she didn't have the energy for any of it. In the end, she took Patrick for a walk on deck after breakfast and told him the truth.

'When Finbarr's hand slipped out of yours on the way up the stairs, he heard someone say there was flooding down below and you know how curious he always was. There was nothing for it but he had to go and have a look. He couldn't help himself. Then he got lost down there and by the time the steward, Reg, found him it was too late to get on a lifeboat. If it was anyone's fault, it was his own. He couldn't resist sticking his nose in.'

'Where has he gone, Ma? Will I ever see him again?'

'One day you will, but not for a long time. We'll all go to heaven when we die and Finbarr will be there waiting for us.'

'I wish I could go to heaven now,' Patrick whispered, and Annie pulled him to her. Whoever said that children's emotions weren't as powerful as those of adults? Behind his quiet demeanour, Patrick was missing his brother just as much as Annie was missing her son.

'You have to be brave and strong. Finbarr would want you to build a specially happy life for yourself to make up for the fact that he can't. Just think about what he would want you to do, and I'll do the same, and we'll be strong for each other. That's how we'll get through this.'

If only it were that simple, Annie thought afterwards. She was dreading the moment when they stepped off the ship in New York and she would have to tell Seamus what had happened. He'd been so proud of his eldest boy. He used to pore over the schoolbooks where his teacher had written 'excellent work' or 'well done'. 'Did you see this essay he's written, Annie?' he'd say, or 'Look how long this sum is, and he's got it all right!' That's why Seamus had come to America to build a new life for them all. *If only he hadn't bothered. If only they had stayed at home.*

She felt sure Seamus would blame her for losing Finbarr, because she blamed herself. She shouldn't have taken her eyes off him for a second, and she shouldn't have got into the lifeboat without him. She said as much that afternoon when one of the Mayo party, Mary, came over to sit with her on deck.

'No one's to blame,' Mary told her. 'It was madness back there. Sheer pandemonium. It was all down to the luck of the draw who survived. Do you know how many are saved from the fourteen of us that were travelling together? Just me and my young niece Elizabeth.'

Annie was horrified. 'But what happened to Eileen and Kathleen? They were ahead of me. Kathleen was one of the people who talked me into getting in a lifeboat. Where did she go after that?'

'We're not sure but we think Kathleen might have gone back to look for her brother.' Annie clutched her face: more guilt for her to bear. 'And Eileen decided she wasn't leaving her man. When the officer said her Eoghan couldn't get on board, she said she wasn't going to either. I heard her myself. But at the time we didn't know for sure what that would mean, did we? No one said that the ship was sinking and you'd die if you didn't get into a lifeboat. Maybe they should have.'

Annie touched Mary's hand. 'To lose twelve friends all at once must be hard. Eileen and Kathleen were lovely women. You were so kind to me. I can't tell you what a difference it made.'

There was no comfort they could give each other, no words that would make it better. They sat in silence for a while, holding hands and looking round at the other survivors, each grieving their own losses. Mildred appeared from a tour round the deck with the children and when baby Ciaran saw Annie he stretched out his arms towards her with a wail. Roisin's eyes were bright with recent tears and she was clinging to Mildred's leg, her thumb in her mouth.

The children are lucky to be able to cry, Annie thought. Apart from that burst of communal grief at the religious service, most adults on board were keeping their tears in check. It was as if they couldn't afford to let go yet. Maybe they were concerned that their own sobs would disturb others with even greater losses to bear. Once they got home to their families on shore, they could let it all out over the coming weeks and months and years.

The atmosphere in the dining saloon couldn't have been more different from that on the *Titanic*. The lively chatter and laughter had been replaced by lowered voices and the clatter of knives and forks, or of the stewards piling dishes on top of each other. Annie at last managed to eat some small meals: bland, invalid food that was easy to chew, like scrambled eggs, or soup and bread. Mildred and her husband sat with her, helping Patrick and Roisin to cut up their meat and chatting about their life at home.

'Did I tell you that I have a car dealership back in Milwaukee?' Jack asked Patrick, and Annie saw her boy looking animated for the first time since the sinking as they discussed Model T Fords, the brand new Chevrolet and the various Ramblers on the market.

'Come and visit us some time and I'll take you out for a test drive,' he promised.

'Can we, Ma?' Patrick asked Annie.

'Maybe we'll take you up on that,' she agreed.

Sometimes there were moments – never as long as a minute,

198

but fleeting windows of time – when she forgot about the terrible thing that had happened, but then it came crashing back again with all its rawness. *I've lost Finbarr. He's gone for ever.*

'It will get easier,' Mildred told her. 'It will never leave you but the weight of your grief will become less crushing over the years.'

Annie hoped that would prove to be true, but in the meantime she still had one of the worst moments to face – telling Seamus.

Announcements were made on Thursday morning about the arrangements for disembarking. No one would have to clear US customs at Ellis Island; apart from anything else, few people still had the necessary papers with them. They were pulling into Pier 54 on New York's North River. Each class would disembark in turn and relatives would be standing at a prearranged spot. There would be help on hand for those left destitute by the sinking. Reporters and photographers were expected to turn up but they would not be allowed inside the pier.

Annie tried to rehearse what she would say to Seamus when they walked out to meet him, but her courage kept failing her. She'd had almost four days to get used to the unbearable pain that he would soon experience for the first time. She wished there was some way to spare him. If she could have carried it alone she would have done so gladly.

They watched from the deck as the *Carpathia* passed the southern tip of Manhattan and headed up the North River. Appropriately, it was raining, with a heavy grey drizzle that blurred the tall buildings people called skyscrapers. Progress was excruciatingly slow, but they docked around nine-thirty on Thursday evening, and first-class passengers began to file off. Annie could hear cries of delight as some families were reunited but there must also be many whose dreams for the future were being cruelly snatched from them in that instant when a wife appeared but no husband, a sister but no brother. She hadn't heard of any other cases such as her own, where a mother survived but not her child. *All the other mothers stayed with their children*, she thought bitterly. *All except me.*

Mildred and Jack were remaining on the ship, which would turn round and set sail for the Mediterranean just as soon as it had been cleaned and restocked with supplies. They sat with Annie and the children until the call went out at eleven o'clock at night for third-class passengers to disembark.

Slowly, Annie picked up the baby, looped her handbag over her elbow and got Roisin to hold onto her coat on one side while Patrick held the other. Her feet dragging, they queued to shuffle step by step along the gangway. She looked over towards the area where third-class families were queuing but there were too many faces to pick Seamus from the crowd.

He found her, though. The minute they stepped off the ship and onto the pier, he vaulted a wooden fence that marked the route to the exit and rushed over to them, joy written all over his face. It was heartbreaking to watch his broad smile fade as he first of all met her eyes and read the expression on her face, then looked at Patrick, Roisin and the baby. His eyes travelled over her shoulder and he searched the area behind them then he looked at Annie again and it was as if something inside him broke in two.

'No!' he yelled with such anguish that people around them turned to stare.

'I'm so sorry,' Annie whispered.

He pulled her to him, wrapped his arms around her and buried his face in her neck. All through these long months apart she had dreamed of their reunion, their first hug on meeting, their first evening alone together, but never in her wildest imaginings could she have envisaged this: that her husband of thirteen years would be shaking with uncontrollable grief, unable to speak, as all their careful plans for the future were swept away in a devastating roll of the dice.

Chapter Thirty-Five

Reg returned to the doctor's surgery to have the bloodied bandages on his feet changed. Underneath the toes were purple and swollen, with blackened nails. They looked monstrous, as if they didn't belong to him.

'Keep clean dressings on them,' the doctor advised. 'They will form blisters as the tissue heals and if you don't keep them clean, they could become gangrenous.'

Reg found he could get his own shoes on again so long as he didn't fasten the laces. He didn't bother to pick up his steward's uniform, though. He wouldn't need it any more. The grey suit he'd been given would be much more use to him in New York.

The *Titanic*'s crew were told that they would disembark after all the passengers had left, at which time they would be taken by tender to the *Lapland*, another vessel on the pier. They would be assigned cabins there while they waited for the ship that would take them back to England. Reg felt like a prisoner. Once they had docked, he couldn't bear being stuck on the water a moment longer. He wanted to flee the *Carpathia* onto dry land and take his chances in the city.

When the third-class passengers lined up to disembark, Reg slipped into the queue, just behind an Eastern European family. With his dark hair, he thought he could pass for one of them, and so it was. They were waved through and he followed as the family walked down the pier towards the exit.

The street door opened and Reg shrank back at the flashing lights and sounds that were like explosions, like the rockets that had been fired on the *Titanic*. He began to breathe heavily, terrified of what lay in wait outside. He pressed his hands to his ears feeling confused and scared.

'Are you all right?' a woman's voice asked.

'What are those lights? And the noise?'

'That's photographers taking pictures. Their flares provide light so the images come out. It's the last thing you want to be dealing with, I'm sure.' She looked at Reg and took in his pale skin and wide, staring eyes. 'Are you on your own? Is anyone meeting you?'

'I don't know anyone in New York,' he told her. 'I don't know where to go.'

She nodded. 'Don't worry. I'll fix you up. I'm Madeleine Butterworth from the Women's Relief Committee and we're here precisely to help people like you. Do you have a job to go to?'

Reg shook his head. 'I'm planning to look for one as soon as possible.'

'No money?'

Reg decided not to mention Mrs Grayling's fiver. That was his emergency fund. He shook his head.

'You look done in,' the woman remarked. 'I'm going to take you to a hostel to sleep tonight and get you some cash to tide you over. If you give me your details, I'll also help you to lodge your claim against White Star. I assume you've lost all your belongings? And your papers?'

Reg nodded. He had the fragments of his own passport, but he needed papers in John's name.

'Come this way,' she said. 'I'll take down your details while we're in the automobile.'

Reg blinked. He had never been in an automobile in his life before.

'We'll have to run the gauntlet of the photographers. Are you up to it? I'll be right beside you.'

He agreed he could cope, and as they walked through the door he covered his face with his hands so his picture wouldn't be taken. A row of black automobiles stood waiting. Madeleine Butterworth spoke to the driver of the one at the front and they climbed in.

She smiled at Reg. 'You see? We women of New York will look after you. Almost every Manhattan family that possesses an automobile has sent it down tonight to help *Titanic* survivors reach their destinations.'

'Where are we going?' he asked timidly as the automobile began to shudder on start-up then rolled away from the kerb.

'I'm taking you to the Municipal Lodging House on East 25th Street. It's not far at all. They'll look after you there until you find something else. Now' – she pulled out a notebook and pen – 'what is your name?'

'John Hitchens,' Reg told her. The lie made him blush, but if she was going to help him to get new papers, then John it had to be.

'Where are you from, John?'

'Newcastle originally, but I've been away from home a while.' He wondered if she would recognise that he didn't have a Geordie accent, but she didn't question it.

'And what class were you travelling in?'

Reg hesitated. 'Actually, I was crew. A first-class victualling steward.' Would she turn the car round and take him back to the *Lapland* where the crew were meant to be staying?

'Didn't White Star Line arrange somewhere for their crew to stay tonight? That's outrageous.'

'They did,' Reg admitted, 'but it was on another ship and I couldn't face it. I can't go back to sea. I've decided I want to get a job and stay here in New York.'

'I'm not surprised,' she said. 'I can't begin to imagine what you've all been through. Well, I'm here to help. Now I can give you four dollars tonight, which should be enough to tide you over for a couple of days. You'll get breakfast in the hostel and you can ask the men there to show you to our offices down at the pier when you get up tomorrow and I'll see what else I can do for you. First of all, I'll get in touch with White Star and tell them that you're safe.'

Reg bit his lip. What if someone from White Star was there when he went down to the pier, and ordered him to rejoin his fellow crew members? What if someone recognised him and blurted out that he wasn't John Hitchens? His plan to get work with a clean record would fall through. He would have to think carefully about this.

Their car pulled up outside a tall grey building with lots of windows, and Madeleine Butterworth cried, 'Here we are!' She walked into the vestibule with him and had a word with the superintendent.

'Do you want something to eat or drink?' Reg was asked, but he shook his head. All he wanted was to get into a bed in a building that was rooted in the earth, one that wasn't moving.

He was shown upstairs to a dormitory where at least a dozen other men were tucked up in bunks. Reg realised it must be late because all were sound asleep. He took off his jacket, transferred his money to his trouser pocket, just in case, and climbed into the bed. It had a straw mattress, a hard pillow and a scratchy grey blanket but it was fine. He knew he would sleep. For the last three days on the *Carpathia*, he'd had no trouble sleeping. He felt an exhaustion so profound that it was hard to get up even after twelve hours' sleep.

As he lay waiting for unconsciousness to come, Reg had the strangest sensation. Despite being on dry land, he felt as if he were cast adrift and floating. He was utterly alone in the world, accountable to no one, and with no future obligations. He decided he wouldn't even go to meet Madeleine Butterworth the next day. He would cut himself off from everything else in his life up to that point and reinvent himself, not as Reg Parton, but as John Hitchens. With John's help, he would recover from the strange fogginess in his head and the heaviness in his limbs and he would make a success of his life.

Somehow. When he felt strong enough.

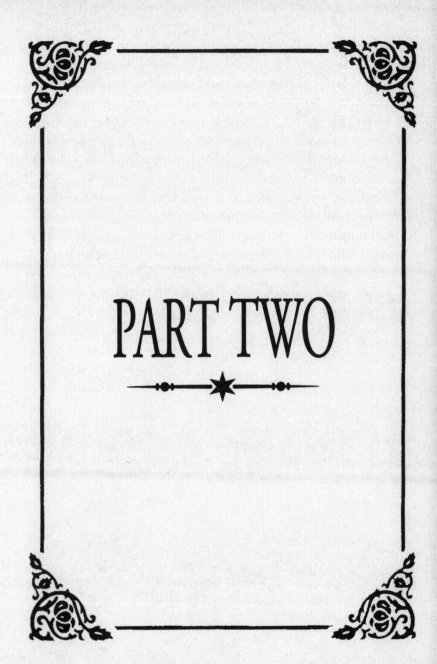

PART TWO

Chapter Thirty-Six

Reg was wakened by a man's voice, an American. 'If you want breakfast, you'll have to get downstairs fast. The kitchen closes at nine.'

'Thank you.'

'Hey, you're English! Are you from the *Titanic*? There were more of you but I reckon they've gone out now.'

Reg sat up and reached for his jacket. 'Thanks for telling me about breakfast.'

'Straight downstairs and across the hall. You can't miss it.'

It was a huge room filled with rows of long narrow tables, and you collected your food – a creamy soup called chowder and a big hunk of bread – from a serving hatch. Reg ate, then asked directions to the bathroom.

He got a shock when he looked at himself in the mirror. There hadn't been any mirrors in the crew WC he'd used on the *Carpathia*, and it was as if someone else was looking back at him. He hadn't realised his chin stubble had almost become a beard, which made him look much older than his years.

'Where can I buy a razor?' he asked and was directed to a drugstore down the street. He also needed soap, a toothbrush, hair oil and a comb if he were to make himself presentable.

On the way to the drugstore, he spotted a newspaper seller. 'Titanic: Survivors' Stories' read one headline, and underneath a smaller headline said 'Heard death chorus for over an hour'. Reg shuddered. It seemed some survivors had been quick to tell their stories to the press, but he didn't want to read their descriptions. He wanted hard facts, so he decided to buy the *New York Times*, which promised a full list of the living and dead. Clutching his paper, he went on to make his purchases in the drugstore then walked back to the hostel. It was empty now; everyone had gone out for the day to attend to their business. He went up to the dormitory where he had slept and opened the newspaper, and found he was shaking so hard he had to sit down.

There was the list in black and white newsprint: Reginald Parton, first-class victualling steward was listed among the dead, while John Hitchens was alive. It was the strangest feeling. Then a terrible thought occurred to him. Would the same list have appeared in the English newspapers? Would his mother and Florence have seen it and already be mourning him? Florence would be devastated. She had hoped to spend the rest of her life with Reg. He was sure his mother would only miss the money he brought home, but his brothers would be upset. He had to write to them straight away.

He thought of Florence's freckled skin, her gentleness, and felt a pang of longing for her. If only she were there right at that moment, he could have buried his face in her neck and held her tight. But their relationship felt like something from his distant past, something that had happened in another country a long, long time ago. He was a different person now. He had to be. He felt confused, and sad, and desperately lonely, but what option did he have?

I'll find out how to send a telegram, he decided. If he sent it that day, they should get it before they'd made funeral arrangements. After that, he could put all his memories of

Southampton into a box in his head and seal it shut while he tried to make a life for himself in New York. He'd need all the strength he could muster to find a job, get a place to stay and keep body and soul together.

He looked at the other names of those lost: Mrs Grayling, Bill, Ethel, James Paintin, and Captain Smith, of course. That lovely old man had gone down with his ship . . . Almost everyone he had known personally was dead. It was unthinkable. Unbelievable.

He closed the newspaper abruptly, and went to the bathroom for a shower and a shave. He wiped down his jacket and trousers, brushed his teeth and combed oil through his hair, then considered his appearance; he didn't look too bad now. Perhaps he could try to find a job straight away? As soon as he'd sent his telegram.

The hostel superintendent told him that the main Western Union office was on Broadway, just before you reached Times Square. He suggested catching a tram but Reg preferred to walk. He'd always liked to walk. It helped you to get your bearings in a strange place. He passed City Hall Park then, following the superintendent's instructions, found himself on Lower Broadway, a street lined with towering buildings, so tall that no sunlight reached the ground. Looking up he couldn't even count the number of storeys, and they loomed over him in a way that made him feel breathless. It was like walking through a narrow, sheer-sided canyon.

The street was full of trams, carriages and automobiles, driving in both directions, and petrol fumes filled the air. Every time a driver parped his horn, Reg nearly jumped out of his skin and his heart began to pound. The pavements were thick with people, all of whom seemed to be in a hurry, with urgent business to attend to. They passed without paying him any attention, as if he were invisible.

It was further than he'd expected to the Western Union office but there was no mistaking when he reached it because of the huge sign over the entrance. He stepped inside and was directed into a hall where clerks in uniform sat behind a long counter.

'Next!' One of them waved him over.

'How much does it cost to send a telegram to Southampton in England?' he asked.

'Three dollars, twelve cents for ten words. Do you need more than ten?' The fellow had a nasal accent and spoke so quickly that it took Reg a few moments to understand what he'd said, then he flushed. He had spent over a dollar in the drugstore so didn't have enough American money left.

'Could you change an English five-pound note?' he asked, pulling it from his pocket. It was in a sorry state, the paper all warped and salt-marked. 'I'm sorry, it got a bit wet.'

'I don't know if I can take that. I'll just go ask my super.' The clerk got up from his chair and disappeared.

Reg rested his elbow on the counter and leant his head on his hand, feeling close to tears. *What would he do if they wouldn't accept his money? Why was everything so difficult?*

'Excuse me, sir.' An older man appeared at the counter a couple of minutes later, with the clerk behind him. 'May I see the banknote in question?'

Reg slid it across.

The man took in Reg's countenance and the state of the money. 'Would you mind telling me how it got in this condition?' he asked, kindly.

'I was on the *Titanic*,' Reg told him. 'We arrived in port last night. I want to tell my mum I'm all right.'

212

The superintendent passed the banknote back to him. 'In that case, sir, we wouldn't dream of taking your money. Please write your telegram on this form,' he handed him a slip of paper, 'and we'll send it free of charge.'

Reg felt overwhelmed. 'Thank you,' he said. 'Thank you so much.'

Now he had to think what to say. His mind went blank. He decided to write to Florence and ask her to pass the message on, and he scribbled down the bare facts, trying to keep it brief: 'In New York [stop] Staying here for a while [stop] Will write soon [stop] Tell Mother [stop] Reg'. He filled in the address of the house where Florence worked and passed it to the clerk.

'Don't you want to give a return address so she can get back to you?'

'I don't have one yet,' Reg said.

'OK, I'll send this straight away. Good luck, buddy.'

Reg hesitated. He should really try to send a telegram to John's mother as well. He remembered seeing their address on John's payslip one time and he knew it was West Road, Newcastle, but he didn't recall the number. The telegraph boy would be bound to know the family, though. What should he say? 'I'm sorry but your son didn't make it and I'm using his name.' He couldn't put that in a telegram. He'd write a letter instead, explaining all the circumstances, and mail it as soon as possible.

He nodded his thanks and left the building, then continued up to Times Square, a triangular road junction. One of the streets running off was labelled Seventh Avenue, and it reminded Reg that he had meant to make his way to Fifth Avenue, where he'd heard there were lots of restaurants. His feet were still swollen and the left one was especially painful but he had to start looking for work if he were to survive here. He asked a passerby for directions and just two blocks down 42nd Street, he came upon Fifth Avenue. There were several restaurants lining the road and Reg stopped to look in some, but they didn't have the grandeur he sought. He had full silver-service training and he might as well use it, rather than handing out eggs and ham in any old diner. Presumably, the smarter the place, the better the pay.

He stopped when he got to the crossroads with 44th Street, because there were two very fancy restaurants facing each other on opposite corners. The nearest one, Delmonico's, had awnings over a pillared entrance, and through the windows he could see that the décor was sublime: red velvet, chandeliers and crisp white tablecloths. It looked as though lunch service was over, and the staff were clearing up. He asked a passerby for the time and was surprised to hear that it was almost four o'clock. That seemed as good a time as any to seek work in a restaurant.

He walked back a few yards and checked his reflection in a plate glass window: his hair was neatly slicked back and his tie was straight. It was now or never. His heart began to beat hard and his mouth was dry. His courage almost failed him, then he heard John's voice in his head: *Come on, man, if you're going to pretend to be me you'd better make sure you do me proud!*

He took a deep breath and marched purposefully to the entrance of Delmonico's, up the steps and in through the front door. The doormen were standing to one side, smoking, and they looked surprised but didn't try to stop him. Inside, he saw someone by a lectern that held a huge book and assumed it must be the maître d'.

'Excuse me, I'm looking for work,' he began. 'Who should I speak to?'

The man raised his head and sneered, as if Reg were an insect recently crawled out from under a stone. 'Did you just use the front entrance? Who do you think you are?'

'I'm sorry, I didn't realise there was any other entrance.'

'Get out. You shouldn't have been let in anyhow. Scram.' He waved his hand in dismissal, and Reg hurried back out to the street, feeling as though he might faint. *You don't want to work somewhere that employs the likes of him anyway. Don't worry. Just try the next place.*

Opposite, there was another smart-looking restaurant entrance, and the name read 'Sherry's'. He wandered over and glimpsed an interior equally as sumptuous as Delmonico's. It seemed worth a try but he didn't want to make the same mistake again, so he walked round until he found an alleyway down the side of the building. He followed it past huge waste bins until he came to some back steps where a man in a white chef's hat was smoking a cigarette.

'Excuse me. Do you know if there's any work for waiting staff?' he asked.

'There might be. What's your experience?'

'I was a first-class victualling steward on the *Titanic*. We just got in last night. I don't want to go to sea any more so I'm looking for work.'

'Jesus Christ! You poor kid! Come on in and have a bite to eat and I'll get the manager to have a word with you. Hell, that's dedication to be looking for work the day after you arrive in dock!'

Reg followed him up the steps and into a vast kitchen, all shiny and modern, where sous-chefs stood preparing food at their stations.

'We've got some roast lamb left over from luncheon, or some

215

canvasback duck. What would you like?' the chef asked, slapping Reg round the shoulders.

'Lamb would be very nice, thank you.'

'Aren't you polite? Listen to his accent, boys! He's from the *Titanic*.'

As he sat at a table in the kitchen eating his lamb, served with Potatoes Lyonnaise and string beans, the kitchen staff gathered round to ask questions. When they heard he had been in the water and had survived on the upturned collapsible, their admiration knew no bounds. They'd read about the collapsible in that morning's papers because Harold Bride, one of the *Titanic*'s radio operators who had also survived on it, had told his story to the press. Someone produced a copy of the newspaper to show Reg but he couldn't bring himself to read it.

When he pushed his plate away, the chef went to fetch the restaurant manager, Mr Timothy, a slight man in spectacles.

'Are you sure you are able to work?' he asked. 'You must be pretty shook up from your experience. Don't you want some time off?'

'I want to stay busy to take my mind off it,' Reg replied.

'I guess you've done silver service?' Reg nodded. 'We'll need to check your references with White Star – if there's anyone left there who can give references, that is – but as far as I'm concerned, you're on for a try-out. What did you say your name was?'

'John Hitchens.' The lie was becoming easier.

'Come back tomorrow morning at ten sharp and you can work the lunch service. We're open six days and the salary is five bucks a week. We'll provide a uniform, but make sure you look shipshape.' He winced. 'Sorry, not a good choice of words. You know what I mean.'

And so it was that within a day of getting off the *Carpathia*, Reg had found work at one of New York's most fashionable upper-class restaurants. As he walked back out onto Fifth Avenue, his legs felt shaky. It was almost too much to take in.

Before he left, he asked Mr Timothy for a sheet of paper and the loan of a pencil, saying he had to write home. He decided to continue a few more blocks up the road to Central Park and find a bench where he could sit to compose his letter to John's family.

If only John were there with him. Reg remembered him saying that he fancied going to Central Park while they were in town. As it turned out, Reg would have to go on his own. He'd have to do everything on his own from now on.

Chapter Thirty-Seven

On arrival at New York's Pier 54, Robert Graham led Juliette and her mother past the crowd of photographers to the spot where his car was waiting. A uniformed driver, whom he introduced as Ted, opened the door for them and Robert helped them inside then they drove uptown to the Plaza Hotel.

'It's gigantic,' Juliette exclaimed as they pulled up outside. 'It's quite the largest building I've ever seen.'

'I believe it has twenty storeys,' Robert told her, 'but it's not New York's tallest building by any means.'

'So long as it's comfortable,' Lady Mason-Parker grumbled. 'I hardly slept a wink in that hard, narrow bunk on the *Carpathia*.'

Robert helped them to check in and, as he said good night, he asked Juliette if he might come by the following afternoon to look in on them and see that all was well.

'Oh, please do,' she cried, unable to disguise her eagerness. 'Come as early as you can.' She wished he could stay in the hotel with them so they needn't be separated. For four days they had spent most of their waking hours together and she knew she would miss his calm presence and the reassuring sense that no matter what happened, he would know how to deal with it. She began to miss him the minute he left.

The Plaza was a lovely hotel. The rooms were large and opulent, decorated in the rococo style, with cream walls and gold swirl carvings on balustrades and dado rails. The service was impeccable too. Despite the late hour of their arrival, a tray of tea and cakes was brought to their room within five minutes of it being requested.

'This is more like it,' Lady Mason-Parker sighed, sinking back into soft pillows and biting into a madeleine. 'I plan to stay indoors for at least a week. My nerves are quite shattered.'

Next morning at breakfast, she spotted some other *Titanic* survivors, the Duff Gordons, in the dining room. Ordinarily Lady Mason-Parker would not have socialised with Lady Duff Gordon since she was a divorcee, but these were extraordinary times. She stopped by their table to introduce herself and they hit it off, retiring to the lounge for coffee together after breakfast. It meant that Juliette didn't feel guilty leaving her mother behind when Robert came to call later.

'Where would you like to go?' he asked. 'My automobile is at your disposal.'

'Actually, I enjoy walking and it's a sunny day. Could we take a stroll somewhere?'

'Of course.' He offered his arm. 'Central Park is just across the road.'

As they walked, they talked about their lives before they sailed on the *Titanic*. Now they were on dry land and no longer surrounded by bereaved passengers, the immediate sense of shock had passed and other topics could be explored.

Juliette asked about his line of work, and he told her that he ran a small investment company helping to raise funds for anyone who had a good idea for a new business. He then took a part share in the business, so it meant he needed to have sharp instincts for the ideas that would prove lucrative. He told her that he lived with his mother and sister near Washington

Square, and that they socialised with New York's finest families – although he wasn't much of a one for fancy parties and balls, finding the conversation rather superficial. Juliette agreed, although in truth they didn't attend many such parties at home, leading a rather more countrified existence.

'You said that you are planning to visit your family in upstate New York,' Robert commented. 'When must you leave for that visit?'

Juliette remembered, with a start, the lie she had told him to explain their trip. 'Not straight away. My mother has sent a telegram and we will wait to hear. But for the time being we will stay in New York and perhaps do some sightseeing.'

'I hope you will do me the honour of letting me show you around. Our tour can begin here, with the Central Park Pond, where many species of fish, insects and birds can be found.' With his tone, he mimicked a guide in a museum, making Juliette laugh. 'Seriously, tell me if you would like to go to the opera, or shopping, to art galleries or museums. What are your favourite hobbies?'

'At home my favourite pastime is horse riding, but I suppose that's not possible in a city.'

'You really like to ride?' He seemed delighted. 'I have stables at Poughkeepsie, just outside New York. Perhaps I could take you there.'

Juliette asked about the horses he kept and told him about their stables at home and they were comparing notes on their favourites when all of a sudden she noticed a young man sitting on a bench writing something and realised she recognised his face.

'Excuse me, aren't you Reg, our steward from the *Titanic*?'

Reg jumped at the sound of his real name.

'I'm sorry, I didn't mean to startle you,' Juliette said. 'Are you all right?'

'Yes, thank you, ma'am.'

'Will you and the rest of the crew sail for England again soon?'

Reg explained his decision to stay and work in a New York restaurant.

'I quite understand you not wanting to go back to sea. I'm not sure how I shall face it myself when the time comes. Have you found somewhere to stay? You are not wanting for anything?'

'I'm fine, thank you, ma'am.'

Juliette remembered the tact with which Reg had helped her when she was sick in the corridor. 'Well, I'm staying at the Plaza Hotel. Please do let me know if I can be of any help. You were so kind to me on the ship.'

'Thank you, ma'am.'

Juliette and Robert walked on. 'I feel as though I should have given him a tip but I didn't know how to do it without embarrassing him,' she confessed. 'I'm sure he will be short of money here. What do you think?'

'That's sweet of you,' Robert said. 'I'll go back and give him ten dollars and say it's from you. Wait here.'

Robert hurried back and she could see that Reg was reluctant to take the money but that Robert eventually persuaded him, and the note was handed over.

'Thank you. You must let me repay you,' she said when Robert rejoined her.

'I don't know why he didn't want to accept it. You would certainly have given him a tip at the end of the voyage.'

'I do hope he will fare well in the city.'

221

'Indeed. Now I am going to take you to a café where they serve rainbow sandwiches. Have you ever had any such thing in England? No, I thought not. Come this way.'

Chapter Thirty-Eight

Reg poured his heart out in the letter to John's mother, using both sides of the sheet of paper to describe the last time he had seen John on the *Titanic*, and tell her that no one on the *Carpathia* knew what had happened to him. He explained why he was using her son's name, and apologised for any distress this had caused to his family. Finally, he wrote about how much he missed John, and sent his condolences on their loss. When he'd finished he asked directions to a post office and mailed it to Mrs Hitchens, West Road, Newcastle, and immediately felt a sense of relief. Now he could get on with making a new life for himself.

On the way back to the hostel Reg used part of his unexpected windfall to buy himself a new white shirt, some fresh socks and underwear. He also treated himself to a sandwich called a 'hot dog', after questioning the vendor to ensure that the meat it contained had nothing to do with dogs.

Still he felt very shaky. Anxieties were screeching through his head. What if he turned up at the restaurant tomorrow and the police were waiting to arrest him for giving the wrong name on the *Titanic*? What if White Star Line sued him for dereliction of duty? What if there was an inquest into Finbarr's death and it was found that Reg had been the cause of it by forcing him to jump overboard when he couldn't swim? All these worries hammered at the inside of his skull, making him feel dizzy and sick.

He crept into his bunk at the hostel, pulled the covers over his head, and slept through till next morning, oblivious to the sounds of other men talking, undressing, snoring and shifting in their slumber.

Reg wakened to the voice of the same man who'd roused him the day before. 'Hey you! It's time for breakfast.'

As soon as his eyes opened, the pounding in his chest began and the worries flooded his head. *You're going to be arrested today. They're going to get you.* It was a continuous chorus of doom that was hard to shake off.

When he reached Sherry's, though, Mr Timothy was remarkably friendly. 'I spoke to White Star Line and they said you are a model employee. They're sad to lose you. I didn't know where you were staying, so they said they will send your final pay packet to the restaurant here. They're also sending temporary documents so that I can apply for immigration for you. Is that OK?'

Reg nodded, amazed it was proceeding so smoothly.

'They'd like you to go down to the office and sign some forms when you have time. I think it's just to say that you won't go after them for compensation.'

'OK,' Reg agreed, knowing that he wouldn't do it. He couldn't risk bumping into anyone who knew him from the old days.

Mr Timothy gave him a uniform of a black shirt and trousers, over which he would wear a white apron, then showed him the routine: the cutlery, linen and plate cupboards, the hot press, the cold buffet and the dessert trolley. He showed him the elaborate table decorations that Sherry's was famous for: asparagus set in blocks of ice, or miniature forests in the centre of the table, all created afresh every day. They sat down to run through the menu and there were several dishes Reg wasn't familiar with: Littlenecks, he was told, were clams, while Lynnhavens and Blue Points were types of oyster; ruddy, golden plover and vanneau were kinds of wild fowl; terrapin was a type of turtle meat; eggplant meant aubergine. Reg concentrated hard, memorising the dishes, because as soon as he was out on the restaurant floor, he would have to answer questions about them. He was grateful that, as on the *Titanic*, a sommelier would deal with the wine orders.

'Do you think you are ready to work this luncheon?' Mr Timothy asked, and Reg nodded, although he was inwardly terrified. What if he got an order wrong or dropped a plate? He'd probably be out on his ear.

There was time for a smoke out the back before service, and someone offered Reg a cigarette. He accepted, but nearly passed out with the buzz from the unfamiliar tobacco, which was much stronger than the type he was used to. He had to hold a handrail until the dizziness subsided. The other waiters gathered round, eager to bombard him with questions about the *Titanic*, fascinated to hear first hand about the story that was filling all the newspapers.

'There's a big stink in the papers about men who barged onto lifeboats so there was no room for the ladies. Did you see any of that?' someone asked.

'Yes,' Reg admitted. 'But I also saw lifeboats go off half-full. It wasn't very well organised.'

'Where was the captain? Wasn't he in charge?'

'I don't know what he was doing. I think they were hoping another ship would arrive in time to pick us up. I thought I saw one, but it never appeared.'

'How long were you in the water?' someone else asked.

'I don't know,' Reg replied honestly. 'It felt like a long time.'

'Were you hurt?'

Reg told them about his frostbite, and they insisted he took off his shoes and unpeeled his bandages to show them his purplish-black toes. There was a collective gasp of shock.

'Are you going to be able to stand on your feet all day? Won't they hurt?'

'I like to keep busy,' he told them. 'I don't want to sit around moping.'

'Why? Did you know anybody who died?'

Reg looked this last questioner in the eye. 'I hardly know anyone who didn't die.'

There must have been something haunted about his expression, because there was a hushed silence and one of the other waiters said, 'Give him a break. Think about what he's just been through.' He turned to Reg. 'My name's Tony. I'll be working the tables next to you at luncheon, so give me a nod if you need a hand or don't know where something is kept.'

'Thanks,' Reg nodded, and managed to squeeze a smile. 'I'll probably take you up on that.'

In fact, it went fine. The training on the *Titanic* had been so rigorous that Reg's standards were higher than those that prevailed in Sherry's and he knew he was doing well. The manager gave him several approving nods. Word spread among the diners that he was a survivor from the sinking and several shook his hand and gave him a generous tip.

'We all share the tips,' Tony advised, and showed him a big earthenware pot in the kitchen that served as a communal gratuity jar. 'The pay is so lousy we need the extra this brings in.

Always smile and hang around when you hand over the bill. It helps to remind them.'

Shame, Reg thought, because he'd have been rich within a month if he'd been able to keep his tips for himself, but it was nice to feel he was part of the team, and everyone was very welcoming.

'Where are you sleeping?' Tony asked at the end of the first evening shift. 'Do you have to go far?'

When Reg said he was staying all the way down at East 25th Street, Tony exclaimed, 'That's crazy! It will take you an hour to get there at night and another hour to get back in the morning. There's a spare room at our place if you're interested. It's a buck seventy-five a week, breakfast and laundry included, and it's only a couple of blocks away. Do you want to come and look around tomorrow?'

Reg agreed that he would. It was extraordinary how quickly everything was falling into place. The only difficulty was remembering to answer to the name 'John'. Several times, he failed to turn when people called out to him: 'Table four, John,' or 'Joining us for a smoke, John?'

He had never known popularity like it. Everyone at Sherry's wanted to be his friend. Another chap called Stefan offered a room at his lodgings and seemed disappointed that he had already agreed to go and look at Tony's. 'If you don't like it, come and check out ours instead.'

The restaurant was huge, Reg discovered, when another waiter called Paul gave him a guided tour between shifts. There was the main dining room on the ground floor, several private dining rooms for smaller parties, and a couple of ballrooms as well as residential suites, all laid out over twelve storeys.

'This is the room where they had the horseback dinner.' Seeing the blank look on Reg's face, Paul exclaimed, 'You must have heard of it!'

Reg shook his head.

'Well, there were thirty-six guys here, all in a circle on horseback, and they sucked champagne through rubber tubes from their saddlebags. The whole room was decorated like a fancy garden, with grass on the floor and birds flying around, and a moon hanging from the ceiling.'

'When was it? Were you here?' Reg asked.

'It was 1903. Before my time, but there are some pictures on the wall.'

Reg gazed at the black and white pictures with astonishment. Beside each rider, a set of steps had been placed so waiters could climb up to serve their meals onto trays attached to the horses. All the men wore dinner jackets and most had bald heads. It was a surreal image, even more decadent than the *Titanic*. Such ridiculous extravagance made him feel slightly sick.

'I bet Mr Sherry, the owner, will want to meet you when he hears we've got a real *Titanic* survivor working with us,' Paul continued.

'I don't want to make a big deal of it,' Reg insisted. 'Please don't say anything.'

Paul was right, though. That evening when Louis Sherry arrived, he came straight into the kitchen to be introduced to Reg.

He was an elegantly dressed man, with grey hair and a waxed moustache curving out from each cheek like a giant superimposed smile.

'You were on the collapsible, I hear,' he said in a slightly foreign-sounding accent, while shaking Reg's hand. 'Obviously a man of initiative. You'll do well in this city if you are prepared to work hard. I started as a waiter myself, back in New Jersey. Keep in with the rich, that's my advice.'

He didn't stop for long, but during dinner service, he summoned Reg to a couple of tables to introduce him to the wealthy clientele, and Reg trotted over meekly to answer their questions.

'Will you testify at the Senate Inquiry?' one man asked. 'I hear it has already started.'

'I haven't been asked,' Reg replied. 'I expect they will focus on the testimony of the officers who survived.'

In fact, he'd only just heard about it and lived in terror of being ordered to attend. How could he explain his actions during the ship's last hours? How could he stand up in court and admit that he saved himself and let Finbarr die?

He was introduced to Morgans and Vanderbilts, Stuyvesants and Aldriches, all of them members of an unofficial set that the other waiters told him was called 'The Four Hundred'. If you were 'in', you received invitations to all the upper-class balls and dinners and to the best boxes at the opera. If you weren't, no amount of money or persuasion could buy your way in. You had to come from a good family with old money, and you needed to have plenty of charm besides.

The old Reg would have been excited to meet such exalted folk. He would have asked the other lads how each gentleman had made his money, what cars their chauffeurs dropped them off in, and how many homes they had. Now, none of that seemed important. The old Reg might have enjoyed his temporary popularity among the other waiting staff but here he wished he could be anonymous. He didn't want to talk about the *Titanic*, didn't want to be told what the papers were saying; he wished he could stop thinking about it and simply get on with earning a living. During the day, he worked harder than anyone else so he didn't have to stand still. He took the room in Tony's lodging house, but when he got back there at night, he fell into bed exhausted and numb instead of sitting out on the steps for a drink and a smoke with the other lads.

He remembered something Florence had said to him. 'When you're upset, you crawl inside your shell like a snail and shut out the world. It must get lonely in there, Reg.'

She was right, of course; God but he missed her! She would be waiting for that letter he'd promised in his cable, but he couldn't bring himself to write. It was too hard to think about her because it made him feel even more lonely. He could eat, sleep and work, and he hoped that if he focused on those three things, the rest would get easier over time.

Occasionally, he picked up a newspaper that someone else had left lying around. He saw a story that claimed Mr Howson, the Canadian man with the flirtatious wife, had dressed in women's clothing to sneak onto a lifeboat. Could that be true? He saw that Officer Lightoller had been testifying at the Inquiry, and he cut out that report to read another time, when he could face it. But he gave a wide berth to any headlines about the hundreds dying in the water. One thousand five hundred dead, including John. There were many moments during those first weeks on shore when Reg wished that he had been among them.

Chapter Thirty-Nine

The apartment that Seamus had found for Annie and his children was at the top of a flight of a hundred and twenty stone steps. The whole suburb of Kingsbridge was built on a hillside and apartment buildings were separated by 'step streets' that led to further buildings on the upper levels. When they came out of Pier 54 the night the *Carpathia* docked, a kind woman ushered them into an automobile, which drove them all the way to Kingsbridge and stopped on the street below. They had to climb the steps by the light of the gas street lamps to get to their new home. Seamus lifted Roisin while Annie took baby Ciaran and Patrick walked by himself.

At least we don't have our luggage, Annie thought. *We'd never have managed.* But then she remembered that Finbarr would have been there to help. He could have carried the baby while she took a case. Everything would have been exciting. Patrick would have loved his first-ever ride in an automobile, bouncing around full of questions instead of staring glumly out the window. They would all have raced up the steps for a first glimpse of the new place. Instead, they trudged slowly, wearily, and Annie's legs were aching by the time she reached the top.

There was a communal hallway to the building. Seamus took out a key and unlocked the first doorway they came to, and as he swung the door open and lit a candle, she watched his face and knew how much he would have been looking forward to this moment. He must have been so proud to find such a smart place for his family. She should try to show some enthusiasm.

The apartment seemed nice. The room at the front had a tall window with a view right down the step street and across their neighbours' rooftops. It was a good size, and what's more, it was clean. She could smell its cleanness.

'Some women from the church cleaned it for us,' Seamus said, reading her mind. 'It's a lovely community.'

'Isn't that nice of them?' Annie looked around the room, then lit another candle and wandered through the next doorway, which led into a big kitchen. It had an oven and a grate and a rack for drying laundry. *Pretend,* she told herself. *You have to learn to pretend.*

'Isn't this grand?' she said. 'Much better than my kitchen back home.' The two bedrooms already had single beds in them and she nearly broke down when she saw the one for Finbarr. The one he would never sleep in. 'It's lovely,' she told Seamus. 'You've done well.'

'I said I would take you down to meet the priest, Father Kelly, just as soon as we've settled in. I was thinking . . . Maybe he could say a mass for Finbarr.' Annie could see it was hard for him to say his boy's name. Everything was going to be hard now.

'I'd like that, but we need to buy some clothes first. We've only got the ones we're standing up in and I can't meet my new priest looking like this.'

'Father Kelly said if we need anything to help us get set up, just to ask. The church helped me to get the beds, and the chairs in the front room.'

'We all need a good wash before we meet him. And I'll have to get some food in.'

'Yes, of course.' They were tiptoeing round each other, scared of saying an insensitive word that might cause any additional grief.

Just look after the practicalities, Annie thought. *That's all I can do.* They fell into bed and once she was in Seamus's arms the tears came to her eyes for the first time, but she fought them back because she didn't want to upset him. Possibly he was doing the same thing, because they lay there without words, listening to each other breathing and feeling the warm familiarity of each other's bodies.

The next morning, Seamus had to go to work. He might just have heard about the death of his eldest son, but the railways would deduct a day's pay and possibly even sack him if he didn't show up. Half an hour after he left, there was a knock on the door and Annie opened it to find a priest standing there. He looked around fifty, with wispy silver hair and kind blue eyes, and she knew at first glance that he was a good man, someone she could trust. You came across some sly priests back in the home country, but this one had compassion written all over him.

'Mrs McGeown, I'm Father Kelly. I've come to say how sorry I am for the loss of your boy,' he said, holding out his hand, and she felt a huge lump form in her throat. 'Your husband looked in to tell me and I came straight away.'

'Please come in, Father.'

She ushered him into the front room and sent the children to play in the kitchen.

'Shall we say a prayer for Finbarr?' he asked, and she nodded, unable to speak. Before he had managed much more than an 'Our Father', the tears began to trickle down her cheeks. Father Kelly carried on with his solemn words, asking God to look after her boy, and at last Annie could see it, she could feel as though Finbarr was in God's hands and that he was safe.

'I'm so sorry,' she said, wiping her eyes with a handkerchief after the prayer came to an end. 'What a sight I must be.'

'All I see is a remarkably brave woman. My heart goes out to you.'

'Father, I must come down to your church and say confession. So much has happened, and I've done a terrible thing. I saved my three younger children and left my eldest boy behind and I don't know how I will ever learn to live with that.'

'Tell me about it,' he said, and so she did. Step by step she described what had happened on the ship and the decisions she had made, and he listened carefully, asking questions to make sure he got the facts straight.

When she finished, he reached out to take her hand. 'You did what any loving mother would have done: you protected the youngest of your children, the ones who most needed protection, and you sent two kind men to look for your eldest. It seems to me that you made all the right decisions, Annie, but the Man above has decided to take Finbarr and nothing could have changed that.'

Annie was still crying, but the weight of her guilt felt slightly less. If only she could fully believe his words then she could grieve without that complication. Maybe the time would come. They discussed the mass Father Kelly would say for Finbarr, when all the family could be present.

'If only his body would be found,' she wept. 'If only I could give him a proper funeral.'

'Don't get your hopes up,' Father Kelly told her, 'but I hear they have sent out ships from Halifax to recover any bodies that can be found. I will make enquiries for you. And even if we don't find Finbarr, we'll keep remembering him in our services. Everyone in our congregation will be praying for him.'

As soon as Seamus got home from work later, Annie mentioned to him what Father Kelly had told her, that it might be possible to get Finbarr's body back.

'He was wearing a life preserver,' she explained. 'He should have floated. There are ships looking for all those floating on the surface so they should find him.'

'He won't be in a fit state for his mother to see after a week in the ocean,' Seamus cautioned. 'He may not be recognisable.'

'I don't care what state he is in,' Annie declared. 'I want my boy back and I know I will recognise him.'

On the 22nd of April, a week after the sinking, Father Kelly told her that a ship called the *Mackay-Bennett* had radioed that twenty-two bodies had been found; the next day there were a further seventy-seven. By the 25th, there were a hundred and ninety bodies in the hold and the *Mackay-Bennett* was heading back to port.

'We have to go up there!' Annie insisted to Seamus. 'It's the last thing we can do for our son. I will not have his bones thrown into an unmarked grave.'

Seamus was hesitant, feeling it would be a harrowing experience and could put terrible images into their heads that would be hard to forget. He was also worried about the expense of the journey, but when he enquired he found that he'd get discounted tickets because he worked on the railways. If he and Annie travelled up on an overnight train and back the same way, without incurring hotel bills, it would be just about affordable. Father Kelly agreed to have the children to stay in his house, where they would be looked after by his housekeeper. And so Annie prevailed.

The seats in third class were rock-hard and the carriage was crowded, so Seamus and Annie only managed to snatch odd moments of sleep on the train. She looked around and wondered if anyone else was travelling for the same reason as them, but most passengers got off at different stops and, besides, they seemed too cheerful as they chatted to each other and handed round drinks and food.

They arrived in Halifax at eight-thirty in the morning and asked directions to the curling rink, which had been turned into a temporary morgue. It was a long walk, but they had no money for a hansom cab. Father Kelly had made an appointment for them at twelve, and they arrived early and sat on the steps outside until it was time, not talking, just looking around at the town that sloped down to the sea in the distance. Two women came out and hurried into a waiting automobile with handkerchiefs held to their faces and Annie's heart went out to them.

Suddenly, she got a strong feeling she wasn't going to find Finbarr here. This was not where his body lay. She didn't say anything to Seamus but she tucked her disappointment inside her. *Wait and see, Annie. Wait and see.*

At the appointed time, they walked into the vestibule of the building and an official came out to meet them. After offering his sympathies, he explained that bodies were laid out in individual cubicles, and he would show them all the ones they had that were male and child-sized.

'Are there many children here?' Annie asked, surprised. 'Surely not many children died? I thought it was mostly grown men.'

'I believe that around half the children on board perished, ma'am. The lists indicate that over fifty children were lost, among them your son.'

'But it was supposed to be women and children first! That's what they said.'

The official consulted a sheet of paper. 'Well, we have nineteen here who could be your boy. I warn you that many of them have deteriorated due to exposure to the elements, while others seem to have remained in rather better condition. There are no guarantees.'

'Of course,' Seamus said. 'Thank you for warning us.' He looked at Annie and she nodded. 'We're ready now.'

Her heart was thumping so hard she felt faint as they walked towards the main room, Seamus's arm around her. *I pray for the strength to do this without collapsing*, she thought. *I pray for any other mothers who have to go through this.*

The official pulled back the curtain on the first cubicle and they saw a canvas body bag lying on a table. He lifted a corner of it, and inside there was a tiny face with a huge dark bruise on the forehead. Blood had congealed under the nose, but the boy had blond hair and would have been perfectly recognisable to his parents. Annie's hopes rose. If Finbarr looked like this, it would be all right. She made the sign of the cross, as did Seamus.

The next body wasn't in such good shape, with the face severely swollen and black and purple in colour, but Seamus and Annie knew it wasn't their son. Despite the disfigurement you could see the type of boy he must have been.

Some of the bodies they were shown were too big, or too small; others were the right size, but had the wrong face. Each time the official pulled back the curtain on another cubicle, Annie's heart was in her mouth and she was whispering to herself: *Please God, please.* But deep inside, she knew Finbarr wasn't going to be there. After all this, their journey was going to be a waste.

'I'm sorry but this is the last child that fits your son's age and description,' the official told them.

'But there must be more,' Annie cried in despair. 'Are you sure some haven't been mistaken for adults? You said fifty were lost. Where have they all gone?'

'If a body was badly decomposed when they found it, then it was given a sea burial. It seems that may be what happened to your son. I'm so sorry.'

'Please, can I look one more time?' Annie begged.

'He's not here,' Seamus told her, squeezing her hand. 'We'd have known straight away.'

'But we've come all this distance,' Annie wailed, tears beginning to slide down her cheeks. 'It can't be for nothing.'

'Ma'am, you can still have a headstone for your son at the cemetery here, even without a body. Many people are choosing to do so. You'll find it's a beautiful spot. I can give you directions.'

'Are you sure there's no mistake?' she begged him. 'Couldn't we just look again? Could I check all the adults as well?'

'Annie, no,' Seamus told her firmly. 'He's not here.'

The official was a kind man, though. 'There are still a few more boats bringing in bodies. If you give me a full description of your son Finbarr, I will make it my personal responsibility to check each one. I'll get in touch with you in the event that any seems as though it could be him. But in the meantime, I think you may find it a comfort to get a headstone for him.'

'We'll do that,' Seamus agreed, and wrote down their address.

The sun had come out when they emerged from the ice rink and a fresh breeze was blowing. As they walked down the road to the beautiful grassy cemetery with wide views over the Atlantic, Annie asked, 'How can we live without knowing where he is? How can we just carry on?'

'Because we have no choice. Because that's all we *can* do.'

And she knew Seamus was right. Finbarr was in heaven and that's what mattered. She prayed that all the poor souls in that grim makeshift mortuary would be identified and claimed by their families. She would have hated to think that maybe Finbarr was lying there on his own and she hadn't gone to find him. But she had done what she could, they both had.

The headstones were expensive but Seamus made a down payment and it was agreed that he would send more money when he could afford it. They were very accommodating.

'Shouldn't White Star Line pay for this at least?' Annie asked bitterly.

'We'll find out. Maybe they will,' Seamus soothed.

When they got on the overnight train back to New York and sat down by the window, Annie felt the strangest sensation. All of a sudden there was a feeling of warmth, as if a blanket had been wrapped around her, and she felt very close to Finbarr, almost as if his spirit was with her. He didn't say anything, but he was *there*, in the atmosphere.

'I feel as though he is with us. Don't you?' she asked Seamus, searching his face to see if he was feeling the same thing.

'He'll always be with us,' Seamus said, his voice husky. Could he feel the peculiar sensation she was experiencing? She wasn't sure.

Annie sank back in her seat, not exactly happy but somehow cushioned from the worst of the pain. When she thought about it, she was glad she hadn't found her son among those blackened, bruised, swollen bodies. She knew he was dead and there was no hope of him being found alive, but now she could think of him as he was: a perfect, beautiful boy, who had become a spirit in the air around them. He had come back to her. He was with his mother again.

Chapter Forty

When Juliette told her mother that Robert wanted to take her to Poughkeepsie to visit his stables, Lady Mason-Parker was pleased, because it looked as though her daughter was getting closer to this man by the day, and her discreet enquiries through the Duff Gordons' New York friends had ascertained that he was an extremely suitable match. She had one concern, though.

'When you see these horses, you know you are going to want to ride them. And you mustn't. Not in your condition. How will you explain that to Robert?'

Juliette hadn't thought of that. 'Why can't I ride? The only thing I mustn't do is fall off, but I am experienced enough to prevent that.'

'All that bouncing around in the saddle would be terrible for the baby. You could damage its brain,' her mother replied.

'I hadn't realised you were such a great medical expert.'

'I think I should come to Poughkeepsie as chaperone in case you are tempted to take any risks.'

'No, absolutely not,' Juliette forbade her. 'I can't bear the way you talk to Robert, always boasting about our family connections and titled ancestors. It's vulgar. You embarrass him.'

'I won't be spoken to like this. Apologise at once!'

Juliette apologised, and managed to marshal all her skills of tact and diplomacy to talk her mother out of chaperoning her. In fact, she sensed that Lady Mason-Parker hadn't really wanted to come. Since they had been in New York, her only outings had been to fashion houses, where she took the advice of Lady Duff Gordon, herself a noted designer, on replenishing her own and Juliette's wardrobe. There were fittings to be attended, accessories to be tried, and Juliette found it very tiresome. She had to select the loosest styles to accommodate her growing waistband, and ignore all the sales girls who urged her to try the season's new slim silhouette. It was embarrassing as they fussed around trying to fasten buttons and squeeze her into impossible sizes. Lady Mason-Parker revelled in it all, though, and had no interest in seeing any more of what the city had to offer.

'I've taken a lease on a house in Saratoga Springs,' she announced at breakfast one morning, looking over the rim of her teacup. 'That's in upstate New York. We'll be leaving three weeks on Friday. I don't see how you can keep your secret any longer than that. Unless, of course, wedding bells are in the air. Are they?'

'Mother, you know they are not. Robert is a good friend and I refuse to trick him into marrying me.'

Lady Mason-Parker sighed. 'Well, you can't expect the "friendship" to be sustained through six months' absence. He will find someone else to befriend as soon as your back is turned. There must be many a New York maiden who would be delighted to become Mrs Robert Graham. At the moment, you seem to have a good chance, but disappear for six months and you will lose any hope you might have had. In love, as in business, one must strike while the iron is hot.'

Juliette knew it was true. She had an ache in the pit of her stomach when she thought of Robert falling for someone else, but what could she do? *Oh, foolish, foolish girl!* Why had she ever succumbed to the charms of Charles Wood, which now looked so meagre compared to those of Robert Graham? When she was with him, she managed to put all thought of her pregnancy out of her head and simply live in the moment. But her mother was right to have taken a house for them. Living in the moment would not be possible for much longer.

When Robert came to collect Juliette on the day of their Poughkeepsie trip, a new worry struck her as she climbed into the back seat of his automobile. She hadn't experienced any recurrence of morning sickness since they'd been in New York, but might a long road journey bring it on? How would she explain it if she started throwing up? Fortunately, it was a beautiful day so Robert's chauffeur rolled the hood back and the fresh air staved off any nausea, although she was forced to clutch her hat all the way for fear of it blowing off.

'We've had a letter from our relatives,' she told Robert, 'and I'm afraid we must leave the city to join them in three weeks. I'm sorry, because I have greatly enjoyed our time together.'

'Where do your relatives live?' he asked.

'Just outside Saratoga Springs.'

'But that's perfect!' Robert exclaimed. 'My sister has some good friends who live there, and she plans to spend part of the summer with them. I will invite myself to join the party and then I will be able to visit you.' He frowned, noting that Juliette had screwed up her face. 'If you would like me to, that is.'

Juliette had to think on her feet. 'I'm afraid that won't be possible. You see, our relatives are very elderly and Mother and I have to assist them with some pressing business of a personal nature. We have promised to devote ourselves entirely to them in order to solve a particular family problem.'

He was puzzled. 'Surely you will be able to slip away for a couple of hours of an afternoon? They can't demand all of your time.'

'But they will. Mother and I have already agreed we will not see anyone else. I'm sorry, Robert. I know I will miss you. But we can write to each other, if you are willing. I would so much like to keep in touch.'

Still he was frowning. 'I can't imagine why your relatives should be so selfish as to refuse to share you for a few hours. I will miss you too. I've never met a woman who has such intelligent, refreshing opinions on all kinds of matters. Most women concern themselves solely with fashion and society, yet you are interested in politics, world affairs, culture – I feel I could talk to you about anything.'

'That's a lovely compliment,' Juliette smiled. 'Thank you.'

It was true that they had wide-ranging discussions when they were together. They never ran out of conversation, or even had to force it. It flowed naturally, and at each meeting picked up where they had left off the previous day. One major conversational thread concerned the testimonies being given at the *Titanic* Senate Inquiry. They were horrified to hear of the string of small coincidences that had led to the sinking, either directly or indirectly. Because the officers' roles had been changed shortly before sailing, no one had made sure the binoculars were in the lookout post so the lookouts had to manage without. It appeared that some of the iceberg warnings sent to the radio room had not reached Captain Smith. And, worst of all, it seemed that a ship called the *Californian* might have been near enough to have rescued all of *Titanic*'s passengers, but her radio operator had gone to bed and the crew on deck had not understood the meaning of the distress rockets they saw on the horizon.

'At least we have clear consciences,' Robert remarked. 'I would hate to be accused of ordering the ship to sail at top speed, as Ismay has been, or of dressing as a woman in order to get into a lifeboat. Do you think that story could be true?'

'I met Albert Howson, one of those accused of it, but I don't know him well enough to speculate on how he might have behaved when his life was at risk.'

'He denies it, and we should take a gentleman at his word, but it has certainly ruined any chance the Howsons might have had of being accepted in New York society. I hear they have returned to Canada.'

'Are *you* a member of New York society?' Juliette asked, with raised eyebrow.

'My mother and sister are, so that makes me a kind of honorary member. But I am a huge disappointment to them, because I don't often attend the opera, I don't go to many of their interminable country weekend parties, and I have refused to marry any of their eligible daughters.' He looked her directly in the eye at this, and Juliette blushed a deep shade of scarlet.

'That's very ungallant of you!' She turned to gaze across the rolling fields, letting the breeze cool her reddened cheeks.

The drive to Poughkeepsie took almost two hours, but they chatted all the way and the time passed quickly. The chauffeur pulled into a large stable yard, and Juliette counted twelve horses leaning over stable doors, and several grooms at work.

'Oh my, they're beautiful!' she exclaimed. 'Just look at them.' She couldn't wait to leap out of the automobile and rush over for a closer look.

Robert led her around, introducing each horse in turn, and she stroked their noses and spoke softly to them. He told her which ones had pure thoroughbred pedigrees, which were top racers and which were retired. It was obvious from their glossy coats, their shining eyes and the impeccable condition of the stable yard that they were very well cared for.

'In England most breeders get rid of their thoroughbreds when they can no longer race. You don't choose to do so?'

'I wouldn't dream of it. They're part of the family and have earned their right to a happy retirement.'

Juliette nuzzled each horse they came to, as Robert looked on. When they reached a gentle bay, he said, 'This is Patty. She's our calmest mare and I thought you might like to ride out on her.'

Juliette looked longingly. 'You're sure she won't mind an unfamiliar rider? I don't want to take any risks.'

'She has never thrown anyone in her entire life. You would be the first! And I have a side-saddle you can use.' He eyed her long skirt.

'In fact, I much prefer to ride astride. I don't suppose you have some breeches I could borrow?' Back home, it was still considered somewhat scandalous for women to ride astride a horse, but Juliette hoped it would be more acceptable in America, with their history of renowned horsewomen such as Annie Oakley and Calamity Jane.

Robert grinned. 'Somehow I thought you would. You may use my sister's breeches.'

It was a tight squeeze to get into the breeches he offered and she had to leave the topmost buttons unfastened, but the hacking jacket she wore over the top disguised her belly.

As she mounted, it crossed Juliette's mind to worry that her mother could be right and she might be damaging the baby's brain, but the theory seemed far-fetched. She rode well and was bounced around little more on horseback than she was in an automobile on a bumpy road, yet no one worried about driving while pregnant. And soon, the dazzling perfection of the day and the congeniality of her companion pushed all anxieties from her mind. For the first time in months she felt a sensation of perfect happiness as she became one with the gorgeous animal beneath her, who was galloping through glorious countryside under a warm sun.

At dusk, it was time to stable the horses and drive back to the city. As Robert took Juliette's hand and helped her into the automobile, he had a soft look in his eyes and his gaze lingered on her in a way that made her shiver with pleasure. She knew he was falling for her, just as she was falling for him.

'I'd like to introduce you to my mother and sister,' he said quietly. 'Would that be amenable? Might I arrange it as soon as possible?'

'I'd like that very much,' she said, then bit her lip. If only this could have been a normal courtship. Robert was everything she had ever dreamed of in a man, but how could they be together with such a huge lie between them? She had been burying her head in the sand, but the moment was fast approaching when their romance would be disrupted and probably destroyed for good.

Chapter Forty-One

On Sundays, when Reg wasn't working, he explored the city street by street, each week choosing a new area and learning it off by heart. He rode on the 'El', the elevated railway on which steam engines puffed all the way up the east side of Manhattan Island, blowing hot cinders into the carriages if you opened the windows. He went to watch the construction of the Woolworth Building, a vast cathedral complete with gargoyles, which someone told him would be the tallest building in the world when it was finished. He could see workmen balancing on narrow girders hundreds of feet above ground, and shuddered at the thought of what would happen if they slipped.

He noticed that immigrants stuck together in their own communities where shops sold the foods they liked: Eastern European Jews were on the Lower East Side, Italians a few streets up in 'Little Italy' and Greeks in Astoria. When you walked in those areas, you barely heard English spoken and the Mediterranean smells of garlic and olive oil permeated the air, making him feel a little closer to home.

It was lonely spending so much time on his own, but he didn't want to stay at the rooming house, where Tony and the other waiters would be playing cards and drinking beer or whisky. He resisted their attempts at friendship and sank deeper inside himself, constantly mulling over what had happened on the *Titanic*. He started reading newspaper reports from the American Senate Inquiry, and once he picked up the first paper he couldn't stop. It was like an addiction. He needed to know it all. He needed an answer to the big question: *Why? Why did all these people die? Why did John die?*

There were several articles about prejudice against the third-class passengers and Reg was ashamed to discover how few of them had made it to the boat deck. There were fewer stewards per passenger down there, and they had been slower to respond. Some third-class passengers claimed the gates allowing them to ascend had been locked, but it was probably more likely that they didn't know the way. The only locked gate he had come across was the one Finbarr was stuck behind and that hadn't led from a passenger area. It's true that some of the catches on these gates could be tricky, though. Why hadn't he gone down to help third-class passengers instead of wandering around aimlessly during the first hour after the collision?

He read Second Officer Lightoller's account of loading the lifeboats, and then the way he had organised the men on the collapsible to prevent it sinking. To Reg, he was a god among men, one of the true heroes of the night. He wished he could somehow get in touch with Lightoller and ask his advice about what he should do with the rest of his life. He couldn't risk it, though, because it would mean owning up to taking a false name. Surely that must be against the law? He would probably be sent to jail if it came out. He had no idea what American jails were like but pictured some grim Dickensian cell where he'd be shackled to the other prisoners and fed only bread and water.

As far as White Star Line was concerned, John Hitchens had survived and Reg Parton had perished. They'd sent official documents in John's name to Sherry's, along with a month's salary of three pounds, ten shillings as severance pay. Reg glanced at the papers, and there was John's date of birth, crew number and the address of the lodgings in which he used to stay in Southampton. Would White Star send Reg's final salary to his mother? He hoped so. She would be very hard up without his contribution to the household expenses.

How would Florence be coping? He knew he must write to her soon – it burned his conscience – but what would he say? He couldn't ask her to come out and join him in New York, much as he would like to, because he had nothing to offer: there was nowhere she could stay and he didn't make enough money to support her. He felt like a burnt-out shell of the person he had once been. How could she love a man who only saved himself and failed to save Finbarr? Her feelings for him would surely change when she heard about that.

One day, Reg walked down to Battery Park, right at the very tip of Manhattan. He sat on a bench and looked across the water towards the Statue of Liberty and the hazy Atlantic beyond. Even being that close to the ocean made him shiver. Someone had told him that you could take the ferry out to the Statue and climb the stairs inside her right up to the observation point in her crown. He quite liked the idea of looking out from that lofty viewpoint, but he couldn't face the idea of the ferry trip across the bay. He never wanted to have water beneath his feet again. The very thought made him feel as though he was drowning. He could actually hear a rushing sound in his ears. It looked as though he would have to make America his permanent home. At the moment, nothing about it felt like home. The food was unfamiliar, with some revolting dishes such as grits, a hot cereal that got stuck between your teeth. The tobacco was strong and harsh, and he couldn't seem to find a brand he liked. And they used words he didn't recognise. 'You got the blues, Reg?' Tony asked one day, and Reg thought it must be some kind of kitchen implement he hadn't been told about; 'I bumped my noodle on the closet door,' Paul told him and it was only because he was rubbing his head that Reg finally understood. Everything felt unreal and temporary. *It will get easier in time*, he told himself. *It has to.*

One Monday, when he reported back for work, he was handed a note addressed to John Hitchens, which had been pushed through the restaurant's letter box. He opened it with shaking hands.

'*Dear John*,' it read, '*I heard from someone in the White Star Office that you are working here and didn't go back to England. I didn't go back either. I'm working at Childs Restaurant on Beaver Street in the Lower East Side and living just round the corner.*' It gave an address. '*We should meet for a chinwag. I'm working Monday to Saturday and I expect you are as well but I'll wait in for you next Sunday. See you then. Danny O'Brien.*'

Reg's face burned. Danny was a room steward with whom John had been friendly. John had been friendly with everyone; he was that kind of a person. Thank goodness Danny hadn't turned up at Sherry's while Reg was there or the story of his assumed identity would have come out. His whole existence was precarious. He was only a hair's breadth away from discovery. At any moment, some old friend of John's might walk through the doors during working hours and, when pointed in his direction, they'd blurt out, 'But that's not John!'

He considered going to see Danny, explaining that he'd taken John's name and asking him for his discretion. They'd never been close, but it would be good to talk to someone from the ship, someone from back home. When he thought about it, though, he knew his story sounded too outlandish. Danny would think he'd gone mad to use a dead man's identity. In the worst case, he might even report him to White Star. It was better not to take the risk. He couldn't go.

The following Sunday, Reg felt a deep sense of regret. He imagined Danny sitting by the window, waiting for John's friendly face to appear round the corner, and then feeling upset that his invitation had been snubbed. If Reg had gone, they could have compared notes about friends on board. They could have discussed the Inquiry findings. They could have talked about the strangeness of this city where people spoke the same basic language yet everything still felt foreign. Not going made him feel even more alone than he had before.

His hours at the restaurant were eleven in the morning till midnight, with just a couple of hours' break between lunch and dinner service, when the waiters could eat a meal and congregate in the back alley for a smoke and a gossip. Reg liked the routine, liked being busy, and when he first heard from the other staff about a possible strike among New York waiters, he paid no attention. One day, Tony spelled it out for him, though.

'We want to join the International Hotel Workers' Union so they can protect our rights, but management are against it. Without them, we've got no guarantees that Mr Sherry won't slash our pay and make us work even longer hours, then fire us at a moment's notice. Unions are important for workers like us. Don't you have them in England?'

'Yes, of course.' In fact, the coal workers had been on strike in England just before *Titanic* sailed, meaning that a number of other crossings had been cancelled and some people had ended up on the doomed ship who might not otherwise have been. Reg was a union member there because you had to be. The

251

union looked after you if you were sick long term and unable to work, or if you had an accident at work. He wondered if the union would be negotiating on behalf of the families of those lost in the sinking? Perhaps they might get a compensation payment for his mum?

'The point is,' Tony continued, 'that the Negroes are coming up to New York from the South and taking our jobs for a whole lot less pay. It's happening all over the city and if we don't stand up for ourselves we won't have jobs to come back to. But if we stick together by joining this union, they won't be able to fire all of us.'

'What are you planning to do?'

'Well, we're threatening an all-out strike. It would hit the restaurant trade so bad I bet they'd cave in before a week's out. It wouldn't last too long.'

That wasn't Reg's experience, though. Back in England, the coal strike had lasted right through March and had still been rumbling on in places when he'd left. He knew that strikers didn't get paid, and although he had some savings put by they wouldn't last indefinitely. So far he had eight pounds, ten shillings in English money, and a few dollars in American currency, but he was hoping to use it to better himself somehow. When he had a decent lump sum, he would be more in control of his circumstances.

In the back of his mind, he had an idea that he might start his own small restaurant one day. Maybe he could specialise in English dishes, like tripe or steak and kidney pudding. The Americans seemed fascinated by all things English. Mr Sherry had started as a waiter after all so it wasn't entirely far-fetched. If he was able to save up enough to take a lease on a property, he could do all the work himself at the beginning. He didn't want to blow his savings having to support himself during a strike or he'd never get there.

Also, Reg was reluctant to get into a dispute with his new employer, Mr Sherry, and the restaurant manager, Mr Timothy, who without fail had been kind and understanding towards him. Mr Timothy had chased White Star for those crucial immigration papers, and had found a doctor to change the dressings on Reg's feet once a week, for which the restaurant paid the fee. How could he reward them by joining a union and going out on strike? He decided to keep his head down and hope it all blew over before long.

Far from blowing over, the talk of a strike got louder and more strident until, towards the end of May, the staff of seventeen New York restaurants, including Sherry's, told their managers that they would walk out within two weeks if their demands weren't met. Reg was distraught, but how could he let his co-workers down?

'You *are* in this with us, aren't you, John?' they asked, and he mumbled, 'Yes. Of course.'

In private moments, he felt an overwhelming sense of panic. What could he do? How could he survive? He had no one to fall back on. He couldn't be the scab who broke the strike and came in to work, but how would he fill the empty days? How would he manage? He'd starve in this foreign country, where he had no family or old friends, no one to invite him for a bowl of soup or let him sleep on their floor. His connections in New York were fragile and tentative. *I need someone to look after me,* he thought. *If only I could speak to Lightoller. If only I could talk it through with John.* He woke at night in a cold sweat, then dozed off into fitful sleep, only to waken with a sense of dread already upon him.

The strike date approached and the atmosphere in Sherry's became tense. Mr Sherry slammed doors and wouldn't speak to any of his staff. Mr Timothy did his best to negotiate with the hardliners, but to no avail. Reg's anxiety grew with each day that passed.

And then one evening, he was asked to wait on a couple who were eating in a private dining room upstairs.

'Be discreet,' the manager instructed him. 'Just take the order and don't stop to talk.'

That suited Reg fine because he felt shy when diners tried to make conversation with him. He picked up two of the day's menus, climbed the stairs to the private room, opened the door and stopped dead in his tracks. Inside, holding hands across the table, were Mr Grayling and the beautiful girl from the boat deck.

Chapter Forty-Two

'My goodness! What brings you here?' Mr Grayling looked startled and quickly pulled his hand away from the girl's.

'I work here, sir. I decided I couldn't face another Atlantic crossing so soon after the *Titanic*, so I found a job on dry land.' He placed a menu in front of the girl, and caught a strange expression on her face as he did so.

'You were on the *Titanic*?' she said. 'So were we. Aren't we all the lucky ones to have survived! It was such an adventure.'

Close up she was even more stunning than he remembered: her chin a perfect little curve, her eyes an intense blue and sparkling like sapphires, her hair a deep copper colour, her lips painted in a Cupid's bow. But how could she be so vacuous as to describe the sinking of the *Titanic* and the loss of all those lives as 'an adventure'?

Reg moved round the table to give Mr Grayling a menu, wondering whether to offer commiserations about his wife or not. *Better not*, he decided.

'This is Miss Hamilton,' he told Reg. 'We met on the *Carpathia* and are just catching up . . . I'm afraid I've forgotten your name.'

Reg hesitated, thrown by the lie, and unsure whether Mr Grayling might have known his real name. His wife had used it often enough, but had he paid any attention?

'John Hitchens,' he told him and tensed for the reaction.

'Of course! I remember now.' He turned to Miss Hamilton. 'John was our dining saloon steward. It's a small world, isn't it?'

He'd got away with it, thank goodness. 'I hope you didn't lose any loved ones on the ship, ma'am?' Reg asked politely.

'No, thank God!' She gave a tinkle of a laugh and some ostrich feathers in her headdress swayed. 'We were very lucky.'

'I'll give you both a moment to decide on your order,' Reg told them and backed out of the room. His brow was damp with sweat and his hands shook. He leant against the wall in the corridor to catch his breath. It was bizarre to bump into someone from his old life, and it took him right back to the *Titanic*'s grand dining saloon. He could almost feel Latimer's eyes on him and hear the gay chatter of the first-class passengers. Would Mr Grayling suddenly remember that his name was in fact Reg? Would he report him to the restaurant manager for passing himself off under a false identity? He would be out on his ear if that happened, and Reg Parton didn't have immigration papers. Reg Parton had no rights now.

And then he became angry. It was only six weeks since the *Titanic* sank. What was Mr Grayling doing dining out with another woman? Mourning for a spouse should last a year at least, should it not? Perhaps that was why they were in a private room. Reg wasn't surprised that they didn't want to be seen together. There had been some stories in the press castigating Mr Grayling for surviving while his wife did not, so the last thing he'd want would be to be caught courting a girl less than half his age. The scandal would finish him off in the city.

When he went back in to take their order, he could tell they had been talking about him. Miss Hamilton's eyes looked him up and down with something like amusement, but he remained strictly businesslike and didn't linger. He tried to seem as though he was in a hurry as he brought in their entrées, placed them carefully so as not to disturb the intricate table decoration, then turned immediately to head back to the kitchen.

When he brought their main courses, though, Mr Grayling stopped him and asked whether he was going to go on strike with the other waiters. Reg answered honestly.

'I don't rightly know, sir. I can't afford to live without any wages coming in, but I don't want to let my fellow workers down either. I'm hoping it will be resolved before it comes to that.'

'I can't see any sign of a resolution, frankly. Mr Ettor is not in any mood for negotiation.' Mr Grayling was referring to the Italian-American spokesman for the Industrial Workers of the World, which was behind the strike call. 'He'll have all of us forced to turn Socialist if he gets his way.'

'I hope not, sir,' Reg replied. 'Can I order any more wine for you?'

'Yes, why not? Ask the sommelier to bring the list and I'll choose something different to go with our beef.'

Miss Hamilton giggled and rolled her eyes. 'What are you trying to do to me, George? You are a very naughty man.'

Was he drowning his sorrows? Reg wondered. *Or trying to compromise the lady's honour by making her inebriated?* The latter seemed to be more the case, because Reg couldn't detect any evidence of sorrow.

At the end of the meal, when Reg brought the check, Miss Hamilton excused herself to go to the powder room and Mr Grayling seemed stone cold sober when he spoke his next words.

'I have an offer for you, John, that might help you out of your present difficulty. You seem a very dedicated worker and I would be delighted to offer you a job at my own establishment in Madison Avenue. I don't keep a large staff but there's only me to look after so you would have plenty of free time. I see from the newspapers that waiters at top establishments earn about five dollars a week. Well, I would give you ten. What do you say to that?'

Reg was astonished. He hadn't expected that at all. 'Thank you, sir. I don't know what to say.'

'I run a very happy household and I'm sure they would be pleased to welcome you. You'd have your own room, of course. We're close to Central Park, and you would eat well because I have a French chef. But from your point of view, I imagine it could see you through the strike and perhaps help you to build up a nest egg.'

'Really, you are too kind.'

'I'd like to help you, John. I know my wife was fond of you, and I believe I should support you in her memory. She would want me to. I'm sure she would want you to accept the help as well.'

Reg wanted to refuse, but couldn't think of a way to do so politely, so he hesitated. 'I've never worked in service before, sir,' he said eventually.

'I assume Sunday is your day off. Why don't you come over at three and look around? You could let me know your answer after that.'

Miss Hamilton re-entered the room in a cloud of freshly applied scent, her eyes questioning Mr Grayling. *She knew he was going to ask me*, Reg guessed. *They'd discussed it. She left the room on purpose to give him the opportunity to talk to me.*

'Here's my card, John.' Mr Grayling handed it to him. 'I'll see you on Sunday.'

Reg nodded and held the door for them then watched as they walked down the staircase arm in arm and out to a waiting automobile.

Chapter Forty-Three

A date was set for Juliette and her mother to take tea with Robert's mother and one of his sisters at their family home. Lady Mason-Parker reacted with great excitement.

'If they approve of you, he'll certainly propose. Gentlemen don't invite you home to meet their mothers unless they have serious intentions.' She eyed Juliette up and down. 'We must get you a tighter corset. He might not notice your swollen belly but the women certainly would, and if they put two and two together your chances will go up in smoke.'

Juliette felt sick with nerves at the thought of meeting them. So many things could go wrong. 'Mother, you mustn't drop any hints about marriage. And you must back me up in the story that we are spending the summer with elderly relatives who need us with them at all times. Just say there is a pressing matter to be resolved but that we are not at liberty to discuss it.'

Her mother sighed. 'If only you had made Robert fall in love with you a bit sooner, it would have been possible to convince him the child was his. I fear it is getting rather late in the day now. But maybe . . .'

'I would never have tricked him. Never.'

'You and your misplaced sense of morality. You'll be the death of me.'

When they arrived at the tall, brownstone house Robert shared with his mother and sister, Juliette felt faint from the pressure of the corset her mother had squeezed her into, which seemed to force her innards up into the space normally occupied by her lungs. She wondered how the baby was coping with this constriction. Surely this must be worse for it than riding had been?

A footman showed them into a large, sunny drawing room decorated in blue, with handsome velvet chairs. Robert's sister Eugenie came over to shake their hands then introduced them to her mother, who was close behind.

'It's a great pleasure to meet you at last. Robert has told us all about the close friendship you've developed since meeting on the *Carpathia*. We are so grateful that he had someone to talk to during those awful first few days when you must all have been in terrible shock. Please, sit down.'

Lady Mason-Parker smiled graciously. 'Robert has been invaluable to us, helping to solve all the tricky little problems that arise when you lose your luggage and need to replenish it in a foreign country. He almost feels like a new member of our family.'

Juliette willed her mother to stop talking. They had barely sat down and already she was dropping hints. Above the fireplace there was a painting of a pot of white flowers with some yellow pears around the base. 'What a beautiful picture!' she exclaimed. 'It looks just like a Cézanne.'

Robert's mother smiled. 'You obviously know your art. Yes, it is a Cézanne. We're very lucky to have it.' She launched into the story of how they came to possess it, and Juliette sighed with relief at her lucky guess, which had successfully redirected the conversation.

Juliette's mother began to describe some of the paintings they had at home in Gloucestershire – dark portraits of ancestors and a couple of landscapes with horses – and as she spoke, she never missed an opportunity to mention their titles. 'Lord Mason-Parker, the Earl of Gloucester, says . . . and my daughter, Lady Juliette . . .'

Mrs Graham noticed, of course. 'An earl indeed! How wonderful to have aristocratic blood!' she exclaimed. 'Over here, we are all more or less peasants.'

Juliette cut in: 'In fact, it means very little. The title was given to a great-great-great grandfather of mine who donated a house to a mistress of King Charles II so she was close enough for him to slip out and visit in the middle of the night. Actually, I think there are many more "greats" in there, because it all happened two hundred and fifty years ago. We've personally done nothing at all to deserve it!'

The ladies laughed, but Lady Mason-Parker wasn't amused. 'Of course we have, Juliette.' She turned to Mrs Graham. 'There are a huge number of responsibilities associated with running an estate the size of ours, and we take the welfare of the local people very seriously.'

We're making fools of ourselves, arguing like this, Juliette worried. *How can I steer the conversation to safer ground?*

Before she could introduce a new topic, though, Robert's sister was saying how disappointed she was to hear that they wouldn't be able to visit her while she was in Saratoga Springs. 'We'll be there throughout July and August to escape the heat of New York. My other sister Amelia will visit with her husband and children, and I know she's dying to be introduced to you. Are you quite sure you won't be able to come over for afternoon tea even?'

Juliette shook her head. 'I'm so sorry. It's imperative that we devote ourselves to our relatives.'

'Do let me write down our address for you just in case you manage to slip away,' Eugenie insisted. 'There are some charming walks around the area and I'd love to spend more time getting acquainted.'

The whole meeting lasted under two hours but Juliette was on edge the whole time, certain she would inadvertently give herself away. Either that or her mother would alienate the Grahams with her snobbishness and pushiness. But at last, Robert arrived to convey them back to their hotel and the farewells seemed genuine and affectionate. He was silent throughout the journey and at the entrance to the Plaza Hotel, he asked if he might take Juliette out for dinner that evening.

'He'll check what his mother and sister say, and when they tell him they adore you, he will propose,' Lady Mason-Parker predicted.

'No, he won't,' Juliette frowned, but there was a kernel of hope inside her. *If only.*

'I promise you. I'm more experienced in affairs of the heart and I know that's how respectable men operate.'

With this thought in mind, Juliette was even more nervous going down to meet Robert that evening than she had been meeting his mother and sister. Her hands were shaking as he helped her into the automobile and she couldn't meet his eyes. Conversation between them felt unusually stilted, although he assured her that she had been a great hit with the Graham family women.

If he proposes, I must confess straight away that I am pregnant, she decided. *I will lose him, but at least he will respect my honesty.*

It seemed the only decent thing to do – and yet, she couldn't bear to lose him. She would never be able to see him again, a prospect that felt unbearable. Wasn't there any way she could put him off and ask him to wait six months for her hand? If he proposed, that was. Maybe he wouldn't.

In fact, they had barely sat down in the restaurant than Robert opened his heart. 'You must know how I feel about you.' He gazed into her eyes. 'I think about you day and night and can hardly concentrate on my work for remembering some clever thing you have said, or recreating your smile in my mind's eye.' He took her hand across the table. 'The circumstances in which we met could not have been more inauspicious but out of something quite so awful, surely some good can come?'

Juliette felt hot all over.

'I might have waited longer to speak but I can't bear the thought of you disappearing to some gloomy relatives for the whole summer, leaving me to exist on letters alone. I love you with all my heart and now we've got to know each other, it's as if the sun has stopped shining when you are not with me. If only you will consent to marry me before you leave for Saratoga Springs, then I will become a member of your family and can help to solve your relatives' problems. Please say yes.'

She covered her face with her hands, trying to still the pounding of her heart. 'Oh God, I can't tell you how difficult this is. I love you too, but I can't invite you to my relatives' this summer. I simply can't. Mother and I have to do this on our own.'

'Even if I were family?'

'I'm sorry, but that's the case.'

Robert looked crestfallen. 'I fear that I will lose you during such a long separation. You will forget me and in the fall you'll return to your family in England and I'll never see you again.'

'That won't happen. I swear.' *How could she convince him?*

263

'Would you consider setting up home with me in the States? Would you not be homesick?'

'I'd be happy to live wherever you were. I want to be with you, Robert. I do. Please believe me. I just can't be with you this summer.'

He kissed the back of her hand and she shivered with pleasure. 'In that case, let's get married before you leave. The weeks will be easier to bear if you are my wife and I know for sure that you will come back to me.'

Juliette felt giddy with delight. 'Yes,' she gasped. 'Oh yes, let's!' It seemed the answer to all her worries, if Robert would accept that he couldn't see her for a few months but would be waiting for her return.

But then, she began to see problems. 'There's no time to organise a wedding. My father and brother would be terribly disappointed not to be invited, and my mother will have a huge list of acquaintances to be included. I don't see how we could manage it with less than three weeks before we go.'

'They can all wait,' Robert said, in a husky tone that brought goosebumps to her skin. 'I want to marry *you*. We can go to City Hall next week and get legally married without telling anyone else. At least, we can simply tell them that we are engaged, if you like, so your mother can start her elaborate plans. We could then have a formal wedding in the winter some time, and I'd be delighted to come over to England for the ceremony. That's traditional, isn't it? The wedding is at the bride's local church?'

'Is it really possible to get married at City Hall without giving more notice? I don't mind if you would rather just get engaged for now.'

The passion of his response amazed her. 'I want you, Juliette. I want you so much that I can't wait six months. Please say you'll marry me just as soon as I can arrange it.' He fished in the pocket of his waistcoat and pulled out a small box. He opened the lid and she could see the glitter of a diamond inside.

'I will,' she said firmly. 'I can't wait either.'

He leaned over the table to kiss her on the lips, and she thought she was going to faint with happiness.

Chapter Forty-Four

Annie found life in Kingsbridge a struggle. The practicalities were easy enough: Father Kelly got Patrick into a good Catholic school, which he seemed to like, and he introduced her to a local woman who would look after the little ones sometimes to give her a break. She bought black mourning clothes for them all, even the baby, and every morning she stopped in the church to pray before going to buy groceries or do any of her other errands. She was a country girl, though, and she missed the green fields, trees and birdsong of her home in Cork. Everywhere she looked was grey and brown and black, the air smelled of gasoline and rubbish (which they called 'trash'), and the sounds were of traffic and street sellers and sometimes the loud honking of a fire truck rushing to an emergency. A few spindly trees struggled out of holes dug through the concrete alongside the step streets, and Annie sometimes mused that she felt just like them. She'd been planted in the concrete herself and was finding it difficult to survive.

The one blessing was that she felt Finbarr around her a lot of the time. She heard his voice in her head, and sensed that he was content. When the others weren't there, she kept up a running monologue with him: 'Why do you think this dough won't rise, Finbarr? What do they put in their strange American flour?' 'How long do you think it will be before my

266

old knees give out, what with climbing these steps twice a day, sometimes more?' 'Did you see that your little sister drew a picture on her bedroom wall? I was going to give her a piece of my mind and then she told me it was the *Titanic* sinking and you in the water, so I've left it. You'd never guess if you saw it, but she says that's what it is, bless her.'

Those were the good moments, when she talked to him in her head. During the bad moments, the burden of her loss came crashing back and she crouched in a corner of the apartment sobbing so hard she strained the muscles between her ribs and made herself hoarse. She never let Seamus or the children see her like that; she only succumbed to it on her own, and most of the time she tried not to because it was so excruciating. She often cried with Father Kelly, either in confession or when she talked with him in the sacristy. He encouraged her to talk and to cry whenever she felt the need, and that was healing crying. She felt better afterwards.

Father Kelly encouraged her to make friends and become involved in the local community, so she donated some loaves of soda bread to a yard sale to raise funds for the church, and she began to help by arranging the flowers in the church. A local florist brought them the blooms that were too overblown to sell, and she would select the colours that went together and arrange them into pretty bouquets. It was an uplifting task, and she suspected that some of the other women were jealous, but Father Kelly insisted she was the best person for the job.

'You've got an eye for colour, Annie,' he told her, and she replayed the compliment over and over in her head afterwards, repeating it to Seamus that evening.

'You should do some embroidery to show him,' her husband suggested. 'I haven't seen you embroidering since you got here. Maybe you should, because it always seemed to make you peaceful.'

She turned her head away. *How can I be peaceful when my son is drowned and his body is floating in the Atlantic?* But Seamus was right. She used to feel at peace when she was absorbed in her creations. Perhaps she should find a shop in which to buy a couple of embroidery threads and some needles. Maybe it would be good for her. Maybe she could start by making a sampler for Father Kelly to thank him for his kindness to her family.

She was overjoyed to find a pack of six assorted embroidery threads at a bargain price in a local discount store. Lovely colours they were too, with an emerald green, a deep blue, scarlet, primrose yellow, steely grey and white. She decided to make a picture of the church, surrounded by flowers, leafy trees and songbirds. Along the top she would embroider Father Kelly's name, the name of the church and the date. Surely he would be pleased with that?

It was good to have a project to throw herself into, and she spent all her spare moments on it, taking the opportunity to talk to Finbarr in her head. 'Do you think there should be clouds in the sky? Just one or two?' 'I'm putting in a bluetit, although I haven't seen one here yet. Do you think they have them in America?' Seamus was right. It definitely made her feel more peaceful.

Within two weeks of starting, she had finished her picture. She couldn't afford to frame it but hoped that Father Kelly would be pleased all the same. Seamus had the glint of a tear in his eyes when he looked at it and pronounced it perfect.

She felt a little embarrassed as she handed it over to Father Kelly, explaining that she wanted to give him a gift to say thank you for all his support and she hoped he didn't think it was frivolous.

He carried it over to the window so he could examine it properly in the light and for a while he didn't say anything, making Annie feel nervous. Had she done something wrong? Broken some church law?

At last he turned and beamed at her. 'I think this is the most precious gift I have ever been given. I had no idea you were so talented. Every stitch is perfect, and the design is glorious.'

'Oh good, I'm glad you like it.' She began to sort through some flowers, but he hadn't finished.

'I'm moved beyond measure that you would give this to me. I'll cherish it for ever.'

Annie bit her lip with pleasure.

'I would love to see more of your work,' he continued.

'I could do some for the next yard sale if you like,' she suggested.

'Your work's far too good for that!' he exclaimed. 'No one round here could afford to pay what it is worth. But I wonder . . . I have a parishioner who works for one of New York's top dressmakers, Camille Ozaney. Can I show her this picture and ask if she would like you to help embroider her ladies' dresses?'

'Oh, I'm not sure I'd have time what with the children and Seamus to look after.' Annie thought for a moment. 'But I suppose the money would be useful.'

'Why don't you have a chat with her?'

Camille Ozaney found Annie's sampler charming and offered her a trial job embroidering two hundred tiny silver butterflies onto white taffeta for a ballgown. Annie had to shift a table over beside the window in the front room and cover it with white sheets to keep the costly fabric clean, and she sat there where the daylight was brightest, painstakingly creating her butterflies. There wasn't a stray end of thread or an imprecise stitch, and the spacing between each butterfly was geometrically precise. She wrapped the finished work in tissue paper and took it down to Father Kelly, who delivered it to Mrs Ozaney.

More work followed: she was asked to stitch colourful oriental designs onto purple velvet collars, elaborate curlicues onto evening jackets, and flowers of all shapes and hues onto gowns of brocade and satin, chiffon and lace. Sometimes she was given jet beads or seed pearls to incorporate into the pattern, or sequins that looked like tiny mirrors. Camille would send a sketch with rough pencilled instructions, but Annie was the artist who rendered the images and brought them to life.

The work was absorbing and didn't leave her much time to think, but she always felt as though Finbarr was around while she was embroidering. Roisin and Ciaran would play on the floor nearby, Patrick was at school and Seamus at work. She looked forward to those moments when she was at peace with the world.

'Is it all right where you are?' she asked Finbarr one time, in her thoughts.

Immediately an answer came: 'Ma, it's wonderful here. I'm with yer da and he sends his love. He's been looking out for me since I arrived.'

Annie's father had died ten years earlier, when Finbarr was just a baby. 'That's good. I hoped he would. It's nice to think of the two of you together.'

She smiled at the image and carried on with her stitching.

Chapter Forty-Five

The night following Mr Grayling's offer of employment, Reg lay in bed wondering what to do. Why had he offered such a thing? Was it really because he felt sorry for Reg as a fellow survivor? Or was he trying to buy his silence? The last thing he wanted was Reg gossiping about his new romance so soon after his wife's death. *Before it, in fact.* Maybe he wanted to be able to keep an eye on him. 'Keep your friends close and your enemies closer,' the saying went.

Reg had formed a distinctly unfavourable impression of Mr Grayling's character since first encountering him on the *Titanic*. He didn't want to be under obligation to such a man, and reliant on him for food, shelter and wages. Yet he had agreed he would go to the house on Sunday. He had better go, or else Mr Grayling might complain about him to the restaurant. He could probably get him fired with one telephone call if he took it into his head to do so.

'Have you ever worked in service?' he asked Tony on the way to work the next morning.

'Yeah, for a while.'

'How is it different from the restaurant trade?'

'It depends on your boss, but it's pretty different really. At least with the restaurant we can get back to our own place after work. If you live in, you never get away. You're at their beck and call day and night.' He looked suspicious. 'Why, you're not thinking about it, are you?'

'I've had an offer,' Reg admitted. 'It's good money, so I'm tempted.'

'Yeah, but *service*.' Tony drawled the word contemptuously. 'It's one step up from slavery if you ask me. Who'd you get the offer from?'

'Someone I knew on the *Titanic*. Mr Grayling. He has a house on Madison Avenue. Is that a good address?'

'You must be kidding. George Grayling, the guy who saved himself and let his wife drown? What a heel! You can't go there, John. He's not even one of the Four Hundred so you wouldn't get to meet all the best people. Sure, he's got a grand house but it's like a mausoleum.'

'I told him I'd visit on Sunday so I'd better go. But thanks for your advice.'

Reg had more or less made up his mind he was going to turn down the offer, but at work on Saturday, a union representative came to the back door of the restaurant for a word with the waiting staff. 'These goldbricks aren't even listening,' he said, referring to the restaurant bosses. 'They've got trainloads of Negroes lined up down South. We have to be ready to walk out for the long haul. The bosses never do any work at all, but they want us to take a pay cut. The only way to beat them is to stick together. Are you with us on this?'

'Yeah!' 'Too right!' The waiters at Sherry's were a vociferous crowd.

Reg shrank back, his chest tight with nerves. He'd read in the papers about a mill workers' strike earlier that year in which a woman was shot and killed. Passions ran high at strikes and Reg wanted to steer well clear. He was an illegal immigrant, after all. He was there under false pretences. What if he got arrested while standing on a picket line with his fellow waiters? He'd be sent to jail then thrown out of the country on his release.

Reg slipped away to the men's room and locked himself inside a cubicle. He sat on the seat and bent double, hugging his knees. He was sweating and could hardly breathe, while his heart was pounding hard. What's worse, there was a pain in his chest that was making him feel sick, and he began to worry that he was having a heart attack. *What can I do? What can I do?* He'd started down one particular path on the *Carpathia* when he took John's name, and now there was no way to get off it again. All he wanted was a calm, quiet situation where he could save some money, keep himself to himself, and gradually, when he felt better, create a better life. This strike seemed to threaten everything. But the alternative was working for Mr Grayling and that seemed scary too.

'You in there, John?' Tony banged on the cubicle door. 'It's time to get to our stations. Mr Timothy's looking for you.'

Reg stood up carefully and opened the door.

'Christ! You feeling all right? You look terrible. Want me to tell Timothy you can't work tonight?'

'I'll be fine. I just need to wash my face. Tell him I'll be right out.'

Reg splashed cold water on his face and the back of his neck, and gradually he could feel his heartbeat slowing and the deep pain in his chest easing, but still he felt fragile. He wasn't himself. Somehow he got through the evening shift without incident and hurried home on his own without waiting for Tony. He needed solitude. Why wouldn't everyone leave him alone?

The following afternoon, he made his way to the Upper East Side and walked along Madison Avenue until he reached the address Mr Grayling had given him. He was over an hour early, so he sat on a bench across the street. The house was a big brown square box, three storeys high and covered in ivy. There were half a dozen steps up to a double doorway lined by pillars. The building sat on a corner and he could see it was three windows deep as well as three windows high. There must be dozens of rooms inside. The shutters were closed on the ground floor but upstairs he caught an occasional sense of movement inside.

At five minutes to three, he stood wearily and walked round to the back of the house, where he found the tradesman's entrance and rang the bell. It was opened by a tall, skinny man in a chef's hat.

'*Ah bonjour!* You are the new footman from the *Titanic*, yes?'

This was obviously the French chef Mr Grayling had mentioned. He had a heavy foreign accent. Reg nodded shyly. 'Maybe.'

'You look good. That is a start. Come this way.'

The chef led him through a large, airy kitchen and up some stairs to a hallway, where he introduced him to a man in wire spectacles who seemed to be the butler, a Mr Frank.

'John Hitchens? I've been expecting you. Let me take you upstairs first and show you the room that would be yours, then we can work our way down.' He smiled in a friendly fashion. 'Perhaps there will be a cup of coffee on offer when we get to the kitchen.'

Right at the very top of the house, there was a room with a slanted skylight window through which Reg could see clear blue sky. As well as a bed there was a writing desk, an armchair, a wardrobe and a china washbowl.

'This would be yours,' Mr Frank explained. 'You'd share a washroom with Alphonse, the chef, but otherwise you'd have this floor to yourself.'

It was quiet up there, a million miles away from the hustle and bustle of the rooming house where he and Tony lived, a million miles away from the clattering and shouting of the restaurant kitchen. *I could think up here. I could get my head sorted out.*

'You'd have a lot of free time,' Mr Frank told him. 'Your duties would be to serve breakfast, luncheon and dinner to Mr Grayling, when he is at home, and occasionally afternoon tea if there is a visitor, but that is very rare. Between times, you could help Alphonse with food preparation, but most days you are likely to have several hours of free time. Would that suit you?'

Reg nodded. *Yes, it would.* 'And the wages?'

'Mr Grayling said he agreed that with you. Ten dollars a week, paid every Saturday.'

As he followed Mr Frank down the stairs, Reg wondered what John would think of this place. '*It's a bit dull, man, but think of all that money.*' Is that what John would have said?

At least I'd be safe here, Reg thought. *I wouldn't have to go on strike or get arrested.*

Down in the kitchen he was given coffee in a cup with a Japanese pattern painted on it, and a piece of cake. It was good cake: moist and tasty. A girl came in wearing a maid's uniform. She had reddish-blonde curly hair and a broad smile that showed pretty white teeth.

'Are you the guy from the *Titanic*?' she asked. 'What a shocker that was. I'd be in a hell of a sweat if that was me. I hope you're going to work here. We need someone new to talk to. It's easy work. Alphonse and I will look after you. Have you met Alphonse? He's the big guy with the funny accent. Come on, say you'll take the job, John. You'll take it, won't you?'

'Yes,' Reg said. 'Yes, I rather think I will.'

275

Chapter Forty-Six

'It appears to be about two carats.' Lady Mason-Parker eyed the engagement ring. 'May I have a closer look?'

Juliette slipped it off her finger and handed it over.

'The clarity is good. No visible flaws. It's an old-fashioned kind of setting. Did he say if it's a family ring?'

'Honestly, Mother, I don't give a fig about the ring. Surely it's more important that I am engaged to be married to the man I love and want to spend the rest of my life with?'

'Well, of course. There is that. You won't do anything foolish like telling him about your condition with some misguided notion that you should be honest about it? Promise me you won't.'

'Of course not. I wish I could, but I can't risk it.'

The news of the engagement came at just the right moment to revive her mother's spirits. She was deeply disturbed by newspaper stories about her erstwhile friends, the Duff Gordons, who had been testifying to the British Inquiry into the sinking of the *Titanic*, and who were not coming out of it smelling of roses. They had escaped, along with their maid, in Lifeboat 1. It was smaller than the other boats, but was seriously underfilled with only twelve people on board, including crew. It looked as though the Duff Gordons had personally commandeered it for their own use.

After the ship sank, witnesses claimed Lady Duff Gordon had stopped the crew going back to pick up survivors despite all the space they had and – most damning of all – her husband had paid them the sum of five pounds each in a gesture that seemed calculated to buy their silence. In her testimony, Lady Duff Gordon claimed that she hadn't heard any cries from those dying in the water after the ship sank, and they both insisted that the money they paid was a mere gesture to help the crew replace their lost kit. The verdict of the press was damning, though.

'I can't believe I misjudged them so badly,' Lady Mason-Parker cried. 'They seemed such an upright, distinguished couple. I do hope no one of importance saw us together. Since we only took tea in the hotel and went to fashion houses together, surely I won't be associated with them in the public view?'

'Our case was completely different from theirs, Mother. We didn't behave selfishly that night. You have nothing to berate yourself with.'

With a deep sigh, Lady Mason-Parker turned her attention to the more pressing matter of organising a Christmas wedding back in Gloucestershire, to which it seemed virtually the whole county would be invited.

During those final weeks before her departure for Saratoga Springs, Robert came to call every afternoon, and he took Juliette out for dinner each evening. Every second was precious as they talked about the house they would buy in New York (they would stay in his family home until the perfect one was found), the honeymoon they planned (both had a hankering to see the Egyptian Pyramids and perhaps cruise down the Nile) and the American guests who would cross the Atlantic to come to their English wedding. He had applied for a licence for them to marry in secret at City Hall and when it arrived, he made an appointment for an afternoon just four days before she and her mother were leaving for the country.

'Are you sure you want to do this, my love? I don't mean to pressure you,' Robert said gently. 'The haste is merely born of my insecurity that you might change your mind during our long separation. But as I get to know you better and understand the type of person you are, I see you would not trifle with me.'

Juliette blushed. 'I understand your reasons, and mine are the same. Let's get married now so that neither of us has any doubt about the other's commitment. Leaving you behind would otherwise be unbearable.'

And so it was that at four o'clock on a Monday afternoon in early June, they rode in Robert's car down to the south of Manhattan, to a domed building with a statue of Justice holding her scales on the very top. A wide set of stairs led up to the entrance, and Juliette felt short of breath as they climbed them, her corset squeezing her inwards so she still had a semblance of a waist in the cornflower blue dress and jacket she wore. The simple ceremony lasted only fifteen minutes before the city clerk pronounced them husband and wife and Robert kissed her full on the lips.

Straight afterwards, they went to the Waldorf Astoria for a glass of champagne in its plush drawing room.

What have I done? Juliette wondered, feeling light-headed. But she had no regrets when she looked at the wonderful man who sat beside her on a velvet sofa, holding her hand and gazing into her eyes. She wanted the moment to last for ever. She was so much in love with Robert, and so perfectly happy, that she felt she could explode.

'Shall we dine here?' Robert asked. 'The food is rather good.'

'I'd have to go back to the Plaza to get changed first. I'm not dressed for dinner.'

'You look wonderful to me,' he said, 'but I know how much you women care about wearing the correct style for each occasion.'

She opened her mouth to deny this, then saw that he was teasing her. She'd often told him how ridiculous she found the dictates of social etiquette.

'I have another suggestion,' he said quietly. 'If you don't want to, that is absolutely fine and I will quite understand, but now that we are married we could legitimately take a room here and have an intimate dinner on our own. Then it wouldn't matter what you were wearing.'

Juliette blushed deeper than ever and he stroked the pinkness of her cheek, looking deep into her eyes. He was asking her to have marital relations with him. It was his right now. She wanted to be intimate with him, yearned for it in fact, but how could she risk him feeling her swollen belly and guessing her condition? Surely it would be obvious?

'You're shy,' he murmured. 'It's only natural. We won't do anything you don't want to do, but I would love to get you on your own so that I can give you some proper kisses, husband to wife.'

'I'd like to . . . to be with you,' she said quietly. 'But I fear you will not like me so much. I've . . . I've put on weight recently with all the fine dining and lack of exercise and I am afraid you will find me rather plump. I promise that once I can ride and walk more regularly, I will shed my excess flesh.'

'I adore your figure,' he whispered in her ear. 'You are a woman rather than a spindly creature who looks as though she would break in two.'

279

He kissed her neck, and Juliette was overcome with such a wave of desire that the decision was made. *I can refuse him nothing,* she thought. *Especially not when he kisses me like that.*

He paid for a room and when the door closed behind them they devoured each other with kisses. Any shyness on Juliette's part, Robert took for female modesty. They slipped under the bedcovers to make love, and afterwards lay wrapped up in each other's limbs, kissing and talking softly, then making love some more. At one o'clock in the morning, they knew they could linger no longer but must get Juliette back to her hotel or risk arousing Lady Mason-Parker's suspicions.

'I never thought a love like this was possible,' he whispered as he said good night. 'You have made me the happiest man in the world.'

Chapter Forty-Seven

Reg was astonished but pleased when he saw a story in the *New York Times* that Lady Juliette Mason-Parker and Mr Robert Graham had become engaged to be married after meeting on the *Carpathia*. He assumed that was the man she had been with in Central Park, the one who had given him ten dollars. It was less than two months since the *Titanic* sank so they hadn't known each other very long but it was heartening to hear of love blossoming out of tragedy like that.

Theirs was the only good news regarding the sinking. The British Inquiry was now in progress and Reg was aghast at the testimonies that seemed to imply Captain Lord of the *Californian* had been told of a ship on the horizon firing rockets and had done nothing to ascertain whether they needed assistance. Surely he must be cast for ever as the villain of the tragedy? If he had only asked his radio operator to get out of bed and turn on his set, he would have heard the desperate distress messages the *Titanic* was firing out right up until power was lost around twenty minutes before she sank. He was close enough to have come alongside and saved every single passenger and crew member. He could have saved Mrs Grayling. He could have saved Captain Smith. He could have saved John. Reg was overwhelmed with fury when he thought about it. How could that man live with himself?

He would have liked to vent his rage by discussing it with the other waiters at Sherry's, but he wasn't very popular after announcing that he was leaving. Mr Timothy was understanding when he explained that he couldn't afford to be out of work during the strike, and expedited his immigration papers so he could take them with him, but Tony implied that he was seen as something of a traitor among the ranks of the workers. Fortunately he only had to work a week's notice, then he packed his few belongings and headed uptown to take up residence at Mr Grayling's mansion.

Molly answered his knock at the back door and led him up to his room, chatting all the way. 'We're so glad you took the job. Me and Alphonse are dying to hear all about the *Titanic*. Mr Grayling doesn't talk about it much, but Miss Hamilton sometimes spills the beans when you get her alone. She's been shopping for all kinds of new clothes and jewels because she lost her old stuff on the ship. She's having them delivered here and I get to unpack them. The material is out of this world – just wait till you see them.'

'Why are they delivered here? Does Miss Hamilton live here?'

'No, of course not.' Molly rolled her eyes as if he had said something silly. 'She lives in a hotel. She comes around here all the time, though. Mr Grayling's been helping her get back on her feet. Well, that's what he says. If you ask me, it's really the opposite.' She giggled at her own joke.

'But isn't it sad about Mrs Grayling? I'd have thought Mr Grayling would be in mourning.'

'She was a good mistress and a nice lady, but we aren't allowed to talk about her now. Mr Grayling's orders. He'll probably tell you the same thing. I better not say any more.'

She paused, and it was clear that not talking about something was difficult for her. She was one of life's born talkers.

She watched as Reg hung his only spare shirt in the wardrobe, and put his one spare pair of socks in a drawer.

'Is that all you got? You better buy some more clothes because Mrs Oliver only does the laundry once a week, on Mondays. I can show you the best stores for getting some cheap stuff if you want. Or I could even go and buy things for you.'

'I haven't worked out what I need yet, but thanks for the offer.'

'Just let me know. I love shopping, especially with other people's money. My sister and I always check out the new fashions on Fifth Avenue and then we go and find them cheaper someplace else.' She chattered on about how much she liked nice clothes, and the best places to find bargains, as Reg opened the drawers and cupboards to see what was inside. There was a Bible in a chest under the skylight and a candlestick and candles by the bed, although there was electric light throughout the house, operated by switches beside the doors. The candles must be a precaution in case of power cuts.

'Are you ready to come downstairs and meet Alphonse?' Molly asked. 'He's from Provence. That's in France. He can be a bit grouchy because that's the way French people are, he says, but he's a top-notch chef.'

Alphonse shook Reg's hand, gave a quick nod of the head and asked if he would like something to eat. They'd already had lunch but there were some leftovers still warm. Reg was feeling a bit peckish so he said yes, and was served a portion of a delicious savoury tart made of eggs, cheese and leeks. It was as good as anything he'd had at Sherry's, with buttery pastry and moist filling.

'This is delicious,' he told Alphonse.

'Of course,' came the reply. 'It is my grandmother's recipe.'

'He's been trying to fatten me up,' Molly giggled, putting her hands behind her head and thrusting her hips to one side like a model in a saucy Victorian postcard. 'A girl's got to watch herself around here or she'll get into *all* kinds of trouble.' She was curvy, Reg noted, with a prominent bosom and hips that were verging on plump. He noticed Alphonse was ogling. Maybe it was a while since he'd had a girlfriend.

The butler, Mr Frank, came in to tell them that Miss Hamilton would be dining with them that evening, and when he saw Reg, he shook his hand and welcomed him to the house.

'When you've finished eating, I'll show you round and explain your duties.'

Reg ate his last mouthful of tart and leapt to his feet. 'I'll come now,' he said, eager to get started.

First Mr Frank demonstrated how to use the dumb waiter that carried food from the kitchen up to the dining room above so it would be piping hot when served. Mr Grayling was most particular about his food being hot. He showed him the cabinets where cutlery, crockery and glassware were kept. It would be Reg's job to set the table for meals, to serve and clear away, and between times to do any odd jobs Mr Frank requested, perhaps running errands out of doors, or helping Alphonse.

The public rooms were decorated in old-fashioned, dark fabrics and seemed gloomy, especially since the shutters were pulled across. Reg looked at the paintings – mostly landscapes and the occasional still life – and couldn't see much of a woman's touch in them. Nowhere was there a hint of Mrs Grayling's influence. There were no flower arrangements, no photographs grouped on a side table, no shawls draped over lamps or decorative flourishes such as the women he'd seen in first-class suites on his voyages seemed to like. This house was plain and no-nonsense. On the first floor, he was shown Mr Grayling's office, and Mr Frank pointed to a couple of doors that were locked, explaining those rooms were not in use at present.

'Were they Mrs Grayling's?' Reg asked.

'Did you meet her?' Mr Frank asked, giving him a curious look.

'Yes, I was very fond of her.'

Mr Frank nodded. 'I was as well. But Mr Grayling doesn't want the staff gossiping about her. He's dealing with his bereavement in his own way and has asked for our discretion. I hope you'll respect his wishes.'

'Of course,' Reg agreed.

That evening, he laid the table for two and was there to hold a chair for Miss Hamilton when she and Mr Grayling came in for dinner. She looked stunning in a slim black satin sheath, with diamonds dripping from her ears, looped around her slender neck and swathed around her wrist as well. Her copper hair was swept back from her forehead by a silvery headband, and Reg saw that her face was a near-perfect heart shape.

'I'm so glad George managed to tempt you away from Sherry's,' she told Reg. 'We *Titanic* survivors have to stick up for each other. We have our own private club.'

'Yes, ma'am,' Reg agreed. Her accent was plummy. *She's probably from London or the Home Counties*, he decided.

'What's more, you and I can wave the British flag and gang up against these Yankees with their strange words and funny accents.'

'I object!' Mr Grayling cut in jovially. 'You're in our country now, so you're the ones with the funny accents.'

'Where are you from, John?' she asked, and he had a moment of panic. If he said Newcastle, she would realise straight away he was lying, because he didn't have a Geordie accent, but if he said Southampton, would Mr Grayling remember when he looked at his immigration papers and find him out in a lie?

'I was living in Southampton before we sailed,' he compromised. 'But my folks come from the north.'

She was barely listening to his response, though, because all her attention was focused on Mr Grayling. He looked mesmerised by the sparkle of her diamonds and the perfection of her features, like a man in a trance. *He can't believe his own luck,* Reg thought. *Neither can I. But then those diamonds can't have come cheap.*

Serving dinner to two people was easy work and Reg found himself hanging around a lot. After they retired to the drawing room, he went out to sit on the back door step for a cigarette and Molly came to join him.

'Are you OK, John?' she asked. 'You seem down in the dumps. It must be really lonely for you, going through such a bad experience and then not having anybody you can talk to about it. I hope we can be friends.'

Her face was tilted towards him and she was staring straight into his eyes, her face just inches from his and her lips slightly pouted. Reg sensed she would have let him kiss her if he'd tried. She was pretty enough, and she seemed nice, but he was wary of getting into an awkward situation in such a small team as the staff at the house. Besides, the thought made him feel disloyal to Florence.

'Yes, I hope so too,' he replied. He finished his cigarette and ground it out under his heel before standing up to go back inside.

Chapter Forty-Eight

The morning of her departure for Saratoga Springs, Juliette woke with a sense of deep anxiety. When Robert asked how long she must stay with her relatives, she had blithely replied 'Just till the autumn' but in fact, the baby wasn't due till the beginning of November and it was only mid June. That meant there would be five months before she would see him again; five months cooped up with her mother in a little cottage in the middle of nowhere. The prospect was unbearable.

'I'll write to you every day,' Robert promised, and she said she would do the same, but she knew how much was left unsaid in letters. They could never be a substitute for nestling into his chest and inhaling the scent of him, for looking into his eyes and seeing his love and desire for her, which reflected her own.

He joined them for a farewell breakfast in the Plaza Hotel, at which Lady Mason-Parker chatted interminably about the wedding plans – the flowers, the hymns, details which neither of them cared about.

'I wish you had let my chauffeur take you,' he reiterated. 'Ted's a very good driver and I don't want to risk any harm coming to either of you.'

They couldn't accept his offer, though, because then Ted would report back that rather than staying in a large family home, they were in a tiny two-bedroom cottage on the outskirts of town that had the sole virtue of being close to a maternity hospital. Their subterfuge would be revealed.

'I'm sure the driver our relatives send will be equally diligent,' Lady Mason-Parker replied.

Juliette barely spoke over breakfast, afraid that her tears might start to flow. Robert held her hand and stroked it gently, sensing her emotional distress. It wasn't just that she would miss his conversation and caresses; without him, she didn't feel safe in this foreign country. Her mother would be useless if anything went wrong, while Robert was eminently capable. His calm pragmatism had helped her to recover from her severe shock on the *Carpathia*. Talking through the tragic events with him had helped her, if not to make sense of them, at least to come to an acceptance. She felt that with him by her side she could face anything; without him, she would feel vulnerable and lonely. And gradually, as her waistband grew, she was beginning to think about the fact that there was a baby developing inside her, and that it was going to have to come out somehow. Women died in childbirth, so the prospect was terrifying. She wasn't sure if American doctors were as good as British ones. If only Robert could be nearby when the time came, rather than her mother. But that wasn't possible. Of course it wasn't.

Porters carried their bags to the waiting car, and Lady Mason-Parker tactfully went ahead to give them time for a last embrace.

'Goodbye, my beautiful wife,' Robert whispered to her.

'I'll write to you on arrival,' she promised.

And then it was time to go and as their car pulled out into the New York traffic, Juliette gave in to the tears.

Lady Mason-Parker opened her handbag and passed her a handkerchief, then waited for the intensity of the sobbing to abate. 'Now, now, you are a very lucky girl to have such a handsome fiancé to come back to. He's a good man and I know your father will like him.' She pulled an envelope from her bag and passed it to Juliette. 'A letter arrived from your brother yesterday but I saved it to give you today as I thought you'd want some distraction on the journey. He will have heard the news of your engagement from the Marconi-gram I sent and I expect he wants to congratulate you.'

Juliette dried her eyes before tearing open the envelope. '*Well, well,*' the letter began, in her brother's large, untidy hand. '*Who would ever have thought that my ugly big sister would find herself a husband? Seriously, Jules, I'm over the moon to hear your news. Bring him home for a visit and I'll tell him all about what an annoying child you used to be.*'

Her brother continued with news of the local cricket team, someone who had just been made partner at the law firm where he was taking articles, and about a party where a man she didn't know had fallen into a fountain wearing a dinner jacket. He didn't mention any new girlfriends on the scene, but he wrote about the woman who had broken his heart the year before. Juliette had met her through some horse-loving friends and felt guilty about the fact that she had made the introductions.

'*Venetia's been up to her old tricks. Did you know she was engaged to Lord Beaufort? Well, she disappeared two days before the wedding and hasn't been seen since. All the wedding guests turned up, and until the last moment poor Harry thought that she would reappear so he stood like a lemon at the altar of some Italian church under the pitying gaze of the priest and their nearest and dearest.*'

'I think he's finally seen through Venetia,' Juliette remarked to her mother. 'She's pulled the same stunt on someone else.'

'Indeed, I heard about it from Lady Duff Gordon, because her fashion house made the wedding dress. Venetia is quite incorrigible. Her name is utterly ruined in polite society. She will have to dig deep to find any more poor saps prepared to put a ring on her finger.' She glanced over with satisfaction at Juliette's ring.

Juliette read on. '*When will you be back, old sport? I don't understand why you have to spend quite so long there with some distant cousins I'd never even heard of before. Cut the visit short and bring Robert to Gloucestershire before the summer is over so I can challenge him to a tennis match and assess the cut of his jib. Love to Ma. Your brother, Wills.*'

Juliette passed the letter to her mother to allow her to read it and settled back to gaze out the window. They headed north on the same road she had taken with Robert for their trip to Poughkeepsie and she recognised some landmarks – a soda fountain with a huge ice-cream-cone sign; a police training camp where officers learned to ride horseback – but it was more than twice the distance to Saratoga Springs, and the driver warned them it would take about five hours. Once the initial tears had passed, she occupied herself by imagining how it would be when she introduced Robert to her father and brother, showed him round their family home (what would he think of the fact that they didn't have electric lights?) and took him out riding in the English countryside. She imagined the house they would buy together in New York and wondered how many staff they would employ and what paintings they would hang. Might they own a Cézanne one day? She loved his work with its bright modern colours. And then she began to cry again, but quietly this time, because the pain of not being with Robert was so acute.

'It will get easier.' Her mother patted her knee kindly. 'I promise.'

What does she know? Juliette thought. It was impossible to believe that her mother, who cared about appearances and manners, could ever have experienced emotions of the intensity Juliette felt at that moment. Surely her mother had never been in love.

Chapter Forty-Nine

A couple of days after starting work for Mr Grayling, Reg took a tray of coffee to him in his study. It was a high-ceilinged room lined with books, and he sat behind a large leather-topped desk by the window, with a pair of spectacles on his nose. In front of him were a newspaper folded open to a page with columns of share prices and a sheet of plain paper on which he had been writing down lists of numbers. Reg was curious to know what he was doing. Was this how you ran a business?

'Put the tray there, please,' Mr Grayling said, making a space for it on the desk. 'And take a seat.' He indicated a chair on the other side of the desk and took his spectacles off.

Reg hesitated, then sat down. There was a smell of furniture polish and ink in the air, and a grandfather clock ticked loudly in the corner.

'How are you finding it here? It's not too dull for you, I hope?'

'It's perfect, sir. I enjoy the peace and quiet.'

Mr Grayling was examining him in a way that made him feel uncomfortable. 'Do you still think about that night on the *Titanic*?'

'All the time, sir.'

'It's hard reading about it in the newspapers, don't you find? The inquiries seem interminable and the press won't stop digging up one story after another. You never did find that friend you were looking for on the *Carpathia*, did you?' Reg shook his head. 'Were you very close?'

'We'd been working on the same ships together for seven years. I was closer to him than to anyone in the world. But you lost your wife, sir. I don't know how I would have coped with that.'

Mr Grayling leant his chin on his hand. 'It's been tough, I don't mind telling you, and it's been made ten times worse by the scurrilous newspaper stories about me. Have you seen any of them?'

'Not really, no, sir,' Reg lied.

'There are all kinds of fabrications about me being a coward and rushing to save my own skin while leaving my wife behind. It's terribly hurtful, and quite unfair.'

'The newspapers have condemned any men who survived, sir. It's not just you.'

'Tell me, John, how did *you* make it into a lifeboat?'

Reg told him about jumping overboard and swimming to the collapsible, but he omitted any mention of Finbarr.

'And you were injured, weren't you?' Mr Grayling asked. 'I remember your feet were bleeding. Are they quite recovered now?'

'Yes, thank you, sir. I had frostbite, and I've lost a few toe-nails but they're growing back just fine.' *Shut up, Reg! He doesn't want to know about your feet!*

'Good, I'm glad. If you need to see a doctor, tell Mr Frank and he'll arrange it.' He paused and tapped a finger on the surface of the deck. 'There was so much confusion on the boat deck towards the end that I haven't been able to establish exactly what happened to my wife. It would be extremely helpful if I could find someone who saw me helping her into a lifeboat and heard when the officer refused me permission to enter it myself.'

'Do you remember the number of the lifeboat, sir? They've been compiling lists of who was in each boat. The other ladies there would surely have noticed Mrs Grayling, especially as she got off again and went back onto the ship.'

Mr Grayling shook his head. 'Of course I should have noted the number but I wasn't thinking straight. I suppose I was concerned for myself, and then I got a place in a boat on the other side, and – well, you know the rest. I just wish . . . John, I am going to ask you a favour. You are under no obligation to agree, but it would make me very happy if you would give an interview to a reporter and tell him about the general air of confusion on the boat deck during the last hours of the *Titanic*. Explain how difficult it was to stay with your loved ones. I expect you would have liked to stick with your friend, but you got separated in the crush.'

Reg froze with horror. A reporter writing a story about him? He'd been doing his best to avoid attracting attention to himself and now Mr Grayling wanted him to talk to the press. What if they wanted a picture? He couldn't risk any such thing in case someone recognised him. But how could he refuse his new employer? 'I'm very shy, sir. I wouldn't know what to say . . .'

'I could arrange for someone sympathetic to come to the house here. It would only take five minutes of your time, no more.'

'Would they want to take a photograph, sir? I really wouldn't like to have my photograph taken.'

'There's no need for a picture if you don't want one. I'll arrange an appointment for later in the week, then. Thank you, John. There's just one other thing . . .' Once again he paused, tapping his finger on the desk and narrowing his eyes as if planning what he was going to say next. 'It would be best if you

294

avoid mentioning Miss Hamilton. You know what reporters are like: they might leap to the wrong conclusion.'

Reg gazed down at his lap, embarrassed by his knowledge of the closeness of the relationship. Mr Grayling didn't know he had seen them kissing on the boat deck, or stepping into a lifeboat together.

'Female company is helpful at times like these, because women are better able to talk about emotions. Miss Hamilton has been consoling me in the loss of my wife . . .'

Consoling? Reg thought cynically. *Is that what you call it?*

'I value her opinions and judgment highly. She's a very sensible woman.'

Not from what I've seen, Reg thought. From where he was sitting, she seemed like a social butterfly who didn't take anything seriously.

'Perhaps you should try talking to Molly? She's a good girl – I know the family – and I expect she could be a comfort to you. It would be nice if the two of you got along.'

Reg felt very awkward throughout this exchange. It was almost as if Mr Grayling felt the need to justify himself to Reg, which was strange from a man in his position, a man of his wealth, talking to one of his staff.

He obviously decided this himself, because he ended the discussion abruptly. 'Mr Frank will let you know when the reporter will be coming. Thank you. That will be all.'

He returned to perusal of his newspaper, and Reg stood up quickly and hurried from the room. *What on earth have I agreed to?* he worried. *What will the reporter ask? I'll really have to keep my wits about me so I don't give myself away.*

Another thing preyed on his mind. Why had Mr Grayling dropped that hint about talking to Molly? What did he mean by that? Was he implying that he would turn a blind eye if they became romantically involved? It was becoming obvious that she was interested in him. Every time Reg went out to the back step for a smoke, she seemed to appear as if by magic and her flirting was becoming more direct.

'Have you had many girlfriends, John? Any of them serious? I bet a nice-looking fellow like you has a girl in every port. I bet you can't even count all the girlfriends you've had.'

He shook his head. 'Not me.'

'Don't think you can pull the wool over my eyes. I wasn't born yesterday. I bet they throw themselves at you, and what man would be able to resist? It would be only natural.'

One evening, just before bedtime, he went into the pantry to put the butter on a high shelf, and Molly slipped in behind him. It was a cupboard rather than a room, and they were pressed up against each other.

'Did you want something?' he asked, confused.

'Yes. I did, actually,' she said, then leaned in and kissed him quickly on the lips. He could smell wine on her breath. 'That's what I wanted,' she laughed, before skipping out of the larder again and off to her room.

Reg climbed the stairs to his own room, feeling close to tears. He'd been keeping the protective carapace around himself, not letting anyone get close, but between them Mr Grayling and Molly seemed set to puncture his defences. He'd thought he would find peace in the quiet, gloomy household, but instead the fact that there were fewer people meant he was forced to engage with them. He didn't feel ready but it seemed he wasn't being given any choice.

Chapter Fifty

Reg liked to keep busy and there wasn't much to do in his new job, so between meals he sat in the kitchen helping Alphonse with food preparation. Alphonse showed him how to knead dough, how to trim string beans and the best way to whisk eggs for a soufflé.

'Use your wrist. *Comme ça.*'

Occasionally Reg tried to use the smattering of French he'd picked up on his Mediterranean cruises: '*Les oeufs sont prêts.*' But Alphonse imitated him, mocking the accent with a cheeky glint, and he soon gave up.

Alphonse never asked about the *Titanic*, never enquired about his life back in England, and that suited Reg just fine. Their only conversations were about food, and a lot of the time they worked in silence, punctuated only by Alphonse's swearing when a pot overheated and his oil began to smoke, or if he dropped a vital ingredient on the stone floor.

Reg watched the way he worked: marinating meats for hours before cooking; throwing together a delicious sauce with just some butter, wine vinegar and shallots; seasoning then tasting then seasoning again. All this would be useful to know if he ever got his own restaurant.

The atmosphere changed in the kitchen when Molly swept in, though. She was like a mini whirlwind of energy and chatter, with her stream of observations on the weather, the latest news from the society pages of the papers, the jewellery and gowns she would like to own one day, or the menu for dinner that evening. She could talk a blue streak, seldom pausing for a response. Reg found it curiously relaxing because it required little of him and Alphonse seemed to find her entertaining as well. He might be grumpy with everyone else but Molly could always raise a smile. He seemed to have a soft spot for her.

'Mr Frank says there's some reporter coming to see you later,' she said to Reg towards the end of his first week on the job. 'I guess he'll want to ask you all about the *Titanic*. They should give you some money for that. Lots of other people got paid and you know more than most of them because you worked there. You had the inside scoop. It's a wonder they didn't call you to testify at the Inquiries. I hope they give you a big front page with a nice picture. Give me a call when they're doing the picture and I'll make sure your hair's looking good.'

'I'm not having a photo taken,' Reg chipped in, but she was off again:

'I was in the newspaper once when I was five. I was picked as the cutest little girl at the fair on Coney Island and I had to have my picture taken, but when the flash went off I started crying. They gave me a rag doll prize and my picture was on page three of the newspaper the next week. My mom cut it out and saved it.'

There hadn't been a repeat of the kiss in the pantry, but they'd slipped into a routine in which Molly would accompany Reg outside while he had a cigarette after the dinner had been cleared away. Miss Hamilton dined at the house almost every evening and Molly liked to ask which gown she'd been wearing and the jewellery with which she accessorised it, so Reg had to do his best to remember the details. If he could recall a snippet of the conversation for her, all the better.

'You will tell me what the reporter says, huh? I can't wait to see the story. Find out when it will be in the newspaper so we can run out and buy it. Alphonse and I want to know what you're saying about us.' She grinned at Alphonse, and he gave one of his exaggerated Gallic shrugs to show he couldn't care less, but his eyes twinkled benignly.

The reporter's name was Carl Bannerman, and he was not much older than Reg, with dark hair swept back from his forehead in a similar style to Reg's. Mr Frank led him into the front drawing room and Reg followed, feeling very self-conscious. They sat opposite each other in the big armchairs by the fireplace and Reg didn't know what to do with his hands. He rested them on the arms of the chair, then linked them in his lap, but however they were placed they felt awkward. Mr Frank offered to bring them a refreshment, but Carl said no thanks, he wanted to get on with things.

While Carl took out his notebook and pencil, Reg noticed that some photographs had been placed on a side table, and were clearly visible from where they sat. There was Mrs Grayling smiling at the camera in a high-necked blouse with a cameo brooch at her throat. He felt sad to see such a good likeness, almost as if she were in the room. There had been many folk lost on the *Titanic*, but surely she had been one of the kindest among them? Another picture appeared to be a wedding photo of her and Mr Grayling, although they were both so much younger they were almost unrecognisable. One thing Reg was sure of: these photographs hadn't been there the day before when he served an after-dinner brandy in this room. They'd been placed there deliberately for the reporter to see.

Carl began with some questions about his background: 'How long were you at sea, John? What made you want to work on the liners? Was the *Titanic* as magnificent as they say she was?'

Reg answered as briefly as possible. 'Seven years. I grew up by the sea and liked watching the ships going in and out of port. Yes, she was the height of luxury.'

'And you became friends with the Graylings when you waited on them in the first-class saloon?'

Reg hesitated. He couldn't say that Mr Grayling had been a friend. 'I'd met Mrs Grayling the previous year on a Mediterranean cruise. She was very nice to me.'

Carl moved on quickly to ask about the night of the sinking, and since Reg continued to answer in one-liners, Carl began suggesting words he might use.

'I bet you were terrified when you realised the ship was going to sink. You must have been out of your mind with worry.'

Reg agreed that he had been and Carl scribbled it down. He was using shorthand so it didn't take long. Reg could just see some of the impenetrable squiggles on his pad.

'And there were people hurrying around on the boat deck, but nobody to tell you what you were supposed to do.'

'That's right.'

'I bet you helped show the passengers to the boats, didn't you?' Reg nodded. 'But lots of the women didn't want to get on without their husbands?' He nodded again. 'Do you think that's why Mrs Grayling got off the boat her husband had helped her into? Was she going to look for him to make sure he was safe?'

'I don't know exactly. She was a very kind lady and she always worried about other people.'

'Maybe she gave up her place for someone who needed it more? A pregnant lady, maybe, or somebody with a little child?'

'I suppose it's possible,' Reg agreed doubtfully, and Carl wrote that down.

'Now tell me about your escape, John. You were on the upturned collapsible, weren't you? What was it like?'

'It was hard. I thought we weren't going to make it.'

'You were injured, I hear. Your feet were bleeding.'

'It was just frostbite. They're OK now.'

'But you could have lost your feet to gangrene if you'd been out there any longer. You are lucky to be alive.'

Reg felt tears come to his eyes and blinked them away furiously, but he saw Carl writing something down. 'Yes, I suppose so.'

'I bet you really appreciate Mr Grayling giving you a job and place to stay.'

'I didn't want to go back to sea again,' Reg explained. 'I couldn't face it.'

'I'm not surprised,' Carl said, then looked up and smiled. 'Terrific. That's all I need from you.'

Reg was surprised because he felt he'd hardly opened his mouth. 'When will the story come out?'

'It's hard to say because it depends on what else is going on, but I'll write it this afternoon so it could be tomorrow or the next day. Thanks a lot.' He put his notebook and pencil away, and looked at Reg closely. 'Off the record, are you OK? I'm talking to lots of *Titanic* survivors these days and they're all shot to pieces. It must have been hell out there.'

'Yes, it was,' Reg told him. 'I'm fine. I'm just trying to keep myself busy.'

'Have you got family in New York? Or any friends?'

Reg shook his head. 'Not really. Not yet.'

'Well, you take it easy. Look after yourself.'

They stood up and shook hands, then Carl hurried off to his next appointment.

'What was he like? What did you say? Did you talk about us?' Molly wanted to know as soon as he walked into the kitchen, but Reg didn't feel like discussing it.

'You'll see when the article comes out in a day or so.'

That evening as they sat on the back step after dinner, he asked Molly if she had placed Mrs Grayling's photographs in the drawing room.

'I saw them,' she said. 'But I didn't put them there. They've all been tidied away again now. I guess he just wanted the reporter to see them.' They both knew who she meant.

'It's peculiar that there aren't any signs of Mrs Grayling around the house. There are no women's coats or outdoor boots in the cloakroom, none of the things you'd expect in a woman's house.'

Molly glanced over her shoulder to check whether anyone might be listening from inside the kitchen. 'Mr Grayling made us pack away all her stuff as soon as he got back. It's all in her bedroom and dressing room upstairs, and he locked the doors.'

'I find it strange that he's not in formal mourning. Back in England, husbands mourn their wives for at least a year, wearing a black armband and staying at home, yet he dines out and entertains Miss Hamilton most evenings.'

Molly lowered her voice and inched closer. 'They weren't happily married. I've been here three years and I never once saw them kiss or hug or anything.' She shook her head for emphasis. 'I used to hear him biting her head off and her crying sometimes. She kept sleeping potions by her bed, ones the doctor prescribed, so I guess she was sad about things. Did you know they had a daughter who died?'

Reg hadn't known and was upset to hear it. 'That's awful. Poor Mrs Grayling.'

'It was seven years ago, so you'd think she would have got over it. But I heard he wanted another kid and she was too old to give him one.'

He raised his eyebrows. 'Where do you get all this, Molly? Were you crouching with your ear at the keyhole?'

She sniffed. 'I pick stuff up as I go along. My mom knew about them before I even started working here. She says Mr Grayling only married her for her money. She came from a way richer family and it was her cash that helped him to set up his company.'

'Well, she was a kind woman. I liked her very much.'

'Gosh, yes, you should have seen the Christmas presents she used to give us. Last year I got a new coat and a necklace with a real pearl on the chain. I bet we won't get anything like that next Christmas, not from Mr Grayling. But I used to wonder why she didn't have dinner parties, with that big dining room and the drawing room too. She could have had great soirées with lots of glamorous ladies, but she ate all by herself most nights and he went out to his club.'

'Had you ever seen Miss Hamilton here before Mrs Grayling died?' Reg asked.

Molly was surprised. 'Don't be an idiot! They met on the *Carpathia*. I thought you knew that.'

Reg threw caution to the wind. 'No, they didn't. I saw them together on the *Titanic* two nights before we hit the berg. *And* I saw them getting on a lifeboat together.'

Molly's eyes widened. 'You're kidding! They were fooling around while she was still alive?'

Reg nodded. 'Yes, they were. I don't know whether Mrs Grayling knew about it or not, but I'm sure they were.'

'That's incredible. Oh my gosh, I wonder where they met? Hey, no wonder he didn't have any time for his wife with such a gorgeous gal on the side. He's crazy about Miss Hamilton. Alphonse and I reckon they'll probably get married. It's kinda handy that Mrs Grayling is out of the way and they don't need to get divorced. You don't think they bumped her off somehow, do you?'

'Molly! Don't be ridiculous!'

'All I'm saying is that it's pretty easy for them that she's not around any more.'

The thought had never occurred to Reg before, and at first it seemed far-fetched, but in bed that night he began to wonder. Why hadn't Mrs Grayling been seen that last day on board the ship, or on the boat deck, or in a lifeboat? Was she already dead by the time they struck the iceberg? Were they planning to throw her body overboard in the dead of night? The image of Miss Hamilton tossing her fur coat over the railings on the boat deck came back to him. Was that a dress rehearsal? Was she checking how an object would fall when thrown from there? If that were the case, the sinking of the Titanic had been mighty convenient for them.

Could it be that when Reg knocked on the cabin door that night, Mrs Grayling was already lying dead inside, leaving Mr Grayling free to escape with his mistress? He shivered. If that were true, he was living in the house of a murderer.

Don't be silly. You're getting carried away, he told himself. But a niggling doubt had taken root in his head.

Chapter Fifty-One

Mr Frank came into the kitchen holding a newspaper. 'Your article's on page five, John. I thought you would like to see it.'

Reg sat at the kitchen table to read, with Alphonse peering over his shoulder.

'Millionaire's wife gave up her place in lifeboat', the headline read. Underneath, the article claimed that Mrs Grayling had been seated in a lifeboat that was full and ready to be lowered when a young woman who was pregnant and carrying a small child appeared. 'Give my place to her,' Mrs Grayling had cried, and leapt out of the boat. 'I will find my beloved husband and our fates will be entwined for ever.'

Unbeknownst to her, though, her husband had been ordered to board a lifeboat on the other side of the ship, and so she drowned while he was saved. All this was witnessed, according to the reporter, by a first-class steward called John Hitchens, whom they had befriended on board. In a unique twist of fate, the story continued, after the *Carpathia* docked Mr Grayling bumped into John, who was limping along the street on badly injured feet, and offered him work at his luxury mansion, which is when the truth came out.

Reg winced. 'That's not what I said at all.'

'Reporters write what they want to write. They want everything to be a sensation, *n'est ce pas*?'

'I just hope Mr Grayling doesn't mind. I'd better apologise to him.'

Far from minding, Mr Grayling seemed very pleased when he read the newspaper. 'Well done, John. I appreciate it.'

I bet you do, Reg thought. *Especially if I'm helping you to cover up a murder.*

Molly had many more questions, though. She seemed to have got the bit between her teeth. 'Did you even see Mrs Grayling near the lifeboats?' she wanted to know, and Reg admitted that he hadn't. He mentioned knocking on the door of their cabin and getting no reply, then trying the handle and finding it locked.

'That sure is suspicious.' Molly frowned. 'Where the heck was she?'

'It might be possible to work out which lifeboat she was on,' Reg mused, 'because I saw Mr Grayling and Miss Hamilton getting onto Lifeboat 5, which was quite an early one to launch, and he says he put Mrs Grayling in a boat on the other side *before* that. Hang on a moment.' He ran all the way up to his room at the top of the house and retrieved a page he had torn out of a newspaper that estimated the time at which each boat had been lowered and who had been on them. He sat down beside Molly at the kitchen table and they pored over it together.

'Boat 5 was lowered from the starboard side at twelve-fifty-five, according to this,' he told Molly. 'The first one to leave the port side, at around the same time, was Lifeboat 6. Look, it was full of women: Helen Churchill Candee and Elizabeth Jane Rothschild.' He read a few more names from the list.

'My sister works for the Rothschilds,' Molly said thoughtfully. 'She's a maid, like me. She wasn't with them on the

Titanic, but she can probably ask Mrs Rothschild if she saw Mrs Grayling on the lifeboat. I think they knew each other.'

'What harm can it do?' Reg agreed.

'I'm going to see my sister on Sunday so I'll ask her then.'

Suddenly Alphonse banged a mixing bowl down on the table, making them jump. 'This is gossip,' he snarled. 'I hate gossip in my kitchen. It makes the sauce curdle. Don't you have any work to do?'

Molly stuck out her tongue at him. 'Who got out of the wrong side of the bed? Don't get grouchy with me.' However, she rose to her feet and picked up her dusters. 'I guess I'd better get going with the upstairs.'

'Here!' Alphonse threw a sack of peas at Reg. 'Shell these. It will keep you out of mischief.'

Reg pulled out the first pod and split it with his thumb-nail, then scraped the peas into a pan. He didn't like the awkward atmosphere between them so he tried to explain. 'Molly's getting a bit carried away with this mystery,' he said. 'I expect there's a completely rational explanation.'

'All I know is that it is not your business, and it is not hers. You have not worked in a house like this before, but I am telling you it is best to keep out of other people's *affaires* or you can get yourself in *beeg* trouble.'

'I agree. You're right. I will.' They carried on working in silence but Reg sensed that Alphonse was still cross because he continued thumping pots and pans with gusto. He and Molly had better avoid discussing Mr Grayling's private life in front of him in future. Alphonse seemed to object to it.

That evening, Mr Grayling and Miss Hamilton were dining out, so after the staff had eaten Reg was at a loose end. It was sunny so he decided to go for a walk in Central Park but by the time he crossed the street, he found he was sweating in the black jacket he wore to work, so he turned back to leave it at the house. He'd be fine in his shirt sleeves.

He entered by the back door and walked up to the cloak-room on the ground floor where outdoor clothing was kept. As he opened the door, Molly jumped back with a cry of surprise and Reg saw that she was holding one of Mr Grayling's wallets in her hand.

'What are you doing?' he asked.

'Mr Grayling . . . wanted me to find something . . .' she began, stumbling over her words.

'But he's not here.'

'He . . . erm, asked me before he left.' Reg looked down at her hand again and saw that she was holding a dollar bill.

'I'll split it with you,' she said quickly. 'He never notices. He keeps wallets in all his coats and he never knows how much money he's got in them. Here – you take this.' She tried to thrust the money into Reg's hands but he backed away.

'I won't tell on you, Molly, but I don't want anything to do with this. You should be careful, because he could call the police if you're caught . . .'

Molly cocked her head to one side. 'You're a nice guy, John. You're a good influence on me. Look! I'm putting it back.' She pushed the money into the wallet and replaced it in Mr Grayling's coat.

Reg took his jacket off and as he stretched his arms up to hang it on a peg, Molly slipped her arms around his waist and pressed her body against him. 'I like you,' she whispered. 'I like you a lot.' Flustered, Reg was unable to move away before she leaned in and gave him a lingering kiss on the lips. She had a sweet smell about her, and her touch felt good, but when she tilted her head back to look at him quizzically, he said, 'Molly, we can't do this. I'm sure Mr Frank wouldn't like it. It could get complicated.'

'We don't have to tell the world, do we? I like you, you seem to like me, and if we kiss and hug every now and then to make the day go faster, it's not exactly a crime, is it?'

'I have a girlfriend back home.'

'Do you really? When are you going to see her? She's on her way to visit you, is she?'

Before he could answer she kissed him again, and this time he couldn't help responding. It felt wonderful to be in a woman's arms. He'd been walking around for two months like an invalid or a person in a trance, but Molly's kisses brought him to life. He gave in to the feeling and kissed her back.

Chapter Fifty-Two

A sign announced 'Welcome to Saratoga Springs, district of Saratoga County' and Juliette was surprised to find they were in a town, with hotels, shops, a racecourse and several bath-houses advertising health treatments with the local spring water. Southeast of the town there was a large lake and every-where she saw pretty gardens in bloom. It seemed an attrac-tive area, but quite different from the backwater she and her mother had been led to expect. Everywhere she looked there were fashionable ladies walking the streets shaded by parasols, and gentlemen standing beside the latest models of automobile.

'Is this a busy place?' Juliette asked their driver.

'It's quiet in winter,' he replied, 'but in summer it attracts many visitors from New York.'

Juliette and her mother exchanged glances. If that were the case, she would have to be a virtual prisoner in their home. She wouldn't be able to come out to shop in the stores or sip a soda in a café for fear of being recognised by someone who knew of her connection to Robert. Besides, his sister would be arriving in a couple of weeks to spend the months of July and August there, so she certainly couldn't risk going out then.

The house they pulled up in front of was isolated down a dirt track, within a large flower-filled garden. It had a shady verandah out front with a swinging seat on it, and inside the rooms were freshly painted and sunny. A local woman called Edna had been hired to shop, cook and clean for them, and she was waiting to greet them.

Juliette wandered from room to room. There was a drawing room, a dining room, a kitchen and scullery, to which Edna's room was attached, and a bathroom for her use; upstairs there were two bedrooms, a dressing room and a bathroom for her and her mother. This was to be their home for the next five months. It was neatly furnished and had electric lights, but it was much less luxurious than they were used to and suddenly Juliette realised, with a pang of guilt, what she was putting her mother through. Her predicament was entirely her own fault and it was fair that she should suffer, but her mother had done nothing wrong and she would be a prisoner in this place as well. *I must be nicer to her,* she reprimanded herself. *I must remember her sacrifice.*

Edna brought them tea on the verandah, and Juliette asked her mother about the relatives they had told everyone they were visiting.

'I promised to write to Robert on arrival,' she explained. 'But what can I say? I suppose I must describe these elderly relatives we are supposed to be staying with. How can I not?'

'I will have to do the same when I write to your father and brother. We should get our stories straight. I haven't seen them since I was a child, but they are the son and daughter of my grandmother's cousin and have lived in America all their lives.'

Together they invented a likely kind of house, very dark and brimming with antiques, and two frail grey-haired people, a brother and sister, seeing out their final days together.

When Juliette wrote her first letter to Robert, she merely said that the relatives were in poor health but had seemed pleased to see them and she devoted the rest of her letter to the journey, her first impressions of Saratoga Springs, and how much she missed him already. Her mother wrote to her father and brother to tell of their safe arrival, and when both letters were signed and sealed, their driver was despatched to town to post them. He lived above a garage down at the end of the track, just where it left the main road. They were keeping him on for the summer so that he could drive Edna to buy food. He'd pick up the newspapers and mail every day and be on hand to fetch a doctor if Juliette needed one.

'I'm only just beginning to realise all the lies we are going to have to tell!' Lady Mason-Parker exclaimed. 'I must keep a note or I'll forget.'

'I'm sorry, Mother,' Juliette said. 'Truly I am. This has been horrid for you too, and we still have five months to go.'

'I expect we'll be able to sail back before the end of November. That will only give me a month before the wedding, though, so I shall endeavour to make most of the arrangements from here. We can do it together. We'll get you a dress in New York and have it altered by our dressmaker at home once you lose the pregnancy fat. I hope Robert will be able to sail with us. He was so comforting on the *Carpathia*, and I know I will feel nervous getting on a ship again.'

'I'll ask him,' Juliette promised, but her mind was on yet another lie she was telling. Her mother had no idea that they were already married. Would that mean they couldn't get remarried in the local church at home? Would they have to confess to the vicar what they had done? Her mother would be devastated at the deception.

The day after their arrival, a doctor came to examine Juliette. He took her blood pressure, felt her stomach and asked a number of questions about her diet and sleeping patterns.

'I've been getting a strange fluttery sensation in my belly,' she told him. 'But I expect it's nerves brought on by the journey.'

'On the contrary,' the doctor said. 'I expect what you can feel is the baby kicking.'

Juliette started back in her chair, open-mouthed with surprise. 'Really? That's the baby?' Until that point she had given it little thought, but if it was kicking her from within, she would have to start accepting it was a real living creature.

'These feelings will get stronger and more definite over the next weeks until it is too big to move any more.'

'May I ask you a question? I think you understand my situation, that I am unmarried and the child is to be offered for adoption.' He nodded, tight-lipped. 'Will my future husband be able to tell I have had a child?'

'That depends. If you give birth normally, there should be no visible signs, but if we have to operate to remove the baby by Caesarean section then there will be a scar.' Juliette sighed. 'It will also be important if you have children in the future to tell the doctor that it is not your first time.' His tone made his disapproval clear. He would look after her physical needs but she couldn't expect any sympathy.

In bed that night, she couldn't sleep. The baby was kicking, and she stroked her belly trying to soothe it. Every letter she wrote to Robert that summer would contain yet more lies and glaring omissions. She wouldn't ever be able to tell him what was foremost on her mind. There was nothing she could write that was true, apart from the fact that she missed him. And then after the baby was adopted and they were reunited, their marriage would be founded on a huge lie. When they had a child of their own, she would have to pretend to him that it was her first pregnancy. She would have to swear the presiding doctor to secrecy. And if, heaven forbid, she needed a Caesarean, she would have to keep her belly concealed or invent some other procedure that might have necessitated such surgery. A problem with her ovaries perhaps?

It all felt horribly wrong, but she knew that she had no choice. If it came out in society that she had an illegitimate child, she would be ostracised both in England and America. Robert would either have to divorce her or forfeit his own position, his business connections, and possibly his relationship with his family. In that situation he would surely divorce her. When he found out she wasn't the honest, intelligent girl he'd thought she was, he would fall out of love faster than he had fallen into it.

There was no course she could take other than the one she was already on. She just wished time would speed up and the months would pass quickly so that it would all soon be over and she could relegate her pregnancy to the shadowy realms of ancient history.

Chapter Fifty-Three

Reg had very mixed feelings about his flirtation with Molly. On the one hand, he enjoyed their stolen kisses in corners. It made the working day more interesting. He might be alone in the dining room, polishing cutlery, and she'd arrive with her dusters, check the coast was clear then sweep him into a passionate embrace. When he emerged from the washroom, he'd sometimes find her skulking down the corridor, and they always had their tête-à-têtes on the back step after dinner. It was fun, and arousing, and she was a pretty girl.

On the other hand, he was worried about anyone else in the house finding out. It didn't seem appropriate. There had only been around twenty female staff on the *Titanic* but it would have been a sackable offence to get involved with any of them. Management would not have looked kindly on it, no matter the circumstances, and Reg worried that the same standards might apply in service. Also, he didn't entirely trust Molly since finding her stealing from Mr Grayling's wallet. If she could do that, what else was she capable of? And might she drag him into trouble with her?

Above all, Reg knew she wasn't his type. She was fun to be with but he would never marry a girl who was quite so bold and brash. He liked girls who were quieter and more refined. Like Florence. Thinking about her caused him a physical pain.

If only that transatlantic telephone line they'd speculated about were in service already and he could talk to her, just for ten minutes, he felt she would give him wise advice. He'd have given anything to hear the sound of her voice, but of course it wasn't possible. She must hate him now. He'd promised to write and hadn't. He'd sat down several times with pen and paper but the words simply wouldn't come. What a cad she must think him. He couldn't bear to think about that.

Instead, he tried to imagine what John might say about Molly. 'She's a looker, in't she? Why not go for it? You deserve a bit of fun after what you've been through.'

She was only the second girl Reg had ever kissed. Most of the lads on the ship had kissed dozens – or at least they boasted they had. It's what young men did. Why should he feel bad about it?

'Do you have any plans, John?' Molly asked. 'Are you going to stay in service or do you want to go back to Sherry's when the strike is over?'

He told her about his idea of opening a restaurant one day and straight away she said she'd like to help. 'I could be your maître d' and greet all the diners when they come. I'd be good at that. Everybody says I'm a friendly girl. Don't you think I'm friendly?'

Reg agreed that she was. He didn't tell her he was planning a small-scale venture, too humble for a maître d', and that when he pictured it, he certainly couldn't see Molly there.

She remained obsessed by Miss Hamilton and Mr Grayling's behaviour on board the *Titanic*, and while they waited for her sister to report back about Lifeboat 6, she asked Reg many more questions.

'Where was Miss Hamilton's cabin on the ship? Was it near the Graylings'?'

316

Reg didn't know, but he fetched his newspaper with the list of survivors to confirm that she had been in first class. He ran his finger down the page, but the alphabetical list leapt from Hamalainen to Hansen. He looked again in case it was out of order. 'This is strange,' he told Molly, and she hurried to peer over his shoulder. 'She's not listed here.'

'No kidding! I guess if you are a married man's mistress, you don't use your real name. But who is she then?'

Reg fetched the page that listed the occupants of the life-boats, and there in Lifeboat 5 was Mr Grayling's name – but which one was his glamorous companion? Several women were listed as travelling alone, but some sounded German, two had obviously Jewish names and when he cross-referred between lists he found that the rest appeared to have left family behind on the ship. Perhaps, like him, Miss Hamilton hadn't given her real name to the man doing the roll call on the *Carpathia*? Perhaps she wasn't on any records. The full list of passengers and their cabin allocations didn't appear to have survived so there was no way of checking.

'I wonder if Hamilton is even her real name? Those parcels of clothes and jewels that were delivered here for her – what name did they have on them?' Reg asked.

'Mr Grayling's. He paid for them. Don't you worry, I'm going to keep an eye on her from now on,' Molly averred. 'I'll figure it out if it's the last thing I do.'

In fact, Reg was the next one to see something odd. One afternoon, he was walking down the hall outside Mr Grayling's study. The door was ajar and he heard a noise from within. He believed Mr Grayling to be out and assumed it was Molly, but when he peeked cautiously round the edge of the door he saw Mr Grayling with his face cupped in his hands, seeming distressed. He wasn't crying exactly but his shoulders were shaking and he was moaning. A small side drawer was open in the desk in front of him and he was staring at something inside.

As Reg watched, he sighed abruptly and pushed the drawer shut then turned a key in the lock. He placed the key inside the pages of a thick red almanac, then slid it into the bookshelf behind him. Reg stepped backwards as silently as he could, praying the floorboards wouldn't creak.

Perhaps there had been something to do with his wife in that drawer. Perhaps he was upset about her loss after all but chose not to display it in public. That made Reg feel a little more respect for him, although on the negative side there was still the matter of his affair with Miss Hamilton.

She was spending increasing amounts of time at the house, and was even found there sometimes when Mr Grayling was out. One blazing hot afternoon she rang the bell and asked Reg to bring her some iced lemonade in the drawing room. When he arrived with the tray he found her fanning herself in the faint breeze coming through the open window. She seemed drowsy with the heat and lay sprawled against cushions with her hair tousled and her legs spread in a quite unladylike manner.

Reg put the lemonade on a little table by her side. 'Will that be all, miss?'

'I was just thinking about the *Titanic*,' she said dreamily. 'Lots of men are ashamed to be survivors. Do you feel that way?'

'No, not really.'

'It's silly, isn't it? How could men wait until they were sure every single woman and child was rescued before getting on a lifeboat? They would all have drowned and what good would that have done?'

'Indeed, miss.' He guessed she was talking about Mr Grayling. This must be something he brooded about.

'Has it changed you, John? Do you think it has made you a different person? Have your plans for the future altered?'

'I suppose so. Yes, miss. I've decided to stay in America instead of going home, so that's a change.'

She wasn't listening to him, caught up in her own thoughts. 'Surely it makes sense after a near-fatal accident to create the next generation so as to continue your bloodline? That would be a reasonable reaction. Do you think you will marry and have children soon?'

Reg was embarrassed by the personal line of questioning and mumbled something noncommittal.

'Come now.' She turned the full power of her deep blue gaze on him. 'You are an attractive boy and must have many admirers. I've heard that young Molly is keen on you.' Reg coloured. 'Didn't you know? Surely it can come as no surprise?'

He looked at the carpet, unsure what to say in response. How did she know about that? Who had been gossiping? Could Molly have told her? It was as if Miss Hamilton was drunk with the heat and normal barriers had broken down.

'How long do you think one should know a woman before proposing marriage to her?' she asked. 'What is your opinion?'

'I can't rightly say, miss, seeing as I'm not married myself. I suppose some people wait a year or so?' She made a tutting sound and he felt she wanted another answer, so he continued: 'I heard that Lady Juliette Mason-Parker, who was on the *Titanic*, has become engaged to a gentleman she met on the *Carpathia*. The announcement was in the newspaper.'

Miss Hamilton sat up. 'Dowdy old Juliette? Really? Who on earth is marrying her?'

Reg was surprised to hear that they knew each other. 'A Mr Robert Graham. He's American.'

'Well, well. *She* didn't waste any time.'

Emboldened by her candour, Reg asked how she knew Juliette.

'We used to have a few friends in common.'

'You didn't see her on the *Titanic*? I never noticed you in the first-class dining saloon, miss.'

She gave him a sharp look. 'I stayed in my cabin for most of the voyage. There are times when you want to escape from society . . . I simply wasn't in the mood for it.'

'I saw you one night,' Reg volunteered. 'I was on the way down from the bridge and I saw you throwing your fur coat overboard. I nearly came to offer assistance because it seemed such a strange thing to do.'

She was alert now, listening carefully. 'If you must know, it was a present from an old beau and I couldn't bear the associations. It made my flesh crawl.' She shuddered. 'Were you watching me for long?'

Reg coloured. 'No, miss, I was on an errand taking tea to the bridge, so I couldn't stop.' He hoped he had convinced her. He didn't want Mr Grayling to know he had seen them kissing.

She took a sip of her lemonade, leaving a red lipstick smile on the glass. 'I suppose you have been to America several times before, John.'

'Yes, a few times.'

'You'll know all about American society then. It's a very complicated business.'

'So I believe, miss. Is it your first visit here?'

'No, I was at finishing school in New York for a year. Madeleine Astor and I were there at the same time. It was a ghastly place!'

'But you like New York? Are you planning to stay?' Reg would never have been so forward with an upper-class lady if she hadn't introduced the conversational tone and seemed to want to chat. Suddenly her eyes narrowed, as if she felt she had given too much away.

'That will be all,' she said in a tone of annoyance, and gave a little wave of dismissal.

'Thank you, miss.' Reg bowed and left the room, dying to track down Molly and tell her what he had heard.

He found her in the kitchen. As he walked in, Alphonse was feeding her a spoonful of the sauce he was preparing for that evening. Molly jumped back when she saw Reg and it spilled down her chin.

'You scared me, sneaking in like that!' she exclaimed, wiping her chin with the back of her hand.

'Guess what?' Reg announced. 'I've just been chatting with Miss Hamilton and she was quizzing me about how long I thought it should be before men proposed marriage. You must be right, Molly. She's hoping for Mr Grayling to propose, and she's getting impatient that it's taking so long.'

Molly used a corner of her apron to clean her hand. 'Why was she asking you, I wonder? What do *you* know about proposing?' She laughed. 'But wouldn't it be great if they did get married? We could all go to the wedding and wait on their glamorous friends. I bet that *she* has some glamorous friends, even if he doesn't.'

'I expect she does. She says she went to finishing school with Madeleine Astor, here in New York.'

'Miss Spence's school? Well, isn't that interesting.'

Alphonse was banging pots again. 'You two are very bad,' he snarled. '*Faux-culs.*'

Molly winked impertinently at him, made a face at Reg and mouthed 'See you later' then flounced off to do some housework.

'Can I help with anything?' Reg asked Alphonse.

'Yes.' He threw a bag of carrots on the table. 'I want these *julienne*-style, very thin, so long.' He held out his finger and thumb to show the length.

Reg peeled the carrots, aware from the crashing sounds coming from the stove that Alphonse was still in a bad mood. He began to chop the carrots into little matchsticks and Alphonse came over to supervise.

'*Non! Idiot!* Not like that.' In a temper he grabbed the handle of the knife to demonstrate how it should be done and the blade slid across the palm of Reg's hand. He yelled in pain and looked down. Blood was oozing from a side-to-side cut just below the base of his fingers.

'*Merde!*' Alphonse exclaimed, and went to find the first aid box, but he didn't once say sorry.

Chapter Fifty-Four

Annie hadn't realised how hot it would be in New York in the summer. As she climbed those infernal steps to the apartment every day, carrying the baby, leading Roisin, and with umpteen bags of groceries in her hands, the sweat was pouring off her. She bought a straw sunhat, but it didn't help much. She only had to step out into the sun's glare and she was instantly slicked with a film of moisture. Inside the house was like a furnace, even with all the windows open, and she had to keep drying her hands and face on towels to avoid getting perspiration on the expensive fabrics she embroidered. She'd never thought she would miss the rain that swept in off the Atlantic most days back in Cork, but now she yearned for the freshness of it.

The only place where it was cool was in the church. The cold stone walls and floors and the high vaulted ceiling kept the air at a bearable temperature, and she looked forward to cooling down there during her daily visit. As well as looking after the flowers, she volunteered to sweep the floors on alternate days, and Father Kelly often came over for a chat.

'How are you managing, Annie?' he asked one day.

'This heat is something else!' she exclaimed. 'I don't know how you all cope with it.'

'Personally, I stay indoors. But I meant to ask how you are in yourself?'

'There's good days and bad days.' She felt the tears coming and attacked a cobweb in the corner of a pew to drive them away.

'On the good days, what is it that makes them good? Is there something you can pinpoint that might help on the bad ones? Some thought, or action?'

'Well . . .' she hesitated. 'I don't know if the Church would think this wrong or not, Father, but I talk to Finbarr in my head. Sometimes it really feels as if he is there, answering me.' She stopped to control herself, determined not to cry, then continued. 'I suppose the good days are the ones when I feel he is here with me, and the bad days are the ones when I can't feel him.'

'I wouldn't call that wrong, if it brings you comfort.' He paused, choosing his words carefully. 'Do you believe that Finbarr's spirit is genuinely with you on those good days?'

'I wonder about it, Father. It feels as though he is, not just from his words in my head, but also a sense of his presence around me. Sometimes I think I can even smell the scent of his hair. But I know that the brain can play tricks when you are grieving, and maybe mine is letting me believe his spirit is here so as to get me through this period. I know it's against the teachings of the Church, but I *want* to believe it.'

'Of course you do. And you are right that the Church has pronounced against spiritualism, but I think that's because they were concerned about the charlatans and showmen it attracted. Tell me, when you talk to Finbarr in your head, does he answer you directly?'

'Not always, but a lot of the time it appears he does.'

'And do you talk to any other spirits in your head?'

'Goodness no, Father. I wouldn't do that.' Annie was shocked.

He sat down on the end of a pew. 'I am going to speak to you in confidence now, because this is not official Church doctrine, but I have personally attended a séance at which my mother's spirit came through.' Annie stopped sweeping and stared at him in astonishment. 'There was no doubt it was her. She called me Figgy, which was her pet name for me when I was a boy. My Christian name is Fergus but when I was little I used to call myself Figgy and it stuck. That's something no one in this country could possibly have known. She also talked about a little black and white dog we used to have. It was a profound experience for me, as you can imagine, and it forced me to re-examine my beliefs and the teachings of the Church. But I found that nowhere in the Bible does it say it is a sin to contact those who are in heaven. I expect there are only a few people who have what they call the 'second sight' but if such a gift is given to them by God, and so long as they use it responsibly, I can't see any harm in it.'

'Can it be true? Do you really think it could be Finbarr speaking in my head?'

'I believe it could be,' Father Kelly replied.

'What did you call it, the thing when you spoke to your mother – a séance? What happened at that?'

'I was invited to the house of a Spanish woman who lives about a mile from here. We sat across a table with linked hands, and she concentrated hard, asking the spirits if there was anyone on the other side who would like to speak to me. And then my mother's spirit came through. She spoke to the medium, who repeated the words to me because I couldn't hear her directly, although I was sure, just as you describe with Finbarr, that I could feel her presence in the room.'

Hope swelled in Annie's heart. 'I want to try it. I want to have a séance with this woman. Will you tell me how to contact her, Father?' She was quite definite.

'Perhaps you should discuss it with Seamus first.'

'No. He wouldn't feel the same way I do. He's a no-nonsense, practical man. If I try and it works, I might tell him, but not otherwise. He would just say, "Oh Annie, stop with all yer imagining."'

Father Kelly nodded. 'All right. I will contact this woman – her name is Pepita – and I'll ask when she might consent to see you. But I will come with you for the appointment because I know you are going to find it a very emotional experience.'

Annie was glad of that. She would have been scared to go on her own. As it was, she felt nervous enough when she got on the streetcar with Father Kelly to head to the woman's home.

Pepita was shorter than Annie, with dark hair that she wore loose down her back, and heavy eyebrows above bright hazel eyes. She kept glancing at Annie with a curious expression as she led them down a corridor and into a parlour, which had a round table in the centre. The shutters were closed but she lit a candle and they sat in chairs next to each other. She closed her eyes and remained still, without speaking, for several minutes. Annie glanced at Father Kelly, and he nodded to show this was the normal procedure, and smiled encouragement.

'Now we can link hands,' Pepita said, in a heavy, lisping accent, 'and you can tell me why you are here today.'

Annie cleared her throat. 'I'm hoping to contact my son, Finbarr, who died . . .' She couldn't finish the sentence for a catch in her throat. It was always difficult to say those words.

Pepita sounded surprised. 'But Finbarr is here with you. I could see him by your side as you came in the door. He tells me that he talks to you all the time.'

Annie started to cry, but they were tears of joy. 'I thought so but I didn't know for sure.' Father Kelly squeezed her hand.

'You have the second sight yourself,' Pepita continued. 'I knew it as soon as I saw you. But now that you are here, I am happy to act as a medium if you have any questions you want to ask Finbarr.'

'Is he OK? Is he happy?' Annie asked immediately, through her tears.

Pepita was quiet for a moment, as if listening for the answer. 'He says you know he is. He is in a beautiful place where there is no sadness but he wants to help you to find a way through your grief and that is why he is coming back to visit you.'

Annie cried even harder at that. 'He told me he is with my da. Is that right?'

'Of course it is. Spirits only speak the truth. I can see an older man in the background.'

'How does he look?'

'Finbarr? I can see black hair and a cheeky smile.'

'That's him,' Annie agreed.

'Are his front teeth a bit squint?'

'Yes, that's right. He fell off a rock at Youghal beach and knocked his baby teeth out and we didn't think he'd get any big teeth, but then he did, only they were a bit sideways.'

Pepita started murmuring something, and Annie strained to hear. She moaned as if in pain, but Father Kelly pressed with his thumb on Annie's hand to reassure her.

'He wants you to know he's sorry . . . On the ship, he heard some people talking about the water gushing in and he wanted to see it . . . He tried to follow you but then he got lost . . .'

'Ask him what happened at the end,' Annie requested, barely breathing.

Pepita paused. 'He says he jumped out into the blackness and he remembers being under the water but then he saw a white light and when he looked closely, your pa was there so he pushed his way through the water towards him. He says it didn't hurt. He wasn't scared, not even for one moment.'

Annie's tears were dripping down her face and she had to let go of Father Kelly's hand to find a handkerchief.

'You don't need me,' Pepita told her. 'Any time you want to ask Finbarr something, just go to a quiet corner and ask him yourself. He might not answer straight away but he will get back to you before long.'

'Thank you so much. You don't know how much this means to me.'

On the way home, she felt lighter than she had since the sinking. Mostly they walked in silence, but at one stage she turned to ask Father Kelly a question.

'Did Pepita know beforehand that I'd lost a child on the *Titanic*?'

'I'm not sure,' he replied. 'She might have been in church that time when I told the congregation what happened to Finbarr and asked them to pray for him.'

'But how could she have known that he had black hair and squint teeth? She couldn't have known that.'

For her, that was the proof. Pepita could have learned the other facts elsewhere, but there were no photographs of Finbarr in existence. Only his family knew what he looked like.

When she told Seamus about it later, he said, 'But Annie, nine out of ten children have squint teeth. Whose are perfectly straight? And *you've* got black hair, so that was a pretty safe bet.'

'She's not a charlatan, Seamus. She knew Father Kelly's pet name from childhood, and she knew he had a dog as well. She was very good, and she didn't ask for any money.'

'Uh-huh,' he nodded. 'Oh well, then.'

But she could tell from his eyes that he didn't believe her.

Chapter Fifty-Five

Reg let everyone think the cut on his hand was his own fault, a clumsy accident when chopping vegetables. Mr Frank was concerned, and insisted on rebandaging it himself after dabbing it with a solution of lye. Reg nearly jumped through the roof it stung so much. Molly was offhand about it, merely calling him a 'crazy guy'.

She had become obsessed with finding out more about Miss Hamilton, and proposed they should go down to Miss Spence's school and make enquiries.

'They wouldn't tell us anything,' Reg insisted.

'They might. And if she's going to be my next mistress – and that's looking pretty likely – then I want to know everything about her. If she and Mr Grayling were up to no good on the *Titanic*, I want to know. Especially if they are murderers. We might not be safe in our beds.'

Somehow Mr Frank caught wind of the discussions going on below stairs, and he gathered the entire staff in the kitchen for a stern talk.

'Some of you will have observed that Mr Grayling has formed a close friendship with Miss Hamilton and that she frequently visits the house. I think it likely that an engagement will be announced after a suitable period of mourning for the late Mrs Grayling, but in the meantime if I hear that any word of their attachment has reached the outside world, the person responsible will be fired immediately.' He thumped his fist on the kitchen table. 'And I don't want to hear of any more speculation about it in the house. Is that clear?'

'Yes, Mr Frank,' they murmured in unison.

'That includes you, Molly.' He glared at her.

Molly was not deterred, though. Every time Reg went out to the back step for a cigarette, she would appear with some new theory. It got so he didn't have a minute's peace during the day.

'Maybe she committed some crime in England and she's on the run. Can you remember anything from the newspapers about a rich lady poisoning somebody, or stealing stuff?'

'Look, just leave it alone,' Reg said, eyeing the back door nervously. 'I like a detective story as much as the next man, but you'll put our jobs on the line if you carry on like this.'

'You must be kidding. They'll never fire us. We know too much already.'

She leaned over to kiss him but at just that moment he turned to draw on his cigarette and the kiss landed on his ear. There was a crashing sound behind them as Alphonse pushed the door open so hard it clattered against the wall. He glared at them and Reg wondered if he had seen the kiss or just overheard part of the conversation.

'Luncheon is served in one minute.' He stomped back into the kitchen.

'Molly, you must be more careful. People could see us,' Reg hissed.

'So wha-at?' she drawled.

Lunch was fillets of sole served in a cream sauce and it looked delectable, but when Reg picked up his fork and took the first bite, it tasted very salty. It wasn't like Alphonse to oversalt the food. Usually the seasoning was perfect. He glanced round the table but everyone else appeared to be eating with relish. Maybe he was imagining it? Reg took another bite, but it was virtually inedible. He didn't like to say anything to Alphonse for fear of hurting his feelings, so he poured himself a glass of water from the jug and managed to eat his meal, taking a swallow of water after each mouthful.

As he watched the others eating quite happily, the suspicion entered his head that it was only his food that had been oversalted. He glanced at Alphonse, but the big Frenchman's face was inscrutable. *He's a loyal employee and doesn't like Molly and me scheming behind Mr Grayling's back*, Reg decided. *That's why he's cross with us.*

Later that afternoon, when they were on their own, Reg decided to try and clear the air with Alphonse. 'I owe you an apology,' he began. 'I know you don't like it when Molly and I discuss Mr Grayling and Miss Hamilton, and you're quite right. We shouldn't be doing it. You have my word that it won't happen again.'

Alphonse grunted.

'I've told her I want nothing more to do with her secret scheming. Please can we forget about it and start again?' Reg held out his hand. 'Like gentlemen?'

'*D'accord.*' Alphonse shook his hand with a firm grip, a mischievous glint in his eyes.

'About the fish at lunch,' Reg commented. 'That was an unusual recipe. Maybe not such a big portion for me next time though?'

Alphonse laughed and turned back to his cooking, but he seemed more relaxed. He even sang a catchy song, 'Sur le pont d'Avignon', as he prepared dinner, explaining to Reg that it was about dancing on a bridge and that each verse introduced new characters: shoemakers, laundresses, musicians and soldiers. 'My mother used to sing it to me,' he explained.

Afterwards Reg couldn't get the tune of the chorus out of his head, and found himself humming it as he went to bed that night.

He told Molly about his promise to Alphonse, and insisted that he didn't want to indulge in idle gossip any more, but when she came back from meeting her sister the following Sunday, she drew him to one side in the hallway.

'Mrs Grayling wasn't on Lifeboat 6,' she hissed urgently. 'Mrs Rothschild was one of the first ones to get on board and she didn't see her all night. What do you think about that?'

Reg got goose bumps all up his arms. If she hadn't been on that boat, which one could she have been on? The others on the starboard side all left *after* Lifeboat 5, with Mr Grayling on board. 'She must have been sitting in another one that was delayed for some reason,' he suggested. 'Maybe there was a problem with the davits.'

'You can believe that if you want to. I know what I think,' Molly said darkly. She grabbed his jacket and tried to drag him into the cloakroom for a kiss, but Reg moved away.

'I've been sent to the cellar for some wine,' he told her. 'Better not tarry.'

He might not want to discuss it with Molly any longer, but that didn't stop Reg mulling things over in his own head. The next afternoon when he had a few hours off, he went for a walk and his feet led him down to Times Square and along West 44th Street, where Molly had mentioned Miss Spence's school was situated. He wasn't planning to go in and make enquiries. He just wanted to have a look, out of idle curiosity.

It was a smart grey stone building with arched windows and balconies on the first floor. As Reg watched, a teacher led out some young girls wearing white smocks over their clothing, and they walked in crocodile formation to another building down the block. There was a little walled garden adjoining the school and Reg sneaked a look through the railings. Several girls in their late teens sat chatting under the shade of the trees. They were impeccably dressed young ladies, obviously the products of upper-class families. One of them had an open, friendly face that reminded him of Florence, and it gave him a start. He hadn't thought about her for a while. It was easier not to.

He walked to the end of the street, where there were industrial docks on the Hudson River, before looping back towards the house again.

As he approached, Mrs Oliver, one of the cleaners, was polishing the brass fittings on the front door.

'You've got visitors,' she called to Reg. 'They're waiting in the kitchen.'

Panic gripped him. *Who could it be? Who knew he was there?* His mind raced frantically, before he decided it must be Tony from Sherry's. Tony was the only person who knew where he was. He must have dropped in with one of his friends. Perhaps they had come to tell him the waiters' strike was over and he could return to work at the restaurant. Either that or it might be Danny O'Brien from the ship. He hoped it wasn't Danny because he'd tell them he wasn't John Hitchens, and that would put the cat among the pigeons.

He opened the back door and walked through to the kitchen. Sitting at the table were a woman and a girl he had never seen in his life before. Alphonse had given them coffee and cake. Everyone turned to look at him expectantly.

'Is our John with you?' the woman asked, in a broad Geordie accent.

Reg's knees gave way and he clutched at the kitchen sink to stop himself collapsing.

Chapter Fifty-Six

'This *is* John,' Molly said, to fill the stunned silence in the kitchen.

'No, John Hitchens, I mean. He was on the *Titanic*. White Star Line told us he was working at Sherry's and Sherry's told us he was working here.' The woman had an edge of agitation in her voice.

Everyone turned to look at Reg and for a moment he considered running out the back door, and keeping on running for as long as he could.

'He's my son,' she explained, 'but I haven't heard from him since the sinking, even though I know he survived. He's on the list of survivors.'

Reg couldn't speak for the colossal weight of shame. How could he have been so stupid? What had he done to this poor woman?

'*This* is John Hitchens,' Molly said carefully, 'and he was on the *Titanic*.' She turned to Reg. 'Did two of you have the same name? It would be terrible if it turns out they've come all this way for the wrong guy.'

At last Reg found his voice. 'Alphonse, Molly, do you think you could leave us alone for a while? I need to talk to Mrs Hitchens on her own.'

Molly didn't want to leave. She wanted to be part of this conversation, which promised to be juicy, but Reg insisted. Alphonse warned that he would need to come back in twenty minutes, no more, to check on some meat that was roasting. As the door closed behind them, Reg slumped heavily in a chair and leaned his head in his hands. He couldn't bear to look the visitors in the eye.

'I am so sorry,' he said. 'I wrote to you. Didn't you get the letter?'

'What letter?'

'I sent it to you at West Road, Newcastle, but I didn't know the number. I was sure it would get there.'

'West Road is one of the longest roads in the city. We never got any letter from you. What did it say?'

Reg could barely speak for his shame. 'I can't tell you how sorry I am. I've done something unforgivable and I didn't even realise it till now. John was my best friend and I took his name after the sinking. I've been pretending to be him. But I'm not. My name is Reg Parton.'

The woman was shaking her head in bafflement. 'I don't understand. Why would you do that?'

'I wanted to get work in New York and John had a clean record while I didn't.'

There was a pause while she took this in. 'So where is John then? Whose record is he using?'

The girl spoke for the first time. 'He's dead, isn't he? That's why you used his name. That's what you wrote to tell us.'

Reg nodded slowly. 'I'm so sorry. I don't know what happened to him when the ship went down but he didn't make it onto the *Carpathia*.'

'He *must* be here,' John's mother insisted. 'We've come all the way from Newcastle to find him because White Star told us he was here. They were quite certain of it.'

'That's because they believe that *I* am John. I don't know what I was thinking of. I can't begin to explain this to you . . .'

335

What was wrong with him? John had said they weren't close, but family was still family. It was unbelievably cruel to steal a dead man's identity.

'I'm his sister, Mary,' the girl explained, and when he looked at her, he could see it was true because John's features were there, albeit with a more feminine twist. 'Are you absolutely sure he couldn't be alive somewhere else? Maybe *he* took another name as well.'

'I searched the *Carpathia* from top to bottom. I looked everywhere for him. I was devastated when I couldn't find him. He was my best friend in the world.'

'I know. He mentioned you in letters.' The girl gave a huge sigh and it caught in her throat and turned into a sob. 'He was very fond of you.'

John's mother still couldn't believe it. 'White Star told us he was here. There must be some mistake. We've spent all the money we had in the world coming to find him. We thought he must be too shook up to get in touch. We wrote to him and sent the letters to White Star but he never replied.'

'I didn't get the letters,' Reg told them. 'If I had, I'd have written back and told you the truth. I'll reimburse you for your fares. I'll give you all my savings and I'll keep sending you money until I've paid off everything you've spent. I promise.'

John's mother was pale and her face tight, as the truth began to dawn on her. 'I don't want your *money*,' she cried, her voice getting louder. 'I want my *son*!'

Mary was crying silently, and Reg felt such a deep shame that he wished himself dead. If only he had gone down with the ship as well. Since then, nothing in his life had gone right and it was entirely his own fault. He couldn't think straight. His head was full of fog and he'd made all the wrong decisions.

He'd left his brain in the North Atlantic.

'I wish there was something I could do, something I could say, to make this better, but there isn't. I would do anything,' he pleaded.

'Bring me back my son!' John's mother shouted, angry now, and Mr Frank opened the kitchen door and stepped into the room. He looked from one face to another, trying to fathom the cause of the ruckus.

'What's going on?' he asked quietly.

'He's impersonating my son John. We've come all this way and John is dead. I don't know how he could do that.' John's mother started crying, with huge sobs that made her chest heave.

Her daughter tugged at her arm and said, 'Let's go back to the hotel, Ma. We need to be alone.'

Mr Frank barely glanced at Reg, just addressing them. 'Ladies, please allow me to get our driver to take you to your hotel. You are too distressed to walk the streets. Come with me and I'll show you out the front.'

The women rose to their feet and Reg watched them go. John's sister gave him one last look of reproach, but he was frozen to the spot. Alphonse came in to check his meat. He gave Reg a searching look and patted him briefly on the shoulder but didn't say anything.

Reg sat there without moving for more than ten minutes. He could hear Mr Frank talking to the women in the hall upstairs, then the front door opening. He was in a hole so deep that he didn't believe he would ever be able to climb out again. How could he have been so thoughtless? He'd blithely assumed the postman would deliver that letter and hadn't bothered to check. He could have written to them care of White Star in Southampton – that would have reached them – but instead he'd just put them out of his mind. It was evil, that's what it was. He deserved to die. Just as soon as he could, he decided he would find a way to kill himself. That was the only solution. That way, he could put an end to all this misery.

Mr Frank was tight-lipped when he came back into the kitchen. 'I think we'd better go upstairs and explain this to Mr Grayling, don't you?'

Reg staggered as he stood up and would have fallen over if Alphonse hadn't caught his arm.

Chapter Fifty-Seven

Mr Grayling was in his office. Mr Frank tapped on the door and led Reg in.

'Excuse me, sir. We have an unusual situation here. Can you spare a few moments?'

'Of course. Sit down.'

Mr Frank pointed Reg towards a chair then sat himself and began his explanation. 'Two women came to the house looking for John Hitchens. They are his mother and sister, recently arrived from England to look for him, but it seems that this is not John. He is someone else who has been using John's name, and the real John is dead. Am I right?' He turned to Reg, and Reg nodded, his head hung in shame.

Mr Grayling frowned and sat back in his chair. 'What's your real name?' he asked sternly.

Reg told him.

'And why in God's name did you lie about it?'

In a shaking voice, Reg explained that a mistake had been made in the roll call on the *Carpathia* and he hadn't corrected it because he wanted to start a new life with a clean sheet. He'd written to tell John's family but the letter hadn't arrived and it never occurred to him for one moment that they would try to track him down. He was devastated at the turn of events, he whispered. He didn't know how he would be able to live with himself.

'Tell me about your record with White Star,' Mr Grayling demanded. 'Was it so bad?'

Reg explained about his misdemeanours, and Mr Grayling exchanged a look with Mr Frank.

'I see,' he said, and tapped his finger on the desk while he considered the situation. 'I should dismiss you on the spot for lying to us. Don't you agree, Mr Frank?'

Mr Frank said nothing, but the two men continued to look each other in the eye.

'However, I feel a sense of responsibility for you now. Everyone who was on the *Titanic* is struggling to come to terms with it, and I see you are having more trouble than most. But if you are to remain in my employment I need to be sure you will not tell me any more lies.'

Reg was trembling. 'I . . . I can't carry on, sir.'

'You have to carry on, Reg,' Mr Frank told him firmly, but his tone wasn't unkind. 'You have to keep working so you can repay these women every penny they've spent coming here, including the cost of their hotel and sustenance. I told them I will send you down there to talk to them tomorrow.'

'I can't.' Reg's eyes welled up. 'They can have all my savings, all my wages, but I can't face them again.'

'It's the very least you can do,' Mr Frank told him. 'When they get over the shock, they are going to want to hear the whole story and anything you know about what happened to John. You owe it to them to tell them every last detail.'

Reg covered his face with his hands and started to cry bitterly. He was crying for what he'd done to John's family, and crying for himself, but most of all he was crying because he missed John so badly. The wound hadn't begun to heal and maybe it never would.

Mr Grayling spoke to Mr Frank. 'I think we need to keep an eye on him tonight. He's in a bad way. To be honest, he's not the only person I've heard about who took on a different identity on the ship. The Duff Gordons booked themselves under the name of 'Morgan' and there were supposedly a number of card sharps travelling under assumed names. I'm sure the survivors list has many errors in it because everyone on the *Carpathia* was in a state of shock and the chap going round with the roll call wasn't the world's brightest spark. Come, come, lad. Pull yourself together.'

Reg took out his handkerchief to wipe his eyes and struggled to regain control. How humiliating to cry in front of his employer. What must they think of him? Before the *Titanic* sank, the last time he'd cried was as a young boy. Now he couldn't seem to turn off the waterworks.

Mr Grayling continued: 'So, tomorrow you will go and visit these women and tell them everything they want to know. Make sure you get the correct address in England so you can send them some money every month until they've been reimbursed. You can't ever make it up to them fully, but they will be able to see how remorseful you are, and that will help.'

'Yes, sir. I will.'

'Next week we are going to my summer house on Long Island for a vacation and I think the sea air will do you good. Tonight you may take the evening off your duties. Go to your room and rest. Someone will bring your dinner on a tray, and I'll see you at breakfast tomorrow.'

Reg went upstairs and lay on his bed, watching the sky gradually darken through the skylight. Molly came up with a tray of food and slammed it on the chest, snapping, 'Here you go, *Reg*' in a tone that showed she had heard the news and was furious

341

with him. He could see how it must look to her. They'd been speculating about Miss Hamilton taking an assumed name, and all the time Reg had one himself. He had kissed Molly on several occasions, yet he hadn't trusted her enough to tell her his name. No wonder she was cross.

He couldn't eat, couldn't take so much as a sip of water. Suicide was the most appealing of the options in front of him, but he couldn't do that until he had reimbursed the Hitchens family. In the meantime, it looked as though he would have to go to Long Island with Mr Grayling, but that was a terrifying prospect as well. To get to an island he assumed they would have to go on a boat, and he still had a terror of water. Whenever he thought about it, he could feel the ocean gushing over his head, swallowing him up, and the burning pain in his lungs as he struggled for the surface.

I thought I had reached the depths of misery on the Carpathia, Reg thought. *But that was nothing compared to how I feel now.*

Chapter Fifty-Eight

In Saratoga Springs, the temperature shot up into the nineties and Juliette's belly grew bigger by the day. She didn't sleep well at night, partly because of the heat and partly because her bump wouldn't allow her to lie in her favourite face-down, spread-eagle position any more. During the day, she went for short walks in the vicinity of the cottage but was usually driven back by biting insects. The air was thick with buzzing, stinging, flapping creatures and before long her face and hands were covered in swollen, itchy lumps.

'Rub your skin with some lemon juice before you go outside,' Edna advised, and that helped a little but wasn't foolproof. Some of the 'little critters', as Edna called them, seemed to have a taste for lemon.

They had brought books with them but it was hard to summon the concentration for reading. The entire focus of Juliette's day lay in writing a letter to Robert and waiting for the mail to arrive so she could read his replies. They were her umbilical cord with the outside world where people went out for dinner and rode horses and formed friendships and fell in love.

Robert wrote about his business, about the choking heat of the city, about a young niece who was visiting town whom he had promised to show around, and about events in the news. Captain Scott still had not been found and all parties

343

had given up hope of finding him alive. The US government had instituted an eight-hour working day and many companies feared it would put them out of business. And during an eventful marathon at the Summer Olympic Games in Stockholm one runner went missing while another died of a heart attack. At the end of his letters, Robert never failed to say how much he loved her and was looking forward to seeing her again.

Juliette pored over the *New York Times* so she had interesting items to write back to him about. She devised witty descriptions of the biting creatures who were so desperate for her blood. She wrote about her family, drawing character sketches of each. In one letter, she described the cynical way in which Venetia, an old acquaintance, had seduced her brother Wills two years previously, hoping to get him to propose – until she found out that the Mason-Parker estate had a lot of land and property but not enough cash to keep her in ballgowns and jewels, at which point she promptly disappeared. Juliette wrote that Wills had become cynical about women since then, seeing them as scheming, heartless, untrustworthy creatures, and had not entered into any further affairs of the heart.

When she finished the letter she sat back to read it through and was overcome with guilt. Wasn't she being a scheming, untrustworthy creature herself? Who was she to say that of another woman? The difference between her and Venetia was that she loved Robert whereas her erstwhile friend had only ever loved herself, but there were times when it felt like a fine line. How could she trick Robert when she cared about him so deeply? She ran through the arguments again, but always came up with the same conclusion – that she had no choice.

More than two months after it sank, women's magazines still dwelt endlessly on the *Titanic*. Each issue had a new story about the plight of some passenger or other. Juliette read about Ida Straus, who had refused point blank to leave her husband of forty-one years. Many had heard her announcing 'We have been together these many years. Where you go, I go.' Juliette decided that she would almost certainly have insisted on staying behind with Robert, because when she was with him she felt safe. On the other hand, he would mostly likely have tried to order her into a lifeboat, as many other husbands had done.

What was strange was that it all felt like a story now, rather than something that had happened to her only ten weeks earlier.

'Do you still think much about the *Titanic*, Mother?' she asked over luncheon.

'Of course. Every morning when I wake up, I look for my mother's locket and when it's not there by my bedside it makes me start the day in a melancholy frame of mind. It was all I had left of her that was personal.'

Juliette hadn't known her grandmother, who died before she was born, but she suddenly realised how much her mother must have loved her. When Lady Mason-Parker complained on board the *Carpathia* about the loss of her family jewellery, Juliette had been embarrassed by her seeming crassness in the light of the huge losses others had suffered. But now she could see that it wasn't so much the objects themselves as what they represented that her mother mourned.

Perhaps, if nothing else, they would come to a greater understanding of each other during this summer of forced detention. Perhaps they would even become friends.

Chapter Fifty-Nine

Mr Frank insisted that Mr Grayling's chauffeur drove Reg downtown to the hotel in which John's mother and sister were staying. It wasn't far from the hostel where he had slept on the first night he came ashore. He took with him all the money he had in the world: Mrs Grayling's five pounds, the three pounds ten shillings which were John's final salary from White Star, and almost fifty dollars he had saved on his own account. He reckoned that should cover the cost of their tickets across to America if they had come in a third-class cabin, but he would need to save as much again for the return trip and more besides for their hotel bill.

On the way, Reg didn't plan what he would say. All he could do now was be completely, uncompromisingly honest, and apologise from the bottom of his heart.

The women were expecting him and he was shown into a dingy drawing room. They'd chosen a very cheap hotel. Both were red-eyed and looked as though they hadn't slept much, but Mary rose to shake his hand in greeting.

'I'm sorry if we got you into trouble at your work yesterday,' she began. 'We were in such shock we weren't thinking about your position.'

'Please,' Reg begged them. 'Please, whatever you do, don't apologise to me. If I were to apologise to you a million times it could never be enough for what I've done to you and your family.'

'Sit down, lad. If you don't mind, we have a lot of questions for you, but first I'll ask if they can bring us some tea. We have a lot of talking to do and I don't want us getting dry in the throat.'

Reg took a seat opposite John's mother, self-consciously smoothing his jacket.

'You look all in,' she commented. 'It was a bad night for us all. I know you and John were great pals to each other. He said you used to go swimming, and he told us wherever you went the girls were always chasing after you.'

'That's not true,' Reg shook his head, but he described to them the friendship they'd had, from the night when John first helped him get the dessert trolley out of his bunk. He told them about the hours they spent exploring foreign ports, and the way they looked out for each other on board, and he said he had always hoped to persuade John to help him start his own restaurant one day, the two of them in business as partners.

'He'd have liked that,' his mother nodded. 'I could see him going for that.'

His sister Mary asked, 'We don't want to upset you, but would you mind telling us what happened to John after the *Titanic* hit the iceberg? When did you last see him?'

Reg told them about bumping into John on the boat deck about an hour after the collision and their plan to swim to one of the half-empty lifeboats. They'd been scared, but thought they could make it since they were both strong swimmers. 'We wanted to stick together, but then we were sent on errands and I promised an Irish woman that I would look out for her son, who was missing, and when I got back up on deck I couldn't see John anywhere. We'd said we'd meet at the captain's bridge but as far as I could see he wasn't there. And then the ship started to go under and we had to jump. I don't know where he was then.'

'He didn't make it to any of the lifeboats?' Reg shook his head sadly.

'Mary and I were trying to decide this morning whether to go up to Halifax and put up a headstone for him there, among the other crew from the ship, or to have one for him back home in Newcastle. What do you think he would have liked, Reg?'

I think he would have liked to be alive, Reg thought to himself, but he answered tactfully: 'Newcastle. Near his family. That's where he'd want to be – with the living rather than the dead.'

'Aye, you're probably right. That's what we'll do then.'

Reg explained as well as he could about the way his mind had been working when he gave John's name on the *Carpathia* and then decided to pretend to be John. He told them about his fear of the water now, which meant he couldn't return to England even if he wanted to. He described the fogginess in his head and the difficulty he had making any decisions.

'Your mum must have had a right scare when she saw your name on the list of the dead. Did you manage to get word to her before the lists were published?' Mary asked.

Reg looked down at his lap and the guilt flooded over him yet again. These weren't the only people he had hurt with his self-ish actions. There were his mother, his brothers, and Florence. His Florence. 'I sent a telegram the day after we docked but I haven't written since.'

The women were aghast. 'She must be worried sick about you.' They stared at each other and then at him, in open-mouthed disbelief.

'Do you not get on with her?' Mary asked.

'We're not very close, but it wasn't that. I couldn't think what to say because I'm not sure what I'm doing here or how long I'm staying.'

'All you needed to say was that. She'll be imagining all sorts.'

He was the most selfish person in the world, he now realised. Everything had been about him and what he wanted, with no thought to those he'd left behind.

'You have to make amends. You need to write to her, lad.'

'She'll never forgive me,' Reg told them. 'She'll hate me.'

'She might be furious but her anger won't be as strong as her relief. I'm speaking as a mother myself. You write a letter apologising and trying to explain. She'll understand, just as we do.'

'I had a girl back home, called Florence. We'd been stepping out for two years and she hoped we were going to be married. I need to write to her too.'

Mary gave him a withering look. 'If you have your letters ready soon, we could take them for you. We're going home on the next ship we can get a place on. We have to tell John's father, you see. He's waiting for news.'

Reg clasped his forehead. *Another person he had hurt.* 'I'm so sorry,' he repeated. 'I know it can't compensate in any way, but I've brought you all the money I have.' He handed it to Mary, who put it on a table without counting it. 'If you give me your address I'll send you more every month to cover the cost of your trip.'

The women looked at each other. 'We talked about it this morning and decided that we'll take this money from you, if only to make you feel better. We'll put it towards John's headstone and get him a fancy one. He'd be happy you'd done that.'

Least you could do, man, Reg imagined him saying.

'I can't explain properly why I did all this,' he told them, 'but in a funny way I felt as though the old Reg died on the *Titanic*.

I haven't been myself since then. I'm scared of everything, and I never used to be. Life feels unreal. I've missed John so much and I've got no friends here, not real friends. I sometimes wish I went down with the ship as well.'

'Don't you ever say that again!' John's mother was cross with him for the first time that morning. 'You are young and strong with your whole life ahead of you, and if I hear of you doing anything silly, I will never forgive you. You know what I'm talking about.' She glared into his eyes. 'You write your letters, send your money, make your amends, then pick yourself up and start living again.'

As he walked back to Madison Avenue, Reg wondered why John hadn't been close to his family. They seemed like incredible people to him. How could they forgive what he'd done to them? How could they be kind to him after that? Maybe independent types like him and John needed to break away from their families first before they could look back and appreciate them. Maybe his own mother was a good woman who had struggled to do her best in difficult circumstances after his dad left, and if she never seemed to pay him any attention, it was because she had no energy left after working to feed and clothe them and looking after the younger ones. Maybe he had been uncharitable in his opinion of her.

Back at the house, he wasn't surprised to find that the story had got around and hardly anyone was speaking to him. Mr Frank asked if everything had gone as well as could be expected at the meeting, and Reg said yes, he thought so. Molly and Alphonse turned their backs when he walked into the kitchen, and the other staff ignored him as well. When he served luncheon to Mr Grayling and Miss Hamilton, he could feel her eyes on him and he suspected she had been told what had happened.

The only thing Mr Grayling said to him was that he was taking legal advice on how to get Reg immigration papers in the correct name. It might take a while to resolve. Reg gave him the surviving fragments of his old passport and thanked him humbly for his trouble.

That afternoon when he had a couple of hours free, he sat down to write to his mum and Florence. 'Dear Mother,' he wrote, then stopped. These were going to be the hardest letters he would ever have to write in his life.

Chapter Sixty

———◆———

Annie couldn't stop thinking about the séance and analysing everything the medium had said to her. Whenever she had a quiet moment, she began asking Finbarr questions in her head, and more often than not she found the answers came to her.

'Can you see your brothers and sister?' she asked. 'And your da?'

'I can't see them in the way you mean, but I have a sense of them. I know when they are happy and when they are sad, just as I do with you.'

'Do you eat food up there in heaven?'

'We don't need food any more.'

'How do you spend your time?'

'We don't have time here in the way you understand it. Everything is different.'

A part of her kept questioning whether she was simply making up answers in her head, but she was desperate to believe it was Finbarr. If that were true, it would be as if he were in the next room, just out of sight but still with her. He could never finish his education and get a good job, or meet a girl, get married and have a family of his own; his death was still a huge tragedy. But if his spirit was genuinely able to speak to her, the loss would be a little easier to bear.

She told Father Kelly about her deliberations. 'I ask a question and wait and the answer comes into my head, but how can I tell whether Finbarr put it there or if I imagined it myself?'

'You'll only find that out when a spirit tells you something you couldn't possibly have known otherwise. Is there anything like that you could ask Finbarr?'

Annie racked her brains. 'I could ask whether it was him who ate the bacon I left out for his father's supper one night, and not a dog that ran in from the street, as he claimed. But no matter what answer came to me, I wouldn't know for sure if it was the truth.'

'I have an idea. Pepita said that you have the second sight yourself. Why don't we conduct our own séance and you could try to get in touch with my mother? You don't know anything about her, so if you came up with any fact that is true, it would have to be coming from the spirits. That would prove it.'

'I couldn't possibly, Father.' Annie was embarrassed. She'd feel like a fool. It wouldn't seem right to intrude in a priest's personal life like that.

'I'm interested in finding answers, Annie. You'd be doing me a favour by helping with my research. No matter what is said in the course of the séance, it won't affect our relationship as priest and parishioner, if that's what you're worried about. Will you give it a try?'

'But I wouldn't know what to do. Pepita seemed to have some way of getting in touch with spirits, but I wouldn't have a clue where to start.'

'I've questioned her about that, and she says she just clears her head of other thoughts then asks if any spirits want to communicate. You could try that.'

Annie didn't like to refuse, but she had serious misgivings. It felt as though it would be sacrilegious to conduct a séance with a priest. She would be uncomfortable if she discovered any personal information about him, but on the other hand she would feel she had let him down if nothing transpired. He seemed dead set on the plan, though, so she agreed to try it one afternoon while Roisin and Ciaran were being looked after by a neighbour. She was dreading it.

At the appointed time, she walked down the step street and along to the house where the Father lived with a housekeeper and a curate. He opened the door and led her into the dining room, a small room dominated by a table, with just enough space for chairs round the sides. He had already closed the shutters and placed a candle in the centre of the table, and as he led her in, he produced some matches and struck one to make a flame.

Annie was trembling as she sat down, but she made an effort to still her thoughts and empty her head of worries. It was hard. The more she tried to imagine her head as an empty space, the more thoughts came flooding into it. What would she make for dinner that night? Was she running out of flour? Did she remember to give her neighbour a change of nappy for Ciaran? Diapers, they called them here.

Father Kelly took both of her hands in his, and she closed her eyes and began to ask the question in her head: *Are there any spirits out there who want to communicate with Father Kelly?*

For a while, nothing came to her except a jumble of mixed-up thoughts. She tried to focus on what she knew about the man she was sitting with, and suddenly a thought came through that was louder and clearer than the others.

'It's not enough to be good. You have to be perfect.'

354

She didn't know where it had come from, but she repeated it out loud.

Father Kelly gasped. 'That's exactly what my father used to say to me. Is he there?'

'I don't know,' Annie replied. In her head she asked 'Are you Father Kelly's father?' but no answer came. She couldn't hear anything else, but she felt she had to say more. 'He's very proud of you. You're a credit to him.'

Father Kelly squeezed her hands, and she could tell he was moved, so she continued. 'He says you are to look after your own health, that you worry too much about other people instead of yourself.' In fact, this was something Annie often thought about the Father, but he was nodding and pursing his lips as though it all made sense.

I mustn't lie to him. He is doing honest research. She scanned her brain for any possible communication from a spirit, but all she could think about was her own embarrassment, the spluttering of the candle and a niggling pain in her right knee.

'I'm not getting any more,' she told him, after a while.

'That's fine,' he said. 'What you did was very impressive for a first attempt. You certainly have the gift, Annie.'

He rose to open the shutters and light filled the room. She saw that one wall was lined with huge books on religious subjects. They had serious titles – *Summa Theologica, Apologetics, A Dissertation on Miracles* – that made her feel even more of a fraud.

She tried to backtrack. 'I'm not sure it's a gift, Father. They're just thoughts that come into my head. I can't hear voices. I didn't hear a man's voice when you thought it was your father. I just repeated what I was thinking.'

'But I believe that's the key to it. That seems to be how it works. I have no doubt at all that my father spoke through you.'

He smiled at her, his eyes twinkling. 'You hadn't any idea you were so talented, did you? Was there no one else in the family who had the second sight?'

'I don't think so, Father.' She shook her head, running through all the aunties and grandparents she could remember.

'I wonder if you might be willing to talk to any of my other parishioners who are struggling to cope with a bereavement? The combination of the wisdom you have gained from your own experience, plus your ability to talk to spirits, could surely help folk through their dark times. Is it something you would consider, Annie? You could hold séances in this room so they don't have to come to your home. I would sit in when I have time.'

'Oh, really, Father, I don't feel I could be any use . . .'

'Of course you could! Think how much comfort you have gained from talking to Finbarr. You have the power in your hands to give that same comfort to others who are grieving. It would be a Christian thing to do.'

Despite her unease, Annie promised she would think it over. That evening, once the children were all sound asleep, she told Seamus about it, and he was deeply troubled.

'You'd be playing with the feelings of vulnerable people going through the worst of times. You could upset them more if you said the wrong thing. What if they felt you hadn't been able to contact their relative? They'd think "Why is he or she not getting in touch?" and feel slighted. In my view it's a dangerous game.'

'I know, but what if I just told them general things – "Your ma is at peace, she's looking down on you, she wants you to take care o' yerself." They might find that helpful.'

'People will want more. They'll ask you direct questions and you won't have the answers so you'll make things up to try and satisfy them. I don't like it a bit, Annie. It's dishonest.'

356

'I know. I agree with you.'

The problem was that she didn't see how she could possibly refuse Father Kelly without appearing selfish. He had made it sound as though it was her Christian duty. It was a troubling dilemma. She wished she had never mentioned to Father Kelly that she talked to Finbarr. She wished she had kept it entirely to herself.

Chapter Sixty-One

Reg completed the letter to his mother – a simple recitation of the facts followed by a heartfelt apology for the distress he had caused – but found he couldn't write the one to Florence. He started dozens of times, then ripped the paper into pieces because it sounded wrong. He wanted to send both letters at the same time so that one of them didn't arrive before the other, but he couldn't find the words to write Florence's letter. The problem was that he couldn't bear for her to hate him, and every time he imagined her reading his letter that was the only reaction he could predict: fury, followed by hatred. The days went by and it was too late to send them with John's mother and sister. A week passed and still he couldn't find the words.

After Molly's initial condemnation, her curiosity got the better of her and she tried to wheedle the story of his assumed name out of Reg, but he saw her in a different light now. She was a dishonest, gossiping troublemaker, and he should never have kissed her or told her anything about Mr Grayling and Miss Hamilton. He resolved to keep his distance, but it was easier said than done when they worked in the same house. She was like a dog with a bone as she tried to get him to talk about things.

'You should have told Mr Grayling that he's one to talk about false names when his own paramour did the same thing on the *Titanic*,' she insisted. 'I wouldn't have been able to keep my mouth shut. He's got some nerve.'

'I wouldn't dream of saying anything of the sort.' Reg glanced at Alphonse. His back was turned but Reg could tell from the set of his shoulders that he was unhappy with the subject of conversation.

'But what if it turns out he was a murderer? If he killed Mrs Grayling, I would like to know. Maybe none of us are safe in our beds.'

Reg was surprised she was talking this way in front of Alphonse and realised she must have told him all about it. 'That's a bit far-fetched, Molly. He's an upper-class gentleman and they simply don't do things like that.'

Molly folded her arms and quoted a story that had been in the papers the previous year about a man who murdered his wife's maid. Reg was caught up in his own thoughts and wasn't really listening. He couldn't bring himself to believe Mr Grayling was a murderer, but he knew he had a secret he wanted to protect. That's why he hadn't sacked Reg. That's probably why he felt 'protective' towards him – so that Reg wouldn't go back to that reporter and tell him he'd got it all wrong about Mrs Grayling being on a lifeboat, and what's more that Mr Grayling had a young girlfriend on the *Titanic* with him. He'd never risk Reg telling anyone about that.

Molly sensed she had lost Reg's interest. He no longer followed her into cupboards for a quick kiss when she beckoned, and if she joined him on the back step he quickly finished his cigarette and came indoors. All the same he was surprised when, the day before they were due to leave for Long Island, he walked into the kitchen and found her kissing Alphonse. He almost laughed out loud, because Alphonse was at least a foot taller than her and had to bend at an ungainly angle to reach her lips. As she broke away, Molly gave Reg a calculating look.

She wanted me to see that, he thought. *She wants me to be jealous.*

In fact, his main emotion was relief. Thank goodness her attentions were directed elsewhere now. Alphonse looked happy and was humming 'Sur le pont d'Avignon' under his breath as he stirred the soup. *Good luck to them,* he thought.

That night, Reg lay in bed thinking about Molly, with all her tricks and subterfuges, and it made him miss Florence terribly. She would never have played any of those games and it wasn't fair that Reg was being dishonest with her. He couldn't hope for her forgiveness but he owed her a bit of honesty, if nothing else. He got out of bed, sat at his writing desk and wrote the letter in a great burst of emotion.

Dear Florence,

I'm sorry I haven't written before. I wanted to write lots of times but I couldn't do it because I couldn't bear you to hate me. I wish I could make you understand what I've been through but as you know I'm not a big writer.

Do you remember saying to me that when I'm upset I crawl inside my shell and hide from the world? Well, that's what I've been doing. On the Carpathia, *the man who took the roll call thought I was John, so I pretended to be him. John had died. I don't know what I was thinking. It was a terrible thing to do.*

John's mother and sister came out here to find him and it was only then I realised what I'd done to them. My brain is not working properly. Maybe it got damaged when I was in the water. They are wonderful people and seem to have forgiven me but I have not forgiven myself.

I think about you a lot and wish I could talk to you again but I can't face getting on a ship. The thought is terrifying. I have no choice but to stay here for now. Anyway, I'm not the person you used to know. I'm very shook up and I don't know if I'll ever get better again. I've got nothing to offer you any more, but I miss you and will always cherish the memories of the times we had together.

I hope for your sake that you find someone else who can give you everything you deserve. I hope you won't hate me too much. I will always love you and wish nothing but the best for you.

Your loving Reg.

As soon as he finished, he sealed and addressed the envelope without including a return address. He would give both letters to Mr Frank in the morning. He was staying behind to look after the New York house, so he could arrange for them to be mailed.

Afterwards, Reg couldn't get to sleep. He lay in bed worrying about the effect his letters would have. He tried not to think of Florence's face when she received it. He couldn't bear to hurt her. His younger brothers would feel terribly betrayed. Maybe he should have written separately to them as well. And goodness knows what his mother would do. She'd probably disown him.

On top of his concerns about the letters, he had a feeling of foreboding about the journey to Long Island. He hoped the crossing wouldn't take too long. All his worries swirled around his head, and when he eventually drifted off he dreamed that he was standing in a small boat as it sank inexorably beneath him. No one on shore could hear him even though he was screaming at the top of his voice.

Reg woke up with a dry throat and covered in sweat. Could he have yelled in his sleep? It felt as though he might have.

The dream seemed familiar and he realised he had had it many times since arriving in New York. It was a landscape that hovered in his subconscious even during waking hours.

Mr Grayling had two automobiles and he and Miss Hamilton were travelling in the front one, while five members of staff, including Reg, Molly and Alphonse, came along behind. They headed downtown through the New York traffic onto a huge bridge that crossed high above the East River, just near the quays where the *Carpathia* had docked. Suspension cables curved from two huge turrets at either end. It was a stunning construction and Reg turned from side to side as they crossed so he could take in the views on all sides.

'That's us on Long Island,' Molly announced as they drove off the bridge. 'My mom lives in Brooklyn, pretty close to here. My school was just over there, at the end of that road.' She pointed as they drove past.

'This is Long Island?' Reg queried. 'We don't have to go on a boat?'

'No, silly. Just the bridge. Long Island is huge. It's way more than a hundred miles long, all the way up to Montauk Point. It'll be at least two hours until we get to the summer house. You'll like it there. It's right on the beach. *You* like it, don't you, Alphonse? I can't wait to get away from the hot city.'

Alphonse shrugged. 'It's OK. Good seafood. We have our own pots for lobster in the bay.'

The buildings were thinning out and Reg could see green fields and trees. The air smelled cleaner and fresher already as they sped away from the city smog. They stopped at a diner for luncheon, and Reg ordered a hot dog. He'd developed a taste for them.

'Did you know they have a hot dog eating contest on Coney Island every summer?' Molly asked. 'You could sign up, Reg,

362

but I warn you that the guy who won last year ate sixty-two hot dogs in ten minutes. Think you could beat that?'

Reg smiled. 'I doubt it.'

'Oh look, they've got Pepsi-Cola! I'm going to try one of those. Did you know it's supposed to be good for you? It gives you energy.' She ordered the drink and when it arrived, she took a long slurp. 'Taste it, Reg.' She flicked the straw towards him. 'It's yummy.'

Reg was curious, so he took a quick sip and found the drink was pleasantly sweet and refreshing.

'Get one for yourself if you want,' Molly suggested. 'Mr Grayling gave Alphonse lots of cash to buy our lunch.'

Reg did as she suggested and drank a whole glassful. He wasn't sure if it gave him energy or not, but he felt relaxed as they continued the journey and he smelled the first hint of salt in the air. The ocean came into view, a deceptively warm shade of blue stretching out to the horizon, quite different from the oil-black, freezing water in which Reg had almost drowned back in April. All the same he shivered.

The houses along the shore were further apart now, and between them and the ocean there was a pale sand beach licked by frilly white waves. Small groups of bathers were paddling in the water, or sitting on the beach shaded by huge umbrellas.

At last they pulled up outside a white, two-storey clapboard house surrounded by a lawn and a low white picket fence. Like the house in New York it was square and boxy, but there was a long verandah on the ocean side and the garden butted right onto the beach. It was a peaceful spot, not overlooked by any other houses and when the driver turned off the engine, the only sound was the shushing of waves on the sand.

Molly jumped out of the car. 'Come and look at the beach, Reg. The water's lovely. I've brought a bathing suit. Maybe we can go swimming later. Do you like swimming?' Alphonse nudged her in the ribs and she stopped. 'What? What do you want?'

Reg hurriedly picked up his bag. 'I think I'll just go in and unpack. Thanks all the same.'

As he walked off, he heard Alphonse remonstrating with her. 'He was on the *Titanic* three months ago. You think he wants to jump in the water and have a swim? You must be crazy.'

'He might. How would I know?' she replied in a sulky tone.

Chapter Sixty-Two

Mr Grayling hadn't been to the house since the previous summer but the caretaker, a man named Fred, lived there all year round to keep an eye on it, and he'd made sure it was cleaned and prepared for their arrival. When Reg wandered in through the kitchen entrance carrying his bag, it was Fred who showed him to his room. He could have been any age between forty and seventy, with the deeply tanned, weather-beaten face of a man of the sea, topped by bristles of silver hair.

'You're the new footman? I am putting you on the first floor, near the garage. It's only a little room but you probably won't be in there much.'

There was a single bed, a chest of drawers and a wooden chair under the window, which looked inland towards the coast road.

'This is fine, thanks.'

All the staff would share one bathroom, while there was another for Mr Grayling and Miss Hamilton on the first floor, where they had adjoining bedrooms. *Are they sleeping in the same bed?* Reg wondered. *Surely not? What upper-class lady would risk her reputation by staying in a situation like this without a chaperone?* It was most unusual. He'd never heard of the like.

When he wandered into the kitchen, Alphonse was unpacking a big box of provisions he'd brought from New York, so

Reg set to helping him. As he worked, he realised they could hear Mr Grayling and Miss Hamilton talking on the verandah. Their voices drifted in through the open window.

'Won't you come for a sea bathe, George? I'm sweltering after the journey but I don't want to go on my own.'

'I'll sit on the beach and watch you, my dear.'

'Plea-se,' she wheedled, drawing out the syllable. 'Aren't you simply boiling?'

'I don't like sea bathing. The water's cold and the salt makes your skin itch. But I would very much like to watch you.'

'Oh, you killjoy! Very well. I'll go on my own but if I am eaten by a shark it will be all your fault.'

Alphonse and Reg caught eyes, and Alphonse raised his eyebrows.

Ten minutes later, Reg wandered out the kitchen door to a little yard where laundry was hung to dry. Miss Hamilton was in the ocean, shrieking as she jumped over waves. She picked up a clump of brown seaweed and hurled it in the direction of Mr Grayling, who rolled over on the sand to get out of the way.

'You'll have to try harder than that,' he yelled.

Suddenly Miss Hamilton emerged from the water, her navy-blue swimsuit clinging to her tiny figure. She sprinted up the sand to drop a frond of seaweed directly on his balding head, where it lay like a lock of new brown hair, before running back to the water again, out of reach of his flailing arms.

'Touching, isn't it?' Molly whispered close by.

Reg grunted noncommittally. He had been thinking about Mrs Grayling. Did she often come to this summer house while she was alive? Did she enjoy sea bathing? Miss Hamilton had stepped extremely quickly into a dead woman's shoes. Surely it must feel odd to her at the very least?

Looking around the summer house, Reg found a few items that he guessed must have belonged to its former mistress. Under a cupboard on the verandah, there was a pair of faded blue canvas plimsolls. There were still some grains of sand inside, and the insoles were worn into the shape of dainty feet. *Mrs Grayling's feet.* On a shelf, there was a collection of seashells: dark purply-blue mussel shells, ridged white clam shells, fluted pink and cream conches, and long white razor shells. *Presumably her collection.* On a bookshelf, there were some women's romance novels. *Also hers,* he guessed. The summer house hadn't been as efficiently stripped of her possessions as the house on Madison Avenue. The last time Mr Grayling had visited, he must have been there with his wife.

The next day, Reg found another object from the past. Alphonse was planning to boil some lobsters that had been hauled in from the bay. Their pincers groped the air, opening and closing, as they struggled to escape the tank into which they'd been thrown, and Reg gave them a wide berth.

'Find me the biggest pot you can,' Alphonse asked, so Reg got down on his hands and knees to explore the pot cupboard and there, in a corner at the very back, he found a child's rag doll. It was discoloured with mildew and covered in the remnants of spiders' webs, but he could make out blonde hair fashioned from strands of wool, a face painted on canvas fabric and a hand-knitted dress and coat.

'Whose was this, I wonder?' he asked Alphonse, holding it up.

Alphonse grunted without looking. He was preparing a hollandaise sauce, and didn't like to be disturbed at the tricky moment when he dripped wine vinegar and lemon juice into his egg and butter mixture.

Reg hauled out a large brass cauldron for the lobster and took the rag doll outside, to where Fred was repairing a lobster pot in the yard.

'I found this,' he said, holding it out. 'Could it have belonged to the Graylings' daughter?'

Fred looked up and his eyes widened. 'Aw heck, I was supposed to throw out all of Alice's things years ago.'

'Alice. Was that her name?'

Fred glanced around to check no one was listening. 'Yeah. Beautiful little thing, she was. When she died – must be seven years ago now – it broke their hearts clean in two.'

Reg got goose bumps, despite the warmth of the sun. He remembered the sadness in Mrs Grayling's eyes, which he had thought was caused by her troubled marriage. 'What happened?'

'Scarlet fever carried her off. Mr Grayling can't stand to be reminded of her. Thank goodness you found that doll and not him or I never would have heard the end of it.'

'What age was she when she died?'

'Seventeen, and one of the prettiest young gals you'll ever see. She took after her mother's side, not her father's,' he added in an aside. 'That Miss Hamilton was a school friend of hers. Came here with the family one summer.'

'Miss Hamilton!' Reg was flabbergasted. 'She was a friend of the family?'

'That's right. Everyone called her Vee back then, like the letter "V". She was always a bit snobby, if you ask me – just like she is now.'

'Are you sure it's the same girl? She can only have been a teenager.'

'They were both sixteen. It was the summer before Alice died. Those two were always giggling together, running along

368

the beach, or sitting on the verandah combing their hair dry after going swimming.'

So Miss Hamilton is twenty-four now, Reg calculated. *Older than he'd thought. Quite old for a woman to be unmarried. Many would consider her to be on the shelf.* 'I wonder why she has come here with Mr Grayling? It must be strange for her to return to a place where she used to be so happy with her friend.'

Fred tapped the side of his nose. 'Over the years I've learned not to wonder about the affairs of upper-class folk. They don't like it, and it does nobody any good. I have my own opinion about what's going on, and I have a hunch you do too.' He winked. 'But we'll keep it quiet, won't we?'

Reg was disappointed. He'd have liked to hear what Fred thought. But he put the rag doll in the garbage can and went back to help Alphonse. This made the situation in the house all the more bizarre. How could Mr Grayling be having an affair with a friend of his daughter's? It was almost akin to incest.

Alphonse had water bubbling in the pan, ready to cook the lobsters. He picked them up one by one just behind those lethal-looking front claws and placed them into the boiling water head first. Their tails flicked frantically as they tried to escape, but Alphonse put a lid on top to hold them there until he had the next one ready to drop in. Reg found it disturbing, but at the same time decided he'd like to try some if the staff were offered a taste of lobster for their meal.

He went to the drawing room to tell Mr Grayling and Miss Hamilton that dinner was served and as he approached, he overheard them quarrelling.

'It may well be the most stunning necklace in the world, but nothing is worth that much. Do you realise a working man could live quite comfortably for a *year* on five hundred dollars.'

369

Reg cleared his throat and tapped on the open door. 'Dinner, sir, miss.'

'We'll be right there.'

Everyone was living in much closer proximity than in the New York house and the walls were thinner, so Reg was able to hear their argument continue over dinner. Some of her friends had chartered a yacht in the Mediterranean and she wanted him to come with her on a cruise in September. He pointed out that it would still be only five months since his wife had died and far too soon for him to be seen in public with another woman. Besides, he had a business to run. She said she would die of boredom stuck out there on the beach for more than a few weeks, but that it was too unbearably hot to go back to the city. What did he expect her to do? They stopped bickering when Reg brought each course, but started again as soon as he closed the door, unaware that he could still hear them.

When the staff were summoned to eat, Reg was pleased to see that they each had half a lobster on their plates, smothered with Alphonse's creamy sauce. He took a bite of the tender meat, and it was divine: sweet yet with a hint of saltiness, and the texture was satisfyingly chewy.

'It's very good,' he told Alphonse.

'Of course,' the Frenchman agreed, in a tone that implied 'How could it possibly have been otherwise?'

Chapter Sixty-Three

The days when Juliette could wear a corset were long gone. Her waist had completely disappeared and her belly bulged as if she had a plump cushion secured under her petticoat.

'It's a girl,' Edna told her. 'I can always tell from the bulge. Boys have a rounder shape and stick out much lower. I've never been wrong yet.'

Juliette could clearly feel the creature moving now, and was amazed at this life form that she was nurturing with her own cells. The weight of it slowed her and made her back ache. Its kicking, in combination with the heat, kept her awake at night. She began to feel curious about the new little person who was forming fingers and toes, organs and bones inside her. What kind of personality would the child have? Who would it take after?

'Better not think about it,' her mother advised, 'or it will be harder to give it up when the time comes. I am its grandmother and I know I will feel the loss keenly, so it will be even worse for you, the mother.'

There was precious little else to think about, though. Every morning, Juliette rose early and took a walk in the fields round the house before the heat of the sun became too fierce. She ate her breakfast then sat on the verandah reading the newspaper, which their driver would fetch daily. She could make it stretch most of the morning if she read it from cover to cover, including the sports and business news. After luncheon, she would begin her letter to Robert, writing several drafts to make it as entertaining as she could. His own letter would arrive some time before afternoon tea, and she would reply to any questions he asked before sending the driver to the post office with hers, carefully copied out in a neat hand. Most of the time their letters arrived exactly four days after they were written, but on some agonising afternoons there would be no mail at all then the following day two letters would arrive together.

Juliette felt jealous of Robert's life. He had business meetings with interesting people, he could stop by his gentlemen's club and have a drink with friends, and he could dine out in New York's finest restaurants. The only people she saw were her mother and Edna, the driver and occasionally the doctor. Robert complained of the fiery heat of the city in late July and wrote about how much he missed her, but Juliette knew that there was a difference between the way he missed her and the way she missed him. His life was full, while she had nothing to do except miss him. She felt a profound loneliness, like a huge empty cavern within. Sometimes she paced from room to room feeling as though she would go mad with longing for him.

And then one morning, she spotted her own name in the newspaper's gossip column. Her eye was drawn down the page as if by magnetism. 'Lady Juliette Mason-Parker should consider cutting short her trip out of town and hurrying back to keep an eye on her fiancé, Mr Robert Graham. He was seen at the Poughkeepsie racetrack yesterday with a very fetching young actress on his arm, and the pair seemed inseparable.'

The pain felt as though someone had plunged a knife into her chest. 'No!' she screamed, so loudly that her mother came running. Juliette clutched her neck.

'What is it, dear?'

Juliette handed over the paper, pointing to the paragraph. Her mother sat down to read, and her face fell.

'I don't believe it! I've made so many wedding plans already. The church is booked and the invitation list drawn up . . .'

'Shut up!' Juliette screamed at her with such force that she hurt her throat. She rose and ran across the lawn down to the flowerbeds, where she would be out of earshot. She couldn't bear to listen to one more word from her mother's mouth. *Who could it be? He had never mentioned knowing any actresses. Could he have met someone at the theatre? Why hadn't he said?*

She walked along the flowerbed to the picket fence, racked with a hideous jealousy, the likes of which she had never experienced before. As a child she'd been jealous of her brother, because he was allowed to try activities that were forbidden to her and because he would one day inherit the estate while she would not, but that was nothing compared to the intense physical jealousy she felt when she thought of another woman kissing Robert, or lying in his arms. She wanted to rush straight back to town to confront him and make him promise that she was the only woman he made love to. If only the baby would come early. If only it would come *now*.

Suddenly she lifted her skirts, climbed over the picket fence and began to run full tilt across the field. Out of the corner of her eye she could see her mother frantically gesturing to come back but she ignored her. She leapt over rocks, swerved around trees and kept running as fast as she could with the midday heat pounding on her bare head. In the back of her mind was the reckless thought that maybe the exertion would bring on labour and she could get this child out of her. No matter that it was too premature to live. She began to get breathless and felt a sharp, stabbing pain in her side, which forced her to stop and bend double. Could it mean she was in labour? It felt more like a stitch. She slumped to the ground in the shade of a tree and leaned back against the trunk.

Had Robert got tired of waiting for her? Did he possess so little patience? Perhaps he was a Don Juan type who liked to carouse with many different ladies. She had only known him for three months, after all, and she hadn't met any of his friends. Maybe they would consider this normal behaviour in New York? But it didn't ring true of the man she loved. He was a gentle, honest soul – as far as she could make out.

He will read the newspaper, she decided, *and if he doesn't spot the item himself then someone will bring it to his attention. He knows that I read the same paper, so surely he will send me a telegram to explain that it's all a misunderstanding?* She wondered how long it would take to receive a telegram in Saratoga Springs that had been sent from New York. It could be delivered within a few hours, certainly by dinner time. She would wait.

On return to the house, she was bright red in the face and breathing heavily. Her mother wanted to call for the doctor but Juliette refused.

'I'm going to lie down for a while, and I don't want to discuss that article with you any further. There's obviously been some mistake.'

'I hope so,' her mother replied, pursing her lips as if dying to say 'I told you so'.

Juliette lay on her bed all afternoon, watching the minutes tick by and listening for the sound of the telegram boy's bicycle coming down the track towards their house. She should hear his bell, or the crunch of the tyres on loose stones. Edna brought tea on a tray but she refused to eat.

'Miss, if I might say something?' Edna ventured. 'Your mother told me what's upset you and even though it's perfectly understandable, you should know that the people who write such things often make mistakes, or don't know what they are talking about.'

Juliette was cross with her mother for discussing it with their housekeeper. What was the world coming to? But she took some comfort from the words. 'I still think he should send a telegram to explain it to me.'

'Maybe he will, or maybe he'll think it's beneath his notice.' Edna folded her stout arms.

'I suppose so.' She narrowed her eyes. 'Is there a telephone exchange in the town from which I could make a direct call to New York?'

'There's one on Main Street, but it's only open in the morning.'

'I can't risk it.' Juliette knew that Robert's sister was now on holiday close by. She had written giving her address in case Juliette was 'able to escape for an hour or two'. 'I'll have to wait for him to get in touch.'

Not only was there no telegram that day, but the mail didn't bring a letter either, and the fact that there were two the following day did little to reassure her. Later in the week he mentioned that he had attended the Poughkeepsie races but he wrote only of the horses, without mentioning any companion. His tone sounded more distant now and the letters were shorter, although he never failed to say at the end that he missed her.

He's slipping away from me, Juliette thought miserably. *We only had four days together as husband and wife. I can't lose him. It's not fair.*

Chapter Sixty-Four

From the first day at the summer house, Molly started flirting with Reg again, trying to resurrect their former intimacy. He kept her at arm's length, not least because he didn't want to tread on Alphonse's toes, and she soon became frustrated at his lack of response.

'What a stuffed shirt you are!' she jibed. 'Come for a walk on the beach. It's a beautiful day and they're flying kites over in the next bay.'

Reg pretended he had to polish some glasses, hoping that would get rid of her, but instead she hovered in the doorway to chat as he worked.

'Hey, guess what! I can hear Mr Grayling and Miss Hamilton upstairs at night,' she told him in a stage whisper. 'My bedroom is right underneath hers. Don't you want to know what they are up to?'

'It's none of our business,' Reg replied, but that didn't deter her.

'He's crazy as a bedbug about her, but she holds him back, saying he can't touch her until she has a ring on her finger.' She paused for effect, but Reg carried on polishing the wine glasses without comment. 'He thinks it's too soon after Mrs Grayling's death for him to get married again, but meanwhile she's costing him a fortune in jewellery and clothes and I get the feeling he's paid off lots of her debts from back home. There's no fool like an old fool, my mother always says.'

'And you've heard all this through the bedroom floorboards, have you?' Reg was dubious.

Molly shrugged. 'That, and when they're sitting inside while I do the housework. They've been arguing a lot since we got here. Didn't you even notice?'

Reg shrugged.

'Those glasses are sparkling like diamonds. If you polish them any more you'll wear the surface off. Won't you come out for a walk with me? I need to talk to you about something. Please? We don't have to go near the ocean if you don't want to.'

Reg really didn't want to be on his own with her. He glanced round, racking his brains for another job he could pretend was urgent. Alphonse had gone to market, Fred was fishing, and Mr Grayling and Miss Hamilton were sitting on the verandah reading the newspapers.

'What if they ring for something?' He gestured in the direction of the verandah.

'Mrs Oliver is upstairs. She'll tend to them.'

'OK, just for ten minutes,' he agreed at last. 'But I don't want to talk about Mr Grayling's affairs any more. I'm lucky I still have a job here and I don't want to push my luck.'

He didn't own any canvas deck shoes, so Molly persuaded him to strip off his leather lace-ups and socks and walk barefoot on the sand. It was very fine-milled, golden sand, which felt soft and cool between the toes. He rolled up his shirt sleeves, unfastened his top button and let the sea breeze ruffle his hair. Molly linked her arm through his and he felt uncomfortable but didn't like to push her away.

'It wasn't Mr Grayling I wanted to talk to you about,' she said, her voice low and husky. 'It was us. I'm sad that we're not friends any more, the way we used to be. I like you, Joh . . . I mean, Reg.' She laughed nervously. 'It's taking me a while to get used to your new name. You suit Reg better, though. It's a proper English name, isn't it?'

'I suppose so.' They walked along the top of the beach, with the spiky grass of the dunes to their left, but he kept glancing out towards the ocean. There were gentle little waves at the shoreline but beyond that there was a flat calm, just as there had been the night the *Titanic* sank. That was partly why they hadn't spotted the iceberg on time. Normally, waves lapping against a berg would have made it more visible, but there weren't any that night.

'What do you reckon? Can we start again?' Molly squeezed his arm and tilted her head to one side to look up at him with a girlish pleading expression.

Reg took a deep breath. 'Molly . . . I'm sorry. I should never have fooled around with you before. I don't want to get involved with any girls right now, and I don't feel right having a girl in the house where I work. Especially since there are so few of us here at the summer house. Everyone would notice.'

'Is it because of your girl back home?' she asked in a small voice. 'Are you still in love with her?'

Reg nodded. 'Yes, I love her, but it's not that. I just need to be on my own. Besides, I saw you with Alphonse. He seems keen on you.'

'Oh, *him*!' She waved her hand dismissively. 'He's always had a thing about me, but he's not my type. It's *you* I like.' She sniffed loudly, and he turned to see there were tears pooled

378

in her eyes, ready to spill over. 'Do you think I have a chance? When you are ready?'

Reg detached his arm from hers. He had to make himself clear once and for all. 'You deserve someone much better than me,' he told her. 'Look at you! You're pretty and clever and good at your job. You'll find a wonderful husband some day.'

'I have lots of plans for us, Reg. Let me tell you them, because you might change your mind.' He started to interrupt, to say that nothing would change his mind, but she talked over him. 'Remember when you told me that you want to open your own restaurant some day and I said I would help you in front of house? I think we'd make a great team. Well, I've been thinking of ways we could raise the money to get started and I've come up with a super idea.' She gave a self-conscious little laugh and turned to face him. He stopped walking. 'My idea is that we go to Mr Grayling together. We tell him that we know he didn't put his wife on a lifeboat on the *Titanic*. We know he was having an affair on the ship with a lady who is less than half his age. We know that there was no Miss Hamilton on the list of survivors, so she was using a fake name, which means she might be running away from something. We could say we suspect that he killed Mrs Grayling, but I don't think we need to. We'll have his attention by then. Anyway, we can say that if he doesn't pay up, we'll go to the newspapers together and spill the beans. We need to figure out how much cash we want. I don't know . . .'

'Stop!' Reg was shocked. He raised his open hand as if to push her away. 'Don't say another word.'

'I thought you'd be happy. It would take us years to save up enough money from our pay, but this would be a short cut. Nobody gets hurt. He has lots of money to spare. He wouldn't exactly miss a few thousand bucks.'

'It's blackmail. You can't seriously think I would go along with this. It's against the law. If he had any sense, he would call the police straight away.'

'But he can't, can he? That's the beauty of it all. He wouldn't even dream of calling the police.'

Reg regarded her with horror. She had absolutely no sense of morality. He knew his own standards had fallen well short of ideal recently, but what she was suggesting was criminal. Any guilt he had felt for leading her on faded at that moment.

'Molly, what you are suggesting is wrong and dangerous and I would never be a party to it. I want nothing to do with your plan, and I'll deny all knowledge if you say anything of the kind to Mr Grayling. Please keep away from me.' He turned to head back to the house.

'You're kidding, aren't you?' she called after him, sounding bemused. 'Think how easy it would be.'

He didn't reply but hurried along the sand, anxious to put physical distance between them. He noticed Alphonse standing on top of a dune and waved, but didn't go over to say hello.

Chapter Sixty-Five

Father Kelly knocked on the door one morning and asked Annie if she would consider conducting a séance for a woman whose two-year-old daughter had died of cholera the previous year.

'She's still beside herself with sorrow. The poor woman just keeps repeating to me that little Dorothy won't be able to look after herself in heaven, that she is too young to be without her mother, and all the wisdom I can offer from the Scriptures brings no relief. I told her about you and she has set her mind on meeting you and asking if you can contact her little girl.' Father Kelly smiled winningly. 'I understand your reluctance, but in this case I know you could do so much good just by telling the woman that her daughter is safe in heaven. Will you do it, Annie?'

Annie had severe misgivings but she had been brought up to believe that the parish priest was the next best thing to Jesus. Whatever he asked of you, you should do without argument because he knew best. That's what was in her mind when she said 'All right, Father. When would she like to meet me?'

'How about this afternoon? Three o'clock. At my house.'

At least that didn't give her much time to worry about it. She had some embroidery work to do that morning and after lunch the children could go to her neighbour. It would mean an extra journey up and down the step street, and Annie had been trying to keep them to once a day because her knees had begun to swell, especially the right one, but there was no getting around it.

She arrived at Father Kelly's house early and sat in the dining room on her own, trying to get into the right frame of mind for the séance. She imagined what it must be like to lose a two-year-old: just past baby stage and still so helpless that they wouldn't survive a day on their own without adult help. The little girl would barely be able to talk. How could Annie report what she was saying if it was all baby talk? She decided she would just have to use her instincts as a bereaved mother to judge what to say.

The woman who came into the room was shaking with nerves and Annie's heart went out to her.

'Please sit down. Take my hand.' She smiled warmly to show that she wasn't scary. You read in magazines about some mediums who spoke in strange voices and vomited a white airy substance called ectoplasm, but that would never be her style.

Father Kelly sat beside her and linked hands with the two of them. Annie gripped the woman's hand to try and calm her, then she bowed her head, closed her eyes and focused, just as Pepita had done. Instantly, she could hear the word 'Mama' in her head, with the accent on the second 'a', so she repeated it.

The woman gasped. 'That's what she called me. Just like that.'

Annie concentrated hard. 'I can see a tiny girl with a much older woman, perhaps her grandmother. She is sitting on her knee.'

'She must be with my mother,' the woman exclaimed.

Annie found some words in her brain and repeated them. 'Your mother says Dorothy is a little sweetheart. They play together every day. She says Dorothy comes to visit you when

382

you are on your own at home. She puts her arms round you but she is not sure if you feel it.'

'I do. Many times I've thought I felt her but I didn't dare to hope.' Annie could hear the woman was crying, so decided to keep the séance brief.

'Your mother wants you to start living your life again. She says none of this was your fault. There's nothing you could have done to save Dorothy. You will always carry this sadness, but there will be happy times as well if you let them in. She and Dorothy will be with you for ever, both in this world and the next.'

She opened her eyes and released the woman's hand to offer a handkerchief that she had thought to conceal up her sleeve. They chatted for a while afterwards, then as she stood up to say goodbye the woman grabbed Annie in a fierce embrace.

'You're a saint, so you are. You don't know what you've done for me.'

'I hope it helps,' Annie told her. The strain of her suffering was etched all over the woman's face. 'You look after yourself now.'

In retrospect, she felt it had probably been the right thing to do. Father Kelly certainly thought so.

'You have great sensitivity and compassion,' he said. 'Seeing the way you handled her, I would have no hesitation in recommending you to others.'

'Please, not too many, Father; only those who are in most need. It's very hard for me.'

Stepping into another woman's grief had been arduous, taking her into some of her own darkest moments. She knew only too well that desperate yearning for one last hug with your child, and the guilt that you had failed as a mother because you were unable to protect them through to adulthood. These were feelings that tortured her every day.

When Annie got back to the apartment she felt utterly drained. She sat and stared out the window for half an hour without seeing anything, unable to concentrate on her embroidery or talk to Finbarr or think a single coherent thought, until Patrick came home from school saying he was famished.

Once she had given one reading, the requests began to flood in. That woman must have talked to her friends, who passed it on, and it seemed everyone in the parish knew someone in heaven they wanted her to contact. Even with Father Kelly acting as gatekeeper, she was overwhelmed by the demand for her services.

'I will do one séance a week,' she told him firmly, 'but they will all be brief. I will leave it to you to choose the most deserving candidate.'

Most of her readings were for women who had lost husbands or children, but occasionally a man came. By concentrating and listening hard, Annie found she almost always had a picture in her brain and sometimes words came into her head as well, so she passed them on. She discovered that the recipients wanted to believe so fervently that they never doubted her ability. Without fail, they were grateful for the comfort she offered.

Word spread beyond their little parish. Camille Ozaney, the dressmaker for whom Annie did the embroidery, told some of her upper-class customers and instantly a fresh avalanche of requests for readings came through to Father Kelly. Most of them he turned down, especially if the person concerned was not Catholic, but there was one he asked her to consider: Mrs Marian Sheldon was a wealthy Park Avenue lady whose husband had died on the *Titanic*, and she hadn't set foot out of her house since then. She was so overcome with grief that she barely got out of her bed and her doctor was seriously concerned for her health. She would give anything for Annie to come to her home and conduct a séance there, and Father Kelly strongly urged her to do it.

'Her husband didn't make it onto a lifeboat and she's worried that maybe he is still alive somewhere but has lost his memory. He was last seen on deck with two of his friends, and their bodies have been found but not his. She hopes that you will be able to tell her once and for all if he is dead or alive. Of course, he must be dead. . .'

'I can't tell her that.'

'Of course you can, Annie. You didn't find Finbarr's body but you know his spirit is no longer on this earth. All you need do is give the same certainty to Mrs Sheldon.'

So insistent was he that Annie began to wonder whether some donation to the church had been promised. Under the circumstances, she felt she had no choice but to agree. Mrs Sheldon said that her driver would collect her and bring her home again afterwards so that was at least one less thing to worry about.

Annie wore her Sunday best for the trip to Manhattan. She was nervous getting into the shiny automobile that stopped down at the bottom of her step street. The only other time she'd been in one was the night they arrived in New York. She found it much more comfortable than taking a tram, and a much smoother ride than in a pony and cart. Finbarr would have loved it. He'd always been fascinated by motor cars.

They pulled up outside a huge house with all the shutters drawn. Inside there was an air of melancholy, with dust motes dancing in shafts of light that crept round the edges of the shutters, and a heavy silence, broken only by the chiming of a clock every quarter hour. The carpets were deep and luxurious, just as they had been in the *Titanic*'s first-class dining room, but there were no bouquets of flowers or glittering chandeliers. Everything was sombre.

The butler led Annie upstairs to a small bedsitting room where there was a table with a candle already burning. A woman sat behind the candle. At first, from her slumped posture and the shawl pulled tight around her shoulders, Annie thought she must be elderly, but as she drew closer, she realised Mrs Sheldon's face was unlined. She was probably only in her twenties.

Annie sat down and greeted the woman before taking both her hands. She didn't stop to chat but bowed her head and began to concentrate hard. She thought about those last moments on the *Titanic*'s decks. She had visualised what it must have been like so many times that she could see it clearly in her mind's eye. Then she pictured a well-dressed man in his twenties or thirties, and a scene came into her head.

'He's wearing a dinner suit. There's a pocket watch in his waistcoat pocket.'

Mrs Sheldon gave a little gasp. 'That's him!'

'He is helping women onto lifeboats, offering his arm to assist them across the slanting deck. He's talking to them, helping to reassure them.' The picture changed. 'Now he is standing with two friends. They're holding onto the railings. He's not afraid. They are joking with each other.' Suddenly Annie could hear some words in her head, and she repeated them verbatim. 'It's the darnedest thing, Marian. A wave swept across but I didn't even feel how cold it was. I was instantly in another world where it is light and beautiful, and I knew I had died but it was easy to pass over. It wasn't hard.'

There was the sound of a strangled sob from across the table.

Annie continued repeating the words that came into her head. 'My dear, you must get up and face the world again. You are spoiling your own health. You are young and beautiful and I want you to remarry, as soon as you are ready. Choose a good man, have children with him, and name the first son after me, if you will. I will watch over you and yours until we meet again.'

The woman was breathing heavily, and Annie decided that was enough. 'He's gone now,' she said, releasing her hands. 'I hope you heard what you wanted to know.'

'That was incredible!' Mrs Sheldon said, clearly stunned. 'Not only did you speak in his words but your voice began to sound like his. I can't tell you what a relief it is finally to know the truth. Thank you from the bottom of my heart.'

A footman brought a tray of lemonade and Mrs Sheldon asked Annie about her family, about Finbarr and about her life in Kingsbridge. She offered money, which Annie refused to take.

'My husband and I have discussed it and we feel very strongly that we should not profit from séances,' she explained. 'It wouldn't seem right.'

'You are a good woman indeed. I will try to start living again, as my husband wants me to, and I will never forget your kindness in coming to see me today.'

The next afternoon, Annie was working on her embroidery when there was a knock on the door. There stood Mrs Sheldon's chauffeur and a footman carrying three huge boxes. They were scarlet-faced and panting with the effort of carrying them up the step street.

'Mrs Sheldon hopes you will accept these presents for your children,' the chauffeur said. 'May we come in and put them down somewhere?'

Annie couldn't believe her eyes. There was a clockwork train set for Patrick, a wooden rocking horse for Ciaran and a doll's house full of exquisite furniture and tiny china dolls for Roisin. She couldn't possibly refuse such wonderful gifts. The children were overcome with excitement, and even Seamus was moved when he saw them.

'What a smart lady. She realised that you wouldn't be able to refuse gifts for the little ones.'

Annie was less happy a few days later when Father Kelly showed her an item that had been printed in the *New York Times*: 'Kingsbridge Woman Contacts Spirits of Those Lost on *Titanic*', the headline read. Mrs Sheldon had spoken to a reporter. If there had been massive demand for Annie's services before, it was about to get out of control.

Chapter Sixty-Six

In early August, a storm blew up the Atlantic coast of America. At Mr Grayling's summer house, they could feel it approaching a day in advance as the atmospheric pressure dropped and the skies clouded over. Headache pills were consumed and nerves became frayed. In the middle of the afternoon, a shriek erupted from Miss Hamilton's bedroom followed by raised voices and everyone rushed out to the hall to see what was going on.

Miss Hamilton ran down the stairs crying, 'She's a thief! I caught her red-handed, George. I watched her tucking my diamond brooch into her bodice when she didn't know I was standing in the doorway behind her.'

Molly stood at the top of the stairs. 'It's not true, sir. Miss Hamilton is mistaken. I was simply dusting the dresser.'

Reg knew from one look at Molly's pink cheeks that it *was* true, though. *Silly girl. She was in trouble now.*

Mr Grayling asked Molly to come into the drawing room and ordered everyone else back to their duties. Reg and Alphonse went into the kitchen, but they could clearly hear what was being said, as the voices drifted through the wide-open windows.

'I've been suspicious for a while,' Miss Hamilton said. 'Remember I lost those sapphire earrings? And I've noticed that I never seem to have as much money in my purse as I thought I had. I suspect this has been going on for some time.'

Molly stuttered in mock outrage. 'I have never in all my years in service taken a single thing that wasn't mine, sir. It's not in my nature.'

'But I *saw* you with my own eyes,' Miss Hamilton insisted. 'I know I wasn't mistaken.' She demonstrated where she had been standing and the clear view she had of Molly's actions.

Mr Grayling listened to both women before making up his mind. 'I'm afraid I'll have to let you go, Molly. You're lucky that I'm not going to call the police. I'll arrange for you to be driven back to New York this afternoon, and Mr Frank will supervise as you pack your belongings at the house.'

'You can't fire me, sir,' Molly said, and something about her sly tone made Reg nervous. 'There are too many secrets around here that you wouldn't want me to let slip.'

'What on earth are you talking about?'

There was a pause before Molly took the plunge. 'I have a hunch that the newspapers would be very interested to hear that Reg saw you kissing Miss Hamilton on the *Titanic* before your wife's death. Except that she was travelling with a fake name, wasn't she? What is she trying to hide?'

Reg sat down hard on a kitchen chair, and Alphonse whirled round, his face furious. 'This is all your fault. You have turned her head. Since you came to the house, there has been nothing but gossip and *malheur*.'

Reg sank his head into his hands as Mr Grayling shouted and Molly responded with sullen obstinacy. The volume rose, and Reg could hear the word 'blackmail' being bandied about. Mr Grayling must be furious that Reg had blabbed. He was part of this now whether he liked it or not.

Reg got up and walked out the back door and through the yard onto the beach. The wind was whipping the waves into swirling white foam and lifting clouds of sea spray that he could feel dampening his cheeks several yards back from the shore-line. The air was darkening, and to the south the sky was purply-black. He sat down on the sand to smoke a cigarette, preferring the impending destructiveness of nature to that of human beings, but when the rain started to fall suddenly and heavily, he had to repair indoors. It was time to lay the table for dinner.

Reg passed Mr Grayling in the hall, but nothing was said. In the kitchen, Alphonse was furiously hurling pots around the stove. Reg bumped into Molly in the hall near the staff bathroom.

'Did you hear what happened?' she whispered. 'I'm being asked to leave, but he's giving me a hundred bucks severance pay. If he thinks that's the end of it, he's got another think coming because I'll just come back and ask for more when that runs out. I told you my plan would work.'

Reg stared at her, aghast.

'Are you sure I can't change your mind? Come away with me and we'll get old Grayling to subsidise us to set up our own restaurant. That money would be nothing to him.' She held out her arms as if to embrace Reg, but he heard Alphonse coming down the hallway and stepped out of reach.

'I don't want any part of this,' Reg told her quietly. 'You're on your own.'

'Are you all right, Molly?' Alphonse asked, barging against Reg. 'Is he bothering you?'

She gave a little laugh. 'Oh, I'm fine. I'm staying here tonight because the driver doesn't want to drive in the storm. Bring me some dinner in my room, could you? And a glass of wine. I'm not working and I deserve a little treat.'

Alphonse agreed that he would, and she cooed 'Thank you, my hero.' She stood on tiptoe to kiss his cheek, making sure Reg could see. He turned away in disgust.

When Reg served dinner to Mr Grayling and Miss Hamilton, he found them in sober mood. They ate in silence, bar the odd comment on the food, and neither of them looked at Reg. Once when he opened the door he caught them whispering to each other, but they stopped as soon as he came into the room. He couldn't work out if he was *persona non grata* as well as Molly, or if they realised that he was a different type of person, with higher standards. He wished Mr Grayling would raise the subject so that he could make his own position clear, but he wasn't brave enough to bring it up himself.

In bed that night, he lay awake, wondering how this new turn of events might affect him. Mr Grayling must be cross that Reg had talked about seeing them on the *Titanic*. He had every right to be upset since he had given Reg a second chance only for him to turn out to be loose-tongued. He had betrayed his trust yet again. Perhaps he would be fired the next morning.

Outside, the storm had exploded into a frenzy of howling wind and horizontal rain that battered the wooden clapboard and rattled the shutters. It was like a huge deadly animal trying to attack them and Reg huddled under his blankets, grateful for the roof over his head.

He was beginning to drift off to sleep, when all of a sudden he heard a sharp, high-pitched scream, a woman's scream. He opened his eyes, fully alert. Through the noise of the storm, he made out angry voices but couldn't work out whose they were, then he heard another scream and to his ears, it sounded like a scream of terror. It was coming from the garage, which was just through the wall from him. Reg jumped out of bed, pulled some trousers and a jacket over his nightshirt, slipped his feet into his shoes without lacing them, then hurried down the corridor.

The house was in silence. He opened the back door as quietly as he could and stepped out into the cold. The wind buffeted him and rain plastered his hair to his head as he walked round to the garage entrance, picking his way in the moonlight. The door was open and as he peered in, he saw Molly in the passenger seat of the car.

'Molly? What are you doing?' he called, over the noise of the wind. 'Are you all right?' She didn't turn round, didn't seem to hear him.

He took a step into the garage towards her, and was dimly aware of a movement over his left shoulder. Before he had time to turn, something heavy hit him on the head and he blacked out.

Chapter Sixty-Seven

Somewhere in the depths of his brain, Reg became aware that he was in an automobile, being driven along a bumpy road. He was lying at an odd angle, virtually upside down and curled in a foetal position. He couldn't force his eyes open but he could hear the rattle of the motor and feel the vibrations and the roughness of the road surface. His head was knocking against something hard but he couldn't shift himself to a more comfortable position. It was a bizarre feeling to be vaguely aware of his surroundings but paralysed and unable to affect them, as if in a nightmare.

No one was talking. Was Molly still in the passenger seat? Who was driving?

The automobile stopped and he heard the door open and someone get out. He felt strong arms beneath his shoulders, lifting him upwards and hauling him over from the back seat into the front. His arm was trapped beneath him and it wrenched in its socket. He tried to resist but his muscles wouldn't obey. Still nothing was said. Surely if Molly was there, she would be talking? Ordinarily, the girl never shut up.

The door slammed, and he felt the automobile rolling forwards. Suddenly the earth disappeared beneath it. There was a moment when Reg was flying through the air, then he was thrown backwards violently as they hit something hard, and cold water began to gush around him.

Am I dreaming? Reg wondered. It was reminiscent of the recurring dream in which he was standing on a rapidly sinking boat.

The automobile somersaulted forwards and now he was submerged upside down in icy water and knew he had to fight for his life. It was pitch-black and he thrust out with his arms, frantically groping at the surroundings. The steering wheel was beneath him and something hard was directly above. To his left he felt a soft yet immoveable object, but on his right he found a narrow gap he could crawl through. He hadn't had time to fill his lungs with air and they were burning with the pressure. His brain was burning. He couldn't see which way to go but he kept struggling till his body was free of the automobile.

Just keep swimming. Just keep swimming. It was as if he was back on the *Titanic* again and he only knew one thing: that he wanted to live. How stupid to survive that and die so soon afterwards.

Suddenly he realised his head was above water. He took a huge gulp of air just as a wave broke over him, making him choke and splutter. The moon glinted on the ocean and he saw that he wasn't far from shore, but the coastline was rocky and the heaving ocean was threatening to wash him onto some jagged outcrops. A current was dragging him away from the automobile and he fought against it, treading water, trying to work out what to do for the best.

At that moment a terrible thought occurred to him: had Molly been in the automobile with him? Had she been hit over the head as well? She had seemed unnaturally still and silent when he called to her from the garage door, and he hadn't heard her voice once they were on the move. Could she be trapped unconscious in the wreckage? Was that the unyielding obstacle he had felt to his left? He had to go back and check.

The road ran at least twenty or thirty yards above the water at that point and he peered up, trying to make out the spot at which the automobile might have crashed down. He focused on a likely headland, swam back against the current towards it and dived down. The water was only around ten feet deep but it was rough and he couldn't find any sign of wreckage. There was no visibility underwater.

He swam further out and tried another spot, then another. The current kept sucking him down the coast and each time he had to swim hard to get back to the point where he thought the wreck might be. He dived ten, twenty, thirty times, all around the area, until his arms were leaden and he had no strength left. If Molly was still down there, she couldn't possibly be alive. There was no more he could do, so he turned on his back and let the current pull him along, past the sharp black rocks and further up the coast.

Once he stopped swimming, he began to shiver. It wasn't cold in the way the ocean off the *Titanic* had been cold, with a heart-stopping shock that you could feel sucking the life out of you. This was just a few degrees below comfort. It was August, after all, and the water wasn't deep.

He saw a glint of pale shingle and used the last of his strength to swim towards it before the current could sweep him past. He couldn't see any lights that would indicate there were houses nearby, but he needed to get on dry land. He crawled through a swamp of slimy seaweed that had been washed up into the shallows by the storm and staggered out onto a stony beach.

It was still raining, but not so fiercely. At the edge of the shingle, there was a wooden beach hut. Reg hurried up to it and yanked the door open, ripping it partly off its hinges. Inside there was a big pile of musty-smelling towels. He removed his jacket and trousers, and that's when he noticed his shoes were missing. They must have come off in the automobile. He rubbed himself down with one towel then wrapped himself up in some of the others and lay on the floor. Within seconds, he was sound asleep.

Chapter Sixty-Eight

Juliette couldn't stop torturing herself with visions of Robert escorting an actress around town. How could he believe that she wouldn't hear about it? How could he be so careless of her feelings? He was her husband and should have been protective towards her. Yet in truth, their acquaintance had been brief: a mere eight weeks spent together and nearly as long again apart. They didn't know much about each other at all.

She thought of all the things Robert hadn't discovered about her. He hadn't met her friends and didn't truly understand her English sense of humour. They'd never played tennis or cricket so he hadn't encountered her fiercely competitive streak. They hadn't chosen gifts for each other. Suddenly she realised she didn't even know when his birthday was. It must have been written on the marriage certificate, but he had kept the sole copy for fear of her mother coming across it in her luggage. She had no proof they were married. Even a flimsy piece of paper would have been comforting at that juncture.

In his letters, Robert always sounded busy. He was going into business with a man who had invented machines called 'air conditioners' that would cool the air in a room on a hot summer day. It seemed a good idea, and Robert was talking to manufacturers who could make them and department stores who would sell them. He seldom mentioned his social life, and the omission made Juliette suspicious. Surely he was doing *something* in the evenings? Did he eat at home on his own every night? He seemed a sociable person. Didn't he miss conversation over his meal? Or was he dining every night with a certain attractive actress and that's why he didn't mention it in his letters?

Juliette questioned herself closely. If he wasn't in love with her, was it true love that she felt for him? Or had her shock at the sinking of the *Titanic* led her to make a foolish mistake? At least part of her strong attraction to him had its roots in the way he made her feel safe again after the appalling experience of having a man die in her arms. He knew how to quell her anxieties. His conduct on the *Carpathia* and while they were staying at the Plaza had been irreproachable but now that the crisis had passed, perhaps he was reverting to his true nature. He must be a playboy. Juliette's parents had a sound marriage and she was determined to find the same for herself. She knew some women were prepared to turn a blind eye to marital indiscretion but she certainly didn't want a husband who had affairs.

How easy would it be to get divorced in America? Would she be able to do it without her mother finding out that she had ever been married? The thought provoked a fit of bitter weeping and she retired to her bed for a morning, causing her mother such concern that she called out the doctor. He took Juliette's blood pressure, listened to the baby with his stethoscope and noted her reddened eyes.

'You must take better care of yourself for the sake of the child,' he cautioned. 'It is understandable that you are anxious, given your unfortunate circumstances, but you must not endanger your health. Perhaps you should take up an interest to occupy you? My wife finds cross-stitching a most engrossing task. I expect your housekeeper could supply you with the materials.'

Juliette bit her tongue in irritation and after he had gone, she made an effort to come downstairs and rejoin her mother. She must pretend to be well, if only to prevent that doctor being summoned again, because his judgmental attitude was infuriating.

When a ferocious storm blew up one evening in early August, Juliette welcomed it for the change it brought. She sat at the window and watched the wind bending nearby trees and tearing off branches, while huge puddles of rainwater formed in the parched garden. Lightning crackled across the sky and thunder boomed around their cottage. Once her mother had retired to bed, Juliette crept out to sit on the verandah at the height of the storm and she could feel the electricity in the air. It made the skin on her arms prickle. The rain was pounding the earth so hard that it bounced up again, causing a white-out. All the stale heat of the last few weeks was swept away in a single destructive stroke of nature. She began to choose the words with which she would describe the storm to Robert in her letter the next day, and it was the early hours before she crept up the stairs to bed.

She was drowsy next morning, and her head rolled forwards a couple of times as she read the newspaper. But then she reached the gossip column, and was instantly wide awake. 'Mr Robert Graham was seen with actress Miss Amy Manford again, this time dining at Delmonico's. Could it be that his engagement to fellow *Titanic* survivor Lady Juliette Mason-Parker has hit the rocks?'

Juliette threw the paper to the floor. It was the final straw. She couldn't sit in the countryside suffering this torture any longer. Enough was enough.

She could send Robert a telegram demanding that he tell her who Miss Amy Manford was and why he was dining with her – but then it would be the following day before she could possibly expect a reply, and besides he might lie. Mere words in a telegram were easy. She could risk going to the telephone exchange in Main Street and trying to place a call, but she only had his home number and by that time he would surely be at the office. Besides, if he was a proficient liar he might be able to fool her on the telephone as well.

Any patience she'd had was spent and impetuosity took over. She had to see him and ask him to his face what was going on. Of course, he would realise her condition straight away. He would have to decide whether he loved her enough to remain married to her when she was carrying another man's child. It was perhaps the greatest test of all. If he wanted a quiet divorce, she would give him one without complaint. So be it. She would rather lose him because of the mistake she had made in allowing Charles Wood to make love to her than lose him to another woman.

She went up to her room and packed a small overnight bag then wrote a brief note to her mother, saying that she had gone to New York because she had to see Robert. She propped the note against her pillow then waited until she heard her mother in the kitchen talking to Edna about the evening's menu before sneaking down the stairs. She crept out the front door, across the verandah, and down the track that led to the main road. The driver was outside the garage, waxing his car.

'I need to go to New York right now,' she told him. 'I'll make it worth your while if you will take me.'

'Of course, miss,' he nodded, without so much as a raised eyebrow.

During the journey, she planned her next move. Robert would still be at the office when they reached town and she didn't know where that was. She decided that she would reserve a room at the Plaza and send a message to his butler. The butler could phone and inform him of her whereabouts and if he still loved her, he would surely hurry straight there to be reunited with her. She shivered at the prospect. In just a few hours she might be in his arms again – or she might have lost him once and for all.

She knew she was taking a huge gamble, but it was as if the storm had cleared her head as it swept across the countryside. She needed to be honest with this man if she was going to spend the rest of her life with him. She had to tell the truth and suffer the consequences, and she would demand that he did the same.

Chapter Sixty-Nine

When Reg awoke, it was daylight outside and the storm had abated. Through the crack of the door, he could see the sky was pale grey and overcast, while the wet shingle was a dark tan colour. He tried to sit up but the movement brought on a pounding headache. He pressed his temple against the door frame then his stomach muscles contracted and he threw up violently, only just managing to push the door open in time so it spewed onto the sand rather than inside the hut.

Reg glanced up and down the beach. It was deserted. He wiped his mouth, lay back on the towels and let the events of the previous night wash over him.

Was Molly dead in the wreck of the automobile? Had she been unconscious in the garage when he saw her sitting in the front seat? Reg was pretty sure that must be the case, and there was only one person who could be responsible: Mr Grayling. He had no intention of letting Molly go after she made her blackmail threat. He probably intended to kill Reg as well. If it was true that he had murdered his wife on the *Titanic*, he couldn't risk anyone finding out, especially now that several weeks had passed and he thought he had got away with it.

The question was, what should Reg do next? If he went to the police, would they believe him? He fingered the back of his head and there was a painful gash where he had been hit.

That proved something. If they found the wreck of the car and Molly's body was still in it, surely that was evidence enough? Alphonse would be able to back up his story that Molly had been trying to blackmail Mr Grayling; they'd both overheard the conversation.

But what if the police thought Reg was guilty? Molly's interest in him had been common enough knowledge in the household for it to have reached Miss Hamilton's ears. They might suspect he had murdered Molly after a lovers' tiff and driven the car off the road to hide the evidence. Reg had no love of the police. He knew that in England they always took the upper classes' word against that of the lower classes, and he assumed that it would be the same in America. Mr Grayling would be sure to hire a fancy lawyer while Reg would have to defend himself. The odds weren't good.

Maybe Molly was still alive. He wished fervently that would turn out to be the case. He hoped she had got out of the car before it rolled into the sea, or she had escaped from the wreck and swum to the shore. In that case, she would go to the police with her story and Mr Grayling would be arrested. Reg decided to walk back and try to find the spot where the car went off the road so he could check whether there was any sign of her in the area.

His nightshirt was still damp but it had at least been warmed by the heat of his body; the soaking jacket and trousers were freezing cold when he pulled them on. He searched the beach hut and found a pair of men's canvas deck shoes. They were several sizes too big for him but it was better than going barefoot. He tidied himself as best he could then peeked outside the hut. At the far end of the beach, he spotted someone walking a dog and ducked down, terrified. What if Mr Grayling had seen him swim clear of the wreck the previous night? He might be hunting for him to try and finish him off. Reg would have to stay out of sight.

He skirted round the corner of the beach hut and zigzagged between the rocks, constantly checking in each direction. When a solitary automobile drove past he hid, and was relieved when he heard the motor continue down the road without pausing.

It was a quiet morning. Holidaymakers were staying indoors because the sky seemed to threaten more rain and the temperature had dropped several degrees. He scrabbled along the rocky slopes until he found a headland where there was a drop from the road down to the water. A sign read 'Sea Cliff'. Could that be the place where they had crashed into the sea? He scanned the surface, which was grey and choppy, but could see no sign of any wreckage.

Reg ducked behind a boulder and examined the surrounding coast. If Molly had been washed ashore there, she would have been dashed against the rocks. He could see no sign of any clothing or red-blonde curly hair floating on the waves. *Please let her be alive*, he breathed. He didn't know who he was asking, but he asked all the same. If Molly was alive, they could go to the police together. If she was dead, he couldn't face going on his own. As Mr Grayling would no doubt point out to them, Reg didn't have a great record of telling the truth in recent months.

The only alternative was to reinvent himself all over again. He would have to start from the bottom, accepting the kind of job where they didn't ask for a reference. It would help if he could at least retrieve his spare clothing from Mr Grayling's New York house. He couldn't apply for a job wearing a nightshirt and beach shoes, and he had no cash with him. Perhaps his new immigration papers, in the name of Reg Parton, would have arrived. He'd have trouble getting a job without them. Could he risk confiding in Mr Frank? No, he decided. He was too loyal to his boss. But there were only a few staff members left in the house, so he might be able to slip unnoticed through the cellar window, which was usually left ajar to keep the wine cool.

First he had to get to New York somehow. He had no idea where he was but sensed it was far too far to walk. He would have to ask someone for a ride and cross his fingers that the person he chose was trustworthy.

The next two automobiles that came along were black and shiny, similar to Mr Grayling's vehicles, so Reg kept out of sight. After a while, a yellow and green painted Ford truck came into view. The cab at the front had space for a passenger beside the driver, and there was a cage of chickens on the flatbed behind. As it drew near, Reg stood up and ran out to the roadside.

'Hey mister!' he yelled, waving his arms in the air. 'Mister, please stop!'

The driver pulled up. 'You want a lift?' he asked, eyeing Reg up and down. 'Where y'all going?'

'New York City.'

'I'm only going as far as Brooklyn, but I can drop you by the bridge. Any use?'

'That would be very kind. Thank you so much.' Reg opened the door and climbed in.

'You're wet,' the driver said. 'I've got a blanket you can wrap yourself in. Don't want you dying of the cold. My wife and I are church people. We believe in helping those who are down on their luck and you seem more down on your luck than most. I bet you haven't eaten today.' Reg shook his head. The man reached behind him for a paper bag. He pulled out a loaf of

406

bread and tore off a big hunk, which he gave to Reg along with some thick slices of ham and a flask of water. 'Be my guest.'

'I can't thank you enough,' Reg said. He heard another motor approaching and looked over his shoulder, anxious to get moving.

The driver started the engine. 'I'm guessing you are in some kinda trouble. I'm not gonna ask your story because I don't wanna get into trouble myself. You look like a good kid and from your accent you're a long way from home, so I'll just take you where you want to go. If you want to thank anyone, thank the good Lord.'

Reg gulped down some water and pulled up the blanket, fearful they might yet pass Mr Grayling on the road. His headache was worsening by the hour. He ate a few mouthfuls of bread but they made him feel sick again, and before long the rhythmic vibrations of the truck had sent him off into a disturbed sleep.

Chapter Seventy

Juliette scribbled a very simple note: 'Am in New York at the Plaza Hotel. Come as soon as possible.' On the outside, she wrote: 'Please deliver message to Mr Robert Graham urgently.'

Her driver took it to Robert's house while Juliette checked in to the hotel. She twisted her engagement ring so that the stone faced in towards her palm and requested a double room, saying that her husband would join her when he could. The desk clerk agreed without question. She was so obviously pregnant that how could she be anything but married? Juliette was led up to a sumptuous room overlooking Central Park and she sat by a window to wait. It was five o'clock in the afternoon. He should be there within the hour.

She was wearing a mauve silk dress that flared outwards from the bust and she arranged the folds carefully so as to disguise her shape. He would discover her condition soon enough. If only there could be a warm embrace, perhaps a loving kiss before he noticed. She felt a little faint and, realising she hadn't eaten since breakfast, she rang the bell for some tea and cake. Her stomach was in knots and she tried not to think about what would happen later. The evening would either bring a joyous reunion or a desperately sad break-up and she genuinely could not predict which it would be.

We were foolish to have married so soon, she thought, *no matter the reason.* He seemed like a good man, but she hadn't seen him in enough circumstances to judge his true character. A long engagement would have been best.

The tea came and she poured herself a cup and sipped it. The hands of the clock were moving hideously slowly, and she had finished the entire pot by half past five, along with two of the chocolate cakes they called 'brownies'. He might just be leaving the office at that point. She peered at the street outside, where traffic came and went, occasionally stopping to deposit a passenger, but she was three floors up and couldn't make out the figures emerging from cars below.

Perhaps if he was in a business meeting, his butler had been unable to pass on the message so far – but surely no one worked beyond five-thirty? They would have no time to get home and change for dinner. Perhaps he had stopped by his club after work. But the club must have a telephone. Surely he would get the message there? Had she made it sound urgent enough? Could it be sitting unopened on his desk at home while he sat in his club unawares?

As the minutes and hours passed, Juliette had to invent further excuses for him. She'd been hoping that they would dine together but when eight o'clock came and went, she rang the bell and asked for a light meal to be brought up to her. She didn't want to risk eating in the dining room, where someone might recognise her and spot her condition.

'Could you check that there are no messages for me at the front desk?' she asked the steward who brought her food, but he came back to say there were none, and that's when she sank into despair.

Was Robert dining out with the actress? Had he gone to watch Amy Manford appearing on stage? What did she look like? Juliette imagined her as petite and strikingly beautiful. Juliette was quite tall for a woman and felt as big as a horse. Her hair was a nondescript mousy blonde and although she was told she had rather fetching grey-green eyes, she had never been described as a beauty. If Robert chose women based on looks alone, then she would certainly lose him to Miss Amy Manford. He had said he appreciated her intelligent opinions and general knowledge, though. Were actresses clever? She had never met any and had no idea.

Outside, the sky was darkening and the gas lamps were being lit in the street below. She lay down on the bed to rest, and when it reached nine o'clock without any sign of him, she began to cry. *What had she been thinking? She should never have come to New York. Had she no pride? If he had fallen for an actress, the last thing she should be doing was humiliating herself by pursuing him.*

She'd sent the driver back to their cottage so that her mother and Edna weren't left without transport, but she decided that first thing in the morning, she would ask the hotel to arrange a car to take her back to Saratoga Springs. Once there she would write to Robert and release him from their marriage. They could claim it was never consummated and seek an annulment. Maybe her name wouldn't be completely ruined then. Maybe she would still have a chance of finding another husband some day.

Chapter Seventy-One

It was getting dark as Reg walked over Brooklyn Bridge. A sign read that it cost a cent for pedestrians to cross but thankfully there was no one manning the tollbooth. The gas lights of the city flickered and down below he could see some huge transatlantic liners docked in the piers. He was too far away to make out which ones they were, but he felt a tug of homesickness. Maybe he should think about going down to ask if he might work his passage home? He looked out in the direction of the ocean and shuddered. It was so vast and deep and cold, and they'd be sailing over the bodies of John and Mrs Grayling, Finbarr and Captain Smith. None of them had been found, so they were out there somewhere. He wasn't sure he could face that.

On the other side of the bridge, he considered trying to find the address where his old shipmate Danny was staying. It would be good to see a friendly face from back home, but there was too much to explain. Besides, Danny might have moved on by now. Instead, he made his way to the Municipal Lodging House on East 25th Street, where he had stayed when the *Carpathia* docked. The superintendent recognised him and took him in without question, giving him some dinner and a bed for the night. Reg was able to have a wash and rinse off the salt water that was making his skin tight and itchy. He soaked congealed blood from his hair and carefully cleaned the wound in his scalp. His clothes had dried but were stiff with salt. There was nothing he could do about that because if he washed them they wouldn't dry overnight. Wearing his salty nightshirt, he climbed into a bunk and fell into a deep sleep.

When Reg woke the next morning he lay in bed thinking about everything that had happened to him, and considered yet again whether he should go to the police. That's what any law-abiding person would do, and the fact that he hadn't done so already would surely make him seem guilty. But he was scared they wouldn't believe him, scared that he could end up in jail.

Over breakfast, he noticed the superintendent had a newspaper on his desk and asked if he could borrow it for a few moments. He flicked through the pages, and on page five, his worst fears were realised. 'Lovebirds steal car from boss and crash into ocean' read the headline. The story claimed that Reg and Molly had pilfered some money from Mr Grayling and escaped in one of his cars, only to hurtle off the road at a notorious accident spot. Molly's body had been found in the wreckage but they speculated that Reg had been swept away by the strong current. A brief sentence at the end mentioned that he was a *Titanic* survivor.

Reg sat transfixed by horror. So it was true that Molly had been in the car. She was dead and he had failed to rescue her. He was filled with rage against Mr Grayling. During all those weeks Reg had been living under the same roof as him, serving him meals and watching him drool over Miss Hamilton, he hadn't been able to bring himself to believe he was working for a cold-blooded murderer. Now he realised his boss didn't care what he did so long as he got his own way. Mr Grayling couldn't risk Reg and Molly telling anyone the inconvenient truth about his conduct on the *Titanic*, so he got rid of them with as little conscience as he would shoot grouse on a country estate.

And Reg was believed to be dead again, for the second time that year. At least it meant they weren't out hunting for him. But Molly, poor silly girl, had been found. He thought of their secret kisses and felt desperately sad for her. Her mum and that sister who worked for the Rothschilds would be in mourning. Alphonse would be upset as well. He wondered if anyone would contact his own mother back in Southampton to tell her that he had perished. She'd just have received his letter explaining he was staying in New York and then she'd get another saying he was dead – and labelled a thief to boot. No doubt she would get word to Florence. He resolved to send them both a telegram as soon as he could raise the cash.

After breakfast, Reg set out for the long walk uptown to Madison Avenue. He slipped past Sherry's, worried in case anyone he knew would see him in such a state, dressed like a tramp in a nightshirt and salt-marked jacket, stiffened trousers and oversized canvas beach shoes. He checked any clocks he could spot through office windows along the way, and managed to arrive at the house just after one, when the staff should all be sitting down to luncheon. He crept round to the back door and made sure he could hear their voices in the kitchen before he slipped down to the cellar window, which was hidden behind a coal bunker. As usual, it was slightly ajar. He had to remove his jacket in order to squeeze through the narrow opening. His heart was pounding. If he were caught, he would tell Mr Frank the truth and throw himself on his mercy, but he didn't greatly fancy his chances of a sympathetic hearing.

Once inside, Reg listened carefully at the cellar door before slipping up the steps into the hall, and then up the main stair-case, storey by storey, to his old bedroom. There was a bulky letter for him on the bed, from the immigration department.

His new papers had come through, thank goodness. He changed quickly into his spare suit, with clean socks and a shirt, and pulled on a pair of old shoes he had left in the cupboard, the ones he'd been wearing on the *Titanic*. He bundled all his other clothes into a paper carrier bag along with his passport and a few dollars he had saved for Mrs Hitchens. Before he left, he remembered Florence's St Christopher was still in a drawer by his bedside, so he stuck it in his pocket.

Reg crept down the stairs as quietly as he could, but paused on the first floor. The door of Mr Grayling's office was ajar and a thought came to him. *I could go to the police if I had some evidence against him, if it wasn't just his word against mine.* He remembered how distressed Mr Grayling had seemed when he gazed inside the side drawer of the desk. Maybe there was something in there that would explain how and why his wife died. It was a long shot, but worth a try.

Still Reg couldn't hear any movement in the rest of the house. With Mr Grayling out of town, the staff probably took a long luncheon. He tiptoed into the office. The almanac was on the same shelf and, tucked inside the flyleaf, he found a small key. He turned it in the lock of the side drawer and slid it open. Inside there was a bundle of letters addressed to 'Mr George Grayling' and a small cloth bag.

As he lifted the bag, he could feel there was a key inside. He opened it and knew straight away what it was before reading the engraving on it: B78. It was the key to the Graylings' suite on the *Titanic*.

Why would he have thought to bring that with him when everyone was rushing to the lifeboats? Passengers never locked their doors on cruise ships. Did Mr Grayling really stop to worry about the risk of theft while the *Titanic* was sinking?

That hardly seemed plausible. He must have locked the door because Mrs Grayling was lying in bed, either unconscious or already dead, and he didn't want her to be found. The sinking of the *Titanic* had been extremely convenient for him. He'd hit her over the head, just as he'd done with Reg, but he didn't have to risk being caught when he tossed her body overboard because he could just let her go down with the ship. It was almost the perfect crime.

A line from a Sherlock Holmes story came into his head: 'Every murderer makes at least one mistake.' Mr Grayling might have thought he'd got away with it, but he should never have kept the key. That gave Reg enough evidence to go to the police.

He slipped the letters and cabin key into his carrier bag, relocked the drawer, replaced the almanac, then crept down the stairs to the cellar and back out through the window. No one in the house heard a thing.

Chapter Seventy-Two

As soon as Juliette woke the next day, she rang and asked a steward to enquire at the front desk whether a message had been left for her. When the reply came back that there was none, her spirits hit rock bottom.

'I'll be leaving the hotel this morning,' she told him. 'Please organise an automobile and driver to take me to Saratoga Springs.'

She hobbled into the bathroom clutching her lower back, which ached from sleeping in an uncomfortable position. In the mirror, she saw purply-grey shadows beneath red-rimmed eyes. She had fallen asleep without pinning her hair into curls and it hung in limp, wayward strands. There was a stale taste in her mouth so she polished her teeth then splashed her face with cold water and got dressed. She didn't feel like eating but knew she had to for the sake of the baby, so she rang for some baked eggs and corn bread.

'I'm afraid we can't get a driver for you until three this afternoon, ma'am,' the steward told her when he brought the food. 'Will that suffice?'

'It will have to,' she said. That meant it would be after dark when she got back to their cottage. Her mother would be going out of her mind with worry, so she scribbled a telegram, which merely read 'Back later this evening [stop] Juliette' and gave it to the steward, along with a tip.

Where are you, Robert? she kept asking in her head. *How could you do this to me? Were you really so easily distracted?*

Suffragettes had succeeded in getting women the vote in New Zealand, Australia and Sweden. Maybe Britain would follow suit one day. But women would never be equal when it came to affairs of the heart. Men held all the cards. They decided whom to marry and when. If they chose to have an affair or even get divorced, society might label them a rogue but they would still be invited to dinners and house parties. She, on the other hand, would have ruined her chances of making a good match. She might be able to hide an illegitimate child given up for adoption, but she doubted that she would be able to hide a divorce. Word would follow her back to England, and she would live her life a lonely spinster relying on her brother's goodwill for a roof over her head and food on the table.

Juliette couldn't bear to sit cooped up in that hotel room a moment longer, but it was only eleven and her driver wasn't due for another four hours. She decided to go for a walk in Central Park to pass the time. If she met someone who recognised her and her pregnancy was revealed, so be it.

She tucked her hair under her hat and buttoned her boots, then walked down the stairs and crossed the road outside the hotel. The weather was cool and fresh after the storm, and sunlight rippled through the leaves, forming dimpled patterns on the path. She wanted to walk and walk and keep walking. It was her first taste of freedom in months. She'd been trapped within the suffocating heat of the cottage since early June, and before that she hadn't gone anywhere in New York without Robert by her side. It felt good to stretch her muscles and fill her lungs with fresh air. She was slightly nervous to be alone in a strange city, but reckoned that if she stuck to a main path she should be safe. She could simply turn and come back the same way so she didn't risk getting lost.

After a while, she came upon a beautiful fountain with tiers like a wedding cake. There was a statue of an angel resplendent on top with four cherubs huddled beneath, and the water cascaded over the tiers and splashed into a pool below. She sat for a while to admire the effect, and remained there resting on a bench until she began to feel thirsty. She remembered passing close to the café where Robert had bought her some rainbow sandwiches, so got up and headed back in that direction.

As Juliette entered the café, she was aware of a young man sitting with his head bent over a letter but it wasn't until she sat down and looked closely that she realised she knew him.

'Reg!' she exclaimed. 'It's you, isn't it? How are you?'

He looked alarmed, and quickly folded the letter he'd been holding. 'Excuse me, miss. I'm fine, thank you.' She saw him noticing her belly. Her condition was instantly obvious.

'I don't suppose I could join you? I feel rather awkward sitting on my own.'

Reg leapt up to pull out a chair for her, embarrassed to be caught reading one of Mr Grayling's letters. She was a genteel, titled lady. What would she think if she knew he was on the way to the police to report a murder?

'I'm leaving the city in a couple of hours but I wanted to see the park first. It's beautiful, isn't it . . .' Her voice tailed off as her attention was caught by the letter Reg had been reading. She recognised the signature straight away. 'My God, that's Venetia Hamilton's signature, isn't it? Why on *earth* would you have a letter from her?'

Reg coloured and pulled it towards him. Of course. He remembered they knew each other. So her first name was

418

Venetia? Juliette was waiting for an answer. 'She is living with Mr Grayling, and I've been working for him. Do you remember him from the *Titanic*? They've been having an affair.'

Juliette snorted. 'But he's twice her age. I suppose it must be his money. Venetia only likes men with loads of money. She has a history in England of making men fall in love with her then leaving them if she finds out they aren't wealthy or generous enough.' She rolled her eyes. 'Honestly, her reputation is atrocious – especially since she broke off her last engagement – so I imagine she decided to try America. It seems somewhat disrespectful to Mrs Grayling that she pounced on him so quickly after his wife's death, but Venetia never did stand on ceremony.' She glanced at the letter again, wondering why Reg would have it. 'Are you delivering this for her?'

'No.' He hesitated for a moment, not wanting to upset her in her condition, but Juliette didn't seem the hysterical type. She knew Venetia and might be able to shed more light on her behaviour. Reg decided to tell her about seeing her with Mr Grayling on the *Titanic*'s boat deck and then watching him help her into a lifeboat on the night of the sinking.

'She was on the ship? But we never saw hide nor hair of her.'

'I believe she stayed in her cabin. She told me she wasn't in the mood for society.'

'I bet she wasn't! She had just jilted Lord Beaufort, left him standing at the altar, and no one on board would have given her the time of day.'

A waiter came by and Juliette ordered a glass of lemonade, then asked Reg how he came to be working for Mr Grayling.

He explained that, then described his shock that Mr Grayling didn't appear to be mourning his wife's death. He told her that Molly had tried to blackmail him over his affair with Miss

Hamilton, and that the night before last, he had killed her and attempted to kill him as well. That's how determined he was that the truth shouldn't come out.'

Juliette gasped and clapped her hand over her mouth.

'I'm sorry to talk of such distressing matters, ma'am, but I'm still rather in shock about it.' He described what had happened in the garage and then his escape from the automobile as it plunged to the ocean bed. 'I've just been in his house collecting my belongings and I found the letters and this.' He showed her the key. 'It's the key to their suite on the *Titanic*.'

'Why would he have the key with him?' Juliette asked, wide-eyed. 'Mother and I never used ours.'

'My theory is that he killed his wife and left her in their suite when the ship sank. She was never seen in a lifeboat. It all makes sense. He wanted to be free to marry his mistress but she refused to give him a divorce, so he hatched a plan to kill her on the *Titanic* and throw her overboard. The sinking of the ship made it easy for him. He just locked her body in their suite and left her there.'

'But that's simply awful! How could he? I didn't know her well but my mother said Margaret Grayling was a charming woman. Still, Venetia Hamilton does seem to have a knack for turning men's heads.' *They can be so weak,* she thought bitterly. *How can men be so easily fooled by external appearances?*

Juliette's lemonade arrived but she no longer felt like drinking it. 'I still can't believe we sat and conversed at dinner with a murderer!' she exclaimed. 'You've had a narrow escape, Reg. Will you take this evidence to the police?'

'That's what I'm planning to do next. I sat down to get things straight in my head, because Mr Grayling is a distinguished gentleman and I fear they may be more likely to take his word than mine.'

'I would be happy to write you a character reference,' Juliette offered. 'Let me give you our address.' She took a notebook and pencil from her bag and wrote out the address in Saratoga Springs. 'Please let me know what happens. It's a shocking story.'

Reg still felt very anxious at the thought of going to the police, but the fact that one person believed him was reassuring.

He offered to pay the bill for their drinks but Juliette wouldn't let him. 'Please, allow me. You'll need your money for whatever you decide to do next. Perhaps you would be so good as to escort me back to the Plaza Hotel?'

They chatted as they walked. Reg plucked up the courage to ask when the baby was due, and she waved her hand and said, 'Oh, not for ages yet.' Then she asked: 'What are your plans? Will you stay in New York?'

'I don't know,' Reg said. 'I've been feeling homesick, but the thought of the voyage is daunting.' He fingered the St Christopher in his pocket. 'And I don't think I have much to go back to.'

'Yes, I'm dreading crossing the ocean again. How strange it will be.'

When they reached the hotel entrance, he walked her up the steps, past the footmen and into the plush reception hall. Robert Graham was sitting with his eyes glued to the door and as soon as they walked in he jumped to his feet and rushed across the room to throw his arms around Juliette, who looked rather stunned.

Reg stood for a moment or two, feeling awkward. They were locked in their embrace and she seemed to have forgotten he was there, so he took a step backwards then melted out of the door and back into the street.

Chapter Seventy-Three

Juliette didn't have time to be nervous as Robert dashed up to her and swept her into his arms.

'Darling, what's happened? Are you all right?' he asked. Feeling the bump between them, he looked down. There was a moment when she watched the truth sink in, then he exclaimed, 'Oh, my love, is it really possible? But that's marvellous news!' He kissed her on the lips, oblivious to the hotel guests and staff milling around. 'I've always wanted to be a father, but I never dreamed it would happen so soon. Thank you. Thank you with all my heart.'

Juliette was dazed. How could he believe that their one night of passion two months ago could have made her so massively pregnant? This wasn't the place to tell him otherwise, though. Minutes before she had believed that their relationship was over, and now this . . . It was hard to take in.

'Where have you been?' she asked. 'I'd quite given up hope of seeing you, and have a car booked to take me back to Saratoga Springs at three.'

'Didn't you receive my message? I was in California, trying to find premises for some new branches of the air conditioner company. I rushed back on the very next train when I heard you were here, but I asked my butler to send a message telling you I wouldn't arrive until today.'

'I didn't receive any message. I thought you weren't coming.' She was confused.

'You didn't? But that's preposterous.' Linking his arm through hers, he marched over to the reception desk. 'Do you have any messages for Lady Juliette Mason-Parker?'

The clerk looked at his pile of messages and instantly pulled one out. 'Yes, sir. Here's one.'

'And why didn't you pass it on?'

Suddenly Juliette realised what had happened and tugged at his arm. 'I checked in as Mrs Robert Graham. I wanted a double room in case you could join me.' She clutched her forehead. 'What an idiot!'

'Goodness, no, I'm the one at fault!' he exclaimed. 'I should have guessed you might do that. Oh, poor you.' He smiled tenderly. 'What must you have thought?'

Juliette blushed, remembering how badly she had misjudged him, and he took her hands.

'Might we not spend some time together now that I have dashed across an entire continent to see you? Must you really leave at three?'

'Let's cancel the driver and go up to my room,' she suggested. 'I think we need some time alone.'

As soon as the door closed behind them, Robert started kissing her and her entire body strained towards him. They moved sideways towards the bed, entwined in each other, lips on lips and legs wrapped around legs. All thoughts of actresses and annulments left Juliette's head as she dissolved into passion. She couldn't stop kissing, couldn't stop touching him, and he was the same. There was no time to be self-conscious about the expanse of her belly, no time to worry whether lovemaking was safe in her condition, because of the urgent need to be joined together.

As they lay in each other's arms afterwards, Juliette waited for him to comment on the advanced stage of her pregnancy, but instead he stroked her face and spoke with awed wonder about how marvellous it was to see her and how much he had missed her.

'You didn't mention what it was that brought you to town,' he questioned. 'Your note made me concerned that there was an emergency, but perhaps you came so that you could share your happy news with me in person?'

'No,' she replied. 'You will think me foolish, but I came to ask you a question.' She took a deep breath. 'Who exactly is Amy Manford and what is she to you?'

'My niece,' he replied straight away. 'Why?'

She stared at him, bemused. 'The gossip column in the paper kept saying that you had been seen out at the races and having dinner with an attractive actress named Amy Manford . . . I wondered why you didn't mention it. That's all.'

He frowned. 'I'm sure I told you that my niece, my older sister's girl, was in town and I was showing her around. I had no idea that she wants to be an actress. It's possible she has mentioned that ambition to her friends but I very much doubt my sister will allow it.' Suddenly his mouth widened into a broad grin. 'You were jealous, weren't you? Admit it.'

'Of course I was! Why didn't you write to tell me the papers were wrong?'

Still grinning, he touched the end of her nose lightly with his finger. 'I have never read one of those columns in my life and don't intend to start. Perhaps they are taken more seriously back in England, but here they are viewed as pure fiction. Were you really upset by them?'

Juliette was embarrassed. 'Well . . . a little.'

'But at least it has meant we are together now. How are your relatives? Must you rush back today? Might I not claim you for a while longer?'

'I think you might,' she breathed. She lay back in his arms in a glow of perfect happiness. She had forgotten how safe she felt with him, how much she liked the smell of him, and how his touch stirred every cell of her body.

And then he ran his hand slowly over her belly, feeling its expanse, exploring its contours. Juliette tried to suck it inwards as much as she could, but it was so huge, there was no disguising it, and just at that moment the baby chose to kick. She felt his hand falter and when she looked up into his face, he was frowning. Now was the moment when she had to confess. She closed her eyes and tried to summon the courage. She couldn't bear to lose him. But what chance would their marriage have if it were based on a lie?

Before she could speak, Robert rolled over and got out of bed. 'Please excuse me, but I have some business I must attend to this afternoon,' he said and started to pull on his clothes. He wasn't looking in her direction and his tone was noticeably cool.

'Shall I see you later?' she asked.

'Yes, of course. I'll pick you up at six for dinner. The staff should be able to prepare something at the house. We don't want to. . .'

He didn't finish the sentence, but Juliette knew what he had been about to say. They couldn't risk being seen in public.

When he came over to kiss her goodbye, she turned her mouth towards his but instead he pecked her forehead, briefly.

He's guessed, she thought, as he hurried out of the room and closed the door without looking back. *It's over. If only I had been brave enough to tell him myself.*

It wouldn't have made any difference, though. How could any man accept another man's child? What had she been thinking? She turned her face into the pillow, too distraught to cry.

Chapter Seventy-Four

Reg didn't know where to find a police station. In England, he might have looked for a bobby on the beat but he couldn't see any around so he asked a newspaper vendor.

'West 54th and Eighth Avenue is the closest.'

'Thank you.'

His heart was pounding as he walked down Eighth Avenue, trying to rehearse what he would say. Where should he start? What if they didn't believe him? Could he go to jail over this? He had stolen the letters, and they thought he was responsible for Molly's death while driving a stolen car.

He was so scared he thought his knees might give way as he walked up the steps and into the lobby of the station. He stuttered as he spoke to the policeman standing behind the desk. 'My n-name is Reg Parton. I was in the c-car that crashed off the road in Long Island, Mr G-Grayling's car, but I didn't steal it. The papers are wrong. . .'

'Hold on a second. Do you mean that car crash where two of Mr Grayling's employees died?'

'Yes, I'm one of them. Reg. I escaped.'

'Well, I'll be damned!' He looked Reg up and down. 'I guess I'll find somebody to talk to you. Come with me.'

Reg was led into an interview room and as he waited, he fingered his St Christopher. It made him think about Florence, with her freckles and her ready smile. The more he learned about the wiles of women, the more he realised how unusual her openness and honesty were. She had no sides, no secrets, no artifice. But it was over four months since he'd seen her, and she would almost certainly have another beau by now. He'd virtually told her to find someone else.

There was a clock on the wall and the minutes ticked by slowly. Half past two. Three o'clock. At ten past three, the door opened and a very tall man walked in. He must have been about six feet six, a whole foot taller than Reg, with silver-grey hair, a reddish complexion and a bumpy nose that appeared to have been broken at least once.

'Reg Parton?' He held out his hand so Reg shook it. 'Detective O'Halloran. Sorry to keep you waiting. You told the sergeant that you escaped from the car that went into the ocean off Long Island?'

'That's right, but it wasn't me who stole it. I was hit over the head and bundled into it. Look!' He turned his head and parted his hair with his fingers to show the gash.

'That's OK. Sit yourself down. We know it wasn't you. We've got the man responsible. He walked into a police station and confessed.'

'Mr Grayling did?'

The detective gave him an odd look. 'No, Alphonse Labreche. The chef.'

'It can't be true!' Reg was stunned.

'Yes, it seems it was a classic crime of passion. He was in love with Molly, she was leading him down the garden path and he couldn't take it any more. After he strangled her, you happened to walk in and he had to shut you up too. He's broken up with guilt.'

'Alphonse,' Reg repeated, as if in a daze. How could he have lived in the same house as them and not realised Alphonse loved Molly? Now he thought about it, it should have been obvious. She'd been flirting with Alphonse the same way she flirted with him, but it seems he'd taken her seriously. He must have been seething inside as he watched her pursuing Reg during all those weeks. And then on the night of the storm, he snapped. Poor Molly, and poor Alphonse as well.

'Are you OK? We should get somebody to look at that cut on your head.'

'I'm fine. I'm just astonished. Alphonse wasn't a bad person.'

'You'd be surprised what being spurned can do to a guy. I've seen it over and over again, even when they are peaceable types beforehand. So you escaped from the automobile after it crashed in the water?' Reg nodded. 'What did you do then?'

'I wasn't sure but I thought Molly might be in there so I dived back down over and over again trying to find her. It was useless, though. I couldn't find the wreckage any more because a current kept pulling me away.'

'That stretch of water is nasty in a storm. It's damn lucky you managed to save yourself never mind anybody else. Besides, we think she was already dead before she hit the water. Where did you come ashore?'

'On a rocky beach somewhere. I slept in a beach hut, then the next morning I went back up the coast to look for Molly but couldn't find her. So I asked a truck driver to give me a lift to New York.'

'Why didn't you go back to Mr Grayling's?' The detective was watching Reg closely, making him feel uncomfortable.

'I was scared.'

'What were you scared of? Did you think Mr Grayling may have had something to do with it?'

Reg chose his words carefully. 'Molly had been trying to blackmail him about the young woman who was staying with us at the summerhouse. Her name is Venetia Hamilton.'

The detective gave a long, low whistle. It seemed there was a lot more to this case than he'd thought. 'So what grounds were there for the blackmail?'

'You know his wife died on the *Titanic*?' The detective nodded. 'Well, I think he might have killed her.' Reg explained that she hadn't been seen during the final day, that their suite door was locked and he saw Mr Grayling and Miss Hamilton escaping together. 'Then I found this in the house.' He handed over the key, and put the letters on the table.

'Whoa! That's some accusation you're making. Mr Grayling told us that Miss Hamilton is a friend of his late daughter's and he's been looking after her while she gets over a broken engagement.'

Reg pursed his lips. 'I believe you'll find a different story in these letters.'

'You reckon she's more than a family friend?'

'I know she is. I've seen them kissing.'

He picked up the letters thoughtfully. 'I'll have a look through these, and if I think there's a case I'll bring Mr Grayling down to the precinct for a little talk.' He stood up. 'Let me find some-body to come and look at your head, then I'll get you some tea – that's what you English like, isn't it?'

The doctor put three metal stitches in Reg's gash, and the pain was teeth-clenching. His blood soaked through the towel he'd been given to hold and made him feel queasy. The doctor handed him some Bayer's aspirin powder dissolved in a glass of water, and he drank it gratefully.

When they'd finished O'Halloran came back in to chat. 'Mr Grayling's on his way back to Manhattan at the moment, so we'll call him later. You've had quite a year, young Reg. Saved from the *Titanic*, then this happens. I guess you lost friends on board, did you?'

Reg nodded. 'My best friend John.'

The detective nodded. 'It leaves a big hole inside, don't it? My best buddy was stabbed on duty last year. There's not a day goes by when I don't think about him and wish I could talk to him one last time.' He patted Reg's arm. 'Hey, did you hear there's an Irish woman in Kingsbridge who they say can talk to the spirits of people who died on the *Titanic*? They reckon she's pretty good. What about trying that? You could see if she can contact your buddy. What was her name again? . . . Annie McGeown.'

'Really? Annie? I knew her.'

'Is that so? What's she like? A bit of a loony?'

Reg hadn't heard the phrase before but could guess what it meant. 'No, not at all. She was a nice woman. Very kind.'

'Well, if you want to get in touch with her, I hear you can make an appointment through Father Kelly at St John's Church in Kingsbridge. Drop by the station and tell me how it goes!'

When it began to get dark outside, Detective O'Halloran telephoned Mr Grayling's number and was told that he had just arrived home.

'Can you request that he comes down to the Eighth Avenue precinct? Tell him to ask for Detective O'Halloran. Yes, right away, please.'

Reg imagined Mr Grayling's expression when he got the message. It wouldn't be well received, he was sure.

Chapter Seventy-Five

Reg had a lot of time to worry while the detective was interviewing Mr Grayling. He felt scared being in the same building. For a start, he would be furious with Reg for stealing the items from his secret drawer and then accusing him of murder. How easily the tables could be turned; any moment now, Reg might find himself arrested for theft. Even in the best-case scenario he would be out of a job, with no prospect of a reference from Mr Grayling to help him get a new one. He was back at square one, and didn't think he could find the energy to raise himself up yet again.

I have to go back to England, he thought. *The time has come to face my fears.* He tried to imagine how he would feel on a cruise liner in mid-ocean, and straight away he heard the rush of water in his ears and felt a burning sensation in his lungs. Maybe he'd be all right if he didn't look out across the water. He could keep himself busy below deck and perhaps he'd be able to manage that way.

Would his mother take him in, or would he find himself homeless on arrival? At least he had friends in Southampton who would let him stay till he found his feet. It made sense to go back to his roots. And Florence . . . he tortured himself thinking how he would feel if he bumped into her with another man. It was entirely his own fault for letting her slip through his fingers.

The door opened and Detective O'Halloran came in, sat down and got straight to the point. 'Mr Grayling is insisting that he took his wife to a lifeboat on the *Titanic*, and he thinks their door must have been locked by a steward. He says the stewards had keys for all the rooms in their section. Is that the case?'

Reg agreed that it was.

'So he wouldn't have left a body there all day in case the steward came in and found it, would he? There sure is evidence in those letters that he was romantically involved with Miss Hamilton and had been looking for a divorce that Mrs Grayling wasn't going to give him. But without a body, there's no suggestion of any crime.'

He could see Reg wasn't happy with this conclusion.

'Hey, I think you're wrong about him. He seems like a decent kind of guy. He was all made up when he heard that you escaped from the crash, and he wants to have a word with you.'

'No!' Reg cried. 'I can't.'

'Why not? I'll be in the room. There's nothing he can do. I think he really is looking out for you. You should hear what he has to say.'

Reg couldn't stop shaking as he was led to the interview room where Mr Grayling sat waiting. He flinched as his boss stood to greet him.

'Thank God you're all right, Reg. I'm told you have a head wound. Has it been properly taken care of?'

'Yes, thank you, sir,' Reg replied quietly.

Mr Grayling fixed his eyes on him. 'I can understand why you have a low opinion of me, but I want you to know that I've only ever felt protective towards you. My wife thought very highly of you.'

'Thank you, sir.'

'If you were of a mind to come back and work for me, I'd be happy to have you.'

Reg looked at the floor and shook his head.

'Otherwise, I'd like to give you a reference and some severance pay to help you set yourself up in your next situation. Do you have any plans?'

'I'm planning to go back to England, sir.' Still he couldn't meet Mr Grayling's eyes.

'In that case, I'll buy a ticket for you. I believe the *Lusitania* sails in four days' time. Would that suit, or do you want more time in New York to say your goodbyes?'

Reg didn't want to accept anything from him. 'I can work my own passage, sir.'

'Nonsense!' He appealed to Detective O'Halloran for support, but he just shrugged. 'I'm going to leave a ticket in your name at the Cunard office. If you don't want it, they will let you change it for another sailing, or cash it in. Please accept this as your rightful due, Reg.'

'Thank you, sir.'

'Do you need somewhere to stay until then? You're welcome to your old room. . .'

'No, I have somewhere.'

'In that case I suppose I'll say goodbye – and good luck to you, Reg.' Mr Grayling held out his hand.

Reg didn't want to shake hands. He knew Mr Grayling was lying. If he had shown his wife to a lifeboat and she got back out again, someone would have mentioned it by now, either in the press or at the Inquiries. Such things had been scrutinised in detail. But he was a polite boy, there was a policeman present, and it seemed awkward not to shake. He took Mr Grayling's hand and gripped it quickly then let go again as fast as he could.

434

Chapter Seventy-Six

Later that night, George Grayling sat at his desk with a glass of cognac by his elbow, fingering the key with the number B78 engraved on it.

Margaret shouldn't have come to Italy with me, he brooded. *Why did she come?*

Had she perhaps suspected he was going to see another woman? Did she want to spoil his affair? She kept trying to 'save' their marriage, no matter how cruelly he behaved towards her. If she had only given him the divorce he'd asked for, she would be alive today.

He knew he'd been bad-tempered with her on the *Titanic* as he skipped between Venetia, who was safely ensconced in a stateroom on C Deck, and his marital suite up on B. He resented having to return to Margaret in the early hours of the morning when Venetia dismissed him. He was bored with his wife's conversation and couldn't abide the time he spent eating meals in her company. Why did she not bow gracefully to the inevitable?

Her stubbornness had made him cross. As far as he could see, she had been the only obstacle that stood between him and his possession of the exquisite Venetia. He'd planned to marry her in due course and with any luck have a child. Margaret had been too old to give him another child, but Venetia could have.

435

Except now everything was ruined. He picked up the glass and swallowed a mouthful, feeling the warmth of it in his gullet.

There was a knock on the door and Mr Frank looked in. 'May I get you anything before I turn in for the night, sir?' He noticed the expression on his boss's face. 'Are you all right?'

'No,' Mr Grayling admitted. 'I'm not. Come in, Frank. Sit down. Have a drink with me.'

Mr Frank hesitated then obeyed, pouring himself half an inch of cognac from the decanter. 'Thank you, sir.'

'Did you know that Venetia has left me?' He sighed and shook his head in disbelief.

Mr Frank pursed his lips. 'I heard. I'm sorry, sir.'

'I loved her, Frank. I was going to marry her and have a child with her. I thought she felt the same way, but she was playing me for an old fool. She let me shower her with money and gifts before announcing that she's sailing for Europe to join her friends on their yacht, and I'm left with no one: no wife, no daughter, no Venetia. She said she couldn't be associated with the scandal of poor Molly being killed and Reg half-drowned, but it wasn't that. She was bored. I could feel it in my bones.'

'She's still young, sir. It was quiet for her in the house here.'

'I suppose I've always known deep down it wouldn't work. New York society would have mocked us, and Venetia would never have been able to cope with that. I'd have been a laughing stock and she would have been labelled a money-grabber.' *Which, of course, she was*, he thought bitterly. He swallowed another gulp of his drink, resolving never to calculate how much he had spent on her during the three years of their affair.

'Perhaps she will come back, sir. Maybe she will find that the grass is not always greener.'

'Oh, no doubt I'll receive an urgent telegram next time she runs out of money. That's how it's always been between us.'

Mr Frank sipped his cognac, with an impassive expression. 'I take it you met her long before you sailed on the *Titanic*.'

'I know you disapprove, Frank, but you must understand that Margaret and I never had a passionate marriage. I married for money, not for love, so it's ironic that when I fell in love with Venetia, she only wanted me for my money.' He gave a harsh little laugh, like a cough. 'What's sauce for the goose is sauce for the gander, as they say.' He realised that the alcohol combined with his disappointment was making him loose-tongued. *Why was he talking to a member of staff about this? But who else could he talk to? Besides, Frank had always been loyal as they come.*

'Did you plan to divorce Mrs Grayling?'

'She wouldn't let me. God knows I asked her . . .' He reached across the desk for the decanter and refilled his glass with a generous measure. 'Reg thinks I killed her. Can you believe it? Me? A murderer?'

'I heard there had been such talk in the house and I told them all it had to stop.' Mr Frank's gaze was level.

'He went to the police about it!' Mr Grayling exclaimed, his voice rising. 'That's why I was called down to the precinct tonight. Can you imagine?'

'It seems incredible. I expect that's why the police let you go again so quickly. They haven't arrested young Reg, though, have they? I hope not, after all he's been through.'

'He's fine. He's going back to England. I said I'd get him a ticket. But I still can't get over the fact he thought I'd murdered my wife to avoid the expense and scandal of a divorce. In his opinion, I was capable of that . . .' He shook his head, and his words were slurred as he spoke. 'And yet, as it turned out, it almost amounted to the same thing. I might as well have killed her.'

Mr Frank frowned. 'Sir, you're tired. Perhaps you should go to bed.'

'No! I have to tell someone and you know me, Frank. You know I'm not a bad person. OK, I lied, but it's not what Reg thinks. I could never have killed her in cold blood. You believe me, don't you?'

'Yes, of course I do.'

'She'd been ill all that last day on the *Titanic*. Christ, the sound of her vomiting turned my stomach but still I dropped in every few hours to make sure she wasn't in need of anything. You see? I was a good husband in some respects. When I checked on her after dinner she was sound asleep, with the bottle of sleeping potion beside her, so I assumed she had taken some and was out for the night. That's when I went to Venetia's room.'

He closed his eyes and imagined himself back there, in her dazzling presence. They had drunk champagne and talked and laughed. She kept him at arm's length, though. You'd think when they were alone together she might have allowed him a few more liberties, but she ordered him to remain in his chair while she sat in another several feet away.

'What kind of girl do you think I am?' she asked coyly. 'You'll get nothing more from me without a ring on my finger. I have already let you be far too fresh.'

And he was content just to be in her presence, allowed to gaze at her perfect features. Those cat-like eyes! The heart-shaped face! The glossy copper curls! And her pale skin, with the smoothness of pure cream. He adored her laugh. She seemed so witty when he was with her, although afterwards he could never remember any of her witticisms. She was intoxicating and he knew he was addicted to her. When they were apart he counted the minutes until he could see her again.

Mr Frank cleared his throat, interrupting the reverie. 'Are you saying you were with Miss Hamilton rather than your wife when the ship hit the iceberg?'

'It was just a slight jolt. Venetia was anxious but I told her that it wouldn't be anything serious. Then a steward knocked on the door and told us to come up to the boat deck with our life preservers. Just a precaution, he said.'

He was the same steward who brought Venetia's meals to her, and he must have guessed their arrangement was illicit but never gave so much as a hint of it in his composure. He showed them how to fasten their life preservers then led them up the Grand Staircase to the boat deck. Venetia kept her head bowed, her face overshadowed by a hat, and walked behind him for fear of being recognised by any of the English aristocracy on board. She needn't have worried, because everyone was engrossed in their own situation.

'I *specifically* asked him, you know.' Mr Grayling banged his glass on the desk, causing a little cognac to spill onto the highly polished wood. 'I asked whether all passengers would be brought up on deck by their room stewards and he assured me that they would. Assured me. I told him that I had a friend who was asleep in a room on B Deck and he said not to worry, that my friend would be fine. It just didn't occur to me to worry about Margaret after that.'

'So you didn't go back for her.' Mr Frank's voice was cold. It was a statement rather than a question.

'Oh Christ, it all happened so fast. You don't understand. They insisted that Venetia get into a lifeboat and she begged me to come too. She was scared. They said women and children were going first but then they started to lower away and there were loads of places left, so I just got on.' He took a greedy swallow of his drink. 'You must believe me, Frank. I wouldn't have done it if that steward hadn't *assured* me that Margaret would be on another boat. It was his fault. Besides, no one said the ship was sinking. We thought it was just a precaution. It was only when we got some distance away and saw the ship getting low in the water, at a slant . . .' He held his arm at an angle to demonstrate. 'That's when I realised it was serious. And even when she sank, I still thought Margaret would be fine because we were in first class, for God's sake. I thought all these people in the water must be third-class passengers who had dawdled and hadn't made it to the boat deck on time. You expect better in first class.' He peered at Mr Frank, yearning for his understanding.

The butler's face was impassive, his body very still. 'I suppose it was only when you reached the *Carpathia* that you realised Mrs Grayling hadn't made it.'

'Not even then! First of all I had to bribe the staff to find a cabin for Venetia and to calm her down – she was a bit upset.' He hiccoughed loudly. 'Then I went off to look for Margaret. I walked all round the ship but couldn't see any sign of her. I thought maybe she had found a cabin so I asked the stewards, but no one had seen her. It was horrible, Frank. You've got no idea what it was like for me. And then I bumped into Reg, and he told me that he had tried the door of our suite on the *Titanic* and found it locked.' A sob burst from his throat. 'That's when the terrible truth struck me: I'd locked the door when I went out.' He pushed the key across the desk. 'I only did it because I wanted her to sleep undisturbed.' He began to sob properly, covering his face with his hands, shoulders heaving.

Mr Frank picked up the key and looked at it. He felt disgust for the man sitting opposite. What kind of person would leave his wife to fend for herself on a sinking ship? 'Was there another key?' he asked slowly. 'If she wakened, would she have been able to open the door herself from the inside?'

The sobs grew even louder, as Mr Grayling shook his head. 'Oh God, I hope she didn't waken. I pray she just slept on. I did care about her, Frank. I did.' He looked pathetic with his sagging jowls and reddened eyes. A bubble of snot under one nostril flared as he breathed out.

Mr Frank said nothing, his face inscrutable.

'Please don't judge me,' Mr Grayling pleaded. 'I thought you would understand.'

'I do understand, sir. Perhaps it would be best if you let me help you to bed now. You probably shouldn't have any more to drink.' He rose to his feet.

Mr Grayling drained his glass in one long gulp. Mr Frank took his arm and helped him to his feet.

'You're a good man, Frank.' He staggered, and would have fallen if not for the butler's support. 'I'm lucky to have someone as understanding as you.'

'Thank you, sir.' Mr Frank led him, stumbling, down the corridor to his bedroom.

Chapter Seventy-Seven

As arranged, Robert came to the hotel at six and took Juliette's arm to help her downstairs and out to his automobile.

'I'm not an invalid,' she said, trying to keep her tone light, although she was terrified about what the evening might bring.

'You must take care in your condition,' he replied, and his voice was kind but not passionate, no longer the voice of a lover.

During the drive, she longed to touch him, to put her hand on his, but didn't dare. Her lips still tingled with his kisses, but everything between them had changed. She could feel the weight of the lie hanging over her like a sword of Damocles. As soon as they got to the house, she would explain that she was six months pregnant, not two, and offer him a quick and easy annulment. It was the only vaguely honourable route left to her.

The butler showed them straight in to dinner, then a footman came to consult Robert on the choice of wine, and when he left a maid brought their entrée of a light-as-air cheese soufflé.

When at last they were alone, it was Robert who spoke first. 'Have you been receiving medical attention in Saratoga Springs?' he asked.

'Yes. With a doctor who advised me to take up cross-stitching, if you can believe it!'

Robert smiled. 'I certainly can't imagine you doing that. Where are you hoping to have the child? Will you go back to England for the birth?'

'I was planning to have the baby in Saratoga Springs,' she said in a whisper, then took a deep breath and uttered the fateful words: 'It's due in November.' He looked so sad, she wished she could take back the words as soon as they'd been spoken. 'I'm sorry.'

Robert nodded and cleared his throat. 'Will you stay with your relatives for the remaining months?'

She shook her head. 'We have no relatives there. Mother and I have been staying in a rented cottage. I'm so sorry I've lied to you, Robert. I never intended this to happen, not any of it.'

'Yet you married me without saying anything. That's what I find hard to understand.' His tone was hurt.

'I couldn't bear to lose you. I planned to have the baby in Saratoga Springs, give it up for adoption and come back to you as if nothing had happened, as if I had merely spent the summer with elderly relatives. It was a ridiculous plan, I know, but I prayed you would never find out. I swear I am not a dishonest person by nature. You must have such a low opinion of me now.'

'I am surprised by you, indeed. When I guessed this afternoon that your pregnancy was more advanced than would have been possible with my child, I was shocked. I invented the excuse of business to attend to because I needed time to think. I didn't want to blurt out in the heat of the moment words that I might later live to regret.'

Juliette felt desperately ashamed. He was a decent, honest man and she had behaved unspeakably. 'Please let me explain,' she begged. 'I am not a woman of such loose morals as the bare facts of the situation might lead you to assume.'

He reached across the table and put his finger to her lips. 'No. I don't want to know.'

'But I must tell you.'

He shook his head. 'In New York society, there are certain matters that are never discussed between husbands and wives. In particular, it's an absolute rule that we never mention any admirers we might have entertained before meeting each other. I will never tell you whether I considered marrying any other woman before I met you, and I don't want to know about all the many men who must have been head over heels in love with you. Do you understand what I'm saying?'

Juliette was confused. Was he implying that he would stay married to her? How could he?

He continued: 'I was telling the truth earlier when I said that I have always wanted to be a father. I also want to be with you, so I have decided that I will be a father to this baby and that we will tell everyone it is ours.' He reached across the table to squeeze her hand. 'In future, God willing, we will have more children of our own who will be brothers and sisters to it.'

Joy flooded Juliette's whole body. 'But how will we manage? What will people say?'

Robert had an answer ready. 'I'm going to have to spend a lot of time in California over the coming months while I set up the new companies. I suggest we take a house out there and hire a nurse to come and live with us. You can have the baby there and your mother may accompany us if she wishes.' Juliette was gazing at him in astonishment. He continued: 'There's a glorious climate, and we can keep our own stables. When the baby is old enough, we'll make a trip back to England and you can introduce me to the rest of your family then.'

Juliette's head was swimming. 'Mother will go mad! She's already planned most details of an elaborate December wedding in Gloucestershire.'

'I suspect she will prefer the solution I propose to your idea of having her grandchild adopted.'

He must have formulated these plans during the last few hours, since finding out about her condition. Juliette sat back and watched him, full of wonder. He loved her so much that he was prepared to accept that she was having another man's child. It seemed extraordinary to her, and at the same time quite, quite wonderful.

'Can you ever forgive me?' she asked.

He gazed deep into her eyes, and he still looked sad but there was love there as well. 'I wish you had told me before, of course, but I know the person you are and I think I can understand why you made the choices you made.' He lifted her fingers to his lips and kissed them. 'I love you, Juliette. You are my wife and I want to spend my life with you. Of course I forgive you.'

Chapter Seventy-Eight

After the newspaper story about her appeared, Annie was alarmed by the sheer quantity of requests for readings from the relatives of *Titanic* survivors. Many of them made the journey to the church to implore Father Kelly in person, while others sent pleading letters. She hated to disappoint anyone who was recently bereaved but it would have been physically impossible to see them all and, for her own sanity, she wanted to stick to the limit of one séance a week.

It was Father Kelly who came up with a solution: she would write a brief letter to each, explaining that she did not have time for individual readings but that she knew their loved one was at peace. If there was some personal detail she could add, all the better. She perused the letters carefully and found she could usually read between the lines and work out what they wanted to hear. *He didn't suffer. She is with her grandparents. He wants you to be happy.* Sometimes she'd ask Finbarr, 'What shall I say to this one?' and the words would flow into her head. Although her notes were largely formulaic, Annie knew from the replies that the recipients found them very comforting.

Shortly after the newspaper item was published, the Church authorities were alerted that Father Kelly was involved in spiritualism and he was told in the strictest terms that he must cease any connection with séances, and should encourage his parishioner to do the same.

'I think they're wrong to close their minds to it,' he told Annie ruefully, 'but I must follow their orders. We will have to stop holding séances in my house. Still, there's no harm in me simply acting as a mailbox if you want to continue replying to letters.'

Annie agreed that she would, because whatever the Catholic Church said, she knew in her heart it was doing some good. She spent an hour a day writing letters in her big, loopy handwriting, before she settled down to her embroidery. It made her feel strong, to be in a position to help other people. She felt part of a network of *Titanic* survivors, and flattered that people trusted her enough to tell her their stories. Most days, it helped to ease the acuteness of her own grief.

She no longer had time to sweep the church, but she continued to take responsibility for the floral arrangements. After dropping Patrick at school and picking up her groceries from the market each morning, she would drop in to pray, then wander round the church weeding out any blooms that had passed their best and changing the water to make bouquets last longer. It was while she was occupied with this one day, that Reg came into the church and spotted her.

'Mrs McGeown?' he said tentatively, lurking behind a pillar as if he were afraid of disturbing her.

'Will you look at that! If it's not Reg Parton. My, but it's good to see you.' She meant it. She'd often thought of him and felt grateful that Finbarr had been so well cared for in his final minutes of life. 'How did you get here?'

He spoke quickly, nervously. 'I came on the Rapid Transit. Have you tried it? It goes through tunnels part of the way, and it's fast. Much faster than a streetcar.'

Annie smiled. Finbarr would have been equally enthusiastic about the new-fangled kind of underground train that linked them with the city. 'Did you come to see me?'

'Yes, I wanted to say goodbye. I'm going back to England. And I wondered if I might have a talk with you, if you have a minute to spare. I don't want to bother you.'

He wants a reading. Probably about his friend John. I suppose I can do that for him. Out loud, she said, 'It would be much appreciated if you would help me up the steps to my house with my bags of shopping. My old knees have been giving me trouble so I like to take it slow and easy, but you're a young fit lad.'

Reg carried everything up for her and waited at the top as she hauled herself up the step street, flinching at the jabbing pain that afflicted both knees now. 'We've found a new apartment down on the main street but it'll be a month before we can move in. I can't wait.'

She led him into her sitting room and he was immediately struck by the sight of some embroidery lying on a table by the window: a stunning oriental pagoda fronted by cherry blossom trees and a lake with a bridge over it that she was stitching onto a pale pink silk dressing gown.

'Aren't I the lucky wan, getting such a lovely job as this? Will you look at the gorgeous colours of those threads!'

Annie made some tea then sat down opposite him. 'Now did you come about your friend John?' she asked. 'Do you want me to try and contact him?'

'No . . . It's not that.' He seemed troubled by something, so Annie waited for him to spit it out. 'There were some first-class passengers on board called Mr and Mrs Grayling. He survived and she didn't. I think he might have killed her and locked her in their suite. I've been to the police but there's not enough evidence to charge him. I suppose . . . I just hate to see him getting away with it.'

Annie nodded. 'You want me to try and speak to her.'

'I don't really know why I came. I'm not even sure I believe in all this.' He waved his hand in the air.

'I'll tell you a secret: I'm not sure I believe myself.' She smiled conspiratorially. 'But I can tell you it helps. I know it has lifted me out of blackness in the moments when I thought I was going mad, and other people tell me it has helped them to pull through. Well, we will try to contact your Mrs Grayling, but no promises, mind.'

She pulled a small table between them, lit a candle then indicated that Reg should give her his hands. She closed her eyes and began to concentrate. The first words that came into her head didn't sound as though they came from an upper-class woman.

'What are you doing here, man? You're the one who always said religion was a load of codswallop.'

'It's John,' Reg breathed. The hairs stood up on the back of his neck.

'Why don't you get yourself back home, marry some nice girl and have children before you get too long in the tooth? Call your handsomest boy after me.'

'I will,' Reg agreed, close to tears. It was uncanny. Annie's voice was still hers, but to his ears it had the ring of John's about it, a very slight Geordie inflection.

Next she spoke in her own voice. 'Is there a Mrs Grayling who was on the *Titanic*?' She paused for a long time, trying to hear something, but all she felt was a deep sense of exhaustion. It was a while before she realised that tiredness might be a message in itself. 'I think it means she was sleeping when the

449

ship sank,' she said out loud, and then she began to hear a very distant voice. 'Tell Reg not to worry. I'm happy now. I'm glad to be here.'

'Is she with her daughter Alice?' Reg asked.

'Of course. Mothers always meet their children on the other side.'

'Can you ask if her husband killed her?'

Annie focused hard. 'She says, "My husband is foolish but he is not a bad man." I think that's your answer.'

Reg gave a deep sigh. If it were true, he could stop worrying. It sounded like the kind of thing Mrs Grayling might say. He hoped it was.

Annie listened a while longer but there was nothing more so she opened her eyes and let go of his hands. 'Was that what you needed to know?'

'I think so. Thank you.'

'It's good to see you, Reg. You're quite the hero, I believe. My husband said he read about you in the papers recently. You were in a car that crashed into the sea and you kept diving down, trying to save the girl who'd been in the passenger seat. It made us remember how brave you were in trying to save our son.'

Reg blushed to the roots of his hair. 'Please don't say that. I'm no hero. Officers Lightoller and Lowe, and Captain Rostron of the *Carpathia* – they're the real heroes. I only managed to save myself.'

'And yet you *are* brave. I can see it in your soul.'

On his way back on the transit, Reg wasn't sure why he had gone to see Annie. Spiritualism had to be nonsense. How could there be some vast place called heaven where souls went after death and met up with their loved ones again? It would be hugely overcrowded if it contained the souls of all the people who had ever lived throughout the centuries, and it would have to keep expanding every day as more people died. Besides, if it were possible for souls to pass messages to those back on earth, why weren't they constantly in contact? They would be poking their noses in, pestering their families with advice and requests. Murderers would always be caught because their victims could point the finger. It couldn't possibly be true.

Yet it had definitely sounded like John's voice. He felt better for going. He felt as though he'd done all he could.

When Seamus got in from his work that evening, Annie told him about Reg's visit. He remained firmly sceptical about her contacting the spirits but sometimes she chatted to him about a séance to get his pragmatic point of view.

Seamus listened to her description of the conversation as he ate his chipped beef and mash. 'He didn't come here to talk to spirits,' he said when she'd finished. 'He came to check that we don't blame him for Finbarr dying. The spirits were an excuse.'

Annie remembered that Reg had looked nervous in the church when he first arrived, and how relieved he'd seemed by her greeting. 'I've never blamed him. Well, maybe just for a second after I got the news but not once I'd heard his story.'

'No, but he's a good lad and if I put myself in his shoes, that's what I'd worry about. He can go home to England now knowing he has your blessing.'

Annie was suddenly overwhelmed by love for Seamus. He was so good and steady and wise. She got up and walked round the table and embraced him from behind, sliding her arms right round his waist and burying her face in his neck. He'd had a wash when he came in from work and she could smell the soap on his skin.

'There's something I've never told you, Annie,' he said in a low voice, so the children didn't hear, 'and I should have. I've often thought about what happened on the *Titanic* that night and gone over things in my head again and again, and I want you to know that in your place I'd have done exactly the same as you did. That's all.' He raised his fork and carried on eating.

'Thank you,' she whispered.

She thought about the choice she had made fourteen years earlier when she'd seen Seamus standing in the seed shop and asked her friend to introduce them. You never knew the kind of journey life was going to take you on, and she'd been a frivolous slip of a girl back then, but somehow she'd got that decision spot on. No matter the tragedy that had come her way since, she had an awful lot to be grateful for.

Chapter Seventy-Nine

When Reg turned up at the Cunard Line office to see if Mr Grayling had left him a ticket as promised, he was astonished to find there was a first-class reservation in his name.

'Are you sure there's no mistake?' he asked.

The clerk checked. 'Reg Parton, that's right. There's a letter here for you as well.' He handed over an envelope with no stamp but with Reg's name on the outside.

Reg went to sit on a bench in the shipping office and tore it open. Two sides of the paper were covered in small, neat handwriting and the signature at the end read 'Algernon Frank'. His first thought was that Mr Frank had written to say goodbye, and how kind that was, but then he started reading.

The letter began with an account of Mr Grayling's confession about his part in his wife's death. '*In vino veritas*,' Mr Frank wrote, and Reg realised it was the truth. Everything fitted into place at last. That's why he'd had the key. That's why she hadn't been seen on any lifeboat.

'*He was very ill the next day from the aftereffects of his indulgence,*' the letter continued, '*but I insisted that he had a responsibility to look after you, that his wife would have wanted him to, and that is why you'll find he has bought you a first-class ticket for the voyage. Please don't be too proud to accept it because you deserve it after all you've been through. Think of it as a last gift from Mrs Grayling, God bless her soul.*

'On reflection, I have decided that I can no longer continue in Mr Grayling's employment. His wife was a wonderful woman, and I was forced to bite my tongue when he brought Miss Hamilton into the house so soon after her tragic death. I followed his orders and asked the staff to pack away his wife's belongings and refrain from mentioning her name any more, even though it felt wrong that we weren't all in formal mourning for her. But now I know the full circumstances, I cannot contemplate staying in the service of such a man. Mr Grayling understands and says he will write me a reference for my next position.'

The letter finished by wishing Reg all the very best for the future, whatever he decided to do.

He folded it and put it back in the envelope, deep in thought. He hoped Mrs Grayling had slept throughout the sinking because the alternative was unbearable. If only he had knocked harder on the door, or insisted that the room steward open it and check, then he could have saved her. But the room steward on B Deck told him the Graylings must have gone already. It wasn't his fault, and it wasn't Reg's fault; it was her husband's. Mr Grayling wasn't evil, but he was weak and selfish and, from the sounds of it, self-pitying. And Miss Hamilton was every bit as shallow as he had always thought.

Reg decided that if Mr Frank thought he should accept the ticket, then that's what he would do. For a moment, he pictured himself sitting in the first-class dining saloon being served filet mignon by someone just like himself. He'd enjoy sleeping in a four-poster bed and luxuriating in his own private bathroom – but it was ridiculous. He didn't have the right clothes. He wouldn't be able to make conversation with anyone in first class. He didn't belong there.

He went back to the counter and asked the clerk: 'How much was this ticket, and how much is a third-class cabin?'

The difference between the two was four thousand dollars, which was about eight hundred pounds in British money. There was a lot he could do with that kind of cash. It was enough to start a serious business venture back in Southampton. But what kind of business?

The idea came to him straight away. He'd been thinking of opening a British-style restaurant in Manhattan, but why not open an American one back home instead? He could serve hot dogs and Pepsi-Cola. If he liked them, surely other English people would?

On his last day in New York, Reg got up early. The first thing he did was go into a soda fountain and ask who supplied them with Pepsi-Cola. He took a subway to the address he was given and asked if he might speak with the manager. The fellow that came to talk to him was roughly his own age and that gave Reg courage.

'I'm starting my own café in Southampton, England, and I'd like to import some Pepsi-Cola,' he said.

Instantly, the manager fetched some requisition forms, a list of prices, shipping costs and import licences. 'I'll do you a good deal if you order at least a thousand bottles,' he promised.

Reg agreed a price for a thousand and paid cash on the spot. He'd pick up the shipment from Southampton docks in three weeks' time. He caught a subway back uptown and next he bought some popcorn and Oreo cookies and a few bags of potato chips with a free toy inside, none of which he had ever seen back home. He asked the store owners for details of their

455

suppliers but decided to see how popular they were before ordering in bulk. And then he stopped to chat to a hot dog seller in Times Square about the key to his success.

'Pile on the onions, let them help themselves to the ketchup or French mustard.'

Reg wrote everything down in a little notebook, beside addresses of all the contacts he had made. It wasn't bad for a day's work.

He was nervous getting on the *Lusitania* the next morning, carrying his boxes of goods. She was much smaller than the *Titanic*, and although she had only been launched in 1906 and took her first passengers in 1907, the design already looked old-fashioned. Third-class accommodation was smart and clean, though, with pine floors and walls. He had a washbasin in his cabin, and the WC wasn't too far away. Everyone sat at long tables in the dining saloon and the food was standard fare but perfectly adequate.

The minute they set sail, Reg made his way up to the wireless room to send a Marconi-gram to his mother. He chewed the end of his pencil for ages trying to think of something appropriate, but in the end he just wrote: 'Arriving Tuesday evening on Lusitania [stop] Your son Reg'. It cost twelve shillings and sixpence. Reg had to change his dollars into sterling at the pursers' office.

He had thought he wouldn't want to go out on deck, but in fact his feet led him there straight away. He stood at the railing and watched as they sailed past Governor's Island, Ellis Island and the Statue of Liberty out towards the open ocean. It was a clear, sunny day in early September and light sparkled on the water, giving a festive feel. In his head was the song 'Come on and hear, come on and hear, Al-ex-an-der's Rag-time Band'. It kept repeating, over and over. He couldn't think where he had heard it recently and then he remembered that it was one of the songs the orchestra had been playing on the boat deck as the *Titanic* sank. It was a spooky feeling, but he couldn't get it out of his head.

At dinner on the second night it was announced that there would be a religious service the next morning as they passed close to the spot where the *Titanic* had sunk. Reg decided not to go. Nothing he'd been through had changed his opinion that there couldn't be a God. It just didn't make sense. Instead, as they passed the area he went out on the open deck and smoked a cigarette, while looking out across the water and thinking about all those who were lost.

'Cheerio, man,' he whispered to John. 'I'll always miss you.' And to Mrs Grayling, he whispered a simple 'Thank you'.

The crossing to Southampton took seven days. Reg didn't socialise with other passengers but he wasn't lonely. He sat with his notebook making plans for the new business, drawing sketches of the seating arrangement he'd like. Sometimes he wondered what reception he could expect from his mother. Now he was getting closer, he couldn't wait to see his brothers and apologise to them for his lost five months. Was that really all it had been since he set sail on the *Titanic*? It felt like a lifetime.

He was standing on deck when the first glimpse of the English coastline came into sight. He'd already packed his belongings and planned to stay outside and watch as the tugs guided them into harbour. When he worked for White Star Line, he'd been rushed off his feet at this final stage of the voyage, clearing everything up so that they could go home as soon as the last passenger disembarked. Someone else could do the work this time.

The quay came into sight, the tugs chugged out to meet them and the ship's engines were turned off. The air filled with the deafening sound of pent-up steam being released and it was only as it began to die down that he realised there was some kind of celebration under way on the dock. He could hear whistles being blown and see flags being waved frantically in the air. Maybe there was an important dignitary on board. He followed the noise to its source and saw a group of around thirty people jumping up and down, yelling and waving their arms. Some of the *Lusitania*'s passengers began to wave back.

Progress was slow as the tugboat captains manoeuvred round the buoys, steering clear of other ships. Reg was about to go below to collect his belongings, when something about the animated group caught his attention. They had a white banner with words painted on it in huge black letters and he couldn't believe it when he got close enough to make out what it said: 'Welcome home Reg'. Surely there must be some mistake, some other Reg on board? He focused hard, and gradually he realised the group were his family and friends. There was his mum, his brothers. None of them had seen him yet but they were making so much noise he couldn't miss them.

Right at the front of the crowd, standing slightly apart, was a girl in a blue coat and with a lurch he knew who it was: Florence. Just as he realised that, she spotted him, even though they were still a hundred yards apart and the decks were lined with hundreds of other passengers. He could tell she'd seen him from the way she suddenly stood very still. There were a few seconds when it was just the two of them, and he held her gaze. In that magical moment, frozen in time, he knew as surely as he had ever known anything that he wanted to marry her.

Then she turned to the others and he saw her pointing towards him. They all began screaming his name and blowing their penny whistles even more frantically. The private moment was over for now, but he sensed with a warm, certain feeling inside, that there were going to be many more.

Epilogue

Reg and Florence got married a week before Christmas 1912 and their first child, a daughter, was born a year later. By that time Reg's 'New York Café', in central Southampton, was a roaring success. He was thinking of opening another branch when war broke out in August 1914, and the following month he enlisted. In 1916, he was awarded a Distinguished Conduct Medal for his outstanding bravery at the Battle of the Somme, but shortly afterwards he received a serious leg injury that meant he could no longer fight and he spent six months in hospital receiving painful treatments before he could walk again. Florence helped him to reopen the New York Café in 1918 and, riding on the wave of enthusiasm for all things American that prevailed after the war, he was able to open two further branches in the South of England. A son was born in 1920 and Reg called him John, after the friend he'd lost on the *Titanic*, the friend he would never forget.

Juliette and Robert tried hard to make their marriage work but she struggled with homesickness and spent ever longer periods with her own family. They never divorced but he took a mistress in New York, while Juliette raised her son back in Gloucestershire and devoted herself to her horses.

Annie and Seamus had two more children, a boy and a girl. Patrick thrived at school in America and became an office worker, the destiny his mother had always dreamed of for Finbarr. Despite many requests during the Great War, Annie no longer attempted to contact the spirits. Her embroidery was renowned in fashionable New York society and she was kept busy with that, and the demands of her expanding family.

Venetia Hamilton married an Italian count in June 1913 and set up home in his castle in northern Italy, where she held frequent house parties for titled expats. She and her husband argued fiercely over her extravagance, and both took lovers. They never had a child together, but he had a string of illegitimate children.

George Grayling had a stroke in 1915, while sitting in his library with a glass of cognac. He was paralysed down one side and lived for six months in a rest home before succumbing to a fatal bout of pneumonia.

TITANIC

THE FACTS

The *Titanic* set sail from Southampton on the 10th of April, 1912, made brief stops in Cherbourg, France, and Queenstown, Ireland, then headed across the North Atlantic towards New York on a voyage that should have taken six days. She carried 1,322 passengers and 885 crew, who marvelled at the state-of-the-art amenities. All the descriptions of the ship in this novel are factual: there was a swimming pool, libraries, a squash court, a café with real palm trees, chandeliers and mosaic-lined Turkish baths. The décor and food were sumptuous, with no expense spared. But they only had space in the lifeboats for less than half of those on board.

The passengers included several American millionaires, including John Jacob Astor, Benjamin Guggenheim, Isidor Straus (who founded Macy's department store in New York) and George Widener (a banker and owner of a street-car company in Philadelphia). There were British aristocrats, including Lord and Lady Duff Gordon (she owned the fashion house Maison Lucille) and the Countess of Rothes (who later helped to row her own lifeboat). And there were travellers of many different nationalities, from Eastern and Western Europe, North and South America, Japan, Russia, Australia and South Africa.

They took a northern route across the Atlantic, which was prone to icebergs in spring when glaciers in Greenland were melting. During Sunday, 14th April, Captain Smith received several warnings of ice ahead but he ordered his officers to keep to a speed of around 22 knots, trusting the lookouts to spot any icebergs and his officers to steer around them. However, it was a moonless night and the sea was dead calm, so there were no tell-tale ripples in the water around the huge iceberg that loomed seemingly out of nowhere at 11.40 p.m. The lookouts rang the warning bell and Officer Murdoch ordered that the

[The *Titanic* under construction in Belfast's Harland & Wolff shipyard.]

ship be turned "hard a-starboard" but it was too late. There were only 37 seconds between the lookouts' warning and the *Titanic*'s glancing collision with the iceberg.

The mass of ice damaged a 300-foot section of the ship's hull, just 10 feet above the keel, and the immense water pressure caused lower compartments to flood rapidly. Officer Murdoch immediately pulled a lever that closed the watertight doors separating the ship's bulkheads, but as the water continued to rise in the front five flooded compartments, the *Titanic* began to settle by the bow. Within twenty minutes of the collision Captain Smith realised she was going to sink, and he ordered the first "CQD" ("come quickly disaster") message to be radioed at 12.15 a.m. then asked his officers to prepare the lifeboats.

Many passengers felt the jolt of the collision but few were alarmed. No announcement was made that the ship had only two hours to live because it was felt this would create panic. The orchestra played ragtime classics on the boat deck and drinks were still being served in the bars. Officers urged the upper classes to step into wooden rowing boats that dangled 75 feet above the ocean surface but, understandably, many were reluctant to leave the comfort of the ship. Stewards knocked on the door of first-class suites and guided their occupants to the boat deck, second-class passengers were told where to go and what to do, but most third-class passengers had to fend for themselves. Given that the layout of the ship was confusing even for crew, it's hardly surprising that many never made it to the boat deck, and that many others arrived only after the last lifeboat had departed.

The loading of lifeboats was controversial. In keeping with the ethos of the time, the message was "women and children first", but it wasn't consistently applied. On the port side,

LC-USZ 62-64154

[It is thought this may have been the iceberg she struck.]

Second Officer Lightoller upheld the rule strictly, only allowing sufficient men on each boat to row it. On the starboard side, Officer Lowe was more lenient, and he let men board if there were spaces remaining after all the nearby women and children had been seated. However, on both sides the boats set off with dozens of places empty. This was partly because the officers weren't sure whether it was safe to lower a fully loaded boat from the boat deck, and partly because of the general air of confusion. By 1.55 a.m. all the lifeboats had departed, except for two "collapsibles" on the roof of the officers' mess – but more than two-thirds of the passengers and crew were still on board.

In the radio room, Jack Phillips and Harold McBride kept sending increasingly urgent distress messages, some of them using the new SOS call signal, but the nearest ship to respond was the *Carpathia*, and she was four hours' sail away when she first got the message. Some people reported seeing a ship on the horizon, just around 20 miles off, and this was later identified as the *Californian*. Her radio operator had gone to bed so didn't pick up the distress signals, and her crew couldn't understand why rockets were being fired into the sky. Had she come to pick up *Titanic* passengers, most could have been saved.

Passengers and crew who clustered on the *Titanic*'s boat deck at 2 a.m. must have known their chances were slim, but they lined the railings trying to estimate where their best hope of survival lay. Jump too soon, while they were still too high above the ocean surface, and they would die from the impact. But it was thought that when the ship disappeared she would suck all who surrounded her underwater, so they were keen to get as far away as they could before that happened. And yet, it was imperative that they didn't spend too long in the water, whose temperature was below freezing point. It was a tricky decision.

At 2.20 a.m. the *Titanic*'s hull split in two and her stern rose perpendicular in the air before slipping down into the ocean. Those who hadn't already jumped were now hurled into the water and a communal howl of anguish filled the air. Doctors estimate that a fit man would only survive around 20 minutes in such water temperatures, so the clock was ticking. Their sole chance was to get into a lifeboat – and fast. But the seamen in charge of the lifeboats had rowed some distance away and were reluctant to turn back in case they were swamped by survivors trying to clamber on board, which could cause them to sink. Officer Lowe was one of the few who did go back for survivors, but only after the cries of the dying had begun to subside and he was sure they wouldn't be overwhelmed. He picked up five survivors, of whom one subsequently died.

Meanwhile, Officer Lightoller had taken charge of a collapsible which had been washed overboard upside down in the final moments before the ship sank. He got around 30 people to stand up on it and, by directing their movements, managed to keep them afloat for the next two hours.

If all the spaces on lifeboats had been filled, it would have been possible to rescue 1,178 people, but only 711 were to survive. The experience of sitting in a lifeboat listening to 1,496 people dying in the water around you must have been devastating. Most of them perished from hypothermia, as their life preservers kept them from drowning. Passengers on the lifeboats heard them crying for help, calling out loved ones' names, muttering prayers, and then sighing and groaning as they passed away. For the rest of their lives, no survivor could forget that awful, heart-rending sound.

It was around 4 a.m. when Captain Rostron of the *Carpathia*, one of the great heroes of the night, arrived at the *Titanic*'s last known position. He had raced there at top speed, dodging icebergs on the way, but he arrived to find just 20 lifeboats, one of them half submerged and another upside down. The *Titanic* had disappeared. His crew helped to bring survivors on board and *Carpathia* passengers donated dry clothing and even their cabins to help. For the first hours, *Titanic* survivors clung to the hope that their loved ones might yet be found, but gradually that hope faded. Captain Rostron circled the area once then turned and headed back to New York.

There was confusion about the early news that reached the rest of the world, with some papers reporting the *Titanic* was being towed to Halifax and that all were saved. Such was John Jacob Astor's wealth that when word came through that he

[Lifeboats making their way towards the *Carpathia*.]

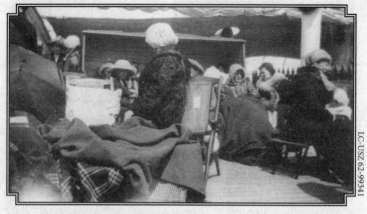

[Survivors sit huddled on the decks of the *Carpathia*.]

had perished, there were initial fears that the American stock exchange might collapse. Survivor lists were sent to shore by Marconi-gram but were filled with inaccuracies. What was known was that the *Carpathia* would dock on the evening of Thursday 18th April, and the pier was crowded with relatives, while photographers and journalists tried everything they could think of to gain an exclusive. The Women's Relief Committee was on hand to look after those left destitute by the sinking, while the rich were met by their chauffeurs.

An American Senate Inquiry into the sinking began straight away, while a British one followed in May and June. Many survivors, both crew and passengers, testified at these Inquiries, and public anger grew at the realisation that the huge loss of life could have been avoided. From then on, it was ordered that ocean-going liners must carry sufficient lifeboats for all passengers. Radio operators were to man their stations throughout the night and SOS became the recognised international distress call, while an international iceberg patrol was established.

There was also questioning of why the survival rate was so poor amongst the third-class passengers: only 16.2 per cent of third-class men survived compared to 32.7 per cent of first-class; more tellingly, less than a third of third-class children survived while all bar one of the first-class children made it to the *Carpathia*. There were tales that the gates allowing third-class passengers access to the boat deck were locked, but no evidence of this has survived. However, there were far fewer stewards per passenger in third class, and the confusing layout of the ship was against them. A combination of these factors led to the high death toll.

Long before the term "post-traumatic stress disorder" had been coined, it is obvious that Titanic survivors suffered from it. At least seven men and one woman committed suicide later in life, a much higher percentage than in the population at large. Many marriages broke down in the aftermath, despite the fact that this was an era when divorce still carried huge stigma. Male survivors were castigated for getting into lifeboats while there were still women on the ship and some found their businesses destroyed when the public no longer patronised them. There were several survivors who simply refused ever to discuss their experiences that night, even with family and friends, and many who never got on a boat again for the rest of their lives.

In this novel, I wanted to explore what it felt like to be on the *Titanic* and to survive. In order to do this, I invented the main characters in my story, but many of their experiences were based on real events.

Reg Parton was inspired by a real-life first-class victualling steward called Reginald Jones. He came from Southampton, was twenty-one years old, and was very handsome. It is reported that a Canadian newlywed on board used to annoy her husband by flirting with him. Sadly, Reginald Jones did not survive.

There was no direct model for Lady Juliette Mason-Parker, but I had in mind a woman called Eloise Smith, who lost her husband on the *Titanic* and married the man who comforted her on the *Carpathia*. She was pregnant at the time of the sinking and gave birth to the son of her first husband, but her second marriage, born out of her shock and despair, didn't last.

Annie McGeown from Cork is invented, but there was a party on board of fourteen Irish people from County Mayo, of whom only three survived. Most of the Irish passengers on the *Titanic* were émigrés, hoping to better themselves in the land of opportunity, and it was common practice for the man to go ahead and establish himself before sending for his family to join him.

The story of the Graylings and Venetia Hamilton is invented, but there were many passengers travelling under assumed names, for one reason or another, and on a ship of that size there were bound to be stowaways. No one is entirely sure how many people were on board and how many survived, although the figures I have given are the generally accepted estimates.

My description of events during the sinking and on the *Carpathia* are based on the reports of survivors, either at the Inquiries or in the press. The story dominated the headlines for many months afterwards and it continues to fascinate almost a hundred years later. There have been ships that sank with greater loss of life, and other ships that sank on their maiden voyage, but with the *Titanic*, there is a combination of factors which makes it so compelling.

[Radio operator Harold McBride is helped ashore on arrival in New York.]

It had been heralded as the safest, most luxurious ship ever built, and some (although not its builders) called it "unsinkable". It was on its maiden voyage and had many of the world's richest millionaires on board, along with several contemporary "celebrities". Those two hours and forty minutes between the collision and the sinking proved a true test of character, as well as a demonstration of the values of the age that would be rejected soon afterwards. But it is in the poignancy of the individual stories that the true fascination lies. What must it have felt like to be there, and to survive? I wrote this novel in an attempt to find out.

Acknowledgements

First of all, I'd like to thank Jason Hook for commissioning my nonfiction book *Titanic Love Stories* and fanning my obsession with all things to do with the ship. Karel Bata suggested I wrote a novel set on the *Titanic*, and has been patient and helpful throughout the months when I tried ideas on him and forced him at gunpoint to read bits of it.

Wilf Sefton told me about his life working in the galleys of big cruise ships; Joyce McElroy advised on all things Irish; Sarah Palmer gave tips on life management; David Boyle acted as a historical advisor; Anne Nicholson, who reads all my novels at an early stage, made some important points; Sue Reid Sexton told me about the symptoms of post-traumatic stress disorder; Kirsty Crawford gave brilliant advice when this book was just an outline; Florence Williams (aged seven) gave me permission to use her name; and Karen Sullivan has, as always, been incomparably magnificent as a reader and sounding board.

Among the books I read for research, I particularly recommend Walter Lord's *A Night to Remember*; John Eaton and Charles Haas's *Titanic: Triumph and Tragedy*; the collection of pieces by John Wilson Foster (ed.) entitled simply *Titanic*; *The Story of the Titanic as Told by its Survivors*, edited by Jack Winocour; and W.B. Bartlett's *Titanic: 9 hours to Hell*. Please note that any inadvertent factual errors are mine and not theirs.

My lovely agent, Vivien Green, was enthusiastic about the idea from the start and couldn't have been more supportive. The team at Avon – my brilliant editor Claire Bord, as well as Caroline Ridding, Claire Power, Becke Parker, Keshini Naidoo, Helen Bolton, Cleo Little, Adrian Hemstalk and Rhian McKay. – have been thoroughly helpful and professional and, among other things, have dragged me kicking and screaming into the 21st century. Because of them I now have a website at www.gillpaul.com, where you can contact me if you wish. I'd love to hear from you.

Huge thanks to everyone involved. I'm lucky to know you all.